THE PRINCE AWAKENS

BOOK ONE OF THE PRINCE OF BRITANNIA SAGA

Fred Hughes

Theogony Books
Coinjock, NC

Chris Kennedy/Theogony Books
1097 Waterlily Rd.
Coinjock, NC 27923
https://chriskennedypublishing.com/

Cover Art and Design by Brenda Mihalko.

Ordering Information:
Quantity sales. Special discounts are available on quantity purchases by corporations, associations, and others. For details, contact the "Special Sales Department" at the address above.

The Prince Awakens/Fred Hughes – 2nd ed.
ISBN: 978-1648555534

For Dundi, who made me believe.

Foreword

This book results from many years of thought and involves many starts and stops. It began as a way to exercise a very busy mind, and I never intended to publish it. But like many people in the Age of Covid, I found myself with an abundance of time and decided to put all of it down on paper (or my laptop). I spent my entire adult life in the engineering field. First as an operator, then as a supervisor, and ultimately as a manager. I never considered myself an artistic person.

The love of my life read early portions and said it was good. Deciding I hadn't a thing to lose other than a few thousand dollars, I self-published it, never expecting any real success. If nothing else, I could claim to be a published author.

Since I had low expectations, I slugged away through the first couple of months, figuring it out as I went along. I received incredibly positive reviews from the few who read them, to my amazement. The people who took the time to post a written review (thank you all) wanted to know when the next book would be out. These readers compared me to David Weber, John Ringo, and Terry Mixon, all writers I admire and respect. So, work began on the second book in the series, and I put more effort into promoting The Prince Awakens.

I found many things I could have done better in writing the second book and getting it ready for an audible version. But hey, I was a first-time writer, after all. I also made changes based on readers' good and bad comments in the written reviews. The story has not changed at all—just a few editorial fixes. Most importantly, I incorporated Imperial dates to help readers understand the unusual way in which I began the book.

Like most science fiction novels, this book contains space battles and gunfights, but it is ultimately about people. The characters I have created are like family to me, and they are the book's core. I wanted to show that the core values most have and admire in others will still be present in the future. While explaining some of the science involved was necessary, I tried hard not to get bogged down in it. For the space battles, which frankly I am immensely proud of, I tried to copy David Weber's style in making it both exciting and realistic. I hope you enjoy it.

Please leave a review and let me know how I did.

—Fred Hughes

Prologue

Empire Date: January 1038

Hazard King had always been a loner, though not entirely by choice. His family situation had always made having friends difficult. So, as he often did, he relaxed alone, pondering the universe. By the Old Earth calendar, which the Empire still used, it was late in the twenty-ninth century, and humanity had undoubtedly come far. The starship he was on was an older-model Imperial destroyer twenty-light-years away from the nearest inhabited world. It was well over one thousand light-years back to Earth.

The tall, lean officer reclined on the observation couch in the navigation blister located at the front of the starship. He had never encountered anyone else there, and he was pretty sure most of the crew didn't even know it existed.

An operations officer could use the blister to take star sightings in the event of a navigation system failure, which could be used to determine where the ship was and theoretically how to guide the ship. Unfortunately, using the ancient handheld devices available in place of computers meant the ship's actual location could only be calculated within several hundred thousand kilometers. This method was not good enough to navigate a ship capable of reaching almost 40 percent of the speed of light, or 0.4 *c*, in standard space, and jumping into hyperspace for faster-than-light, or FTL, travel without navigation computers was impossible.

Earth, the home planet, had been lost long ago. One would think humankind would have finally gotten it right after five or six thousand years of existence, but greed, whether for power or wealth, had always dragged humans down.

Late in the twenty-first century, fusion energy became a practical power source, though not unlimited in supply. Hydrogen was abundant and fusion was clean, producing no radioactive residue. Within a decade, all advanced countries had switched to fusion power for energy. Then the power struggles began in earnest. Countries that had gotten wealthy because of oil or gas reserves found themselves with resources they could no longer sell, and they couldn't eat or drink them. More importantly, these countries had never bothered to develop any other resources. Why should they? They controlled the proverbial cash cow. These countries had built large militaries using their wealth to protect their resources. When their wealth was gone and their economies gutted, they didn't even have enough to buy what they needed to support their populations, and their leaders became desperate. If they wanted to stay in power, they had to meet their people's needs. If they couldn't buy it, they'd have to take it. Small, local wars began, which soon escalated into significant regional conflicts as allies began helping allies. Eventually, every nation became involved in one way or another. Over the next 50 years, wars raged across the globe.

There was hope, though. Many of the advanced countries, led by the United States, Japan, and France, knew that although hydrogen was not unlimited on Earth, there were significant sources of it in the solar system. The space race began again in earnest. Whoever could control the hydrogen within the solar system would become very wealthy and powerful.

Scientists experimented with propulsion systems for spaceships, but most didn't work due to the lack of an adequate power supply. Early ion drives were developed and used, but with the limited power available from a fission reactor, it still took over one hundred days to reach Mars. It would take an ion-drive ship fifteen hundred days to get to Jupiter. Fusion power drastically reduced travel times. The first fusion-powered ion drive ship made the trip to Mars in six days. Over the late twenty-first and early twenty-second centuries, permanent settlements appeared on Earth's Moon and Mars, and mining facilities were built in the asteroid belt and the Jupiter microsystem. Engineers developed new drive systems as fusion technology improved, and the rest of the system was eventually explored and settled.

Improved fusion-drive technology also meant nearby star systems were now within man's grasp. Able to reach speeds of 0.15 *c*, these starships could explore and colonize Proxima Centauri b, though it would take 26.6 years.

Ships were launched, and the crew and colonists were put in cryosleep to minimize the supplies needed for such a voyage. Improvements continued and fusion drives ultimately maxed out at 0.35 *c*, which meant the trip to Proxima Centauri b was reduced to 11.4 years. The new drives also allowed colonies to be established on Gliese 1061 b and c, 34 years, Luyten b, 35 years, and Teegarden b and c, also 35 years. But fusion drives weren't the best way to explore and colonize the galaxy. FTL travel was needed.

Humanity had discovered hyperspace in the middle of the twenty-second century, though it had been theorized well before that. Scientists had been sure it was there but had had no way of accessing it.

It was not until the formal discovery of tachyons and the ability to generate them that access to hyperspace became possible. Like hyperspace, tachyons had long been theorized. The problem was that they were thought to travel at speeds faster than light. During the development of the fusion drive, scientists working for the Old Earth space agency NASA tried various charged particle drives. One of those drives stumped the scientists and engineers working on it. It was producing particles that simply disappeared within nanoseconds. They had unknowingly created a tachyon generator.

Twelve years later, an engineer on that same project, David Little, was assigned to the Jet Propulsion Labs' lunar facility to work on the hyperspace project. The project lead discussed tachyons and how they might be used to open a "door" to hyperspace. The problem was that they had no idea how to create tachyons, which she proceeded to describe.

David was a nuts-and-bolts type of engineer and had never heard of tachyons. The more he heard, though, the more he was sure that the particle generator he had worked on years earlier had been generating tachyons. He approached Katherine Joy, the project lead, and explained the particle generator to her. Though doubtful, Dr. Joy sent a request to NASA. The prototype generator was pulled out of storage and sent to the moon. By the end of the month, the LittleJoy tachyon generator was opening small tears into hyperspace.

Over the next fifty years, the research progressed from probes to human-crewed ships finally entering hyperspace. Now that they were there, researchers had to determine how to navigate through the hyperspace.

The simplest way to interpret the early data was that hyperspace was similar to Old Earth's oceans. It had strong and weak currents that crossed through it, but with energy instead of water. The first probes had found that they could move through hyperspace using just the power of those currents pushing against the satellite itself.

They also discovered that the first generation of drives was not only useless but dangerous if used in hyperspace. Compressed gas thrusters could control ship direction and attitude. The manned probes used the effect of hyperspace on the ship and the thrusters to move around Earth's solar system at velocities at or slightly higher than the speed of light. They also found that gravity affected the hyper generator. The higher the gravitational forces, the more energy it took to open a hyperspace portal, exponentially so.

The age of FTL had begun. Numerous enterprises, both private and government, started sending probes to nearby systems. Colony ships were created, designed for hundreds or even thousands of colonists to be carried in cryosleep until they reached their destination. What eventually became the core systems were settled and developed. But that was only the first step. Moving and navigating in hyperspace still had to be conquered. There were no references, no waypoints to judge speed and location.

By the early twenty-second century, the unrest on Earth and the Sol System colonies came to a head. Like most scientific discoveries, fusion technology could either be used to better humanity or lead to its destruction, and unlike nuclear weapons it didn't leave radioactive fallout. Every powerful coalition, and many smaller ones, had fusion bombs of assorted sizes at their disposal.

Tensions escalated and groups began developing plans to save their cultures. They began building FTL colony ships under the screen that the vessels would be ready by the time hyperspace navigation was solved. In part, this was true; if a solution was found, the ships could be used to speed up the expansion of existing settlements and colonize known habitable planets that were too distant for current methods. Most of the large groups planned along these lines.

ANCUK—the coalition of the old Commonwealth countries of Australia, New Zealand, Canada, and the United Kingdom—created Project Exodus. Ten large FTL colony ships that could each carry ten thousand colonists in cryosleep with a crew of two hundred. The crew would rotate in and out of cryo so forty were always awake to maintain the ship.

In 2141, the king of Great Britain, Henry X, in consultation with the heads of the ANCUK nations, ordered the colonists and crews to board their respective ships. The other necessities of founding a colony—animal embryos, seeds, all types of equipment, and as much knowledge as could be crammed into the computer banks—were already aboard. By this time, two additional countries had added their ships to the mix. Israel and South Africa had built a vessel together, as had the Scandinavian countries of Sweden, Norway, and Denmark.

On November 15, fusion warheads detonated around Earth. The conflagration quickly spread across space as various space orbitals, both military and civilian, were destroyed. The order to commence Project Exodus was given. The twelve colony ships and their six naval escorts transited from Earth Lagrange Point Alpha toward open space, charging their hyperdrives as they proceeded. Forty-five minutes later, eleven large colony ships and escort disappeared into hyperspace. Attackers destroyed one ANCUK ship and four escorts before they could jump.

The journey would be long, but the colonists, like Moses, wandered through hyperspace. When they had finally exited hyperspace to get bearings after four hundred days of travel, they found they had traveled almost eight hundred light-years.

They had arrived at the Orion Cluster.

*****

Chapter One
Empire Date: March 1044

Captain Hazard King sat in the command chair of his Imperial heavy carrier *Constellation*, and surveyed the displays in front of his command console. The Imperial Fleet was spread in an arc in front of Iris IV to prevent the Swarm from capturing and destroying a colony of twenty million inhabitants. The fleet had been battling the Swarm forces for the last three days, and were slowly being forced back across the system.

The war had been going on for one hundred years. To date, seventeen colonies had been taken and destroyed. No communications had ever been received, and no explanations or reasons were ever given. There were no responses to diplomatic offers—only defeats. Deity knows the Empire had tried. Stealth probes sent into defeated systems showed only the destruction of each colony and system, yet strangely there was no Swarm presence.

The Empire had a substantial technological advantage, but the Swarm had untold numbers. Using those numbers, they had overwhelmed every attempt by the fleet to defeat them. Even devastation on a twenty- or thirty-to-one basis was not enough. A single occurrence, early in the war, where the Empire had beaten off an attack, had been followed up within two years by an even larger Swarm attack. The fleet had been annihilated. Fortunately, the Swarm had shown no technological improvements since their first encounter, although its tactics had changed.

Most importantly, they had no FTL capabilities. Imperial ships were able to quickly move around the Empire using their hyperdrive capabilities. After each successful Swarm system attack, due to a combination of the their slower speeds and the need to replace their losses, Swarm forces usually took five to ten years to launch their next offensive. This gave the Empire time to rebuild the fleet, develop new technology, and try again.

Hazard King was a rather unremarkable man. He stood 180 cm, with light-caramel skin due to an East Indies' lineage on his mother's side, and he had the beginning of a receding hairline. He could have blended easily into most crowds, except for the scar that ran from his right earlobe to mid-cheek, a reminder of the battle in Echo System. Hazard could have had the scar healed—modern medicine could easily have taken care of it—but it reminded him of the debt he felt he owed to his lost shipmates. He was becoming "pudgy," to his disgust, because he spent a great deal of time seated, either in his command chair or at his desk handling the deluge of paperwork the navy seemed to sail on, which left little time to exercise. When he did have time, his partially disabled right leg, a souvenir of an attempted assassination, limited what he could do.

King's crew knew—not guessed, *knew*—he was the best commander in the fleet, but he disdained wearing his decorations except on the most formal occasions. When he did, in addition to all his other combat awards, he sported not one but *two* Imperial Stars, the Empire's second-highest award for valor.

At Tarrant 3, he commanded the *Robust*-class destroyer *Cheetah*. When the squadron commander's ship was destroyed, King had taken command of the destroyer squadron. When the battle had turned poorly for the Empire, King had gathered the remaining nearby small ships, and had launched a furious counterattack. For a moment, the Swarm was driven back, but it had been short lived. How long could 23 frigates and destroyers hope to last against the numbers arrayed against them? However, it was long enough to allow the main body of the defending fleet to withdraw from the Swarm's trap. Grand Admiral Henderson had immediately realized what the force was doing and pushed the rest of the fleet through the gap.

Hazard King's group repeatedly ripped through the enemy formation using his small ships like atmospheric fighters, keeping the hole open long enough to allow the fleet to survive. As the main fleet poured through the gap, the battleship divisions turned to engage the Swarm and support King's force. Only eleven of the twenty-three ships remained once the fleet had jumped out. *Cheetah* had been one of them, if one could call what remained a ship. By then, Hazard King had been in a stasis tube in sick bay, seriously wounded when the main bridge was destroyed.

Here he sat, the Hero of Tarrant 3, in command of a heavy carrier, the first of its kind. He was the youngest capital ship captain in the history of the fleet. He had helped design the fighters and the carriers, so it made sense to give him the command. The *Connie*, as everyone referred to her, was the largest hyper-capable ship the Empire had ever designed. She was nearly twice the length of a dreadnought and half as wide at the beam. There were four landing bays that gave them the ability to launch one hundred fighters at a time, and space to hold a complement of five hundred strike fighters. On top of that, *Connie* had her own offensive capabilities. Running three-quarters the length of the centerline were a pair of 800 mm rail guns, each capable of spitting out a heavy metal slug at 0.35 *c*. At that speed, one round could destroy a small moon. Each weapon had a dedicated fusion reactor to charge the firing capacitors, and it took only five minutes to reach a full charge. They were not as effective as long-range weapons, but they were devastating at close range.

Most people—and all King's crew—didn't understand why he hadn't been named a Hero of the Empire, the most significant recognition any person could achieve. A Hero of the Empire took precedence over everyone but the immediate Imperial family. They were entitled to obeisance from the nobility and those in the military were required to salute him. There had only been seventeen in the long history of the Empire, and while no one would dispute that every one of them had deserved the award, King had done much more than most who had earned the honor.

Captain King had a secret, though. A secret that kept him from being named a hero. Only the grand admiral knew his secret—and he only knew because he was King's uncle. King was not who he appeared to be. Empress Elizabeth V had had four children: two sons and two daughters. Her second son, the crown prince, was Henry Alexander Zebulon Arnaud Robert Dimitry Kane. That prince sat stoically in the command chair of the *Constellation*.

He could not be named a Hero of the Empire because he had been born one.

And now that ship and the fleet it served with stood with its back to Iris IV.

* * *

Captain, the squadron is on station and in our assigned position," the navigator announced.

Captain King nodded and turned to the damage-control assistant. "What's our current condition, Jamie?"

King could have looked at the holographic displays arrayed around his chair, but he didn't have the time to give the data the attention it needed.

"Shields are regenerating and are at sixty-five percent. Shield number one has lost two nodes. We'll be able to get eighty-five percent in that quadrant by extending shields two and six, leaving them at ninety percent. All rail guns and phased-array cannons are online. We are limited to ninety percent thrust on sublight engines. The hyperdrive is available and charged for the jump."

King considered their situation for a moment. "Don't extend shield number two. I want it at one hundred percent, at least initially. I want to face the enemy during the next attack. If we need to turn we can show our port side to the Bee Bastards, so those shields need to be strongest. Helm, I hope you're paying attention."

The helm and damage-control officers responded, "Aye, sir."

King looked at the communication station. "Contact the rest of the squadron and get status reports."

A flashing light and a chime on his left console got his attention. King pushed the reply key. A holo display opened in front of him, and an officer wearing the red braid of an admiral's aide appeared.

"*Constellation* actual here."

"Stand by for the fleet commander."

King noticed this was a fleet conference for senior officers. Though the goal of every cadet at the academy was to be considered a senior officer, there were times he wished he was just a plain fighter pilot killing BBs.

Fleet Admiral Henderson appeared. He looked worn. King knew he had hoped the outcome would be different this time. New weapons, new tactics, but the same old results. He would be the first fleet commander to lose two star systems. Then again, most fleet commanders didn't usually last long enough to accomplish that.

"Our development of fighter craft and carriers to launch them seems to have been highly effective," Henderson said. "The new flak rounds for the cruiser-size rail guns have also proved amazingly effective. However, the Swarm changed their tactics even faster than we expected in response to the fleet carriers, and we got caught with our pants down. We didn't have enough support to defend them."

Two hours ago, ten of the smaller Imperial escort carriers had launched almost twelve hundred fighters. The Imperial fighters had proved to be as fast and maneuverable as the Swarm attack ships and had decimated the enemy during their initial attack.

A wave of excitement had enveloped the fleet. Maybe this time they would hold.

That joy was quickly crushed as the Swarm launched an all-out assault on the carriers. The Swarm ships ignored the Imperial escorts and suffered severe losses with less than a quarter surviving, but that was more than enough to take out the ten carriers. The Imperial fighters were rendered useless without a place to refuel and rearm. Then the Swarm showed they could fight a set-piece battle. Since they didn't have enough small attack ships remaining, they moved their capital ships forward and systematically eliminated the Imperial picket ships.

"With the outer pickets depleted," Henderson continued, "my hope is that the Iris IV fighter squadrons can manage the same thing the carrier fighters did. We must provide a screen for the defense fortresses so their fighters can be effective." The admiral's holo appeared to look into the eyes of each officer. "Here we will stand."

* * * * *

Chapter Two
Empire Date: May 1032

The musty smell of recycled air, mixed with the slight scent of human bodies and the ozone produced by electronics, wafted out of the ventilation grate. Two men sat in the cramped living space assigned to newly commissioned junior officers on their first ship. Both were about the same height and weight and had the lean look of men in top physical shape. They were wearing the regulation light blue slacks, white long-sleeved shirts, and light blue ties of Imperial naval officers, and their collar points were adorned with the gold "butter" bars, indicating they were ensigns. The blue Imperial uniform jackets had been tossed on their respective bunks. Covers were not worn routinely aboard ship and had been stowed away.

Ensign Hazard King sat hunched at his desk, a small pull-down affair at one end of the compartment, studying a Type-III passenger shuttle manual. He had been assigned to the Imperial dreadnought *Devastator* two days ago. His initial posting straight out of the naval academy was as a shuttle pilot. A *passenger* shuttle pilot.

"Can you believe this crap? I busted my ass for *four years* at the academy and graduated in the *top five* of my class—to become a taxi driver? I don't usually care what other people think, but I am a trash hauler. It's embarrassing."

His closest friend—really the only friend he'd ever had—reclined on his bunk. Jacob "Jake" Cutter was a security specialist. He'd been appointed to the guard detachment assigned to the fleet commander. *Devastator* was the flagship of the Imperial Fleet, so the fleet commander maintained his HQ aboard, though he spent much of his time planet-side doing whatever a fleet commander did.

"Hank." Jake was the only person who called Hazard by his abbreviated first name. "You knew going into the academy it would be like this. You will never be in a billet that will put you in danger. There is too much at stake. We're lucky we didn't get assigned to a dirtside supply depot counting mess kits. Your father and uncle had to fight like hell to get you this posting. I can still feel the pain of the ass-chewing your mother gave me when she found out you'd taken flight training at the academy."

"If you think you felt pain," Hazard said, "you should have witnessed mine and Father's, but at least Mom controlled her anger enough to do it in private. I love my mother, but she can be a bitch when things don't go the way she wants."

"You realize that some people would consider it treasonous to call her Imperial Majesty, Empress Elizabeth V, a bitch?" Jake chuckled. "You're the second son, the spare heir, and until the succession is firmly established, you have to be protected."

"Yes, I am the spare, but I have two younger sisters who are just as capable of becoming empress. True, they may be a little young right now, but it is not unheard of for someone to become emperor or empress before their majority. Grandfather became emperor when he was fourteen. The crown has a long history of its princes serving in the fleet. I think it is important for us to continue that tradition now, for us to show we're in it with our subjects."

"Henry—" Jake only used that name when he was serious, pissed, or both "—you are second in line of succession. Yes, your brother is twenty-six and is being groomed for the position, but what if something happens to him? Then you would become Crown Prince Henry and your education to become emperor would begin in earnest. The empress is only thinking of the good of the Empire. Quit your bitching. You didn't have to go through the academy twice, like I did. I'll say this: the naval academy was a piece of cake compared to the marine academy."

Jake had become Hazard's personal man-at-arms when Hazard turned twelve. After graduating from the marine academy, Jake did a four-year stint in the Corps then joined the Imperial Guards. Life longevity treatments, which extended one's life by 25 to 30 percent, were typical for the wealthy and noble. Additionally, the apparent aging process was significantly reduced. So it was decided that select young marine officers would receive the treatment and become personal armsmen—male or female; they were always referred to as armsmen—to the Imperial children. Though he was thirty-seven, Jake looked the same age as the prince, and he had gone through the naval academy alongside Hazard. His assignment to the fleet commander's guard was his cover so he could remain close to the prince. The fleet commander was the only person on board who knew their true identities.

"Then I guess I'll become the best damned chauffeur I can be," Hazard said. "Problem is both the marine detachment commander, who owns all the shuttles, and the executive officer think I had to have done something idiotic to be posted aboard the flagship with orders not only to fly shuttles but to specifically *not fly* assault shuttles. They're wondering how the fifth-ranked student in the last graduating class could land such a lowly assignment. Damn, if I didn't want to fly so bad—"

Hazard's wrist communicator beeped. "Ensign King here."

"Ensign King will report to the XO's office as soon as possible," the computer-generated voice stated.

"King acknowledges."

"What did you do now?" Jake asked. "Whatever it was, make yourself pretty and trot on up to see your buddy. I think I'll take a little nap."

"What, you're not coming? I thought you were supposed to be guarding me."

"Plenty of marines up in officer country to protect you, and you don't think it would appear odd if I tagged along after you on this trip? Besides, I'm a little concerned there may be a marine or two on board who might know me. We are supposed to be incognito, remember?"

* * *

King exited the lift onto the single corridor leading to the command center. The central control hub for the ship was buried deep within the confines of the hull amidships fore-to-aft and slightly forward of the vertical center. In addition to the shields and armor of the ship, the command center had separate shields and dedicated life support. It was a protected citadel. The current convention was to call it the command center rather than the more traditional bridge, but most long-serving officers referred to it as the latter.

The corridor was not long. Hazard could see the armored hatch of the command center standing open at the opposite end of the corridor, a marine sentry standing beside it. Only authorized personnel were allowed on the bridge. There were two doors on the port side; the first was for the chief of staff for an embarked flag officer. The second led to the flag officer's conference room. On the starboard side, the first door was to the XO's office and the second was the captain's conference room. There was a marine guard stationed there because the captain's suite and offices were accessible through the conference room. If the fleet commander had been aboard, there would have been a third guard at his conference room door. Both the captain's and admiral's suites opened directly onto the bridge, and was the regular access point for either.

Hazard stood before the XO's entrance and braced himself. After checking his appearance, he pushed the Enter button. The door opened into a small anteroom, where the XO's yeoman, his door-keeper, controlled access.

"Ensign King reporting to the executive officer as ordered."

The petty officer, who was busily typing and hadn't even bothered to stop as Hazard entered, looked up.

"Have a seat, sir; I'll let him know you're here." He promptly went back to typing.

Hazard stood so as not to crease his uniform. After about ten minutes, the yeoman told him the XO was ready to see him. Hazard readied himself, pushed the Enter button, and followed the same routine as before. When the door opened, he marched in, stopped at attention at the required one pace in front of the XO's desk, and said, "Ensign King reporting as ordered, sir."

The commander looked up from his monitor and nodded. "At ease, King. Take a seat."

Hazard sat and looked around the surprisingly large space. He knew from studying the ship's drawings that the XO's private suite was through the door on the right side of the office. On the left-hand wall was a large print of the *Devastator*, showing her when she was launched over seventy years ago. Behind his desk were the obligatory pictures of Hazard's mother, the empress.

There was sufficient room for all the department heads to meet in the office, which explained its size. The XO was responsible for the ship's day-to-day operations, so the department heads reported through the XO to the captain unless there was an issue.

The young prince had an advantage that the typical newly reporting ensign didn't have: he knew all there was to know about the executive officer, Commander Douglas Arthur. All fleet officers had basic biographies that were available for anyone to see. In addition, there was the Fleet Officers Listing, a publication which listed every active fleet and marine officer. Hazard and Jake would be in it when it was updated next year. Though he would probably thought of himself as wiry, Commander Arthur looked frail, with thinning hair and a pencil-thin mustache. Hazard considered him mousy looking.

Despite the war going on for over seventy years, Arthur had never been on a ship in active combat. His first posting had been the *Devastator*, which became the fleet flagship when it was launched, but it had been well away from the front lines and not fired on. With the new ships and men needed after each defeat to the Swarm, Arthur had rapidly progressed to a frigate gunnery officer, then a destroyer XO, then a frigate captain. Finally, he had been promoted to commander and given command of a new light cruiser that was being built. He was there, far behind the lines, when the Swarm had launched their next assault. Fleet didn't assign command of battleships and dreadnoughts to officers who hadn't been under fire, and the XO knew it. It made him petty and embittered, and it was well known that he liked to torment junior officers.

"Ensign King, I wanted to go over these unusual orders that came with your posting," the XO began. "Most officers come to their first posting without a specialty. While it is true that some do come aboard, like your classmate Ensign Cutter, with a specialty that is in demand—security, medical, and engineering fall into that category—graduate line officers are normally put into a rotation through the different departments to determine where they are a good fit. They serve time in the navigation and weapons departments from six to eight months, until we see where they excel. Then we place them in an appropriate role for the remainder of their initial two-year tour. You, however, have these orders assigning you as a shuttle pilot. Do you know how unusual that is?"

Seeing Hazard's blank stare, the XO continued, "There are no fleet officers aboard the *Devastator* who are posted as shuttle pilots. I doubt there are any in the fleet. Marines fly the attack ships and the shuttles, pinnaces, couriers, and tugs, and all the pilots are noncommissioned officers. The commander of the MarDet, Colonel Butler, is also at a loss and has no idea what to do with you, either. He would love to have a marine second lieutenant with your qualifications in charge of the aviation group, not a naval officer. What I need you to do, Ensign," the XO droned on, "is accept a posting to either the weapons or navigation department. That way we can train you as a proper line officer. Since this is an unusual circumstance, I'm willing to let you choose which department you will start with."

Hazard was both stunned and angry that they were trying to take away the flying he loved, but also because so many people had been involved in arranging his orders. Orders that had been carefully crafted to meet his desires while simultaneously fulfilling his mother's wishes. He was stunned that a senior officer would so willingly flout the rules when they were in his favor. King's orders were all about making his life easier.

"Begging your pardon, sir," Hazard said, "those orders didn't come through the normal Bureau of Personal channels. Before you decide to change them, I suggest you check the endorsements on my posting."

The pompous ass rolled his eyes and turned to his terminal. "Very well, Ensign, I'll go along with this—" He abruptly stopped and his face grew red when he saw the final signature. "Would you mind explaining to me, young sir, how it is that the fleet commander himself approved your orders?"

Now Hazard was in a quandary. While maintaining the honor code—at least the truth part of it—he had to explain how he had received the strange orders.

Well, here goes, he thought. "Sir, my mother is a very influential woman." *I guess you could say that about the empress of the Empire.* "She always seems to get her way." *Also, true.* "She was not happy about me going to the academy, but both sides of my family have a history of serving, so she reluctantly agreed to allow me to attend. My mother used her influence to arrange those orders. She would be most upset if her arrangements were circumvented."

Commander Arthur's face continued its color change through every shade of red. "You're telling me that some doting mother has arranged for her cowardly son—who should have never been admitted to the academy, let alone the fleet—to obtain a safe position in the service so he can claim to uphold the family obligation to serve? Your father must be as cowardly as you, not standing up to such a woman."

Hazard jerked up out of his chair and fire blazed in his eyes. He stood at attention in front of the desk and stared down at the poor excuse of an Imperial officer. He glanced into his mother's eyes and thought, *You are not going to like this, Mom.* "Sir, you may think me a jailhouse lawyer, and perhaps I am. I am well-versed in all the requirements of the fleet code, even the most obscure ones, and you have crossed the line. I gladly take your insults against my person; I am required to. I am *not* required to suffer anyone's insults against my honor or my family's honor. Therefore, under the Imperial Fleet Code, I challenge you to either withdraw your insults against my family or be prepared to defend them on the field of honor!"

"You are a pompous little ass!" the XO shouted. "Are you threatening me? You have made it extremely easy for me. I'll run you off this ship and out of the service." The office door opened, and two marines stepped in. "Sergeant, take this officer into custody and confine him in the brig in isolation. He is being charged with conduct unbecoming and threatening an officer."

Hazard looked the XO in the eye. "You, sir, are without honor. Based on your career, I suspect you have always been without honor. You are a blight on the officer corps." He nodded to the sergeant, turned, and left the office. He wondered how long it would take before Jake found out where he was.

*****

Chapter Three
Empire Date: May 1032

"That impulsive, idiotic fool!" Empress Elizabeth raged as she stalked around the room. Grand Duke Henry, her husband and consort, and Edmund Randolph, the Duke of Kara and grand admiral of the fleet, decided that silence while she vented was probably the best course of action, and they remained seated and quiet in the empress' private office.

The grand duke felt this was a case of the pot calling the kettle black. Prince Henry looked like his father, but he had always had his mother's temperament. True, the academy had helped him to manage that temper, but it was still there.

Hazard, or Prince Henry, as he was referred within the confines of the palace, would have been surprised at how fast everyone had become aware of his predicament. Jacob had known the instant it happened; he'd been listening in. Grand Duke Henry and the grand admiral knew within an hour, and his mother shortly after that.

Jacob had rigged the *Devastator's* internal monitoring systems in preparation for their time on board, so he could monitor the prince. No one on the *Devastator* knew of this. Additionally, everything was recorded, so there could be no doubt about what had happened. The grand duke had been tempted to jump on a shuttle and fly up to the *Devastator* to beat the crap out of the XO.

"After all we did to arrange for this posting and allow him to do what he wanted," the empress said. Her husband saw the wheels turning behind her eyes as she slumped into her ornate desk chair. "What do we do now? We obviously can't leave him sitting in the brig. Without our classified recordings, which we obviously can't release, it would be the commander's word against Henry's. I am not concerned about what may happen to that pitiful excuse of an Imperial officer, but I do, honestly, want Henry to have a naval career. One that he earns on his own merits."

Sensing the time was right, Henry leaned across the desk and took his wife's hand. "Beth, I hate saying I told you so. The orders we arranged to protect him only shined a spotlight on him. He wanted to be a marine. It is why he learned to fly the shuttles at the academy. For part of that, I'll take responsibility. He idolizes Jacob. He wants to be a warrior like Jacob, who is Henry's best friend—maybe his only friend. I saw it happening, but I thought it was just a phase, that he would grow out of it as he got older. I should have changed out his personal armsman to break the attachment, but I couldn't crush his heart like that.

"So, what did we do?" the Grand Duke continued. "We got him commissioned as a naval officer because it is safer than being a marine. We arranged to have him stationed on the fleet flagship. Everyone knows the fleet flagship is the most protected part of the formation. It must survive to command. We arranged for a remarkable set of orders to be issued that would allow him to fly shuttles. I find it remarkable that he answered the XO's questions as he did. He didn't tell the truth, but he also didn't lie." *I'll have to remember to ask him if he did that on the fly,* Henry thought, *or if he had worked out the story beforehand.*

"If I may, My Empress," Randolph said. "I may have a solution for part of the problem. It would not be unusual for Commander Arthur to rotate out of his current assignment. He is nearing the window when that would normally occur. I also know that Count Marbury is available to be put in that position. He has been nagging me for three months since his release from the hospital, and he would be an upgrade in the position. Since the count is related to Henry by blood, they can't serve in the same command. These things happen all the time, so we simply arrange a transfer to avoid conflict. We transfer Count Mayberry to the *Devastator* then officially we'll let everyone know that Ensign King will be transferring off because of a familial relationship with the new XO. After all, he has been on board only a week.

"I'll go on board—that's not an issue since it is my flagship—and discuss with the captain and Commander Arthur the rumors that have reached me about the treatment of junior officers aboard my flagship. I'll then point out that the best way to resolve everything is to quietly let things drop and accept the transfer orders. I'm sure he'll see the light."

"I don't want to see that slimy excuse of a serving officer get off free," the empress snapped.

"Nor do I," Henry added.

"And he won't," the admiral said. "I have the perfect spot for him. I'll have him assigned as the staff supply officer to Vice Admiral Choi. Choi is a hard-nosed son of a bitch. He oversees the cruiser screen of the main fleet. Choi lost a leg many years ago, and instead of a normal prosthetic, he stumps around his bridge on a peg leg. Thinks of himself as a pirate. What is more, he's always in the thick of it. So, Commander Arthur will get his chance to see combat with Peg Leg Choi."

The Empress grinned. "I shouldn't feel this way about anyone, but in this case, he deserves it. So, what about Henry?"

"After we spring him out of jail?" Grand Duke Henry chuckled. "I think he needs to spend a day or two here so we can discuss things and set things right." He looked at his wife. "I mean that about setting things right, my love. I don't put my foot down often, but in this case, I am. We can't keep him wrapped in a safe cocoon. Second son or not, he has chosen this career. He must run the risks like anyone else in the service. Yes, we will pull strings to try to mitigate the risk, but we will not erase them. At the same time, he will have to become a regular fleet officer; it's too late for him to change over to the marines; too many people would ask too many questions. If he wants to continue as an officer, he needs to go through the same training they do. After that, he will go aboard a battleship or heavy cruiser as a weapons or operations officer. Admiral, can you make that happen?"

* * *

"So, little brother got himself in a spot of trouble, I hear, Daniel," commented Crown Prince Edward, heir to the Imperial throne, to his personal armsman. "Calling out a senior officer for a duel doesn't look very good on the Imperial résumé, does it?" The prince practically crowed. Edward was four years older than Henry, but unfortunately for the heir, he had lived in his brother's shadow for the last eight years. Henry excelled in scholastics and sports, generating much parental pride. The crown prince didn't do well in either area, primarily because he had little interest in them. That fact was not lost on his parents.

"I am not sure that I'd refer to him as 'the little brother,' My Prince," Major Daniel Shipwright replied. "He is a fleet officer, after all. And yes, I was informed of the incident almost as soon as it happened. All the primary armsmen for the Imperial children share their reports. We do it so we are immediately aware of any shared threats. To answer your next question, yes, Jacob, Henry's armsman, knows everything going on around you, just as I know everything about Henry."

A look of shock passed over Edward's face, which he quickly controlled.

"My Prince, you must realize that anything you do inside the palace, or any other Imperial establishment, is monitored. I swore an oath of loyalty to you, so I don't go running to the empress or the grand duke. They are authorized to pull information, but I don't voluntarily produce it. Regulations precluded me from doing that unless you become a danger to yourself or the empress."

Daniel Shipwright was of Jamaican heritage, like his prince. Dark skinned and muscular, he was ten centimeters taller than his primary at 190 centimeters. He had been the crown prince's armsman for three long years. Unlike the other royal charges, the crown prince was not the most stellar person to work for or with. He was petulant, arrogant, and not shy about using his position to bully people into doing what he wanted. In Daniel's three years, he had pulled the prince out of four situations that would have landed most people in jail or fired from their jobs. From actual physical abuse of staff to sexual harassment, the prince was a piece of work.

"I am only glad that Mother and Father can now see how his charming demeanor has fooled them. I've told them for years that he was a devious bastard that would someday embarrass the family," Prince Edward continued smugly.

Daniel had to work hard to keep from rolling his eyes. The consensus around the palace was that the crown prince would not be a good emperor. He had surrounded himself with sycophants and toadies who only cared about the prince's power and how they could use it. He would not be the first emperor of this sort, but with the war on, Daniel prayed for the empress' continued good health.

*****

Chapter Four

Empire Date: June 1032

Hazard sat at his desk in the small stateroom and thought about how the more things changed, the more they seemed to stay the same. Jake was reclining on the bed, listening to music as he pored over the schematics for the Imperial heavy cruiser *Shinto*. They had arrived aboard the previous morning, and the duty officer had logged them in and assigned them to quarters. After spending a year at the Epsilon V shipyard undergoing upgrades, the ship had only recently arrived in the system. The *Shinto* was an older *Pagoda*-class heavy cruiser, but had been retrofitted with the latest shield generators and point-defense systems. The senior staff was planet-side for meetings with fleet staff, as well as meeting and integrating with their new squadron.

The ship's executive officer had left word Hazard was being assigned to the weapons department as an assistant section commander for the new quadruple 40 mm rail gun batteries. That battery of eight guns ran down the cruiser's port side. The controls for the ship's point-defense batteries were redundant. Typically, fire-control management was handled by the principal defensive fire-control officer on the bridge, assisted by an officer in primary weapons control. The local section commander was responsible for manning, training, and maintaining his section. The section commander could also override fire-control during a battle from his panel in the local control station situated between mounts four and five. As the assistant section commander, Hazard would oversee four mounts and be stationed in either mount one or mount eight.

"Jake, how is it you forgot to mention that you had a total surveillance package set up on me back on the *Devastator?* It would have been nice to know that. I was worried I might be in that cell for a long time."

Hazard's best friend shook his head. "I seem to recall a certain person of noble birth, who shall remain nameless—" he looked at Hazard "—who stated that he didn't want to be bogged down with the nuts and bolts of his security plan, so long as it didn't smother him. The way I see it, if you didn't even know you were being watched, you were not being smothered." Jake brushed his hands together. "Mission accomplished. And yes, before you ask, I already have the same system setup here. So, if you decide to get frisky with someone in our luxurious abode—" Jake waved his hand around the room "—let me know and I'll turn it off. We wouldn't want that footage getting to the palace."

* * *

Jake smiled as he lay in his bunk, thinking of the spy package the prince had discovered. If Hazard knew how long it had been in place and how invasive it truly was, he would not be happy. When he was twelve, the prince had undergone a simple procedure to check on a possible cancerous condition. Or at least that was what the prince had been told. Cancer was eliminated over three hundred years ago, save for one or two particularly rare and nasty forms. The entire procedure had been a cover to implant a nano monitoring system. Every member of the immediate Imperial family was implanted with the system, but only the empress and the grand duke knew about it. The security details assigned to each Imperial knew of the implants and used them as part of their protection.

The system had three distinct monitoring functions. One was a tracking system that constantly broadcast Hazard's location. The second was an audio monitoring system. Jake, or anyone else with the access and equipment, could monitor whatever was being said in or near the prince's presence. The last piece was a biometric monitor that measured blood pressure, body temperature, pulse oxygen levels, and heart rate and rhythm. It wasn't constantly monitored but would alert the security detail if anything strayed outside acceptable limits. In an open environment, the system had a range of almost one kilometer. The inside of a heavily armored starship, with its many electronic systems, cut the range to less than a hundred meters. As a result, Jake had had to make "discreet" arrangements to access the ship's internal monitoring system and use it to track Hazard. Basically, he had hacked into the ship's security system.

* * *

Hazard thought about Jake's comment about "getting frisky" during the evening meal the next day. He was not a prude; he had had a dalliance or two and always in his persona of Hazard King. None were allowed to become serious. He would never wish that life on anyone—hell, he didn't like that life. That was why he was Ensign Hazard King and not Prince Henry. But a woman who was with Ensign King would not have it any easier. There would always be prolonged periods apart and, most importantly, the knowledge that the next battle with the Swarm was always imminent.

* * *

Hiroko Ogowa spotted her cabinmate and friend, Lanre Bassey, a tall Nigerian beauty, looking for her around the crowded dining area. When Lanre spotted Hiroko, she joined her and set her tray down.

Before her friend could even sit down Hiroko said, "Lani, who's that new guy over there?"

Lani looked where she was pointing, shrugged, and said, "Oh, that's one of the two officers who arrived late last week."

Odd, Hiroko thought. *Strange time of the year to get new officers on board. They looked like academy graduates, but all the academy graduates had come aboard three months ago.*

"Hiri, are you interested in him?" Lani asked.

Hiroko dipped her head and tried to conceal her embarrassment and said quietly, "Well, he is rather good-looking."

Lani laughed. "Girl, I didn't know you had a taste for us darker folk."

Hiroko felt her blush deepen.

"Here's what I know," Lani continued. "He's an ensign assigned to the weapons department on the command track, and he's in charge of the first section port defense battery, and his name is Hazard King. I can go over there and ask for his waist and inseam if you'd like."

Hiroko vigorously shook her head, looked up at her tall friend, and said, "Lani, leave it alone. When the time's right, I'll 'bump' into him. I'm not a complete novice."

* * *

Jake and Hazard took their meals in the aft officers' dining room because of its location. Almost all the engineering officers and quite a few weapons officers ate there. For Hazard, it was near to both his stateroom and gunnery station, so it made sense. It also allowed him to mingle and get to know the officers in his department.

A soft soprano got his attention.

"Is this seat taken?"

Hazard looked up and saw the face—and more importantly the eyes—of the most attractive woman he had ever seen.

Hazard jumped up. *Damn, I guess all you have to do is wish for it.* He practically shouted, "It was taken, but now it's not if you want it."

She practically sang as she offered her hand. "Thank you. I'm Hiroko, and I'd be honored to share your table."

Hazard bowed slightly. "I'm Hazard, and the honor would be mine."

Hiroko beamed. "You know the customs of the Honshu home world?"

"Not as well as I should or as I'd like. Maybe you could instruct me?" Hazard replied with a sly grin.

Hiroko chuckled as she took the offered seat. "Hazard, what an unusual—and I'm thinking apt—name. Should I be in fear of my well-being or chastity?"

He blushed. *I had better not get into a battle of wits with her; I am short of ammunition.* "Point to you, my lady," Hazard said. "Point to you."

Later that evening, Hazard strolled down the passageway toward his stateroom. He couldn't remember the last time he'd had such a pleasant evening. Time had flown by as he and Hiroko had eaten and talked. He had told her as much as he could about himself, while trying to be as vague as possible.

Hiroko Ogowa, on the other hand, was a talker. She recounted how she had decided to march to the beat of her drum at an early age. She was a disappointment to her family. She had studied engineering at college and then gone off-world by joining the fleet. Proper young women of Honshu just didn't do such things. Her parents still loved her immensely but would never be comfortable with her life choices.

Hazard suddenly realized all those things attracted her to him. She had gone through or was going through the same things he was. They had much in common—the decision to break from family expectations and pursue their own dreams in the fleet.

When he stepped through the hatch to the stateroom, Jake was waiting with a huge grin on his face.

"Remember, My Prince: I see all; I know all." His friend chuckled. "When you didn't return from dinner at your usual time, I decided I should check, just in case you were in the brig again. I was, of course, surprised to find you acting the Romeo in the mess." Hazard scowled, and he quickly added, "And yes, I tuned you out when I saw you were safe."

Hazard slumped onto his rack. "What should I do? You know how I feel about getting anyone involved in my special circumstances. Most people aren't prepared for the fishbowl that being attached to a royal brings. Hell, *I'm* not prepared for it. And that doesn't include the uncertainty of a long and fruitful life is with the war going on." He sat up and looked at his best friend. "I like this girl. I'm scared, but I want to see if this could go somewhere."

Jake looked at him. "Henry…" Hazard knew he was serious. Jake only used his first name to drive a point home. "First, you are both in the fleet, so you both understand those risks. Second, you're not asking her to be an Imperial princess, at least not yet. There is a saying, from so far back in our past I'm sure no one remembers who said it, that goes, 'It is far better to have loved and lost than to have never loved at all.' However short, it is better to have moments of happiness than to go through life in drudgery. What I am saying, My Prince, is that you should pursue this. Don't let fear stop you from finding out. You have already overcome much in your life. If it turns out it's what you want, we'll make it work."

*****

Chapter Five

Empire Date September 1032

Lieutenant Junior Grade King was in the weapons department conference room with eighteen other officers from the point-defense batteries. Once a month, the group met to share ideas and problems. If someone had a problem in their section, it was likely someone else had dealt with a similar problem before. There was no need to reinvent the wheel if another officer had already figured it out. Captain O'Riley had instituted the meetings two years ago upon assuming command. He was a firm believer in sharing information. He also did a monthly all-hands broadcast to keep everyone up to date.

Today, Hazard was walking into the deep end of the pool. Shortly after being put in charge of his point-defense section, he had reviewed the doctrine and the use of rail gun batteries. There were weaknesses in the philosophy that allowed far too many Swarm attack ships to close to attack range. Hazard believed there was a better way. He had spent two months developing his proposal and had run basic simulations to prove it. Each officer was allowed, even encouraged, to submit topics for discussion. Lieutenant Ushari, his boss, was chairing this month's meeting, and Hazard's proposal was on the agenda. Since he was discussing something out of the norm, the weapons officer himself was in attendance.

"Next on the agenda, Lieutenant King has a presentation regarding point-defense doctrine," Lieutenant Ushari announced.

Hazard moved to the podium. "Fellow officers, I am reasonably sure most everyone knows me, but I'll introduce myself. I am Lieutenant Junior Grade King and I'm in charge of A-section of the port battery. I am sure some of my more experienced fellow battery and section commanders are wondering why the new guy would have the audacity to suggest something different. I would like to think that it's due to a new set of eyes.

"History has always been a passion of mine, and I believe there is seldom anything new in warfare. Currently, we have the central defense targeting system controlling each mount. The system is redundant. Each battery has a local control system and each mount has both local targeting control and manual capability. The entire system is designed to defeat incoming missiles. Now, missiles follow a relatively constant course as they approach the ship. The system can track, identify the best mount to engage, and even account for limited course deviations created by the missile's evasion program. However, they are much less capable against Swarm attack ships. The speeds and severe course changes they use minimize the effectiveness of this type of system."

Hazard looked around the room. Most faces showed either a lack of interest in the topic or skepticism, except for the weapons officer, who showed definite interest. He was also the only one present who had seen combat.

It was time to make it more personal.

"I've prepared a simulation using performance data of Swarm attack ships versus our ship. It has been time-compressed. What you will see is an attack by twenty Swarm ships against the *Shinto*. Our ship will maneuver as it normally would during this type of attack and all available weapons will be in use for defense."

Hazard ran the scenario, which took almost four minutes.

"As you saw, the *Shinto* jumped out after twenty minutes of combat with severe damage. To stay any longer would have meant destruction. If we were in an escort role, jumping out would not have been an option."

He had their attention now.

"All our defensive fire accounted for the destruction of only four Swarm ships. Note that Swarm attack ships don't withdraw during a fight. When they accomplish their mission, they regroup and attack another target. They would have reformed to attack again after the *Shinto* jumped."

Hazard paused and took a breath before continuing, "My proposal is to not attempt to track and acquire targets with the rail guns but to employ a barrage of metal. Each section, and every mount, would be assigned a specific arc they would saturate with slugs, forming a wall of metal around the ship. Then, instead of targeting and intercepting, we let the enemy fly into the fire. The pulse laser batteries would still target and engage, but they will prioritize targets that are the most dangerous. This is a simulation showing this."

Hazard ran it. It ended with all the Swarm attack ships destroyed. "The second scenario lasted almost an hour, and as you saw all bogeys were destroyed. The *Shinto*, while heavily damaged, would have still been considered combat effective."

Hazard spent the next thirty minutes answering questions about his proposal. What were the fields of fire, the fire rate? Hazard emphasized that it was important that each mount maintain fire in its sector, otherwise, gaps would develop.

The weapons officer called the meeting to an end. Everyone began filing out, but he motioned for Hazard to stay.

"That was quite the presentation, Mr. King. I have to wonder how accurate your simulations were."

"They're as accurate as I could make them, sir. True, I'm not a great programmer, but I worked with several people who are," Hazard replied. "Sir, I'm simply proposing this as an option. I think it is good, or I wouldn't have suggested it. I know smarter people on board can crunch the numbers, and I am sure the Weapons Bureau could do it. I want them to. Anything that might give us an edge."

The weapons officer looked thoughtful. "Trying to track a target going point two or point three *c* has always been a gold-plated bitch. It's the reason we have so many point-defense weapons—quantity over quality. I'm amazed that this approach has not been thought of before. It's so simplistic." He turned to look Hazard in the eye. "I like it, and I think it will work. Forward me everything you've put together. You should also be prepared to do this little talk again. I know the captain will want to hear it, and I suspect the commodore and others will as well." His eyes suddenly turned dark. "I've been there, King. A scared, shitless JG feeling his ship come apart around him. I'll do anything to keep that from happening again. Send me that information today."

*****

Chapter Six

Empire Date: December 1032

Hazard and Hiroko sat alone in the deserted pilot ready room. Henry had discovered the location while studying for his officer-of-the-deck qualification. When the *Shinto* was deployed, it used its shuttles and pinnaces for moving personnel, and the on-call crews could use the space to relax while they waited. The room had twenty plush leather reclining seats and a large display screen used for pilot briefings. Henry had set the display to show the starscape outside the ship. Hiroko sat next to him, her head on his shoulder.

These meetings had become a ritual for them. Over the last three months, every third night, when their schedules lined up, they would take their evening meal together. They would talk and catch up on what was going on for each of them. Then they come here and watch the stars.

Henry lived for these moments, having Hiroko next to him. But that feeling was mixed with dread. He knew he loved her and didn't know what to do about that.

I want so much more, but do I dare expose her to my real world? I know, at least I think I do, that she loves me, too, Henry thought. *And I could never allow her to love me, Hazard, without knowing about Prince Henry.*

He suddenly realized that when he was with Hiroko, here in the ready room, he thought of himself as Henry, not Hazard. Was that an omen?

The contemplative prince was suddenly aware that Hiroko had turned to face him. She took his hand and looked at him. "Hazard, I'm in love with you. There, I've said it. It's out there in the universe. I also know that you love me, but I sense something is holding you back."

Henry did the only thing that came to mind, he kissed her. He had intended it to be a brief, almost chaste, kiss. However, it broke the dam that had been holding back both their emotions and became long, warm, and passionate. Finally, after what Henry thought was an eternity, they stopped to take a breath.

"Well, I guess I was right—about you loving me, that is," Hiroko said, panting.

"Hiroko, I've loved you since the end of our first meal together. You don't realize it, but we have so much in common. I have also gone and studied in a field of which my mother disapproves. I joined the fleet, which she didn't want me to do. Fortunately, I had the support of my father." Henry took both of Hiroko's hands. "There's a lot you don't know about me. Things I have kept hidden from you. Not to deceive you, but to protect you."

"My love, My Prince," Hiroko began, "nothing could keep me from loving you or make me run away. There are no secrets that could dissuade me. I decided to make this decision for us. I felt one of us needed to. Tell me I'm wrong."

"Oh, My Princess," Henry said and thought how apt their new pet names for each other were. "No, I won't deny it. I do love you. I would like you to do something for me: when we're alone together, call me

Henry. Hazard is a nickname. Henry is my first name, and only my immediate family and my best friend call me that."

"Oh, Henry, of course. My Prince Henry." She stopped, eyes wide, mouth open.

Henry looked into her beautiful eyes and gave a slight bow. "Yes, I'm your Prince Henry." He could see the wheels turning in her head as she tried to piece everything together. "The problem is I'm also Prince Henry to everyone else in the Empire."

Her hands were trembling in his.

"I warned you I had an influential, strong-willed mother." Henry chuckled.

Hiroko suddenly looked worried. "How can you be in love with me? I'm just a simple girl from Honshu."

"Hiroko, you are anything but a simple girl. You decided on your destiny against your own family's wishes. I never intended to fall in love with you, but it happened. I would not wish being married into my family on anyone. I don't even like it. That's why I became Hazard King, an officer in the empress' Imperial Navy. I'll run the same risks as any other officer. Could you love a simple junior navy officer?" She nodded, and he leaned in and gave her another long kiss.

"All hands, this is the captain," the ship's speakers blared. "Long-range scouts have detected Swarm formations proceeding toward the Echo star system. All available fleet formations have been ordered to proceed to the system as soon as possible. We have recalled all ship's crew that are dirtside. Departure for Echo will be 0800 tomorrow morning."

I guess it is time; Henry thought as he held Hiroko's hand tight. "My love, I'm sure we both have a lot to do between now and then. Remember, I love you."

They left the ready room and raced into the tumult of the coming battle.

* * * * *

Chapter Seven
Empire Date: December 1032

"Defense Minister. High Admiral." The empress looked at her two senior war leaders. "Are we ready for this?"

The admiral, the Duke of Kara, quickly responded, "As ready as we can be, Your Majesty. I have given the order to commence system evacuation. Minister Adams will brief you on that. Initial fleet units are already on their way, and the main fleet body is being organized and will meet in the Tarrant system within the next two weeks. The new fleet monitors will begin their journey by the end of this week and head directly to the Echo System. Based on the initial scout reports, it will take the Swarm forces approximately thirteen weeks to reach Echo."

"My Empress," War Minister Adams said, "the new evacuation ships are already on their way to Echo. They are merely huge container ships. Each ship carries one thousand evacuation pods. Each pod is a heavy-haul cargo lifter attached to a square cargo container outfitted with basic life support and living facilities for one hundred people for fourteen days. They will not be traveling in luxury, but we will be able to get them out. Each trip of the evacuation fleet can move three million people. There are thirty-six million people in Echo System, so with a good turnaround, we should be able to evacuate the entire system before the Swarm forces arrive. We will use the Tarrant system as the temporary waypoint until we can move the people farther away from Echo. Imperial army units are on their way to the Tarrant system to construct temporary camps for the evacuees."

"I'm impressed, Minister Adams," the empress said. "We hadn't expected to get that many people out. I passionately believe the people need to see us doing everything we can to ensure their safety. I carry the shame of allowing the military to dissuade me from doing this previously. I bowed, then, to their opinion that evacuation was a defeatist attitude. Never again."

The empress looked at the grand admiral. "Give me a brief report on your initial plans. I know they'll change as new information comes to light, but I'd like to hear the basic plan to alleviate some of my concerns."

"Of course, Your Majesty." The admiral nodded and began. "Current plans have ten *Monitor*-class defense ships, thirty-five dreadnoughts, one hundred five battleships, one hundred seventy-five heavy cruisers, and two hundred ninety lighter units, which will comprise the Grand Fleet. The monitors are new and about twice the size of our current *Dreadnought*-class ship. They are not hyperdrive capable, so they are towed by hyperdrive capable tugs. The process is time-consuming, and obviously, they will not be able to jump out of the system by themselves. However, they have limited sublight capability, so they can maneuver around the battlefield. They are effectively mobile defense platforms. Not having a hyperdrive frees up space for more weaponry. Each of the monitors will have a fleet built around it, which will consist of three dreadnoughts, eight battleships, fifteen heavy cruisers, and twenty-five light units. The remaining ships will be a maneuver force under my direct command. Seven of the monitor fleets will be arrayed ten million kilometers in front of the planet, facing the approach of the Swarm forces. My maneuver fleet will be arrayed directly behind them. The remaining three monitor fleets will remain close to the planet. They will provide defense against flanking maneuvers, bolster the planetary defense grid, and reinforce the other monitor fleets. It is a defense in depth."

Empress Elizabeth looked at the fleet arrangement on the display.

"It is truly an impressive force. But we've put impressive forces in the field before and been overwhelmed. What's going to be different this time?"

The admiral looked toward his monarch. "Majesty, in the past, we've been overwhelmed with numbers. And yes, the enemy will have superior numbers in this battle, as well; as much as ten or fifteen to one. Normally a lack of numbers means a lack of firepower, and in past battles that was true. We could easily kill the Swarm attack ships, we just couldn't kill them fast enough. They concentrated on our capital ships and ignored the escorts. They're willing to take devastating losses to pass through our escort screen so they could bring overwhelming numbers against our major fleet units. Once they neutralized our heavy units, then they turned around to mop up the remaining escorts. We believe the monitors will make a difference. With their massive armor, reinforced shields, and massive defense batteries, they'll be a tough nut to crack. We'll let the enemy break themselves against our monitor defense wall. After that happens, the heavy fleet units will move in to engage the main enemy body."

"You're putting the fate of the battle and the fleet on these untested assets, Admiral," the empress pointed out. "If it doesn't pan out, we'll have to switch back to the usual ways of losing."

She hoped her statement wasn't prophetic.

*****

Chapter Eight

Empire Date: December 1032

The *Shinto* exited hyperspace at the edge of the Echo System four days later. The monitors were already in position on the far side of Echo 3, along the axis on which the Swarm forces were expected to approach. The *Shinto* had received her fleet assignment during the daylong trip across the system to join up with the monitors.

Seven of the enormous *Monitor*-class ships were deployed a million kilometers ahead of the planet, per the plan. Their formation looked like a capital H: two vertical columns of three monitors, with a single monitor centered between the two columns. The vertical columns were two hundred thousand kilometers apart, with one hundred thousand kilometers between each monitor.

The monitor *Titan* was part of the First Fleet, in the center position, and directing ships to their specific fleets as they arrived. The *Shinto* was assigned to Second Fleet, which was centered around the monitor *Atlas* at the top of the portside column. After contacting the *Atlas*, Captain O'Riley was told he would be in command of a four-ship heavy cruiser squadron guarding the *Atlas'* port side. Only one of the other assigned ships, the *Hanoi*, had arrived in the system. Acting Commodore O'Riley contacted the *Hanoi's* captain to discuss tactics, which would include the barrage defensive fire technique developed aboard the *Shinto.* The commodore had a feeling he would need it.

* * *

The developer of the barrage technique was incredibly nervous, but not because of the Swarm—at least not yet. He was in the flight briefing room waiting for Hiroko. They hadn't been able to see each other since the time when they'd kissed. Hazard worried she had come to her senses and realized just what being involved with him would mean. He loved her and didn't want to lose her. The hatch popped open, and a smiling Hiroko stepped into the compartment. Seeing her smile, he felt relief wash over him. The ever-observant Hiroko noticed.

"Relax, my love," she said. "While I do have doubts about how we'll make this work, the one thing I don't doubt is my love for you. I believe we can work everything else out."

Henry rushed across the room, enveloped her short frame in his arms, and kissed her warmly.

"I would have understood. It's why I've never become seriously involved before. I shied away from women because I didn't want to hurt them. You wouldn't let me do that. Thank you for not giving up on me." They stood and held each other for several moments. Finally, Hazard pulled back and looked into her dark eyes. "I'm in uncharted space, my love. What should we do now?"

Hiroko looked at him slyly. "You've never shown me your cabin."

Later, the two exhausted lovers snuggled together in his narrow bunk.

"Hiroko, as much as I'd love to stay this way until we have to go back to our stations, there are some things we need to discuss. More importantly, there's someone I need you to meet. So, jump into the small excuse of a shower and get dressed." He patted her lovely bottom as she untangled from him and rose.

"You want to introduce me to your roommate?" she asked stepping into the locker-sized sonic shower. "Why is that so important right now?"

Henry motioned for her to wait a moment. He reached behind his left ear and spoke into the air. "Jake, can you come back to the stateroom in fifteen minutes?" He paused, then, "Yes, it's important." After another short pause he stated, "Out," and let his hand drop. She looked at him and he simply said, "It's a royal thing; I'll explain it later."

Fifteen minutes later, there was a light rap on the door. After a pause, the door opened, and Jake entered. Henry was in his desk chair and Hiroko was sitting on his bunk. They were holding hands. Both were freshly scrubbed and clothed, but Henry's bunk was a mess.

Jacob sat in his desk chair and turned to them. "Well, I see the plot has thickened, Hazard. There's something that the two of you want to discuss with me?"

The no-longer-quite-disguised prince began with introductions. "Hiroko, this is Jacob Cutter, my best friend. He also leads an interesting, disguised life." Jake's right eyebrow went up at that statement. "I'm not kidding about the best friend part, but he is also my keeper; Major Jacob Cutter of the Imperial Guard. Jake, I want to formally introduce Hiroko to you, but I'm sure you've already run a deep background check on her and know all there is to know."

Jake grunted, this time in evident amusement.

"And yes, Hiroko pieced together who I am, more by accident than anything else. I was her knight in shining armor, a prince, so that became her pet name for me. Ironic, isn't it? So, I told her Hazard was a nickname and asked her to call me Henry because only my closest friends and immediate family call me Henry. The first time she called me her Prince Henry, things fell into place for her. So here we are, two people in love and a battle on the horizon. Jacob, I haven't asked her, but I intend to marry her."

Hiroko looked at him and said in a quiet voice, "Yes, Henry."

Henry leaned over and kissed her.

"Jake, my friend. I wanted you here to witness this declaration of my love and intention. I also wanted it documented; I want you to put all this into a report and put it in a data dump. I want Mother and Father to know. In case something happens to me, I want them to know that I did find my princess. I also wanted to make sure that Hiroko is taken care of."

Jake sat and looked between the two of them. Henry saw scrutiny and admiration in his eyes. Then Jake rose, dropped to one knee before Henry, and bowed his head.

"My Prince, it would be my pleasure to document your intentions to the empress, your mother. I swear that I'll personally be responsible for watching over the princess if something should happen to you."

*****

Chapter Nine

Empire Date: December 1032

Empress Elizabeth stormed into the office of Grand Duke Henry. Her husband thought his wife, whom he loved dearly, seldom did anything quietly.

Including bedroom activities, the duke thought with a slight smile. He wondered if his son, Henry, was blessed with a woman like that. The report he had read this morning from Jacob indicated his son's love interest was a formidable woman.

"Did you see this report from Jacob?" she asked.

The elder Henry nodded. "Yes, I have, my dear. Jacob only forward reports directly to me, avoiding the normal bureaucracy, when they are highly political or personal. I think this report falls into both categories, so I forwarded it to you."

"And what, pray tell, do you think we should do about it?"

"Nothing. Absolutely nothing." Before she could work herself up further, he went on. "Beth, they've known each other for less than a year. True, Henry has never shown this much interest in a girl before. Yes, he's had his dalliances, as all young men do, but he's never had what could be considered a serious love interest. I emphasize that he has never shown the least interest in getting involved with a girl, and now suddenly he is. So even though I have not met her, she must be a remarkable girl, or woman, I should say, to have hooked our son."

"But she is unsuitable for him and, for that matter, us. She's from Honshu, for deity's sake. A meek woman will never survive in the pressure cooker of the Imperial spotlight. And she's not of noble birth."

"I wasn't either," the duke said, suddenly angry. "And you married me."

"That was different. You were a serving officer at the time, the executive officer on a cruiser. And I loved you."

"She is a serving officer and in love with our son, and he is in love with her. If I didn't know better, I might think you are against this match because of her race. I don't doubt that you love all your subjects, regardless of race, but I think the woman who never worries about what people say is suddenly worried about what they will say about someone from Honshu joining the Imperial family."

The fire went out of the empress, and she sank onto a sofa along the wall of the duke's office. Her husband went to sit beside her. He took her hand and said, "If it makes you feel better, I briefly thought the same thing. Then I decided that I didn't give a damn as long as Henry was happy. According to Jake, he is. Hiroko has done wonders for him. Only a handful of people know about this. Let us leave it at that. I don't like saying it, but one or both may not survive the coming battle, one that may be going on as we speak. I pray they both make it through."

* * *

Prince Edward sat behind his ornate—some would say overly elaborate—desk in his office on the second floor in the executive wing of the Imperial Palace. The way the office, and in fact the entire suite, was decorated was intended to leave no doubt in a visitor's mind that this was the crown prince's seat of power.

A picture of the empress was always prominently displayed behind the desk in every other office other than the empress' own. The image was a subtle reminder that the office's occupant served at the pleasure of the empress. On the wall behind the prince's desk was a sizable solid silver-and-gold device bearing the coat of arms of the crown prince. Her Imperial Majesty knew about the subtle snub to her authority, but since she had never been in the office, she didn't *officially* know about it.

Daniel Shipwright, the prince's personal armsman, stood next to the only door into the office. It was his usual position, and because they were inside the palace, Imperials were only attended by their immediate protection. When traveling outside any secure area, the crown prince was accompanied by six Imperial Guards under Daniel's command. Daniel could supplement this with additional security if required. Of the Imperial children, only the heir was afforded this level of protection. The heir could not overrule any security requirements when outside the palace. Inside, though, he could direct Daniel to wait in an adjacent area to allow him some privacy.

Today he had given no direction, so Daniel stood at his post next to the door, observing. The prince was meeting with one of his principal hangers-on, Count Sergey Todorovich.

The count, whom Daniel knew was not truly a count, was from Moskva in the Marx Federation. During the last days of Earth, Russia and other eastern European countries fleeing Earth had colonized the area and the Marx Federation was created. The colony leadership had been hardcore communists and had set up planetary governments that followed that philosophy. Imperial exploration ships had stumbled upon their federation seventy years ago. Unfortunately, the Marx colony ships had been inadequately stocked to set up colonies on new worlds. The results were agrarian societies with few or no industries, and they were barely able to feed their populations. However, that didn't prevent their leadership from living in the style to which they were accustomed.

The Marx Federation had quickly petitioned to join the Empire. By becoming a member, they could get aid and industrial support to improve their colonies. Unfortunately, the Imperial ambassadors and staff sent to negotiate and investigate quickly submitted unfavorable reports regarding the Marx Federation's admission. The planetary leadership was not willing to give up the controls they had over their populations, so *minor* things such as free speech, free press, a fair court system, and many other "freedoms" were not going to happen. Still, they pressed their case for a vote by the Imperial Senate. The extent of the bribes, fraud, and outright blackmail that ensued was staggering. The Marxists had left Earth with a sizable quantity of old Russia's gold reserves, and they used that gold to purchase goods from Empire members. But that wealth was now running out and they had no means to replenish it. There was significant mineral wealth in the federation, but they could not exploit it. They desperately needed the treaty. As a member system, they would have access to technology, loans, and subsidies.

The motion passed the Imperial Senate by two votes, and the federation's diplomatic group threw a lavish party to celebrate their victory.

The next day, the empress crushed their dream by using her Imperial veto. In her prepared statement, the empress reminded everyone in the Empire of the purpose of the Imperial Charter and the ideals it represented. She stated, swore actually, that her ancestors had passed down the defense of those ideals. Ideals that would never be trampled while she ruled. The Imperial veto could only be overridden by a vote of the system governments, not the Senate. It would take three-quarters of those rulers voting to overrule the empress, something that was unlikely to happen.

The Marxist Federation decided to play the long game after the veto. They knew they could get a vote through parliament through other means, so they just needed to wait for a more sympathetic Imperial leader. Unfortunately, "Count" Todorovich had been cultivating that potential leader for the last two years, which worried both the empress and Imperial Security.

"Daniel." Prince Edward's summons broke him out of his musing. "It's getting late. I have invited the count to dine with me in my suite. I'll not be leaving the palace or conducting any official business. We'll just be having a friendly conversation. You can take the rest of the evening off."

Daniel chuckled to himself. The prince didn't want him to hear the conversation that was going to take place, but it was ironic because he would listen to it anyway.

"Thank you, My Prince. I appreciate it. I have errands that I've been putting off. Now I can do them." Daniel bowed and left the office.

* * *

"That was a magnificent meal, Prince Edward," Count Todorovich stated as he pushed his dessert plate back. "And this wine is remarkable."

"Yes, I believe my chef is even better than Mother's, and as for the wine, I've always been fond of this line. My cellars are amply stocked with this vintage. Please, let me send a bottle or two home with you. A gift from one friend to another."

Sergey Todorovich had been waiting for this opportunity. For two years, he had been cultivating the crown prince's favor, and now it was finally paying off. The Marx Federation desperately needed the resources of the Empire to grow and expand. One person, only one, stood in their way: the empress. Rulers didn't stay around forever. True, Elizabeth probably had another forty or fifty years on the throne thanks to modern medicine and genetics, but the federation could not wait that long, though. Computer models showed that within twenty years, probably sooner, their economy would stagnate, and civil unrest would begin. That unrest would likely topple the Marxists' leadership.

"I'll cherish the gift, My Prince," Sergey replied. "I have a gift for you, as well." He reached into the pocket of his fine outfit and extracted a small electronic reader. "We've discussed our shared love of literature, so I have brought my copy of the works of Tolstoy. I want you to have them. I know your security would frown on you trying to download them onto your network, so please, take my reader. I've included a personal introduction to the works on there for you."

"Sergey, what can I say? I am overwhelmed. There is no Tolstoy or, in fact, much of the old Russian literature that our ancestors saved. It is truly an appreciated gift."

"Think nothing of it, Prince Edward. Besides, it is what friends do for each other, is it not?"

Sergey had set the bait. Now he simply had to wait and see if he could hook the big fish.

*****

Chapter Ten
Empire Date: January 1033

The admiral, the Duke of Kara, gazed at the tactical holo table and observed the Swarm forces as they raced across the system. They had arrived precisely on the heading the scouts had predicted.

"The enemy is arrayed in their standard attack formation, Your Grace," his chief of staff said. Rear Admiral Dustin Conyers stood on the other side of the table. "The enemy count is approximately eighteen thousand attack ships backed by one hundred larger units. We have never seen the larger units in direct engagement, so we have no idea of their capabilities. We have never gotten close enough to do a thorough scan. We do know they are equivalent in size to our dreadnoughts. They appear to be significantly slower than the attack ships. Best guess is that they're a mixture of capital, supply, and troop ships."

"Time to engagement range?"

"Twenty hours, sir. The enemy is concentrating its force. Fifteen thousand attack ships are deployed in fifteen groups with the rest screening what we call the main body. Those fifteen groups are on course to engage First Fleet, just as intelligence predicted they'd do."

"Not a great insight of intelligence there, Dustin—the equivalent of predicting I'll devour a bowl of ice cream." Everyone around the tactical table chuckled; the admiral did enjoy his ice cream. "That's the way they've always attacked."

The admiral pulled up some information on his terminal. "It's 1912 now. Unless the engagement time or enemy disposition changes, they will hit us around 1300 tomorrow. Even if they went to maximum sublight then slowed to engagement speeds, we would not see contact before 1130. What do you think, Dustin?"

"Based on their deployment, Admiral, I think we should move to formation Beta starting around 0200. It should take about three hours for everyone to get into position." Formation Beta reduced the distribution of the current formation. Currently, the spacing was one hundred thousand kilometers between units. Formation Beta required the seven fleets to move together, reducing the spacing to fifty thousand and First Fleet would retreat by fifty thousand kilometers. If the enemy held to expectations, the attack ships would have to run the gauntlet of the vertical sides of the H to get to the center fleet.

"I want to start the move at 0000. If we begin moving and the enemy changes the axis of attack, I want to have time to adjust," the admiral said. "I'd love to wait until the last minute to perform the maneuver, but the monitors are just so damn slow. So, we'll move and see how the enemy responds."

* * *

"Signal from the flagship, Captain," the communication officer reported.

It was well into the second watch, and the captain was typically in his stateroom doing paperwork, letting his executive officer sit in the command chair. But with the Swarm forces in the system, he had stayed on the bridge to monitor the situation. The XO sat in his regular seat to the captain's left. The captain nodded, and the officer continued, "Execute Beta movement commencing at 0000."

"Very well, Comms. Relay that signal to the rest of the squadron. Helm, pull up the Bravo execution orders. Plot them with a scheduled execution time of 0000."

The Bravo formation would place the *Shinto* and its squadron in a battle line 500 km to starboard and 500 km above the *Atlas*. The other two cruiser squadrons would be in the same line abreast and below the *Shinto* at 250 km intervals. The battleships and dreadnoughts would be near the monitor, but would leave clear lanes of fire for the massive ship's numerous defense turrets. The lighter units would be arrayed above and below to pick off stragglers.

This formation would allow the two vertical lines of the H-shaped formation to rake the attack ships as they closed on First Fleet in the center. The whole idea was for the attack force to break themselves against the *Titan* and her escorts. Then the entire fleet could advance against the enemy's main body.

"Number One—" O'Riley used the archaic British term for the executive officer "—you have the bridge. I'm going to lay down; wake me at 2330. I want to be on the bridge when the maneuver begins."

Captain O'Riley stood, looked at the tactical display one last time, and disappeared into his bridge day cabin.

* * *

At precisely 1200 hours, the Duke of Kara appeared on his flagship's bridge. He'd been in his conference room following the enemy's advance with his aides. The admiral knew that when he appeared on the bridge, the tension and anxiety would skyrocket, so he had waited for as long as he dared. Finally, he took his fleet commander's seat, to the right of the *Devastator's* captain's chair.

"They're still coming straight in, Admiral," said Flag Captain Renee Giraud. "They'll be entering the range of the forward units in seventeen minutes. They will enter our escorts' range sixteen minutes after that."

The admiral nodded. "Comms, signal to all forward units: open fire on the enemy at 1220."

The communications officer repeated the message for accuracy and transmitted it to the fleet at the admiral's nod.

The admiral looked at the tactical plot. Everything was going as planned. The Swarm forces were reacting precisely as predicted. So, with everything going so "peachy," why did he have an itch on the back of his neck? That itch had saved his ass on numerous occasions. Something was wrong, but he couldn't see it.

"Communications, open a channel to the entire fleet."

A moment later he heard, "Admiral, you have a hot mike."

"Officers and men of the fleet. Today we meet our old foe again. I'm sure some of you are thinking on how we have never beaten the Swarm. How, at our best, we've only managed one draw, which we saw turned into yet another defeat. We were not prepared for those early fights. Our ships were inferior in numbers and technology, and we have been scrambling for over a hundred years to catch up. Now we have. Yes, we have fewer numbers now, but we have surpassed them in technology, and our ability to destroy them in vast numbers is assured. Here we stand. I am proud of each and every one of you because you don't just fight for the empress and the Empire, you fight for each other. Deities be with you, and good shooting."

The admiral stared at the central display screen. The itch nagged at him as the clock rolled over to the appointed time.

The screen became a blaze of color as the Swarm attack ships died.

* * *

Captain O'Riley sat in his command chair, feeling more like an observer than a participant. Everything was going as planned, so he hadn't a thing to do. He was not sure if he liked that. True, it meant his ship wasn't being damaged and its crewmen killed or wounded, but it felt wrong to be doing nothing in the middle of such a battle.

"Tactical," he said, "I think now would be the perfect time to test the barrage-type rail gun attack, don't you?"

The tactical officer, who was the weapons department officer, nodded. "I think it is, sir. Will the rest of the squadron be joining us?"

"Communications, signal the rest of the squadron to commence volley fire with their starboard rail gun batteries at time—" the captain paused and looked at the chronometer "—1224."

"To Squadron Twenty-Three, commence barrage fire with starboard rail gun batteries at time 1224."

The captain nodded at the repeated instructions, and the officer transmitted the order.

Each ship in the squadron received the barrage fire program. It was unofficially dubbed the King Fire Pattern, after the junior officer on the *Shinto* who developed it. They had test-fired the systems, but this would be the first true test.

At 1224, Captain O'Riley was surprised to feel the thumping as his eight quad-mount rail guns on the starboard side commenced firing. He usually didn't feel the recoil of the guns, but with thirty-two guns going off simultaneously, he did. After fifteen seconds, the vibration was followed by another, then another as waves of 40 mm heavy metal slugs raced away from the *Shinto* at 0.35 *c*.

* * *

Lieutenant Junior Grade King never imagined the captain would use his idea so quickly. He watched the display screen from his control station in the first section of the port rail gun battery. He had shifted it to show the starboard-side of the ship. Flashes of light dotted the screen as Swarm ships flew through the hail of metal and disintegrated. Hazard had known the barrage would be more effective than the track-and-shoot system they had been using, but this surpassed all his expectations.

A flashing light on his console indicated he had a private message incoming.

"King here."

"Do you see this, Hazard?" The familiar voice of his division officer and friend Ken Ushari practically gushed. "This is fantastic. If we could do this on all ships, think what it would mean!"

"Don't get carried away, Ken. It's effective for the rail gun setup on the *Shinto* and the other ships in this squadron. We're all equipped with the new forty millimeter quad mounts. I don't know if it will be effective in other ships with different configurations."

The familiar voice of the captain cut into the circuit. "That's true, Mr. King. But it's easy to install rail guns on a ship." The captain chuckled. "I wanted to personally tell you how important I feel this discovery is and how proud I am to have you as an officer in my crew."

Hazard heard the *click* as the captain dropped out of the circuit.

"Wow," Ken blurted. "I think I'll quietly go back to watching the battle and let you bask in your glory. Ushari out."

Wow, indeed, Hazard thought.

* * *

Rear Admiral Dustin Conyers stared at the tactical display. The 3D display showed the entire sphere of the battle. The Swarm attack force was halfway down the gauntlet to First Fleet and the main fleet positioned behind it. The main fleet was the bait to draw the Swarm forces into the trap.

He addressed the admiral, the Duke of Kara. "Admiral, enemy forces are three minutes from engagement range of First Fleet forces. We estimate we have knocked down about eleven percent of the enemy force. That is less than we had hoped but within the parameters of the plan. The total would be less than that, but Second Fleet destroyed a truly astounding number of attack ships."

"That's Tom O'Riley's squadron at work. One of his officers developed a promising new firing profile for his rail guns. He sent me a private note that he was going to try it. It's working better than he had expected," the admiral replied. "Wish we had it on more ships."

"Aspect change on the enemy attack fleet," the ship's tactical officer said. The admiral and his chief of staff looked anxiously at the 3D display. They waited for what seemed like an eternity—but was really only moments—for the tactical display to update. The enemy force was moving down and to port, relative to the flagship.

"Is the enemy fleet still showing a turn?" the chief of staff asked.

"Negative, the enemy fleet has steadied on an intercept course with Sixth Fleet."

This is not good, Conyers thought. In a low voice that only the admiral could hear, he said "We didn't expect this."

"Opinions or options, Dustin?" the admiral asked.

"Not at this time, sir. Let's see how this develops. I guess we'll find out how tough the monitors are."

* * *

Sixth Fleet was in chaos. Fortunately, all the heavy units were deployed forward toward the attacking fleet and were directing all the defensive fire they had downrange at the enemy. More than thirteen thousand Swarm attack ships were bearing down on a fleet of twenty-six heavy escorts and the single monitor. The monitor crew had faith in their shields and guns, but could they survive against this many? They would soon find out.

Luckily, they didn't have to face all the Swarm ships. Historically, Swarm forces engaged major threats first, then went after the escorts. Which was why the monitor had to be considered the biggest threat in the battle.

Then the Swarm forces deviated from their usual pattern. The Imperial plan was suddenly irrelevant as the Swarm attack ships divided into fifteen groups and attacked the escorts, which didn't last long. When the last dreadnought died in a nuclear fireball, the Swarm attack ships turned and moved toward the next fleet in the column, Fourth Fleet, leaving the monitor behind.

The entire plan was in shambles. But, more importantly, the whole fleet was at risk of being defeated. The admiral's only option now was to save as many as he could.

"Signal to the Third, Fifth, and Seventh Fleets. The monitors are to execute Withdrawal Plan Beta."

The huge monitors had eight fleet tugs that were magnetically attached to the hull when not in use. Together, the eight tugs could get the monitors into hyperspace. However, this process took time, due to the time it took for the eight tugs to generate a warp field large enough to encompass the enormous ship. It could take up to an hour to accomplish, and they didn't have an hour.

Plan Bravo would use six heavy cruisers to accomplish the same thing. The cruisers' larger fusion engines meant the field could be generated within ten minutes, assuming no one was shooting at them. "The remaining fleet units will move to join First Fleet. Admiral Mason in First Fleet will take command of the combined force and deploy it for combat."

The fleet admiral continued giving orders.

"I want Second Fleet to do the same, but I want heavy cruiser Squadron Twenty-Three to merge with First Fleet. Admiral Conyers, I want you to coordinate with the Eighth, Ninth, and Tenth Fleets. I want their monitors to perform a normal Alpha Withdrawal. As they're preparing to do that, have their escorts combine into a single fleet. Figure out which admiral is senior and assign him local command to organize them." He pointed at the single icon indicating the only ship left in Sixth Fleet. "Signal *Prometheus* to move at best speed to join First Fleet. That covers everything for now. I fear there's not much we can do for Fourth Fleet."

The icons were already moving on the tactical display as orders were transmitted and implemented.

"I've given the fleets in the planet's orbit their orders, Admiral," the chief of staff informed him. "The other fleets are on the move now. The Swarm should contact Fourth Fleet in approximately ten minutes. Based on their attack of Sixth Fleet, the battle will last about twenty minutes. With fifteen minutes for them to reorganize and travel to First Fleet, we're looking at forty-five minutes to engagement with the Swarm."

"What are the estimates on the rest of the fleets moving to join up with First?"

"Twenty minutes, Admiral. However, *Prometheus* is going to take at least forty-five and will arrive about the same time as the enemy."

"Organize six heavies from Seventh Fleet and have them coordinate a rendezvous with *Prometheus*, earliest possible timing," the admiral ordered. "Then execute a Beta jump. Unless the Swarm forces divert, they should have enough time. Then find out how many ships have the upgraded forty-millimeter rail gun systems and form them into a single force. O'Riley said that converting the guns to barrage fire was a simple program update. Brevet Commodore O'Riley will be in command of the newly created Task Force Twenty-Three. They are to form a wall of steel which the fleet will form behind. I am not sure if we can win this, but we need to bleed these bastards if we can't. If they win, they'll still have to make up those losses, and that will delay the next attack."

*****

Chapter Eleven

Empire Date: January 1033

"Commodore."

O'Riley reflected on the orders he just received. Form a steel wall and bleed the enemy. He had the ships at his disposal. His original four heavy cruisers were joined by eight more heavy cruisers, four light cruisers, ten new *Rapier*-class destroyers, and three battleships. Not exactly a small force.

He aligned the ships parallel to the system plane. The center force consisted of the *Shinto*, one of the new heavies, and the battleships. Above and below were the ten destroyers in two groups, the remaining heavies in two groups of five, and the four light cruisers behind the leading group. The lights would act as a reserve and allow him to reinforce as necessary.

O'Riley had already discussed the plan with the other ships' captains and transmitted the barrage program. As the ships arrived, they would maneuver into their assigned positions and execute a test of the firing program.

There were still close to thirteen thousand attack ships in the enemy formation. The Sixth and Fourth Fleets hadn't destroyed a significant number. His task force could hurt the enemy—hurt them a lot—but they could easily bypass his units. Or they could simply absorb their losses as they streamed by and move to engage the main body.

Anticipating this, O'Riley deployed his force well ahead of First Fleet. He could deploy a barrage in all directions, including behind them, toward the main body. The bursting charges activated 2.5 seconds after firing to prevent friendly fire casualties, well short of the main body.

Much had gone unsaid in his brief conversation with the admiral, who had directed him to engage the enemy as long as possible and then use his initiative on when to withdraw and jump out of the system. That last bit implied the admiral would not be around to order their withdrawal. The admiral was no coward, so the commodore knew he would not cut and run. If the fleet was destined to lose here, it needed to destroy as many of the enemy as possible, while preserving as much of the fleet as it could for the next fight.

The last of the escorts for Fourth Fleet disappeared, leaving only the monitor *Chiron*. The Swarm forces split into three formations as they turned toward First Fleet.

"Well, Commodore, looks like we're next," his executive officer, Julie Adams, said. "What do you make of their formation?"

"You won't like my analysis, Number One. Two of the formations will pass us. Above, below, side-to-side—it doesn't matter, they will not engage us directly. The smaller force will engage us, if only to pin us down and prevent us from helping the main body.

"Julie, I'll be directing the entire force, so I need you to fight the ship. You're ready. In fact, you should already have your own ship. I am not going to be looking over your shoulder." He leaned over and spoke low enough that only his first officer could hear. "I suspect we're a desperation ploy. I'm willing to bet money the duke will allow the enemy to engage the main body, but will hyper out as soon as he starts taking substantial losses. He wants to buy enough time for *Prometheus* and *Chiron*, if he can, to get out."

Captain O'Riley sat up straight. "Communications, signal to all task force ships. I want them to have their hyper-generators charged and ready to jump. Tell them, yes, I know it's a violation of safety regulations, but when the time to jump comes, we probably won't have time to charge the capacitors. I want to get as many of us home as possible."

* * *

Hazard watched the smaller of the three enemy forces crash headlong into the curtain of steel the task force created. The flashes of dying ships danced across the display. He looked at the numbers. Nearly ten thousand enemy ships were streaming past their formation, outside the barrage field, toward the main body and First Fleet. That left almost three thousand attackers for them. In less than a minute, they had destroyed two hundred of the enemy, which sounded like a lot, but in another minute, they would be within the enemy's range, and a minute after that, the enemy would be passing through their formation. They were going to get hurt, people would be killed. He thought about Hiroko and worried about her safety.

No, I can't do that. Worrying about her only distracts me, and that won't keep her safe. Concentrate.

Hazard saw the Swarm attack ships winking at him on the display, firing their energy weapons. They were concentrating on the lighter units, the destroyers and the cruisers, ships they could dispatch more quickly. The *Shinto*, because she was sandwiched between two battleships, was not being targeted. That would not last.

The weapons officer reported over the intercom, "All batteries shift to rapid fire."

Now, instead of one round every five seconds, they would shoot one round per second. They could only fire at this rate for three minutes. Not only would it rapidly eat through their ammunition, but also rapidly heat the rail gun tubes.

The Swarm ships roared through the Imperial formation. The cease-fire message for his section flashed on Hazard's display. He ensured that all four mounts had indeed stopped firing and that the starboard batteries were now firing in rapid mode. They would not be as effective since the shells were now "chasing" the enemy. A quick count showed the Imperial force had downed 573 attack ships, about 20 percent of the enemy force. None of the vessels in the main battle line, including the *Shinto*, had received damage.

His screen didn't display damage, but it did show gaps in the formation. Only three of the original ten destroyers remained. They had been seriously damaged because they were no longer firing their weapons at all. The last three suddenly vanished from the screen, along with three of the heavy cruisers. Hazard hoped they had simply jumped out of the system.

***

"Have the remaining destroyers jump out. No need to sacrifice ships that can't fight," Commodore O'Riley ordered. "Send the same order to the cruisers *Canberra*, *Juneau*, and *Delhi*." O'Riley looked at his display. "Light cruisers *Cascade* and *Sierra*, join the upper cruiser group. Cruisers *Alps* and *Apennines* the lower."

Once the destroyers were gone there was a more significant gap between the main and cruiser lines.

He opened a channel to the remaining ships.

"We're going to tighten up the formation for the next round. The main line will stay where it is, but the cruiser lines will close the gap to only three kilometers. I know this is tight, but it will allow for a denser barrage and allow the battleships' energy weapons to help cover the other lines. I don't intend to sit still and let them encircle. The upper and lower cruiser sections will maintain station relative to the *Shinto* as we maneuver. We hurt them, for sure, but they got us, too. They're not going to let us off the hook now. Good shooting, everyone."

* * *

The Duke of Kara gazed at the display thoughtfully. He had privately admitted to himself that there was no way he could salvage a victory. He also knew that the more damage he could deal to the Swarm forces, the more time the Empire would have before the next attack. He was walking a fine line between hurting the enemy and wasting the lives of his ships and men.

The main body was not accomplishing much at this point in the battle, but O'Riley's task force was. His innovative fire plan had hurt the enemy. Correction: *Was* hurting the enemy. The admiral could see the enemy was adjusting tactics, trying to find something effective against the task force.

The fleet commander turned to his chief of staff. "Admiral Conyers, the main fleet isn't inflicting as much damage on the enemy as I was hoping. I want the fleet formation tightened. Reduce the spacing between ships. The main fleet needs to stay in play for the time being. Task Force Twenty-Three is seriously hurting the enemy, and I want them to continue hurting it. If the main fleet withdraws now, the enemy forces facing us will turn and crush O'Riley's force. So, we'll sit here and take our lumps. Signal Tenth Fleet in orbit around Echo 3 to assume attack formation Romeo and move to engage the enemy around TF Twenty-Three."

"My Lord," his chief of staff acknowledged, "it will take the Tenth more than an hour to reach them."

"Listen up, everyone," the admiral called out, and the bridge quieted. "I'm going to order Tenth Fleet to help TF Twenty-Three. I don't intend for them actually arrive. It will not take long for the enemy to realize where they are going. I am betting that their countermove will be to detach part of the force attacking us to move and intercept them. When the Tenth gets to this point—" he marked a point on his tactical display "—they will be closer to the main body than the main body is to the TF. When that happens, the main body will jump out. The Tenth will continue toward TF Twenty-Three, engaging the enemy as they go. When the remaining enemy forces commit themselves, either to the Tenth or the task force, the Tenth will jump to hyperspace. TF Twenty-Three will continue to engage and jump at Commodore O'Riley's discretion." The admiral looked around the bridge. "Everyone understand? This keeps Twenty-Three in play for as long as possible and killing the BBs." There were nods, and the admiral turned to the comm officer. "Get me Commodore O'Riley."

* * *

The newly promoted commodore reflected on his conversation with the grand admiral. A great deal of the command burden had been eased from his shoulders. He now knew the task force was not being used as a desperation ploy. He would hurt the enemy as much as possible and then jump away. The admiral was helping by keeping his piece of the pie manageable enough to chew.

"Okay, people," O'Riley announced to the bridge, "the grand admiral is going to line them up for us. Tenth Fleet is headed our way, but it's just a feint. The plan is for the rest of the fleet to keep their part of this shit pie busy while we take care of this group. Don't get nervous—" he chuckled "—or any *more* nervous, when the main fleet jumps out, and shortly after that, the Tenth. We'll hang around a little longer but jump before the rest of the Swarm gets to us. Stay focused. We've done good work this day; let's not screw it up now."

O'Riley could see his portion of the Swarm force turning, lining up for another run. "Comms to all units, immediate execution. Four hundred gravities acceleration. Stay on current heading; maintain guide on the flag." This would put the TF on a perpendicular course, moving across the face of the attackers. The commodore waited and watched as his ships accelerated on their current course. When the ships reached a speed of 0.5 *c*, he instructed, "All ships, ninety-degree turn to port. Maintain formation; maintain acceleration."

The TF was now on course for a head-on intercept.

"Time to weapons range."

"Two minutes, Commodore," the tactical officer said. "Plot is showing the enemy edging slightly up but maintaining head-on bearing."

"He's going after the upper group of cruisers while trying to stay out of our barrage window. Let's maneuver to avoid that." *The problem is, he's faster and more agile than we are,* the commodore thought. *But he's also tied up in that jumbled mess he calls a formation, which will hamper him.*

When the intercept countdown reached forty-five seconds, the commodore called, "All units, cease acceleration, down twenty degrees. Come starboard forty and steady on one forty-seven relative. Commence barrage fire on completion of the turn."

This would have the task force engaging the lower starboard edge of the enemy force.

"The main group just jumped out," Julie Adams informed him as she directed the flagship. "The enemy forces have turned to engage Tenth Fleet."

"Thanks, Number One," the commodore replied, not taking his eyes off the tactical display. He needed to time the fleet maneuvers as close as possible to keep his force intact. O'Riley glanced at the command displays showing the status of the ships in the TF: damage, top speed, acceleration ability, and, most importantly right now, available rail gun rounds. The three remaining cruisers of his original squadron showed their ammunition supplies were just above 15 percent. The remaining cruisers, which hadn't engaged as heavily, still had ample supplies, as did the battleships, which had huge storage capacity. Unfortunately, they would break off soon.

* * *

Hazard watched his display as the TF flashed past the lower corner of the Swarm fleet. He felt the *Shinto* shudder as energy beams struck their shields. The engagement lasted but a moment as the two forces passed each other. The young lieutenant noted this was a new tactic. Imperial ships always stayed in formation around the core fleet; they didn't maneuver against the Swarm.

Instead of letting the attack ships swarm them, the commodore was using movement and the barrages from the ships' batteries to focus attacks on the Swarm while limiting the TF's exposure to their return fire.

Hazard's display showed his guns were dangerously low on projectiles. After the last pass, they were at nine percent. They could not stay in the fight much longer and remain effective. He watched as the enemy forces split. The edge of the formation closest to them turned to pass astern of the force while the rest continued to line up for another attack run. The lead ships in the TF made a sharp turn to starboard to engage the smaller force behind them, bringing them in at a forty-five-degree angle to the enemy.

As the enemy ships came within range, the rail guns again commenced their broadside barrage, raking the enemy. The Swarm ships could only fire forward, and as they turned to engage the attack, they ran into the barrage field. They were allowed to close for a moment and then the Imperial ships turned again to starboard, so the lead ships could maintain the barrage. What started as a small force of only three hundred attack ships was quickly shattered. Only sixty of the Swarm ships passed through the formation. The *Shinto* received no hits.

* * *

Commodore O'Riley looked at the display with satisfaction. He hadn't expected the maneuver to work as well as it had. *Either the Swarm lost their cool or their leader, or maybe both.*

"We can't plan on that working so well another time," he said. "Comms, signal the TF that we'll be jumping before the Swarm can engage us again. All ships, maintain current heading and signal when prepared to jump."

Julie Adams turned to him. "Captain, there's a problem with our hyperdrive. It's charged, but the control systems are damaged. Neither automatic control through the ship's computer nor manual control from the bridge is working. Those last hits we took along the dorsal side aft must have taken out the communication and control circuits in the far aft compartments. The hyper control center is showing dark on the damage-control panel, and we have no communication with them."

Damn. "I'm sure damage-control parties are already on it, Julie. Keep me apprised. Communications, status on rest of the TF?"

"All squadron ships report ready, Commodore."

"All right, people, let's work the problem. I'll wait until the last moment to order the rest of the TF to jump out."

He looked at his tactical display and figured they had five minutes. Amazingly, the TF had destroyed close to seventeen hundred enemy ships, but there were still over thirteen hundred left. More than enough to swamp his heavy cruiser.

*****

Chapter Twelve

Empire Date: January 1033

"Henry," Jake called over their private channel, "I've been monitoring the command channel, and there's a problem; *Shinto* can't jump. Controls and comms to hyper control are out. The hyperdrive is ready to go, but we can't tell it to jump. So far, the DC parties haven't been able to find a way to get to the control center because of damage. They're cutting through bulkheads, but it's taking too long."

Hazard pulled up schematics on his computer.

"My Prince, I'm obligated to try to get you to an attack shuttle and off the ship. The attack shuttles have short-range hyperdrives that could get us out of the system."

"A shuttle! That's it," Hazard responded. "Attack shuttles have breaching collars that can quickly get into a ship, correct?"

"Yes, Henry, and I don't like the direction this discussion is going."

"I'm not bugging out. I am not leaving my shipmates. I'll be in the shuttle bay in one minute. Meet me there."

* * *

"Captain, damage-control parties are cutting their way toward the control center but it's tough going," Commander Adams reported. "They estimate it will take at least twenty minutes for them to get there." The look on her face said everything. They had maybe ten minutes until the *Shinto* was overwhelmed.

"Signal the rest of the force to jump out," Commodore O'Riley ordered. "Julie, speed us up; max acceleration. See if we can buy ourselves some more time. I'm not ready to give up yet."

"Commander, portside shuttle doors have opened, and one of the attack shuttles is launching."

"What the hell is going on? Contact that shuttle," ordered the executive officer.

A voice crackled over the speaker. "Lieutenant JG King here. I don't have much time, XO. I intend to perform a breach entry into the hyperdrive control center. My copilot, Mr. Cutter, has assured me that the breaching ring on the shuttle can punch through the outer hull in under thirty seconds. We might have a chance to get in and accomplish something."

Before Adams could respond, the commodore laid a hand on her arm. "Carry on, Mr. King. Keep us informed."

* * *

Hazard settled the shuttle in the spot the computer had selected as the best access point and activated the magnetic clamps. As soon as the clamps energized, Jake started the breaching mechanism. They were both sealed in pressure suits, just in case. The lights on the device flashed yellow, then auburn, and then finally green, indicating the breach was complete.

Jake opened the upper hatch and disappeared into the breach airlock. Hazard heard scraping as the outer hatch of the lock opened. "All clear, Hazard."

"Bridge, this is King. We have successfully breached the hull and are in the process of entering. I'll keep you informed." Hazard didn't wait for a reply as he scrambled out of the pilot's seat and entered the control center through the new access.

Bodies were scattered around the center. Most of the forward wall had been blown in by a strike, and debris had blasted through the space and cut down the crew where they stood. A lone crewman was still strapped in at the main control panel, a figure Hazard recognized.

"Hiroko!" Hazard rushed to the figure. He removed his helmet and gloves and checked her for life signs.

"My Prince," she croaked, "I knew you'd come. I can't talk to the bridge. Ready to jump." She shakily pointed to the command console. "Push and hold that button for ten seconds."

"Hiroko, stay with me," Hazard whispered as he took her hand. "I love you."

Hiroko smiled at him and passed out.

Jake appeared on the other side of the seat. "My Prince, I'll get her to one of the stasis units on the shuttle. They're designed for wounded assault troops and will keep her alive."

They freed her from the seat, but suddenly the compartment shuddered.

The enemy was back.

There were more shudders and a jagged piece of conduit slashed Hazard's cheek, flaying it open. He ignored it. Jake finally freed Hiroko, hoisted her over his shoulder, and rushed back to the shuttle.

He keyed his suit comms to contact the bridge, but got nothing but static.

"Henry, the shuttle's taken damage. I'm fairly sure comms are out," Jake said over their private circuit. "Hiroko is in stasis, and I've diverted all the shuttle's emergency power to keep it active."

Hazard sensed something wrong. Jake sounded like he was in pain. Before he could ask, the whole ship shuddered again.

"My Prince, hurry."

Hazard used his implant to reach out and find a connection. Finally, after several attempts, he found a link to the main computer.

"Computer, tie me into the bridge comm circuit," he ordered.

"Unidentified user has no access to this circuit."

Deities! Hazard raged. "Computer authorization Hotel four, Alpha two, zeta eight, alpha five, romeo eight, delta. Confirm."

"User access confirmed. Welcome aboard, Prince Henry."

* * *

Commodore O'Riley gripped the arms of his command chair as the *Shinto* shuddered from another wave of hits. His ship was coming apart around him.

"Captain," said a voice over his private channel, surprising O'Riley, "This is King. We made it, and I am ready to jump the ship on your command. It will take ten seconds to initiate."

O'Riley pushed the all-hands comm button. "All hands, jump in ten seconds." The bridge crew looked at him in astonishment. "Do it, King."

Ten seconds later the ship winked out of normal space as it fled to the safety of the hyper bands.

* * *

Even without the displays, Hazard knew they had jumped by the queasiness he always got when transitioning into hyperspace. Now, he needed to check on Hiroko and Jake. He looked at the breaching port and noticed the top hatch was shut and a red light illuminated on the hatch control panel. The shuttle was depressurized.

He donned his helmet and gloves and climbed into the airlock and cycled into the shuttle. He saw Hiroko sealed into one of the stasis units. Everything appeared to be okay. He turned and tears welled in his eyes. Jake Cutter, his best friend, was sitting on the deck, a meter-long rod piercing his body, straight through his midsection.

Hazard, Prince Henry, slumped onto the deck beside his loyal guardsman. Thirty minutes later, the damage-control team found him there, still holding his dead friend's hand.

*****

Chapter Thirteen

Empire Date: January 1033

Hazard maintained a vigil over Hiroko's stasis chamber. He simply sat and stared, sometimes at the readouts, sometimes at Hiroko herself. The right side of his face had been bandaged to cover the wound he'd suffered inside the hyper control center. He had persuaded the corpsmen to bring him his meals, and he left only to grab quick naps.

Three days after the battle, he felt the *Shinto* drop out of hyperspace. A distant part of him wondered where they were. There was a ship-wide announcement about a memorial and burial service being held at 1800. The news shocked him out of his self-pity. He had responsibilities. He would not allow Jake to be buried in space. There were also questions concerning Hiroko.

The *Shinto* didn't have room to store the multitude of dead bodies from the battle. If it had only been one or two, they would have remained on board, but the *Shinto* had forty-eight dead. Only the captain could decide if there would be an exception granted. As for Hiroko, the prognosis was not good. Her injuries could have been healed had she been treated immediately, but she had been alone too long before they arrived. The stasis pod had kept her from dying, but that was all. The chief surgeon said there was little hope of helping her further. She still exhibited brain waves, but her body was in terrible shape. Usually, the stasis tube was off under such conditions so the patient could pass on their own.

Hazard had other plans. Because of who he was, he had access to the best medical care in the Empire, some of it cutting edge. He wasn't going to let Hiroko go. Though, once again, the captain could intervene if he desired.

Hazard needed to see the captain. He rose from his seat and headed toward the sickbay entrance, but a marine orderly stepped in and came to attention.

"Mr. King, Commander Adams requests you attend her in her cabin, sir."

Hazard looked down at his uniform. It was clean but rumpled, and it looked good compared to him. On the other hand, he was worn and haggard and pale. The marine noticed him glance down. "The XO was sort of insistent, sir. I don't think she'll mind you being a bit mussed, considering the whole ship is a bit mussed."

Hazard chucked. "I 'spect you're right, Corporal. Lead on."

He followed the marine and soon found himself outside the executive officer's cabin.

The corporal spoke into the intercom next to the door. "I've got Mr. King for you, ma'am."

The door opened, and the marine motioned him through. The door promptly shut behind him.

The XO's suite was considerably smaller on a heavy cruiser than the one on the *Devastator*, just an office and living suite with an attached berthing area. Commander Julie Adams sat at her desk against the forward bulkhead.

"Ah, Mr. King. Please have a seat." She indicated a chair next to her desk. "While we were in hyperspace having gunnery officers on watch was not necessary, but now it's time for you to be an officer again. Losing people is hard, and friends even harder. What you are feeling is only a part of what the captain and I both feel. You lost one, and I don't want to diminish that, but we've lost forty-eight and will probably lose more from their injuries." She rose and motioned for him to follow. "Now, come along. The captain wishes to speak with you."

Hazard followed her toward the bridge. The bridge hatch was open and the marine guard braced to attention as they passed through. The hatch was shut during battle and while in port, but routinely left open while they were underway. The marine nodded to Hazard as he passed, which he returned. The two-person procession stopped in front of the captain's door, which promptly opened, telling him the captain had been waiting for them.

They entered the captain's day cabin, where he conducted most of the ship's business while underway. The office was large enough for small meetings with the ship's department heads and senior officers, and there were several comfortable armchairs and a sofa along one bulkhead. The captain's desk was a moderately large, simple wooden affair. Its top was almost empty, except for a miniature model of the *Shinto* on one corner and a terminal to the CO's right. The captain looked up from his high-backed chair as they entered, and Commander Adams went to stand at the captain's left.

Hazard stopped at the required two paces in front of the desk and stood at attention. "Lieutenant Junior Grade King, reporting as ordered, sir."

Captain O'Riley considered him for a moment. "Mr. King, I, the *Shinto*, and the crew owe you our thanks for your initiative and actions in the Echo System." He paused. "Attention to orders." The XO came to attention. "Lieutenant Junior Grade Hazard King, for actions during the Battle of Echo, in which you showed great courage and initiative while restoring hyperjump capability to the INS *Shinto*, actions which saved the ship and her crew, you are promoted to the rank of lieutenant, said promotion being in accordance with fleet regulations granting ship captains such authority. Promotion is effective immediately as of this date. Captain Thomas O'Riley, commander, INS *Shinto.*"

Hazard's jaw dropped as he processed what the captain had said.

"Everyone, at ease and take a seat," the captain ordered. He motioned Commander Adams to an armchair to the left side of the desk, just like her seat on the bridge, and Hazard took the straight-backed chair in front of the desk. "Now come the tough questions, which I am sure you knew would get asked, Lieutenant King. Like how you managed to fly a locked-out attack shuttle. Shuttles that can only be flown by certified shuttle pilots, who have to enter their authorization codes into the onboard computer. How were you able to override the launch bay doors? How did you manage to access my personal communications link?"

The captain was right. This *was* what he had expected. When he had started the escapade, he knew he would have to reveal his secret to them.

Hazard looked up; he had never been able to break the habit when he accessed a computer link in a ship.

"Computer?" He was not entirely sure it would respond.

"Yes, Lieutenant King."

The XO bolted out of her chair. "Lieutenant King, how do you—"

Before she could finish, Hazard continued, "Computer, seal this room on my authorization."

The computer responded, "The room is sealed, Lieutenant King."

The XO looked at the captain and then at Hazard. Her tone was like ice. "Do your talents also include computer hacking, Mr. King?" She tapped her wrist comm once, then again. "I'm locked out. Computer, unseal the room." A moment passed with no response. "Computer, I said, unseal the room."

"Unable to comply. The requester has insufficient authorization to override the current order," the computer replied in its monotone synthetic voice.

Adams sat and looked at the captain. Of those on board, the captain's authorization was the only one above hers—until now.

Hazard looked between them. "No, I didn't hack the computer. And the captain can't override it either." The captain had turned to use his desk console but stopped. "Sir, what I am about to reveal comes with the highest of security levels. I predict that both of you will be getting a visit from Imperial Security shortly." Hazard addressed the computer again. "Computer, you are authorized to reveal my access authority to the officers in this room and only these officers."

"Access authority granted to Lieutenant King under Imperial Prince Henry Albert Zebulon Arnaud Robert Dimitry Kane. Voice and code verified. Only the empress and the crown prince may override."

Both command-level officers looked stunned. Finally, the XO rose and started to kneel.

Hazard shook his head. "Commander, stop. I wish only to be Lieutenant King on board this ship, not a prince of the realm." She halted and returned to her seat, although they both now sat at attention. "I know it's hard, but I want both of you to stop it. I am simply Lieutenant King. I want—no, I *need* for you to continue to treat me that way." He could see that they were trying, however awkwardly. "To answer your questions, sir, I had to use my Imperial authorization to get to your comm circuit. It was the only way I could communicate with the bridge to let you know we were ready in hyper control. For the shuttle and the bay doors, I hold a command-grade authorization as a shuttle pilot. It's not in my record, but I was trained in shuttles at the academy.

A command-grade authorization allows a shuttle pilot to override and open bay doors from the shuttle flight deck."

"That clears up about everything, I think, My Pri—Lieutenant King," the captain stuttered. He turned and looked at his XO, whose eyes were still large. "What now?"

"There are a couple of minor requests I have, Captain." Captain O'Riley nodded, and Hazard continued, "First, I need Mr. Cutter's body to remain on board, not buried in space during this evening's ceremony. Like myself, he was not entirely who he appeared to be. He is—or was—Major Jacob Cutter, Imperial Guard. He was my armsman and my friend, and I am obligated to see him buried in the Guard's Cemetery with the honors he deserves.

"Second, I need Lieutenant Ogowa, who was severely wounded in hyper control during the battle, to remain in stasis. I have been informed that she may not recover, or maybe only partially. She is important to me, and I intend to see if anything more can be done for her. I have the means to make sure she gets the best in medical care."

The captain nodded. "Make both of those things happen, XO."

The first officer acknowledged. "I'll personally take care of that when we're done here."

Hazard considered the list of things that needed to be accomplished. "Captain, with your permission, I'll contact ImpSec and apprise them of the situation. I'll arrange for the *Shinto* to be directed to the fleet shipyards in the home system for repairs. They can also arrange for transfer paperwork to reassign me somewhere quiet so I can disappear into the fleet bureaucracy."

Commander Adams asked, "Lieutenant King, why here? Why serve in the fleet as a junior officer on the front lines."

"I believe I owe it to the people. So many families in the Empire make sacrifices for this war. The Imperial family, even if no one knows about it, should make those same sacrifices. Most importantly, I wanted to be a fleet officer and to succeed on my merit, not given assignments or plum positions, but to earn my way. My father had that taken away from him when Mother became empress."

"You know, Mr. King," Captain O'Riley remarked, "I served with your father on my first assignment out of the academy. I doubt he would remember me, but we were acquaintances. He was in the weapons department, a battery commander, and I was a new ensign in operations. Your father was well thought of on the ship."

Hazard nodded. "My father told me that when I received this assignment. He remembered you. He looked you up and commented on how you'd developed a reputation as an excellent ship handler." Hazard shook himself. "I think we've covered everything both we each need to, sir. Computer, release the security hold on this room." Hazard stood, and the other officers did as well. "With your permission?"

"You are dismissed, Lieutenant King."

*****

Chapter Fourteen
Empire Date: February 1033

Two days later, the *Shinto* arrived in the home system and entered dock twenty-two of Fleet Station Alpha, waiting for a repair bay to open up.

The ship hadn't been in the system five minutes when orders arrived for Lieutenant King. He was being transferred to Fleet Information and Technology Unit 45. The transfer was to take place as soon as the *Shinto* docked. Very few people in the fleet knew that FLITU 45 was a cover unit for ImpSec, which meant Hazard was reporting to no one. He was free to take care of any Imperial duties he needed to perform. His mother and father had arranged the cover so he could attend to Imperial family business. Being detached to an official naval unit would not garner any undue attention.

Hazard looked up at the large edifice that was Fleet Headquarters. The office for FLITU 45 was located in the basement. It was natural for a newly assigned officer to report.

It had taken two days of waiting before an available shuttle could take him groundside once the ship had docked. He walked down the corridor. People turned to look at him in his fleet uniform, lieutenant stripes on his sleeves and a scattering of combat ribbons on his chest. Or was it the scar that marred the right side of his face. Most people didn't have scars; they were easily corrected with modern medicine, but Hazard hadn't had the time.

He reached an elevator bank and looked for one that went to the subbasement. Only the lowliest of offices were on this level. He walked to the end of the hall and passed through a door labeled Sub Transport.

The office was not what he had expected. It was the size of a linen closet with a steel security door opposite the entrance. After a retinal scan, the second door opened, and Hazard stepped into an underground tube station. There were only two stops: Fleet Headquarters and the palace. Hazard took the waiting car, entered his access code, and the vehicle zipped off. Within moments, it entered an identical station, and he disembarked.

He quickly passed through the security door. If someone made it this far, they were obviously authorized. Next, he entered a security post in the palace basement. Two Palace Guards inside in full loadout, including armor, were alert. A junior officer stood behind a projectile and laser-proof enclosure. Since Hazard was not recognized, he was required to perform a retinal identity check.

The officer came to attention and called out, "Attention on deck!"

The two guards jumped up and presented arms.

"At ease, men," Hazard said. "Lieutenant, I need an escort to wherever my father is. I don't want to be stopped at every guard post in the palace."

"Your Highness, the grand duke is working in his office in the residence wing. One of the guards on the outer door will accompany you. I've updated the security system to indicate you are in the palace." The officer spoke into his headset to inform the guardsmen. "And welcome back."

Hazard pressed the entry buzzer outside his father's office. The grand duke didn't stand on ceremony, so he didn't have a footman who announced visitors. Even after more than twenty years of being the empress' consort, he still considered himself a simple sailor. The prince heard the door latch click, and the door swung open.

The elder Henry looked up from his terminal, and a broad smile spread across his face. He got up and moved from behind the massive desk.

"Hazard!"

His father had developed the habit of calling him Hazard. The prince suspected it was because both their names were Henry. They grasped hands, and then his father pulled him into an embrace.

"It is so good to have you back safe. We worried—" Hazard's father used the Imperial "we" "—when the first ships jumped back and reported how the battle was going. I knew the *Shinto* was back in home system but didn't expect you in the palace so soon. I know how much you dislike being here; I figured your mother and I would have to force you to visit."

Hazard had always thought of the palace as a combination mausoleum and fishbowl. He didn't like the scrutiny he was always under when he was here. Sycophants and hangers-on trolled the hallways and anterooms, waiting for an opportunity to suck up or acquire gossip. It made his skin crawl. His mother became empress before he was born, and even though the palace was the only place he'd lived, it had never felt like home. He managed to escape when he was sixteen to attend prep school before going to the academy. He hadn't been back in six years, except for brief family visits.

"I'm so proud of you, son. And I am not just talking about the heroism, but of the barrage firing scheme you developed. It shows true intellect, and it's what we'll need if we're going to prevail. Intellect."

His father motioned to one side of his office, his quiet zone, where he had informal conversations with visitors. They sat in a couple armchairs.

"You still drink scotch, correct?" Hazard nodded, and his father moved to the sideboard and splashed golden liquor into two glasses. The grand duke believed in drinking whiskey the right way, straight up with no ice. They each took an appreciative sip.

"There are several things I needed to take care of, things that can only be taken care of here, like arrangements for Jacob and Hiroko. I assume you and Mother were aware of my relationship with Hiroko Ogowa? I'm also sure that since you and Mother were keeping discreet tabs on me, you've seen the after-action report."

His father nodded. "Tell me how I can help, son."

"The first thing is probably the easiest: I need to arrange for Jake's burial with all honors. On the way back, I arranged for his parents to come in from Siri for the ceremony. They arrive tomorrow. I think they need to be there. I'll put them up in my townhouse, which is something *I* need to do… get the townhouse ready."

There was a modest townhome in a prestigious section of the Imperial District that had once belonged to a cadet line of the Imperial family. When the line expired without a direct heir, the property reverted to the Empire. After graduating from prep school, Hazard decided he needed his own place, separate from the palace, where he could at least lay his head. This need had become even more critical when he started using his alternate identity of "Hazard King" rather than the Kane Imperial line. His father had recommended the townhome. However, since it was only ever used as overflow housing for the extended family, it sat empty most of the time.

Hazard had received a not-so-modest allowance since he turned fourteen. He was like his father, a simple person with simple needs, so most of that allowance went into a financial account. The purchase of the manor had put a sizable dent in that account. His mother and father had wanted to gift it to him, but he had insisted that he wanted it to be his, not a piece of crown property. The deed to the property listed Hazard King as the owner, with no attachment to the Imperial family.

The manor allowed Hazard to reward his long-serving personal staff, as well. Oliver Kendrick and his wife, Cecile, had taken care of him from his earliest memory. Oliver had been his valet and Cecile his nanny. Both were friends. When he decided to join the fleet, it was evident he would never live in the palace again. Oliver and Cecile became concerned about what they would do next. Hazard solved that problem by making them the caretakers of King Manor.

His father pushed a button on the table between their chairs. The side door to his study opened and his father's long-serving aide, Jerome, slipped into the room. "Your Grace."

"Jerry, it's 1330. Please inform Colonel Devereaux that I need to see her at her earliest convenience. I'd like that to be at 1400, if possible."

Colonel Yvette Devereaux commanded the Imperial Guard.

"Certainly, Your Grace. I'll contact her at once." He gave a brief nod and turned to Hazard. "Welcome home, My Prince. We are all happy and relieved that you have returned. If you need any assistance, please let me know." Jerome nodded to Hazard and slipped out of the room.

The duke noticed his son's puzzled look over Jerome's offer. "Hazard, you know there are no real secrets in the palace, at least not in the residential wing. They all know what you did and what you've gone through. They're all proud of you and want to help you in any way they can. They consider you an extension of their own families. Your mother and I… well, we're the royals and they treat us with the dignity that we deserve. I would like to think they love us, but you are different. You have always gone out of your way to treat them like people, not invisible servants like some royals do. I think we're well on our way to taking care of your first task. Your townhome has already been opened. When it was arranged for the *Shinto* to be brought back here, I knew you would need it, and I notified Oliver and Cecile you were coming home. What's next?"

Hazard took a sip of his whiskey and stared into the glass. "Hiroko."

Before Hazard could continue, his father raised his hand. "Hazard, I don't want you to explain your feelings for her or your relationship. I need your mother present when you do that. It was a shock to know you had become emotionally attached to someone. I need to know what you want to do about her."

"She has a long way to go, Dad, and I'm not going to give her up. My head knows the odds are exceedingly low that she'll ever be completely whole, but my love for her is not going to change. The plan is to keep her in stasis while the nanobots fix the most serious internal injuries, then to wake her up and perform any additional surgeries or treatments she needs. I'm going to Honshu to see her parents. They are her legal next of kin. I need to convince them to allow me to take care of her. If they agree, I'll convert a guest room at the townhouse into a med suite and move her there. I'll have to arrange for some periodic medical support, but I'm already paying staff to keep the place up."

His father nodded. "I'll arrange for *King Wilhelm* to take you to Honshu. That way, you can get there and back in a reasonable amount of time." *King Wilhelm* was the Imperial yacht, though really it was a light cruiser outfitted with suites to move the empress around her Empire when needed.

"There's one more thing I need to discuss with you, Henry." It must be serious if his father was calling him Henry. "Your brother isn't doing well." He held up a hand. "Oh, physically he's okay, but mentally he's gotten worse. His rages and excesses have become extreme and dangerous. When word gets out about your actions in the Echo System, he's likely to lose control. As parents, we're concerned about his well-being, but your mother also has an obligation as monarch. Both of us are concerned about what he would do as emperor if something happened to your mother.

"We've been reviewing the Imperial Charter, and while it specifically states that a female heir can't inherit if a legitimate male heir exists, it does not specify that the male heir must be the *oldest* male. I bring it up because you will likely hear gossip in the hallways, and I suspect your mother will bring it up."

Hazard was about to question his father when the door buzzer announced a visitor. His father looked at his watch and moved back to his desk. "That must be the colonel."

Hazard rose and moved to his father's side as the door opened to admit the diminutive Imperial Guard commander.

The colonel quietly left his father's study a half-hour later after thanking Prince Henry once again for bringing Major Cutter home.

"I'm sure Yvette understands what you want," his father said. "She'll make all the arrangements, so all we have to worry about is being in the appropriate place at the appropriate time." At his son's look, his father added, "Yes, both your mother and I plan to attend. How could we not? Jake was with you for so long that we considered him part of our extended family. And speaking of your mother…" His father picked up a red phone. "Do you have a minute?" He replaced the phone and waved his son to a side door. "Let's go see your mother."

*****

Chapter Fifteen
Empire Date: February 1033

Hazard sat back in his seat and thought about the past several days, as the luxurious cabin of the fast diplomatic envoy ship streaked through hyperspace on its way to Honshu. The ship would take a day longer to get there than the Imperial yacht, but it wouldn't cause as much of an uproar when it arrived. He decided it was essential to get in and out as inconspicuously as possible, and the diplomatic ship was designed to carry ambassadors or envoys along with their staffs quickly across the Empire.

He was in the forward cabin reserved for the senior diplomats, which held eight comfortable acceleration couches. Further aft was a small conference room, a kitchen, and a dining area. Behind all that, there was another cabin furnished with only slightly less comfortable furniture that could accommodate up to twenty-four staff. Currently, it held six members of his security detail, all in civilian clothing. The berthing areas, provided for more extended runs, were on the deck below.

Jake would have liked the funeral, Hazard thought. *He always enjoyed a military parade, especially if he was a part of it.*

After the eulogy, eight guardsmen in full dress had carried his body out of the chapel, though the anti-grav unit had done the actual lifting, to the waiting guard regiment arrayed on the palace grounds. Colonel

Devereaux, the empress, and the grand duke, mounted on jet-black chargers, had led the procession, followed by a mounted color guard. Jake came next with the eight pall bearers, then Hazard in full uniform on another black stallion. Four hundred guardsmen in formation marched behind.

It was a short march to the small Guard's Cemetery on the palace grounds. Only guardsmen who had made the ultimate sacrifice were buried there. There were only a few, despite how long the Empire had been around. Jake was the fifth interred there.

Yes, Jake Cutter would have enjoyed his last parade.

Hazard thought about his family and frowned. His father had seemed okay, but his mother had looked worn and worried. Unfortunately, it was not the war that was bothering her, but Crown Prince Edward, Hazard's older brother. Hazard had never been close with his brother. Edward was four years older and, from early on, was in training to succeed their mother. But Edward had turned into an entitled, selfish brat. Growing up, the people around him had either deferred to him or ingratiated themselves because they knew he would be emperor.

Then came the disaster of the family dinner. Everyone had been home, so the empress had decided they would all eat together and sent out the notice. Hazard's father had tried to dissuade her, knowing trouble loomed, but she had insisted.

Edward was late. Hazard later learned that his lateness was a planned strategy so his brother could make a grand entrance and focus all the attention on himself. Edward strolled in, his arrogant attitude quickly changing to anger when he saw Henry sitting next to their father at the foot of the table. It went downhill from there. Edward was quick to voice his opinions about anything and everything. He ruthlessly quashed any attempts to argue with him, even from his mother, the empress.

It had seemed like he was trying to bait Hazard, to drag him into a confrontation. That wasn't going to happen, not since Hazard had finished his plebe year at the academy. He'd been provoked by people his brother could take lessons from and hadn't retaliated. It was easy to ignore his brother. Then, before the main course was complete, Edward rose, announced that he had a previous engagement he needed to get to, and stalked out of the room. Everyone at the table breathed a sigh of relief.

Hazard contemplated what he must do. He knew he was acting selfishly. He wanted to be a fleet officer, but was that still possible? He thought about what his father had said in the study: the succession had to pass through male heirs before female ones, but it didn't specify it had to be the oldest male. Hazard was a son of the Empire. He believed in what it stood for.

In his head, he replayed the troubling private conversation he had with his mother and father. Elizabeth had never expected to become empress, her brother Michael was supposed to succeed. From what he knew of Michael, Hazard saw similarities between him and Edward.

Michael had been a vagabond and ne'er-do-well. He'd always looked for the next adventure. Unlike Edward, who was an inside person, Michael had always been outside. Safaris and hunting, skiing, sailing. He was always looking for the next adrenaline rush. He had plummeted to his death in a mountain-climbing accident and suddenly Hazard's mother was heir. Two years later, the emperor suffered a cerebral hemorrhage, and his mother became empress.

His mother had looked him square in the eye. "Henry, I didn't expect to be empress, but I love the Empire and what it stands for. I'll die, if necessary, to defend those ideals. I believe you are the same, else you wouldn't have joined the fleet. I was hoping you could make the same sacrifice your father did, give up your commission and become the heir."

Hazard was shocked. He'd known things were bad. But were they really this bad?

"Mother, Edward is still young. Maybe he'll mature out of it. Maybe counseling would help?" Henry pleaded. "I don't see that he's any worse than before while I've been here."

"It is the Marxist Federation issue, Henry. I don't know if you've been following the political maneuverings that were involved there." He nodded, and his mother continued, "I can't, *will not*, allow that group of gangsters to be a part of the Empire. They are the worst scum, and I believe, along with many others, that they will drag the entire Empire down. They lost the opening round but have not given up. They intend to wait until a more amiable ruler is on the Imperial throne, and they are taking great pains to ingratiate themselves to Edward. They believe he's their ace in the hole."

Henry thought for a moment, then looked at his parents. "What do you need me to do?"

"When you get back from Honshu," his mother began, "we'll hold a private meeting. Your father and I, the lord chamberlain, the lord justice, and the speaker of the Senate. I trust all of them. I'll formally announce to them that I have decided to make you the heir because of circumstances. We'll have the paperwork drawn up, and we'll sign it. We will, however, keep it all under wraps. I don't want anyone else to know, especially Edward. We'll allow him to believe he is still the heir. Henry, I love all of you, and I don't want to hurt Edward. But removing him as heir would certainly push him over the edge. Maybe, as you said, he will grow out of it. But if something happens to me, even if I become incapacitated for some reason, he would be in charge. I can't have that. Will you do this for me? Will you do this for the Empire?"

Henry had no other choice. He agreed. But now, more than ever, it was important for Hiroko to recover and stand with him.

A hand touched his shoulder, and his eyes popped open.

"Your Highness, we will be dropping out of hyper in ten minutes," the steward said. "Would you like anything?"

* * *

Crown Prince Edward stormed into his apartment, muttering under his breath. He was quickly working himself into a rage, and he knew that was bad. His loyal retainers and friends at court kept him up to date on the rumors in the palace and being seen like this only reinforced them. The worst of them painted him as totally unfit to be the next emperor. The best—or, should he say, least harmful—was that, hopefully, he would mature and grow out of his petulant state.

Petulant state! I'll show them petulant. I'm decisive, not testy. Can I help it if they don't understand me? Even Mother!

Then there was little Henry. Now the war hero. The perfect child. And yes, the rumors told him how Henry would be so much more capable as emperor. Edward knew there was a movement in certain circles to have Henry named heir. What made the whole thing ridiculous was that Henry didn't even want it. He just wanted to sail around and play spacer.

Edward forced himself, slowly, to calm down. It was hard. Did everyone think being the heir was easy? He chuckled to himself, remembering his mother's words. If it were easy, anyone could do it. Thankfully, he had a solid group of supporters. He thought of Sergey. Yes, he was a true friend, and he wasn't even an Imperialist.

He needed to think and plan. He needed to secure his position.

Tomorrow, Edward thought. *Tomorrow, I'll call in my closest advisors and decide on a plan.*

The crown prince dismissed all his servants and retreated to his bedroom. He needed to relax and rest if he were to figure this out. He sank into an overstuffed chair in front of his fireplace. He got comfortable, then noticed the tablet Sergey had given him.

"Just what I need," he said. "A little Tolstoy, something new."

He powered up the pad and numerous icons appeared, a directory of the great works on the tablet. One was different, though. It was labeled "Personal Message." He selected it and the screen went blank.

An image formed and spoke.

"Greetings, Crown Prince Edward." It was not Sergey but Peter, the supreme leader of the Marxist Federation. "I hope you are well. These are trying times, and I know you are a devoted friend of the federation. We realize you are going through a troubling time, and friends help friends. This gift is but a small token of our appreciation of that friendship."

"Unknown to you, you are constantly monitored. Anything you say, anywhere, is recorded. Any plans you make are instantly forwarded to Imperial Security. This pad contains an advanced communication device. There is a program in the utility section to write notes. When you save a note, it will be transmitted to Sergey and then erased. Likewise, notes will appear from Sergey or other friends providing information and assistance. After you read a note, it is instantly erased. These precautions are for your and our safety. Yes, we have our own agenda, but in pursuing that agenda, we need your help. To have that help, we need you in the position for which you were destined."

The message went on to detail the plan.

* * * * *

Chapter Sixteen
Empire Date: February 1033

Hazard was on Honshu incognito. There was no official announcement made to the planetary government. He was traveling in civilian clothes under the guise of a diplomatic officer, specifically as a member of the foreign ministry's inspector general's office. This let him breeze through customs and security with his protection detail.

Each planet or planetary system in the Empire was self-governing. There was an Imperial Charter of Rights and Responsibilities that systems had to adhere to, but as long as they stayed within those guidelines, they could govern however they wanted. As a result, the range of government types was vast. Most were constitutional monarchies with a parliament and prime minister in addition to a ruling family, similar to the Imperial model, the main difference being the way power was allotted to the different branches of the government.

Honshu was a constitutional monarchy with an Imperial family of its own. The current emperor could trace his lineage back to the Japanese emperors of Old Earth. The original settlers had come from a Japanese colony established during Earth's early exploration period.

Hiroko's parents had already been informed of her condition by the fleet. Hazard had also exchanged messages with them, and they knew that he was visiting to discuss her situation. From his talks with

Hiroko, he knew her parents hadn't approved of her professional choices. They were traditionalists. Though descendants of the original Japanese were in no way as structured as their ancestors, they still tended to have old-fashioned ideas about the roles of women in society. Women in the military, outside the medical field, were frowned upon, as were women in engineering fields.

Hazard had contacted the Ogowas from orbit and arranged to meet them at an upscale restaurant near the spaceport. He thought about the two stoic people he'd seen in the call. Hiroko's mom was a noted biochemist and her father owned and ran a biopharmaceutical company. Hazard could tell from their hard gazes that they were merely agreeing to see him as a courtesy.

He wondered if Hiroko had told them about him. No, if she had told them about *them.* That could be good or bad. As traditionalists, he suspected that they would not look kindly on his involvement with their daughter.

Hazard stopped en route to don his Imperial Navy uniform and arrived at the restaurant first. Only one member of his security team accompanied him. That had taken some wrangling, but he had put his foot down. His keeper was now doing his best to blend in with the decor at the restaurant's front while Hazard waited. Hiroko's parents finally arrived, and he rose to get their attention. Hazard was wearing his dress uniform, something he had rarely done over the last several weeks, to emphasize his connection to Hiroko and to be more recognizable.

Hazard had studied the protocols for this meeting, in the hope it would avoid unnecessary problems. As the couple approached him, he bowed to Hiroko's father. "Mr. Ogowa." Then Hiroko's mother. "Mrs. Ogowa. You both honor me in accepting my invitation."

Mr. Daizen Ogowa looked hard at Hazard. "Lieutenant King, you honor both myself and my wife with the asking." He gave a short bow. "Let us be seated and discuss what has brought you to us today."

As they took their seats, Hazard could not help but admire how lovely Hiroka Ogowa was. "Mrs. Ogowa, I hope you don't find this impertinent, but it's obvious to me where Hiroko got her beauty."

"Lieutenant King, it is never impertinent to tell a woman that she is lovely."

Hazard looked at them. "I know it's customary on Honshu to speak your piece. Politely, of course, but to the point.

"Hiroko was badly hurt during the battle. In fact, she was near death. If we hadn't gotten her into the life-support unit, well…" He stopped for a moment. "She has a long way to go until she is recovered. I'm sure the fleet has kept you up to date on her condition." Both Ogowas looked at him with blank faces. "I want to take care of her. I know fleet medical would do their best and make her as well as they can. However, I am in a position to do more. My family is well off, and I can afford to make sure Hiroko has the best treatment. The best techniques, the best equipment, best doctors."

"Why are you so concerned about our daughter's recovery, Mr. King?" Daizen Ogowa asked.

"I don't know if Hiro told you anything about us, sir. We are—and I emphasize are—in love with each other. I want the woman I fell in love with back. If I can't have all of her, then I'll take whatever I can get. That is not going to change, regardless of what you tell me today. I'll be a part of her life, and you both need to get used to that idea. I know that when she awakens, she will ask for me. I was the last face she saw before passing out, and the last words she heard were 'I love you.'"

Mr. Ogowa sat up straight in his chair. "It was you. The navy told us a rescue team barely reached her in time to save her."

Hazard nodded. "Yes, sir. She saved the ship. She had managed to repair the ship's drive but lost consciousness before she could inform the bridge. I had my best friend take her to our rescue shuttle and put her in stasis while I restored communication with the bridge."

Hiroka Ogowa reached across the table and touched his hand. "Thank you for our daughter's life," she said softly. "Someday, I hope to thank your friend also."

Hazard tensed and she withdrew her hand. "I'm sorry, Mrs. Ogowa. My friend, Jacob Cutter, died making sure your daughter's life-support chamber stayed energized. I'll miss him."

Hazard saw the concerned looks on Hiroko's parents' faces. "No, don't feel sad or obligated. Jake was an empress' officer and would do it again if he could. More importantly, he did it because he loved me, and he knew I loved Hiroko. It is my debt of honor to carry."

* * *

Noya Hedeo sat at the bar in the Ambassador Hotel. It was where he had said farewell to his son two years ago.

The Hedeo family owned a small but prosperous printing business. Noya had always envisioned his son, Kei, joining and eventually taking over the company. Unfortunately, Kei had developed other plans. After four years of university, he had decided he wanted to explore the stars, so he'd used his degree to obtain a reserve commission in the Imperial Fleet and had gone off on his adventure. Kei would turn twenty-three next month. Noya shook his head and corrected himself: he would have turned twenty-three.

Noya thought about the crumpled letter lying on the bar in front of him. The notification officer and priest had been apologetic and sincere when they arrived to inform Noya and his wife of Kei's death. They told him how sorry the empress was for their loss but that he had died doing his duty, defending the Empire.

Noya had been stunned. It could not have been his son. Things like this didn't happen to his family; it was a mistake. His wife fell apart at the news of the death of her only child. When her sisters and their families had arrived to help, Noya decided he needed to get out, needed to clear his head. He wandered for several hours and then, by chance, found himself in front of the Ambassador and had decided it was fitting. Noya and Kei had toasted his departure in the bar here—why not toast his last departure here?

Noya was on his fourth departure drink, the plum brandy for which the Ambassador was famous. A full glass for Kei sat in front of the empty stool next to him. The bartender informed him there was a limit of four drinks per customer when he served him the current drink. Noya suspected it was a mild hint that he'd already had too much. Perhaps he was right. He dropped a wad of currency onto the bar then grabbed the crumpled notice and stuffed it into his pocket.

Noya could see into the Ambassador's dining room as he rose and turned around. A white uniform caught his eye—an Imperial Fleet officer. Noya was not familiar with fleet rank devices, so he didn't know what level of officer, nevertheless, something about the officer's presence triggered Noya's anger.

Why was he alive and Kei dead? He was probably some rear-area dandy who had used his daddy's influence to stay safe behind the lines. And he was a foreigner to boot. Noya grabbed Kei's drink, lifted it, and toasted—"To you, son"—and downed it in one swallow.

He staggered into the dining room, toward the officer.

* * *

Hazard noticed a flicker of movement from the corner of his left eye. His armsman was moving toward him. Then he felt a hand on his right shoulder that it tried to pull him around and a slurred voice. "How… how do you have the nerve to hide here, safe and sound, while brave men die?"

Hazard stood and turned to confront the man. The average-sized local was waving a crumpled piece of paper in front of him. Hazard recognized it—a death notice. He had delivered one just like it to Jake's parents.

"Sir, I assure you I am not hiding anywhere. As you can see, I am here in plain sight. I proudly wear the uniform."

"Why are you alive and my son dead? You. Safe here, far from the battle."

"Sir, please have a seat and we can discuss this more calmly," Hazard said. "I am sorry for your loss. I lost many friends in the last battle. My best friend died protecting me and another shipmate." Hazard saw the man get control of himself and focus. The man's eyes went wide as he saw the ugly scar and the words finally reached him. "Yes, I was there. Aboard the cruiser *Shinto*."

At the name *Shinto*, a murmur moved through the dining room. Honshu was a proud system. Dating back to their Japanese ancestors, they had a philosophy of nonaggression. But that didn't make them pacifists; quite the contrary. If their home world or system was in danger, they would rally and fight to the death. They had a large and robust self-defense force. They just didn't believe in their sons and daughters going off to fight away from home. The Honshu System had an agreement with the Imperial government to build and provide warships at their own cost and turn them over to the Imperial Fleet in lieu of providing soldiers or spacers.

The *Shinto* had been built twenty years ago as part of that deal. Word of the battle at Echo System had already spread through the Empire. News of another failure, but also news of how a lone force had stood its ground, defying the Swarm. A task force led by the *Shinto.* How that task force, fighting alone, covered the retreat of the rest of the fleet and had exacted an enormous cost from the enemy.

The man finally sank into the offered chair, and Hazard motioned the armsman to back away.

"You were on the *Shinto*?" the man asked.

Hazard nodded and turned to show the left shoulder of his uniform. A patch showing a spaceship emerging from a red chrysanthemum and "Shinto" emblazoned underneath adorned his upper sleeve.

"Yes, I was on the *Shinto.* I came to Honshu to tell Mr. and Mrs. Ogowa about their daughter—" Hazard gestured across the table to the couple "—and how she was seriously injured during the battle. How she helped save the ship from certain destruction." Hazard paused. "Tell me about your son."

The man slumped. His eyes were hollow. "My name is Noya Hedeo, and my son is—was—Kei. He went to university here in the city and studied engineering. I always thought he would follow me in the company business—we own a small printing company—but Kei was headstrong; he wanted more. This younger generation is so different. They go against so many of the old ways." The Ogowas nodded in agreement, and it didn't escape Hazard. "Kei wanted to do more. He thought Honshu needed to be a bigger part of the Empire, so he joined the fleet. And now, he is dead for playing that bigger part."

"There are many sons and daughters who are dead now, Mr. Hedeo. Many more are injured." Hazard looked across the table at the Ogowas. "They all went into that fight knowing they might die but they also knew they needed to be there. Those spacers wanted to defend loved ones and millions of others from an enemy they could never fight. Tell me, sir; do you know what ship your son was on?"

"Kei was on the destroyer *Greyton.* He worked in the engineering department," Noya said.

"The *Greyton,*" Henry repeated. "One of the new *Afrikaner*-class destroyers. Your son must have been an excellent engineer to be assigned to her; she was so new. Mr. Hedeo, the *Greyton* was part of the *Shinto* task force. I want you to know she fought to the very end. The *Greyton* stood with us, covering the rest of the fleet as they withdrew from a battle we could not win. I know that it's not much, but she exacted a high price from the enemy before being destroyed."

Silence filled the dining room as every person listened to Hazard's commentary. "I know it is hard to understand now, but eventually, you will look back on your son's death with a mixture of both sorrow and pride. Sorrow that he is gone but pride in his actions. Pride in his devotion to his fellow man. Years from now, when people talk about the last stand of the *Shinto* and Task Force Twenty-Three in the Echo System, you'll be able to proudly say that your son, Kei, was there and gave his all."

Noya Hedeo looked at Hazard, his eyes red with unwept tears, and nodded. His eyes were no longer the eyes of a man with no hope but those of a man with understanding.

"I believe I have overstayed my welcome, sir. I really should get back and deal with the rest of the family. I can only hope that I can help them as much as you have helped me. Again, Mr. and Mrs.

Ogowa, I sincerely apologize for intruding into your grief. May the spirits shine down on your daughter and grant her a full recovery."

Noya Hedeo rose and started toward the entrance.

"A moment, Mr. Hedeo?" Hazard said. Hazard motioned for his armsman to approach. "My man here will make sure you get outside and help arrange for transportation. Philip, make sure Mr. Hedeo gets into a cab without any legal entanglements." The armsman nodded and led Mr. Hedeo out.

* * *

As he was leaving, Noya spoke to his guide. "You know, I didn't even get his name. Your boss, I mean."

"King, Lieutenant Hazard King," the armsman replied. At Noya's astonished look, he nodded. "Yes, *that* King. The guy who saved the *Shinto*."

* * * * *

Chapter Seventeen
Empire Date: February 1033

Hazard looked across the table at the Ogowas. The dining room was silent.

"Well," he began, "it seems we—or at least I—have overstayed our welcome. I apologize for that. I understand his feelings, though. It's the same way I feel about your daughter." A look of understanding appeared on their faces. He hoped they thought that maybe, just maybe, this stranger loved their daughter as much as they did.

An alarm sounded on Hazard's wrist communicator. "Alas, I'm about to turn into a pumpkin. I am on a very tight schedule, and I need to leave now to make it back to Britannia in time for an important matter. However, we need to continue this conversation. Would you accompany me in my car back to the shuttle pad?"

Mr. Ogowa looked at his wife. "Yes, we can do that, and yes, we need to continue this discussion."

Hazard saw Philip reenter the dining room and motioned him over. "Philip, have the car brought up. The Ogowas will be riding with me to the shuttle pad so we can finish our talk. Then the car can bring them back here or take them home, whichever is more convenient."

* * *

Once ensconced in the car and on their way to the shuttle, Hazard continued their conversation.

"I don't know what details the fleet has given you about Hiroko." By their blank looks, he knew they had been told very little. "Mentally—I should say brain-wise—she is fine. No mental damage. The rest of her—" Hazard paused "—is in bad shape. If she is taken out of stasis, she will die within an hour. There is hope, though. Some innovative techniques have been developed that should help in her recovery. They are not widely known or distributed yet, and they are extremely expensive, but I have the means of getting them for Hiroko. I have a manor in the Imperial District on Britannia. I've already started converting one of the suites into a medical ward to support Hiroko. Unfortunately, since there are no fleet medical facilities here on Honshu, I don't believe the fleet would ever transfer her here. Fleet medical is good—outstanding, in fact—but they don't have all the resources needed to help her."

Now for the final part of the sales pitch, Hazard thought. "I am not her next of kin; I wish I were. When we decided that we loved each other and would marry, we should have had the chaplain perform the ceremony right away. Hindsight is twenty-twenty. As it is, only you can decide on her care. I am not going to ask you to sign that over to me. What I am going to do is ask you to come to Britannia, to be with her and be a part of the recovery. I have plenty of room, and you will want for nothing while you're there. You don't have to decide right now. Go home and discuss it. Then you can come to Britannia, talk to the doctors, and decide for yourselves. When you are ready, contact me through this comm address." Hazard handed Daizen Ogowa a data chip. "The message should get to me within a day, then I'll make arrangements for your trip."

"Lieutenant King—or may I say, Hazard," Daizen replied. "I admit that I came to this meeting with you with a closed mind. Like Mr. Hedeo, I am old school. My wife—" he patted his wife's hand "—if I know her, is already picking out wedding dresses." He chuckled. "I leave our meeting, with everything that happened during it, respecting you. More importantly, I sincerely believe you love our daughter. Not as much as we love her, but love nonetheless. We will go home and discuss this. You are right, we would have made the trip to Britannia regardless. Your graciousness has simply made things easier."

Hazard felt the elephant rise from his chest. "Excellent. I only wish we had a good bottle of wine with which to toast the future. While in stasis, Hiro will not get any worse, but the sooner we start—" Hazard was interrupted by the partition lowering between the front and back of the limo.

"Sir, we just received an all-fleet flash. 'Code Orange.'"

"When it rains, it pours," Hazard murmured under his breath. "What's our shuttle status?"

"It will be at least three hours to get clearance to depart under the code, sir," Philip replied.

"Okay. ImpSec local knows I'm here. Go through them and get *Avon* to launch an assault shuttle to drop to the spaceport to pick me up. They should be dirtside in under thirty minutes, and a quick turnaround means we can be on our way within thirty-five. All they need to know is that they will be picking up a high-priority person—use my diplomatic credentials. Looks like it will be just you and me, Philip." At the guardsman's look, Hazard shrugged. "No time, Phil. Once we're airborne, I can decide what to do next. I would prefer to use the courier, but the destroyer is faster in hyper. The assault shuttle will have secure comms on board so we can figure out what's going on."

Philip nodded and the divider rolled back up.

Hazard had dropped into what he considered command mode and had forgotten about the Ogowas. They looked at him with mixed expressions of awe and trepidation. They had to be wondering who they had gotten involved. In another circumstance, it might have been humorous. He shrugged. "What can I say? I'm a man of many faces: sailor, spy, diplomat—to name a few. There are secrets I can't discuss with you at this time, but soon, very soon, I'll share them with you. And to answer the unasked question, yes, Hiroko knows all about them." *And still loves me.*

* * *

There was no time to change back into civilian clothing before the shuttle arrived. For Hazard, every second counted. He needed secure communications to find out what was going on. The Code Orange was an Empire-wide alert to all senior fleet, diplomatic, and system officials that the empress could not perform her duties and that the heir, his brother, Prince Edward, was acting in her stead. Which was not a good thing in Hazard's mind.

Edward wouldn't have total Imperial power, only limited emergency powers. He could not replace individuals holding office by Imperial decree, except for charges of treason; the Regency Council, with Edward at its head, would be in actual control. The problem was if his mother was incapacitated for a considerable time, over six Imperial months, the Regency Council was obligated to give the heir full Imperial power. There were five members of the council, and Hazard was familiar with all of them. His brother, as head of the council; his father; the Imperial chamberlain; the lord justice; and the majority leader of the Imperial Senate.

The first and last members were who he was truly concerned about. Edward, because of his instability, and the majority leader. When the Emergency Powers Act was created eight hundred years ago, it was decided that at least one member of the council needed to represent the people. The current leader, Joseph Wells, was head of the Legislative Party, and had been one of the supporters of Marxist Federation membership. The Legislative Party members believed that the time had come for revising the Imperial Charter and creating a more democratic society.

To declare that the empress would be unable to perform her duties for more than six months took a two-thirds vote of the council. In Hazard's mind, there were two votes solidly for that. Edwards and Wells. His father would be against it. The wild cards were the chamberlain, Lord Derby, Kendrick Beckham; and Lord Justice Richard Dyess. Both were loyal Imperialists, but they were strict adherents to the Imperial Charter. Even though both knew Edward was a poor choice to be in charge, they would vote based on facts. Hazard needed to get to Britannia and help his father manage the situation.

The aft boarding ramp of the shuttle lowered, and a natty-looking lieutenant commander approached to greet Hazard and Philip. She looked perplexed as she examined the two of them.

"Where's the rest of the party, Lieutenant? Where's the ambassador?" LCDR Aiden Dohany asked.

Hazard saluted. "Lieutenant Hazard King, ma'am. We're it."

Hazard could see his uniform was going to cause problems. He should have guessed that when a backwater picket destroyer got a flash message from ImpSec to perform an emergency extraction of a diplomatic party, its captain would send down a senior officer to greet them.

"You are not what the captain or I expected, Mr. King. Therefore, I'm going to need some validation of your orders."

Hazard quickly ran through possible options. There were no good ones. He could reveal his identity, but wanted to use that only as a last resort. Then he had it: Philip. An Imperial guardsman had the authority to commandeer any Imperial unit to perform the function of protecting a member of the royal family. This was stretching that a bit, but Phil knew what was going on.

"Philip, would you provide your authorization for the commander? That you are 'acquiring' this shuttle in performance of your duty in securing the safety of your charge." Philip immediately understood the direction Hazard was going.

"Commander Dohany, I am an officer of the Imperial Guard performing a mission for the empress. Said mission was to escort this lieutenant to the Honshu System to perform a classified task and promptly return him to Britannia. The mission is classified at the highest levels and only the empress and the lieutenant are authorized to reveal details." With that, Philip handed the commander an identity chip. "Please run this chip through your scanner to verify our mission, but be prompt, we are on a tight schedule."

Dohany huffed, took the chip, and went back up the ramp. Within two minutes, she was back and looking annoyed. Hazard decided she had run the chip two or three times, hoping the results would change; otherwise, she should have been back in under a minute.

"Very well, Captain Myerson. Your identity and authorization for the use of this shuttle are confirmed. Please come aboard and strap in so we can prepare for launch. The captain ordered me to get you back up to the *Avon* as quickly as possible." She turned and strode into the shuttle. Hazard and Philip followed.

Getting takeoff clearance was simple since few ships were flying at the moment. Hazard could tell by the smooth liftoff they had an experienced pilot. He quickly pointed the nose skyward but was using only standard power. Regulations required that small craft, shuttles, pinnaces, and the like restrict speed to 75 percent of standard power in civilian airspace. During emergency conditions, the restriction didn't apply. Hazard had asked for an assault shuttle for two reasons: its onboard security suite and its speed. At the moment, it was traveling at half its possible top speed under emergency power.

Hazard turned to Phil and quietly said, "Too slow. You need to arrange for me to be in command." He could see the wheels turning behind Phil's eyes and then a devious glint.

"Commander," he said, and Dohany turned in her seat to look at him. "You have recognized my authority to use this shuttle in the performance of my mission, correct?"

Dohany nodded.

"I am now informing you that the lieutenant here has authority over me, making him my superior during our mission. Authority vested in him by the empress. I am at this moment placing him in command of the mission and the shuttle."

The glare the commander gave Philip could have burned through armor. "Very well, Captain Myerson. I accept your authority and have no recourse, but to accept Mr. King's." She raised her voice." Attention in the shuttle. As of this moment, Lieutenant King is in command of this shuttle."

Hazard quickly unstrapped and moved to the jump seat just behind and between the pilots. He ignored the stares of the two unarmored marines who had accompanied the commander. Hazard put on the spare headset. "Pilot, I'm authorizing you to use full emergency power to get to orbit. My authority. Adjust to rendezvous with *Avon* soonest practical course."

The enlisted pilot, a marine sergeant, replied tersely, "Negative. I am responsible for the safety of this shuttle and all in it. You may be in command, but I am the pilot in command, and my orders trump yours."

"Well played, Sergeant. Exactly by the book and totally correct." Hazard removed a small data chip from around his neck and inserted it into the flight computer between the pilots and quickly typed in his code. The shuttle's AI flashed a message to the flight crew, informing them that flight command of the shuttle had passed to the senior flight officer on board, who was assuming that responsibility. That officer was Master Flight Commander Hazard King.

"Now, Sergeant, let's get the speed up to emergency and replot the rendezvous. If there is a problem, I'll jump into that seat and do it myself. And just so you know, I flew a shuttle, just like this one, two weeks ago with Swarm ships shooting at me. Now, I know two grizzled veterans like yourselves can handle this without me looking over your shoulders, so I'm going to private mode to use the secure comm link." With that, Hazard switched his headset to access the fleet data net.

Time to find out what the Code Orange was all about. As he scanned the message, Hazard decided he had made the correct decision in pushing the envelope. He needed to get to Britannia as quickly as possible, and he needed the destroyer to accomplish that.

* * *

As the shuttle approached the destroyer *Avon*, Hazard left the shuttle cockpit and moved to sit beside *Avon's* diminutive executive officer. Aiden Dohany showed all the traits attributed to her Irish ancestry. The pale skin, freckles, and red hair were stereotypical of the inhabitants of the planet Eire. Hazard would have wagered that one, if not all, those traits had been genetically engineered into the officer.

"Commander." Hazard nodded respectfully. "I know this has been trying on you, and I thank you for your cooperation. It was a highly unusual situation you were not prepared for and you handled it exceedingly well." Hazard paused. "The hardest part is still to come, though. Once we're aboard, I need you to get me in to see the captain as quickly as possible. Due to the unusual circumstances of this whole flight, I doubt that will be a problem, but one thing I've learned while being in the fleet is never to assume."

The commander giggled. Hazard thought, *Fleet officers don't giggle.* But then she did it again. "Trust me, Mr. King. The Kong will want to speak to you as soon as you get aboard. Frankly, I can't wait to see that happen. It should be entertaining." She giggled again.

Hazard raised an eyebrow and asked, "The Kong?"

"Commander Gathii Kong, my CO. One hundred ninety centimeters, seventeen stones of mean Kenyan. It's why we refer to him simply as the Kong. You know, like King Kong?"

Hazard chuckled at the image of the small XO standing next to the huge CO that materialized in his head. "Well, Commander, I'll make sure you get a ringside seat."

He felt the destroyer's tractor field grab the shuttle and begin the docking sequence which was handled both smartly and flawlessly.

Hazard reflected on the flight so far; everything had been done that way. Unfortunately, he knew that was not the norm in most patrol fleets. The ships assigned to patrol and monitor the space lanes were obsolete but still serviceable. They wouldn't stand a chance in a Swarm attack, but they were perfectly capable of maritime and antipirate patrols. Unfortunately, they were usually staffed with fresh-out-of-boot camp ratings along with lower-performing chiefs and officers. Commander Kong didn't seem to fit that mold, and neither did his crew.

Once the docking sequence was complete, the loading ramp lowered. Dohany hesitated, motioning for Hazard to go first.

"Commander, I realize you are deferring to me as the person who took command of the shuttle, but you are still the senior officer aboard. Please, lead on," Hazard said in a quiet voice. The red-haired commander gave a polite nod and marched down the ramp.

Waiting to greet them was a midshipman and two fully armed and armored marines. Midshipmen were another anomaly of the patrol fleets—a holdover from the old sea navy. The program provided capable and intelligent teenagers from lesser-developed worlds a path to obtain an officer's commission in the Imperial Fleet. These teens would never be able to get the type of education on their home planets that would enable them entry into Fleet Academy or, for that matter, any major university. Several of the fleet's senior officers and ship captains had come from this program, and those officers were considered among the best in the fleet, primarily because of the work ethic they had developed as midshipmen.

After *Avon's* XO had completed the boarding ritual, Hazard followed suit. First he saluted the aft bulkhead of the shuttle bay, where a sizable Imperial flag was painted. Next he saluted the midshipman.

Then, holding the salute, he barked, "Lieutenant Hazard King requesting permission to come aboard, sir."

The young midshipman returned his salute and replied, "Permission granted." They both dropped their salutes. "Commander, Lieutenant, the captain requests your presence in his cabin. If you would follow me?"

The middy turned and led off, with the *Avon's* XO by Hazard's side, then Philip behind Hazard, and the two armored marines. The last two didn't surprise Hazard at all.

When they reached the CO's cabin, the XO motioned for them to remain outside as she made her private report. There was another marine standing guard at the captain's door, wearing a standard shipboard rig. A marine gunnery sergeant was present, and Hazard decided he was the marine detachment CO. Maritime patrol destroyers typically fielded only two squads of marines. A gunnery sergeant typically commanded such a small independent command instead of an officer.

Hazard noticed the gunnery sergeant was sizing him up, checking out his scar, ship patch, and ribbons. "I apologize for the mussed uniform, Gunny. It's been a long two days. Otherwise, do I measure up?"

The veteran gunnery sergeant and Hazard eyed each other.

"Yes, sir, you certainly do. Especially if you are who I think you are," the sergeant replied.

The door slid open again as Hazard responded, "In short, yes, Gunny, I was in Echo System."

"Mr. King, the captain is waiting to see you. The rest of you remain. Gunnery Sergeant, you may dismiss the armored escort." The gunnery sergeant nodded to the commander, and Hazard gave a slight nod to Philip, indicating he should wait outside.

Hazard marched into the CO's office with parade-ground precision, stopped, came to attention at the precise spot in front of the desk, stared twelve inches above the captain's head, and reported. "Lieutenant Hazard King, reporting to the captain of IFS *Avon* as ordered."

Captain Kong let him stand that way for at least thirty seconds as he took Hazard's measure. "At ease, Mr. King. Welcome aboard the *Avon*. Please, have a seat."

Hazard didn't immediately sit. He was finally able to look at the captain of the *Avon*. The XO hadn't been kidding, Kong was enormous. More importantly, he exuded that rare mix of command and competence. Many commanders had one or the other; the number who had both were rare. That made Hazard regret what he was about to do.

"Computer, command override code." Hazard recited his code, and he noticed both the CO and XO rising from their seats as they moved to attempt to stop him. They would fail. "Voice-recognition phrase, 'The Pauper is the Prince.' Computer confirm order and authorization." Hazard felt the immense hand of the captain grab his left shoulder.

Before *Avon's* CO could say or do anything, the computer's electronic voice echoed through the office. "Override authorization confirmed and granted. All shipboard controls are at your disposal."

This taking control of ships is becoming a little redundant. Maybe we need to develop a secret handshake or something, Hazard thought. "Computer, place a complete security lockout on this office, physical and electronic. Confirm when complete."

"Desired security protocols are set."

Hazard felt the captain's hand slide off his shoulder.

"Now, let's all get seated." He looked at the tiny XO staring at him in shock. "I told you I was on a tight timeline, and I was not kidding." He turned to the *Avon's* captain and continued, "I apologize, Captain Kong. I would have preferred to be more diplomatic in my request, but the needs of the Empire forced my hand." Hazard finally paused to gather his thoughts. "Computer, validate the CO and XO my authority to issue the override command."

Without pause, the computer responded in its monotonous, electronically generated voice. "Override authorization is under Imperial Control Override Protocols embedded in this computer's core processing program. Authorization is granted by a recognized command code and a validated voice-recognition phrase. Authorization may only be overridden by Empress Elizabeth or Crown Prince Edward."

There was a look of disbelief on Captain Kong's face. He was still trying to come to grips with the fact that he had lost control of his ship. Hazard was surprised by the reaction of the XO. She had a mischievous look on her face. Maybe she thought they were about to go on a great adventure. Boy, was she wrong! They were about to become an exceptionally high-priced taxi service.

"Computer, identify override user to the captain and exec," Hazard continued. The reply seemed to boom out of the speaker. "Override initiator is Lieutenant Hazard King. Override initiator is also Prince Henry, second in line to the Imperial throne."

He looked at the two senior officers of the *Avon*. "As I said, Captain, I apologize for being abrupt, but I needed to establish my credentials quickly. Are you satisfied I am who the computer says I am and that I have the authority to issue you binding orders?"

"My ship, myself, and my crew are at your disposal, Your Highness," Captain Kong replied, bowing his head.

"Excellent. I love it when a plan comes together. Computer, release command override of the ship. Second, computer, release security lockout of the CO's office. Third, computer, wipe all traces of the command code and all conversations that have taken place in this office since initiation of the override." The computer promptly complied with all of Hazard's commands.

"I have two requests of the *Avon* and her crew. First, I'll be treated as the lowly lieutenant I appear to be. This is not a cover; I am an actual lieutenant in the fleet and was in the Echo System on the *Shinto* two weeks ago. Second, I need the fastest trip to Britannia you can arrange."

*****

Chapter Eighteen
Empire Date: February 1033

Crown Prince Edward, the soon-to-be Regent Edward, sat at his office desk. In twelve more hours, he would become regent. The succession charter defined that if the empress didn't recover within seventy-two hours, the designated successor could assume the emergency powers of regent. The six-month clock was already ticking away the time until he would become the regent emperor with full Imperial powers.

He was not sure how, or what, his Marxist allies had done. He didn't want to know. Somehow, they had accomplished what he had asked. He was in power, and his mother was still alive. Now it was up to him to consolidate that power and fulfill his side of the bargain.

The prince had scheduled a meeting of the Regency Council for the next day. The summons had been sent. Little did the participants know that once they were inside the palace, they would not be leaving. Since they would be ruling the Empire, they would need to be kept secure and safe. At least that was the story Edward would use.

Even though he didn't have regency powers yet, the crown prince had started taking action. Edward had been unnerved by the revelation that he was under constant surveillance. He decided it had something to do with the Imperial Guards. He had dismissed the Imperial Guards from the palace, sending them to their compound adjoining the palace.

The Palace Guard force had assumed all their responsibilities. All the individuals whom Imperial Guardsmen had guarded now had Palace Guards instead. For specific individuals, his father, for instance, those guards were handpicked and loyal to him. Edward had a squad of loyal guardsmen constantly with him.

The key to the whole plan was his mother and making sure she remained unconscious. Edward had dismissed her personal physicians, claiming they may have been complicit in her situation, and assigned his own medical team to ensure she stayed in her current condition. Neither he nor his Marxist friends wanted to wait the full six months to gain total power, which meant Edward had to convince three council members the empress' condition was long-term. He already had two votes he could be sure of. He also knew his father would never support the action. So, he would need to convince the chamberlain or the lord justice to vote for his assumption of power. They would never advocate that without an independent medical review, but his friends assured him they could handle that.

His intercom buzzed. "Your Highness, Guard Captain Reynolds is here as ordered," his aide announced. "I'm sending him in as requested."

A moment later, the short, stocky guardsman who was now the commander of the Palace Guard entered his office. He would not have been Edward's first choice, but he was the senior officer whose loyalty to him was unquestionable.

Captain Reynolds stopped before the desk and made a short bow. Edward waved a hand in acknowledgment, and the guard began his report.

"Your Imperial Highness, we have completed our sweep of the palace. All the Imperial Guards have been removed. We have control of the security stations within the palace, so any listening devices seeded through the palace are under our control. All communications or transmissions to or from the palace are under our direct control or have been jammed. You need not worry about being spied on any longer."

"Excellent, Captain. You have accomplished much in a short time, and I greatly appreciate it. I assure you that your arduous work and loyalty will be rewarded."

Edward leaned back in his chair and considered. He had played all the cards he could, at least until tomorrow. Technically, most of what the prince had done was outside the scope of even his soon-to-be emergency powers, but there was no one to overrule him.

He thought about his long-term plans. He would replace every single Imperial official with ones who were loyal to him. Then he would get down to the real business of changing the Empire into what he thought it should be.

*****

Chapter Nineteen
Empire Date: February 1033

A transition portal opened, and the Imperial Destroyer *Avon* flashed into standard space inside the Britannia System. Within moments, the destroyer was hailed by the local pickets. Because it was the capital system, the arrival of starships into the Britannia System was strictly controlled. Picket stations were positioned around the system along the regular transportation routes. Any vessel that appeared from outside the established lanes was immediately classified as hostile and a force from the home fleet would immediately jump to the location to identify it.

Hazard and Captain Kong had already worked out what they would say. But as with any good story it was primarily based on fact. "Local Control, this is the IFS *Avon*, Commander Kong commanding. We have an Imperial emissary on a classified mission for the empress. He is transmitting his authorization now." Captain Kong nodded to Hazard, who transmitted his orders to the picket. "Control, orders have been sent. The emissary was stranded in the Honshu System due to the Code Orange and used his authority to have us deliver him to Britannia. Request best speed approach to Central Station so I can get rid of him."

The only response they received from local control was, "Acknowledged, *Avon*. Hold your current position and wait."

The CO indicated to his comm officer to cut the circuit. He turned to Hazard, who had remained outside of the video pickup. "You know they're going to kick this all the way up the chain. We could be here awhile."

"It will not be as long as you think," Hazard replied. Before he could say more, control responded.

"*Avon*, you are to use approach vector Able to Central Station. You are cleared for full military power until contacted by Central Approach."

Captain Kong nodded to the comm officer to acknowledge receipt. "All right, boys and girls, it seems our rider has gotten us VIP status. Helm, vector Able, ahead full, engage." Kong chuckled.

Hazard looked at the captain. "I am sure the message is still en route up the chain, but my orders had embedded authorization codes that grant priority passage through Imperial space. Who's in charge may be in flux, but orders are orders. More importantly for us, they will never be able to figure out who issued them."

Kong looked hard at him. "Well, the first part of the plan worked. You do realize ImpSec will be waiting for us when we get to Central, right? They'll want to have a little chat with you and me and probably a few other members of my crew. Those slimy snakes love to ask questions and will keep on asking them till they get answers they like."

Hazard put on a feigned look of surprise. "I can't believe you'd characterize the protectors of the Empire as slimy snakes." Then Hazard chuckled. "I hope they meet us. It will keep me from having to look for them. The head of security on Central is an old acquaintance of mine. He knows *me*. To do what I need to do I'll need access to the security data net, and he can provide that for me."

Hazard rose from the observer's seat on the command deck and moved toward the control-room hatch. "With your permission, Captain, I'm going to use the hyperspace transmitter in your assault shuttle to make some arrangements."

"Permission granted, Mr. King. I've given you run of the ship and everyone knows it. If you need anything, just ask."

Hazard nodded his thanks, motioned for Phil to follow him, and left the bridge.

* * *

Hazard sat in the engineer's seat of the assault shuttle, headset in place. He had pulled out his little black book and was looking through it. Rather than the names and addresses of friends and relatives, this book listed hyperspace communication addresses.

Hyperspace communication, or faster-than-light communication, was a relatively new breakthrough. Most ships in the fleet still didn't have the capability. That the assault shuttle had one was a real stroke of luck. The *Avon* had lost her original shuttle to an accident, and she had received a brand-new one. New ships were equipped with the new comm system, but small craft weren't, except for assault shuttles, since many of the missions they were designed for would be greatly enhanced with FTL comms. Like the old telephone systems Hazard had read about, each unit had a unique identifier. If you knew a unit's identifier, you could signal it directly without going through the central comm system.

Hazard's first call was to Darrel "Snake" Atwater. Darrel was the ImpSec chief on Central Station. Hazard tapped in the number, and after a short wait, the screen in front of Hazard lit up with the face of his old acquaintance.

"Henry, thank the deities. Where are you?" the professional spy asked. "Everyone is trying to find you, and some of them for all the wrong reasons."

"I need to keep this brief, Darrel. I'm not sure how secure any transmission is, even this one. I'm sure you're aware that the *Avon* is inbound to the station with a mysterious Imperial envoy. I am that envoy. I'm sure ImpSec will have agents meet the shuttle to validate the envoy's credentials. I need those agents to be handpicked by you, and then I need to be brought to the security center so I can meet with you. Don't meet me yourself, because that will raise questions. Based on your greeting, you're thinking the same way I am right now. I'll see you soon." Before Snake could reply, Hazard cut the connection.

"Do you think you can trust him?" Philip asked behind him. "I came into the Imperial Guard Force after he left the palace."

"I don't have much choice, do I? That's why I refer to him as an acquaintance, not a friend. However, I do know he's incorruptible and that he takes his loyalty to the Empire seriously." He shrugged. "That will have to be enough. I'll also hedge my bet a bit and have the Kong provide us with a couple marines to cover our backs. About that, make sure you're well armed, including some grenades and flash-bangs. And get me a sidearm."

"I've already beefed up my own arsenal, but I didn't think to get anything for you. I'll remedy that," Philip replied.

Now for the next call.

Getting in touch with the grand admiral was a little more complicated. Grand admirals and dukes didn't answer their own comms. Hazard had to use his envoy's credentials on two aides and the chief of staff before he finally saw the face of Duke Kara, grand admiral of the fleet.

"Your Grace," Hazard said quickly before the admiral could say anything, "this conversation needs to be private." The admiral nodded and left the field of vision, obviously removing people from his office.

Within a moment, the face reappeared. "We are as secure as I can make it, My Prince. You can't believe how glad I am to see you."

"Is it that bad, Your Grace?" Hazard said, frowning.

"It may be worse," the admiral replied.

He gave Hazard a brief rundown on the changes Prince Edward had already made. "Additionally, he restricted shuttle flights to and from the planet unless cleared by his new palace security. All in the name of security of the Empire, he claims."

"He's exercising a lot of power he doesn't have, probably because there's no one willing to tell him no," Hazard commented. "I'm going to be brief. The less you know now, the safer you are. I'll give you details when I see you."

Hazard detailed what he needed the admiral to do.

"That went better than I had hoped. Only two calls, and I managed to get the plan started," Hazard said aloud what he was thinking.

Behind him, Phil clucked. "You have a plan? Do you think you could let your poor, confused armsman in on it?"

"Not yet, Phil. You're in the same boat as the admiral; the less you know now, the safer you and I are. Part one of the plan is to get to ImpSec Command on the station. You need to get me there. Period. The entire plan hinges on that."

*****

Chapter Twenty
Empire Date: February 1033

Hazard exited the *Avon's* central lift as the ship secured into the space station's docking cradle. Across the landing bay, next to the main docking hatch, he saw Philip talking with the two marines Captain Kong had loaned him. The marines were in their standard light-armored shipboard rig. Anything more than that would have raised suspicions as they moved through the station. None of the men noticed as he quietly approached and listened in on Philip's brief.

"Guys, this is a simple VIP escort. I'll have close cover on the envoy. I'll have the two snakes that are supposed to meet us take point; that allows me to watch them. I'm placing my trust in you two to cover our back." One of the marines, the gunnery sergeant, glimpsed Hazard. He used his chin to point out Hazard to the other two men.

"Gunny, it is good to see an old hand on this," Hazard said, reaching out to shake the gunnery sergeant's hand. "Introduce me to your partner."

"Corporal Jerry Rodriguez, sir," the second marine replied.

Hazard patted him on the shoulder. "I am happy to have you both in this little parade with me. Let me flesh out what Phil has already briefed you on. I'm not expecting any trouble, but as I am sure the gunny would say, it's better to be prepared for things to go in the crapper and it not, than to be in the shit with no plan." The gunnery sergeant grunted and smiled. "Gunny, you and Jerry are the heavy lifters if we need it. Have your pulse rifles on stun, but don't hesitate to start jacking that up if necessary. *I need to get to the security center.* Period. I can't tell you why yet, but I'll tell you that the Kong initially wanted to give me all of his marines. That's how important he thinks this is." The last statement got their attention. A horn blast and flashing lights indicated that the main docking hatch was opening. "All right, troops, let us be about it."

The transfer party waited at the hatch as four other marines came through the docking connection to position themselves on the station side of the docking tube. Instead of the usual two marines and a junior officer, Captain Kong had beefed up the detail to four marines with a junior officer and a middy. There was also a security team with the chief and two armed spacers at the ship's end of the tube. If asked, he was prepared to explain that they seldom docked with space stations and he was taking this opportunity for a training exercise.

The chief nodded to Hazard, and the parade began, with Philip leading them out. They exited the docking tube and Hazard noticed the two security types waiting for them. ImpSec had long ago decided it was foolish to try to disguise known security agents, so they went in the other direction. Each agent was dressed in a black coat, black slacks, black tie, and black hat. Hazard wondered why they didn't just stencil "ImpSec" on the back.

The two agents approached. "Mr. King, if you would follow us, we will get to the central office as quickly as we can. We have arranged for a station drill that will isolate sections of our route," the lead agent stated. They were all business. No ID checks, no introductions, just move the package.

Hazard nodded. "Very well, lead on."

They moved out. He began wondering whether he was in a parade or if he had formed a posse. He liked the idea of having his own posse.

They moved quickly through the station. Everything moved smoothly—almost *too* smoothly. When Hazard had developed his plan, he had looked at routes to get to ImpSec Central Station. So far, they had followed the one Hazard had worked out himself, and if he could work it out, others could, too. The security setup was designed to prevent a random attack, not a deliberate one. If someone had learned he was on board, or even suspected he was, there were only a limited number of places for him to go. He motioned for everyone to stop.

"I have a bad feeling about this," Hazard said. "I know exactly where we are. We'll turn left up there into a long corridor with no side exits. It's maybe sixty meters long. If I were setting up an ambush, that's where it would be. Gunny, what do you think?"

The gunnery sergeant's voice, like grinding glass, answered. "Aye, sir, you're right about that." Hazard assumed he was checking schematics in the heads-up display inside his helmet. "It's where I would do it, and this is what I do for a living. The problem is that we have to go that way. It's the only path that will get us to where we want to go. I have to ask this, sir. Do the bad guys want to capture you or eliminate you?"

Hazard thought about that for a moment. He was reasonably sure that anyone after him would have orders to capture him, but if capture was not possible, then termination was fine, too. He also knew that Edward or those around him couldn't let him live if he was captured. He would likely have an "accident" within the next four or five months.

"That is a great question, Gunny. If something happens in that hallway and things go south, I'll either die there or die somewhere else before the month is over."

"If it's a basic ambush, the bad guys will have someone in front of us to both block and distract. Then they'll bring in the anvil behind us to close the trap. The key to defeating it is to attack out of it. We can't stand our ground and wait for them. And it just so happens that Jerry here has just the tool we need for that." The Marine Corps was famous for hanging on to old-style weapons that might be useful in modern situations. This one was a 40 mm grenade launcher with an eight-round rotary magazine. "As soon as he sees the bad guys move in behind us, he'll open up. All his rounds are shaped high explosives with shrapnel. We might have made a slight modification to it from the original design. There is a selector to change the rounds from shrapnel to time delay. Set at two seconds, they'll sail down the corridor and explode in two seconds, sending a blast cone and shrapnel toward the target. When Jerry opens up, the rest of us need to advance and take on the enemy in front of us."

"Okay, does everybody understand the plan?" There were nods all around. Hazard could tell the security guys were not happy. They simply refused to believe that ImpSec might be compromised. "Move out."

They moved forward and turned down the corridor. Hazard heard the gunnery sergeant power up his pulse rifle. He turned and saw him connecting the control cable from his helmet to the weapon. This would allow him to sight the rifle using his HUD.

Hazard drew his pulse pistol and energized it. A glance to his left showed that Phil already had his pistol out. The posse approached the halfway point and four black-suited ImpSec operators and four security types in light body armor turned into the passage.

"Right on cue. Everyone, stay sharp," Hazard said quietly. "Gunny, you take the security guys. Phil and I'll take out the ImpSec, and we'll meet in the middle. We go when we hear the launcher or on my order."

The agent leading the approaching group called out to one of the escort agents.

"Ben, change in plans. The envoy is to be transported planet-side. We have a shuttle all—" The agent never finished his sentence. Jerry fired the launcher and all hell broke loose.

The noise in the corridor was deafening. Hazard heard the launcher *thump* again as he brought up his pistol and took out the lead agent before his gun could clear his holster. Hazard glanced around as he changed targets and saw Phil was already firing on his second target. Gunny's rifle seemed to be hammering right inside his head. Before he could fire on the last agent, pain exploded in his right leg and he went down.

His final thought as he faded away was that it was suddenly extremely quiet.

* * *

Hazard opened his eyes and saw the overhead lighting typical of any bureaucratic office.

I guess I'm still alive. Everyone knows there are no pencil pushers in heaven.

He tried to sit up, but the pain in his leg and the throbbing in his head forced him to lie back down.

"Easy there, champ," the gravelly voice of the gunnery sergeant warned him. "You are in no condition to move. You took a nasty wound to the leg and you may have a minor concussion. When your leg buckled, your head bounced off the wall."

"No time, Gunny; there is too much to do," Hazard managed to croak. "How long have I been out? Where are the others?"

"They are in the next room trying to decide what to do. Phil and some guy named Snake are trying to be cagey and not reveal too much to the rest of us while trying to decide what to do next. As for how long you were out, it's been about an hour since we got you here into the security center. Fortunately for you, they have a well-stocked med bay here, but the morons don't have a medic. Jerry and I patched you up as best we could. We sent an ImpSec agent we could trust back to the *Avon* to get the doc and a corpsman. They should be here any minute."

"Gunny, how bad did we get hurt?" Hazard asked in a low voice.

"We lost both agents who were with us." He met Hazard's stare and quickly continued. "Not your fault, sir. They were too slow. They didn't believe their fellow agents could be the enemy. You took a leg wound. Phil took a through and through in his arm, but he's fine. He's a tough guy, simply switched the gun to his other hand and went on shooting. I took a scrape along the side that hurts like hell, but I'm mission capable. As for the bad guys, we took down all the ones in front of us. Jerry tagged the four behind us and we managed to grab two prisoners from the rear group. Mr. Atwater already has people talking to them."

"Okay, Gunny, lift this bed and then go round everyone up. We have things to do. And have someone get me a grav-chair. Regardless of what anyone thinks, I am continuing with the plan, so I need to be mobile."

* * *

Fifteen minutes later, Hazard entered the security conference room in a gravity chair. Jerry and Sondheim had managed to get him into the chair with only two or three moans from wounded Hazard. The medical team from the *Avon* had arrived, along with four additional marines in full armor and, to his surprise, Aiden Dohany, the *Avon's* diminutive XO.

The conference room was packed with Atwater, two of his agents, the reinforcements from the *Avon*, Sondheim, Jerry, and, of course, Phil.

"All right, folks, we need to get started," Hazard began. "Some of you know pieces of what's going on, but not all of it. I want everyone here to understand what we are about to do." Hazard paused. "Everything you are about to hear is classified top-secret Imperial. Only the empress or I may release you to divulge information." Hazard let that sink in. "Everyone in this room, because of the service they are in, has sworn an oath to defend the Empire. Whether it be fleet, marine, Imperial Security, or Imperial Guard, you have sworn to defend the Empire, the Imperial Charter, and the empress, even at the cost of your own lives. At this moment, the Empire is facing the biggest threat to its existence since we left the home system, and it is not the Swarm, it is internal." Hazard saw the looks of concern on every face. *Good.*

"Snake, were you able to find the recording I asked for?" Hazard asked. Snake Atwater nodded. "Well, that makes things easier. Queue it up and let's show everyone."

The clip was only ten minutes long. When it finished, Hazard deliberately met each person's eyes. There were looks of surprise, confusion, and even awe. He also saw a sense of purpose in those eyes.

"Shipmates, yes, I am Prince Henry. As you saw in the clip, the empress had decided to make me the heir. I am sure most of you have heard the stories about what is going on. However, there is much more that you don't know. Somehow my mother has been rendered incapable of ruling the Empire. Under the Charter, emergency powers have been granted to the Regency Council. The heir heads that council. As far as anyone knows, that is my brother, Prince Edward. However, you saw in the video that the empress had become convinced that he can't be trusted. I believe my brother is in the process of staging a coup to grab those powers before he loses them. He is being helped by people both inside the Empire and by the Marxist Federation. I intend to stop him."

Hazard paused to let everyone absorb what he'd said. "Some might say that I'm the traitor, trying to usurp my brother. Those who follow me and my plan could also be branded traitors if that is the case. Every person here needs to decide for themselves whether to believe me and help stop this. If you can't, there will be no recriminations or hard feelings, but you will be detained here until the end of our operation."

Phil stepped to his side and placed a hand on his shoulder as Atwater approached from the other side. Sondheim came to attention, saluted, and was quickly followed by the rest of the marines and Commander Dohany.

He saw the *Avon's* medical team was apprehensive. "It is all right," he said. "You can patch me up the best you can, so I am mobile, and stay here. Everyone else, take a fifteen-minute break while the docs make me a little more comfortable. Grab a bite or smoke, and then we'll talk about phase two."

*****

Chapter Twenty-One
Empire Date: February 1033

The Duke of Kara, commander in chief of the Imperial Fleet, paced the confines of his office. Since becoming the commanding officer of his first destroyer until today, he had always walked to relieve stress. One of the ancient histories he enjoyed reading had even told the story of how Horatio Nelson, the iconic British admiral, had paced his quarterdeck while he waited for action.

The admiral's wrist communicator chimed. "Randolph."

"*Fleet One* is ready to launch, Admiral," Marine Gunnery Sergeant Hyman Gentry reported. *Fleet One* was his pinnace, and Gunny Gentry had been his pilot for the last ten years.

"You are authorized for launch, Hymie. Godspeed and good luck. Remember, when those rascals over at the palace challenge you, transfer them to me. More importantly, they *must* think I am on board."

His pilot and friend replied, "Will do." After a brief pause, "Airborne, see you on the flip."

Five minutes later, his comm chimed again.

That didn't take long, he thought to himself. "Randolph here."

Gentry said, "Transferring palace security to you, sir."

There was a short click and an unknown voice came over the comm. "*Fleet One*, you are in violation of the new security measure that is now in effect. You are instructed to land at the fleet landing facility immediately and await security."

"Who am I talking to?" the admiral asked.

"Lieutenant Embid. I am the duty palace security officer. You are in violation and must return for inspection."

The admiral felt his anger beginning to grow. "What if I decline your most generous invitation?"

The voice immediately answered, "We will scramble aerospace fighters to turn you back. If that fails, we will have an air-defense battery shoot you down."

"You have no idea why this craft is designated as *Fleet One*, do you?" the admiral began. "Nor do you know who I am. *Fleet One* is the personal craft of the commander of the Imperial Fleet. I am the Duke of Kara, the fleet commander, and I use this craft to routinely shuttle between my offices in the fleet building and the fleet units in orbit around Britannia. I have things that I need to do to keep the fleet going, and I am not going to raise my hand like a schoolboy to get permission from some self-important chair-warmer in the palace to use my pinnace to get up to the fleet. As for the threat of fighters and laser batteries, from whom do you think they get their orders? I guarantee that *they* will know what the *Fleet One* designator means.

"Additionally, if you trace through their chains of command, you will find that they work for me. Now leave my pilot and me alone and do something constructive. Randolph out." With that, the admiral broke the connection.

The admiral waited two minutes and called the gunnery sergeant. "What's up, Hymie?"

"They still have a lidar lock on us, but we don't see any fighters and no weapons locks."

"Excellent, we called the bully's bluff. I took an added precaution of having the cruiser *Melbourne* near your flight track to provide additional cover if you need it. Randolph out."

Well, the hardest part of the plan was on its way to Center Station, he thought. All he had to do now was wait for his two dinner guests to arrive.

* * *

Richard Dyess, the lord justice to the Empire, had been surprised by the dinner invitation. He seldom mingled with high-ranking officers of the fleet. True, Richard had an occasional meeting and even dined with the fleet's judge advocate, but that was more in the line of two legal professionals conferring about matters of justice. A dinner invitation from the fleet commander—and a Peer of the Realm—was a different matter. Moreover, the invitation had been hand-delivered by the admiral's senior aide, which was also unusual.

His escort led him out of the lift and down a hallway that ended at two ornately gilded wooden doors. The left door bore the coat of arms of the Imperial Fleet, the right the arms of the Dukedom of Kara. Two armed marines in dress uniform flanked the doors and came to attention as they approached.

"This is His Grace's private dining room," his escort explained and opened the doors. He ushered the lord justice inside and withdrew, closing the doors behind him.

Richard saw two men at the far end of a table that could have sat twenty. The two men turned as he entered and he immediately recognized the other guest, the lord chamberlain, Kendrick Beckham, Lord Derby.

"Dick, come join us," his old friend and fellow council member said. The two clasped hands.

"I didn't expect you to be here, Ken," Richard commented as he was led toward the admiral.

"I don't believe you two have ever been introduced. Richard Dyess, lord justice, may I introduce you to Edmund Randolph, the Duke of Kara." The two men shook hands. "Now, I think we should sit and drink some of the excellent whiskey that Ed has on hand and discuss some things."

*****

Chapter Twenty-Two
Empire Date: February 1033

Private Toprack Jalbani was the first to notice the strange party approaching the docking tunnel to the IFS *Shinto.* She had only been assigned to the *Shinto* two days ago as a casualty replacement. The stocky female of Pakistani descent was the true definition of a greenie. She had graduated from boot camp only the week before and was teamed with the more experienced Corporal Jaime McFarland. Jaime had been on the *Shinto* for two years and was still wearing a soft cast on his right arm from a wound suffered in the Echo System.

"Corporal, heads up, party approaching. Odd-looking bunch; looks like a security guy leading with two marines armored in standard shipboard rig. The marines are flanking a civilian pushing someone in a grav-chair," Private Jalbani reported.

"Got 'em," the corporal replied as he flipped his helmet visor down and activated the heads-up display. Jaime zoomed in on the party to get a closer look. "Good catch, Jalbani. You are right about the front guy, definitely ImpSec." He focused on the shoulder patches of the marines and used the ship's information network to identify them. "The two marines, one a gunnery sergeant, are off the *Avon.*" Jaime continued scanning. "No ID on the civilian pushing." He paused as he recognized the man in the grav-chair. "Damn, I'm surprised to see him."

"Who, Corporal?" the young private asked.

"You'll see," Jaime said as he switched his comms to the security net. He made sure the private was in the net as well. "Sergeant of the guard, Station Able. We have an armed party, which appears to be friendly, approaching Station Able. Be aware that one member of the party is Lieutenant King. Recommend that the XO and captain be informed."

"Copy that, Station Able," Sergeant Kelly Moore responded. "Hold on."

There was a *click*, indicating Moore was switching to the *Shinto's* command circuit to inform the officer of the deck and probably the marine detachment commander.

The approaching party was twenty-five meters away when the sergeant dropped back into the circuit. "Jaime, hold the party at Able. XO is on the way. Should be there inside two minutes."

"Who is this guy? Why is he important enough for the XO to come down here?" Jalbani asked.

Jaime chuckled. "You are a greenie; I forgot. He's the crazy bastard who flew a shuttle out of the ship in the middle of a Swarm attack run, landed on the ship, and breached hyper control to save the ship. So, we all kinda owe him."

Commander Julie Adams, the XO, arrived just as Mr. King's party arrived. "Seems we can't get rid of you, Mr. King," she said as the party reached the end of the boarding tube. The XO returned the salutes of the marines in the party and then noticed the bandage on Lieutenant King's leg and the pain evident in his face. "Sir, what happened?"

Jalbani was surprised that the XO, the person who sat at the right hand of the demigod who ruled as captain of the *Shinto*, would call a mere lieutenant "sir."

"I can't seem to stay out of trouble despite the best efforts of my comrades." King waved at his companions. "I am glad you're here to meet me, it'll makes things a little less difficult."

"Corporal McFarland is an old hand and recognized you, and Sergeant Moore, the sergeant of the guard, realized that the captain and I needed to know that you had suddenly reappeared under unusual circumstances," Julie Adams said. "How may the *Shinto* assist you?"

"I need to have another 'special discussion' with you and the commodore, ma'am," King said. "And while we're doing that, I thought the rest of my team here could camp out in the pilot's ready room."

"The captain—he was only an acting commodore, Mr. King—assumed you might need to have that type of discussion and directed me to bring you directly to his cabin. The pilot's ready room is the perfect place for them to wait."

* * *

Hazard had only been on the *Shinto* for a brief time before the Battle of Echo System, so he was not well known to most of the crew. However, much of the crew had since made it a point to become familiar with the person who had saved them. Unfortunately, this knowledge resulted in some odd looks as the XO pushed him through the passageways on their way to the CO's cabin. Luckily, this included not passing through the bridge, since they were meeting in his main cabin instead of the ready room.

The hatch closed behind the XO, and Captain O'Riley stepped around the desk and offered his hand. Hazard returned the handshake.

"Your Highness, what is going on?" the CO asked, concern in his voice.

"Since I am already seated—" Hazard gestured at the grav-chair "—I would appreciate it if you two would sit as well."

Commander Adams pushed Hazard to the right of the captain's desk then took a chair across from Hazard on the other side of the desk.

"Commodore," Hazard began, and before O'Riley could correct him, he continued, "you're still a commodore to me, and I have it on good authority you will be that again soon. If you have not been notified, you soon will be that the grand admiral has decided to visit to personally check the status of *Shinto's* repairs and to thank you for your actions in Echo."

"While you were on your way here, Central Control informed us that *Fleet One* was en route, but we have received no other information except that it will arrive in fifty minutes and dock directly using our outboard hatch. I naturally assumed the duke would be on board."

"Before we get into more details, I need for you and Commander Adams to watch this video clip." Hazard passed the data chip containing his mother's discussion about the heir to the captain. "Everything you are about to see and what we discuss afterward is classified as top-secret Imperial. Only I or the empress may authorize the disclosure of said information."

Hazard waited while the two officers watched the video. Their looks when they finished confirmed his trust in them.

"Your Highness, this makes you the heir, as far as I'm concerned," Captain O'Riley stated. The XO nodded. "But how legal is it?"

"I hope to find out in about four hours, sir," Hazard said. "But before we go any further, I need to warn you that there are some who will claim that I'm staging a coup to replace my brother. That means the two of you could be named as traitors for supporting me."

Captain O'Riley interrupted. "Prince Henry—" he paused and looked at the XO, who nodded "—I legitimately believe you to be the heir. Besides, the men and women serving on the *Shinto* owe you a debt. Hell, the whole fleet owes you one. So, we're in."

Hazard, overcome with emotion, responded softly, "We—" this was the first time he had used the Imperial "we" "—thank you for your loyalty and support." He collected himself and continued, "To stop the events currently in motion, I need to borrow some assets from the *Shinto*. Once the shuttle gets here, I need to set up a meeting. Since my party is already privy to some details and are already involved, the ready room seems to be the best place to have it. It was designed for briefings and has the room to hold everyone. In addition to my party, I'll need the two of you, the MarDet commander, the doc, and the two pilots from *Fleet One*."

Hazard noticed Adams' confusion. "No, the duke is not aboard the pinnace, but no one outside this ship must know that. Once *Fleet One* docks, I'll need a total emissions blackout; use the duke's presence as an excuse. Also, the *Shinto* will need to be sealed, no traffic on or off until after the operation. If there are any non-*Shinto* people on board, we need to get them off before then. I suggest sealing the ship, but you and the MarDet commander will know how to best handle that."

He was on a roll; everything he'd been brainstorming started to rush out. "We'll need eight additional marines and at least one corps-man. They'll have to be briefed on the mission, so they need to be people we believe will accept my authority. Commander Adams, would you coordinate that? After the briefing, anyone who decides they can't go along will have to be left behind in isolation."

Hazard looked at his watch. "Twenty minutes until the pinnace gets here. Can the two of you think of anything I might be missing?"

"You act like you have been training your whole life for something like this, My Prince," Commander Adams said.

"I suppose I have," Hazard said. "I always took my responsibility as the spare heir seriously. Fleet Academy only reinforced the training I had while growing up." Hazard thought of Jacob. He missed his friend and mentor. *Thanks, Jake; you are why I can do this. You prepared me for this. I know you are here with me.*

"Then let us be about it."

* * *

Philip pushed Hazard's grav-chair into the ready room just off the *Shinto*'s hangar deck. Hazard noticed the room had stratified. Snake and the two marines from the *Avon* were standing toward the front of the room. The prince chuckled to himself as he realized he thought of the gunnery sergeant and Jerry as *his* marines. They hadn't even been together for an entire day and he had taken ownership of them. *Shinto's* marines were seated to the left of the podium, and the non-marines, including the captain and the XO, were seated to the right.

When the XO noticed Hazard had entered, she popped out of her seat and barked, "Attention on deck."

Those not already standing did so, and everyone braced to attention. Hazard hoped he could remember to thank Julie Adams after everything was over. She had helped set the stage perfectly. There was no doubt about who was in charge.

Phil turned him to face the group and he put the group at ease and had them take seats. "Commander Adams, before I forget, thank you for the courtesy.

"Ladies and gentlemen, and, of course, marines, who don't fall into either category..." Hazard got the chuckles and "oohrahs" he was hoping for. "Before we get to introductions and a discussion of the mission, I am going to share a video that will help explain what's going on." The central display activated and showed what Hazard thought of as the "Rightful Heir" video.

He studied the group as they watched. He saw the surprise and then awe as they realized they were watching their empress in a very private setting. There were covert glances in his direction as they realized he was in the video with the empress and her husband, Grand Duke Henry. Then confusion as they realized the person in front of them was being called "Prince Henry" and "son" by the empress. There was silence in the room when the short clip ended.

"Mr. Atwater, here—" Hazard gestured to the security chief "—is the ImpSec chief on Center Station, and he will validate the authenticity of the scene. It should not surprise anyone that everything in the palace is under constant surveillance, especially when the empress is involved. To answer the first question all of you likely have, yes, that was me in the clip, and yes, the empress is my mother." Hazard paused to let that statement sink in. "I am Prince Henry, second son of the empress. I am also Lieutenant Hazard King, Imperial Fleet. I don't want to get into a lengthy discussion about how I can be both; I just am. The purpose of showing you this video was not to validate that I am a prince, but to show you that the empress intended to change the succession and had named me the heir. I would have already assumed the position, but I had pressing business in the Honshu System I had to attend to.

"Why is this important? The empress, who was in perfect health only four days ago, now lies unresponsive in a coma. Any access to her has been strictly controlled—even her long-term physician has been unable to examine her; she was banned from the palace. The Imperial Guards have been removed and replaced with Palace Guards whose loyalties are questionable. Less than six hours ago, my party was attacked by what we believe were rogue ImpSec agents. That's where I got this." Hazard gestured to his leg. "It saddens me to think that my brother, Edward, is complicit in any of this, but my mother came to a decision four days ago that he could not be trusted to rule. I believe outside powers have used the crown prince's fears to coerce him into these actions. Tomorrow morning, he will assume emergency powers along with the Regency Council. I intend to stop that," Hazard stated with a sudden surge of passion. I don't intend to do this in a vacuum. I intend to validate my claim as the rightful heir. That is the next part of my plan."

Hazard gestured to the pilot of *Fleet One*. "Gunnery Sergeant Gentry flew here in the grand admiral's pinnace. The Duke of Kara was not on board, but we have led the rest of the system to believe that he is. When the shuttle returns to Fleet Headquarters in an hour or so, everyone should believe it's just the fleet commander returning after a visit to the *Shinto*. The shuttle will be carrying my party, augmented with some medical people and as many marines as we can cram on board. The admiral, an essential part of the plan, has arranged for a private dinner this evening with some special guests. A dinner I intend to crash. The duke's guests are the lord chamberlain and the lord justice. I am going to present the same evidence to them that I just showed you. I'll only assume the position of heir with their approval. If they disagree, then I'll halt the entire endeavor."

Hazard waited while everyone considered what he'd said. "I never wanted to be emperor. Hell, I don't want to be emperor. All I ever wanted was to be a fleet officer, like my father. I'm sure most of you remember that my mother never thought she would be empress. But, like you, I swore an oath to protect and defend the Empire, both as a prince and officer. If I have to do this to accomplish that, then I have to put my personal feelings aside."

Hazard glanced at the clock on the forward bulkhead of the room. "In forty minutes, *Fleet One* will have been docked with the *Shinto* for one hour. By then I intend to be aboard and launch. I am asking for your assistance to make that happen. If you can't support that, I understand; there will be no repercussions for you. But for those of you who support me, I tell you now—the Empire thanks you." He gestured and Phil pushed Hazard back down the center aisle.

*****

Chapter Twenty-Three
Empire Date: February 1033

Edmund Randolph, the Duke of Kara, looked at his watch and then at the cabinet ministers seated at his dining table. He was worried. Things were behind schedule. The special guest he was expecting was exceptionally late. He hadn't informed the lord chamberlain or the lord justice about his fourth guest. To buy time, he had quietly told his aide to slow serving the meal, drawing out the time between courses. Even with that, they had finished eating thirty minutes earlier, had sipped their after-dinner brandy, and were now having coffee.

"Your Grace," the lord justice, Richard Dyess, said, "I want to thank you for your hospitality. The dinner was amazing. I really would like to get a bottle of that excellent brandy. Unfortunately, Kendrick and I—" he nodded to the lord chamberlain "—have, in the morning, what may be the most important meeting we have ever been invited to. I, for one, will need time in the morning to prepare, so I need to take my leave."

"Dick, you are entirely welcome," the admiral replied. "I'll have a bottle of the brandy sent over to your office by courier. It has been my pleasure to entertain the two of you." He paused. "I need to be honest, like all social gatherings among people of power, there were other purposes in tonight's get-together. I accomplished one of them by getting to know you both better. A fourth guest was going to attend, but obviously he was unable."

Before the admiral could finish, the dining-room doors opened and a young man in a gravity chair was pushed into the room by a man in a dark suit. A third person entered behind them and closed the door. All three senior officials rose when the door opened.

"My Prince," the old admiral exclaimed, moving around the table to meet the man in the chair. He knelt beside Hazard. "What has happened to you? Are you all right?"

"I'll be okay, Uncle," Hazard said. "I apologize for being late. Palace security was a pain in the ass. It seems they had an air car keeping an eye on the landing pad. We've been stuck circling for thirty minutes waiting for them to leave. We didn't want them to see who was getting off the shuttle, and we could not contact you to tell you why since I am sure they are listening. They finally got tired of watching and left. As for my leg, I took a bullet during an attempt to either kidnap or eliminate me."

The lord justice finally caught on. "Prince Henry, my god. We all thought you were on Honshu."

"I was, Mr. Dyess, until two days ago. I managed to get back to Britannia as fast as I could. With the Code Orange, I knew I needed to be in the home system. I have some information I need to share with you and the lord chamberlain." Hazard motioned toward Kendrick Beckham. "I know you have a meeting of the Regency Council in the morning, and I need to discuss that with the both of you. The Empire stands at a precipice and, gentlemen, the two of you are in a position to save her.

"Let us sit, and I'll elaborate. First, I would like to introduce Darrell Atwater. He's chief of ImpSec on Central Station. Before his promotion, he was the ImpSec assistant chief at the palace. I am sure of his loyalties. I asked him to extract some information from the palace's security system, information you need to have before your meeting. He is prepared to swear on its validity, as am I."

Hazard removed the chip with the palace recording from an inner pocket.

"Admiral, do you have an interface we can use to watch this recording?"

The duke took the drive, went to a long side table, and pushed a hidden recess, revealing a computer input terminal and a large monitor rose from behind the table. The admiral inserted the drive and returned to his seat as the playback began.

* * *

There were several moments of silence after the playback ended.

"Mr. Beckham, Mr. Dyess, I arranged for the admiral to get you here so you could see this. I believe it is obvious the empress didn't feel my brother could rule in her place. Therefore, I have but one question for the two of you: If I were to claim to be the true heir, based on this recording and my word, would you support me?"

Both men stared at the now-blank video screen. Hazard had distilled the entire issue into one simple yes-or-no question. Did they believe the video? Did they believe him?

"Your Highness, the video does not come as a complete surprise to me," the lord chamberlain began. "I knew about the empress' reservations about the crown prince. She had me draft the document—in secret, mind you—to change the succession a month ago. The only surprise for me is that she had finally decided to act on it."

"I have to believe," Hazard said, "that if my trip to Honshu hadn't been so important and time-sensitive, that document would have already been signed and witnessed. Then this would all be moot."

The lord justice jumped in. "I suspected that something like this was in the works. The empress and your father sent for me several months ago and had me look into it. I spent several days researching it and gave them my findings. Prince Henry, my finding was not an opinion but a statement of fact: the initial line of succession is to the direct descendants of the ruling emperor or empress. The only stipulation is that males have precedence. There is no mention of birth order. So, I informed Her Majesty that if she wanted to name you as heir, as a direct male descendant, it was within her rights under the Imperial Charter."

The elderly justice walked around the table and went to one knee in front of Hazard's chair and took his hand.

"I, Richard Dyess, lord justice of the Empire of Britannia, do solemnly swear my allegiance to you, Crown Prince Henry Kane, and recognize you as the true heir to Empress Elizabeth, your mother. I swear this before God and these witnesses."

The sudden oath shocked Hazard to his core. He was overcome with emotion as he placed his free hand on the lord justice's head.

"Richard Dyess, we humbly accept your oath of allegiance. Thank you, sir. Now rise." The minister rose and joined the others. "Lord Justice, a simple yes would have been enough." Hazard chuckled and the three statesmen did as well.

"Now that the easy part is over," the chamberlain said, "how are you going to execute your newfound power, My Prince? Your brother is holed up inside the palace and surrounded by guards who are loyal to him. You know as well as I do that the place is a fortress."

"Not as much as you think, my lord," Hazard replied. "And we don't have to take the whole palace, we just need to get me into the council meeting room. There are two weak points that I intend to exploit. The first one is the underground access. True, it has a security checkpoint and several guards, but once you get past them, there's nothing else on that level. The secure elevator next to the checkpoint only has two stops: the underground access and the main floor across from the council chambers. Remember, the underground tube is designed to allow ministers quick, discreet access to the empress. The second weakness is the palace security system. I have backdoor access that we're going to use. I can't say any more about that because the information is sensitive.

"I have my team working on how best to take advantage of those flaws. Something I learned from you, Uncle." Hazard looked at the admiral. "If you don't know how to accomplish something, assign knowledgeable people to figure it out for you. I have ten marines putting that part of plan together. Your aide was kind enough to provide a conference room for them. Now, I need a place to lay down for a bit. I have a medic with me who needs to take a look at this leg. Do you have a couch I could use, Uncle?"

* * *

Phil Myerson, captain in the Imperial Guard, walked into the conference room set aside for the team's use. The guardsmen had left his prince in the care of the *Shinto's* doctor and corpsmen. They were going to check on Hazard's leg wound and give him a mild pain med to get some rest. Phil had left the ImpSec chief, Mr. Atwater, to stand guard. Atwater would not participate in the next day's activities, so Phil had used him instead of a marine—said marines would need the rest to be sharp.

Two sergeants were standing on either side of the center table, studying computer pads and examining a holographic projection of the palace. The eight other marines were scattered around the room, resting, lying on the floor or leaning against walls. All of them were practicing a marine's learned ability to sleep anywhere at any time.

Gunnery Sergeant Sondheim looked up when Phil joined him at the table and nodded. Phil reached a hand across the table toward the other sergeant. "Sergeant, I'm Phil Myerson."

The slim sergeant shook his hand. "Isaac Baumgardner. Just call me Bummer, it's easier." The sergeant was a wiry, medium-height man of either African or East Indian heritage. He commanded the second platoon of the *Shinto's* marine company and was in charge of that ship's volunteers.

"We are lucky to have him, sir," the gunnery sergeant put in. "Bummer here has spent quite a bit of time in Force Recon, including as an instructor. To our benefit, he had a 'misunderstanding' with a fresh-out-of-academy lieutenant and was promptly transferred to the regular fleet force."

"Sounds like just the man we need, Gunny," Phil said sincerely. He understood the conflicts that arose when amateurs led elite combat troops. "Just so you know, it wasn't that long ago I was a bootneck." Phil used the ancient English term for marine. "I, however, learned the lesson of letting the professionals do their thing. I'm just here to offer advice and information. More importantly, I spent the last four years inside the palace in the Imperial Guard Force."

"And we plan to pick out every piece of info you have, sir," Bummer responded. "Information brings knowledge and knowledge wins battles."

"What have you come up with so far?" the guardsman asked.

"So far, it doesn't look promising," Sondheim reported. "We can drop the two interior guards using sleepy darts, but the checkpoint officer is sealed in a blast-proof room, so he won't be affected. When he sees those guards go down, he'll simply hit the panic button. That drops a security partition in front of both station doors and alerts the rest of the palace. The sealed checkpoint is the nut we need to crack. We haven't come up with a quiet way to do that yet."

Bummer took over. "I have a top-notch hacker with me. Given enough time, he could get through all the firewalls and disable the alert system, but he can't get in from here. The palace security and control net—hell, the whole net—is cut off from the outside with no hard-wired connections outside the palace proper. All outside comms, both wired and electronic, go through the central security comm center. That center is adjacent to the palace in a self-contained bunker. It has only a single data line that crosses the boundary into the palace. All electronic signals are blocked by a combination jammer and exclusion zone, which encompasses the entire palace."

Phil said, "There are ways to get around all that, but there is a big 'but' involved. If I reveal that method—which it looks like I'll have to for the plan to succeed—neither of you will ever be able to go back to your current roles. There are only a handful of people who know it."

The two sergeants looked at each other and then nodded to Phil.

"There's an override access into the central computer system that is only available at the highest levels. This access gives the user complete override authority. All the users need to do is tell the central computer what to do. Only three people have this access: the empress, Prince Edward, and Prince Henry. Yes, our Prince Henry. Prince Edward, fortunately, does not know he has access. And as the old vid commercial used to say: 'but wait, there's more.'" The sergeants chuckled at the ancient anachronism. "The empress and Prince Henry have an embedded neural interface which connects directly into the computer, bypassing all login protocols. The weak spot in the tube station the prince was referring to in his initial brief to you was not about the station itself, it was about the fact that the last five meters of the tube line are actually inside the wireless network of the palace. All we need to do is get him to the right spot then he can take out any system we need him to."

*****

Chapter Twenty-Four
Empire Date: February 1033

Hazard—or should he start thinking of himself as Henry now?—felt better after five hours of sleep. Lieutenant Commander Phyllis Warren, the chief medical officer from the *Shinto,* had been an immense help. Knowing Hazard needed to be alert and clearheaded, she had administered a nerve block to control his pain. In addition, she had given him strict orders to remain seated in his chair. Since he couldn't feel anything in the injured leg, any attempt to use it could result in additional and possible unrepairable damage.

Phil, now in the uniform of a Palace Guard, pushed him along in his gravity chair. His marines—the two marines from the *Avon*, also dressed like Palace Guards—flanked him on either side. Leading the group, and tagged as the assault team, was the breach team, four marines led by Bummer, from the *Shinto.* Two were in guard uniforms, but the other two, including Bummer, were wearing a type of armor Hazard had never seen before. Bummer had told him they were prototypes of the new stealth armor the Marine Corps was testing. Behind Hazard was the rest of the team: the remaining four marines in full combat armor and the three-person medical team from the *Shinto.* The last four marines were the muscle of the operation. He hoped he would not need them.

The team moved quietly through the transit tunnel, along the tracks connecting the palace to Fleet Headquarters. Hazard was intimately familiar with this rail system. He had used it many times to secretly travel to and from the palace to preserve his identity as Hazard King.

His thoughts wandered again. What would become of Lieutenant Hazard King? Would he disappear because he would have to become Prince Henry of the House of Kane?

Hazard shook his head. He had to stay focused on the mission.

He reviewed the mission in his head. It was pretty simple. Once he was within range of the palace network, he would take control and override or isolate the critical systems. The breach team would then secure the station. After the basement was secured, the assault team, augmented by the two marines in stealth armor, would proceed to the main floor and take control of the Regency Council. At that point, if everything had gone as planned, armored marines would escort the medical team to the Imperial apartments and secure the empress.

Sergeant Baumgardner held up a fist to signal the party to stop. The breach team was in position outside the tube station doors to the palace. Because they were on the tracks, not inside a transport, the bottom edge of the door was at mid-thigh. Hazard reached out with his neural link and… nothing. He motioned Philip to move him forward, closer to the door.

Still nothing. Damn.

If he couldn't access the network, they were screwed. He looked at his watch. 0940. Twenty minutes until the meeting. Hazard reached for the chair controls. The chair didn't have any propulsive force, but he could adjust the height. He pulled the control lever back and the chair began to rise. Simultaneously, he searched for a network signal.

He was nearly to the domed roof of the tunnel when he started to get an intermittent connection, but it wasn't sufficient for him to perform the override.

Hazard lowered the chair and motioned the two sergeants and Phil closer. The men's heads were practically touching as Hazard whispered, "I can't get a solid signal. The tube construction must be blocking it somehow. Ideas?"

The four of them stared at each other. Phil's eyes lit up.

"Which side is your implant on?" he asked Hazard.

"Right side."

"Let's try this: raise the chair so that your head is level with the top of the door."

Hazard raised the chair and Phil spun it around so the right side of his head was toward the door, then he pushed the chair sideways until it gently brushed against the door. Hazard realized what Phil was thinking and tilted his head so it touched the door. He searched for a signal and… bingo! There it was, weak but a solid connection. He motioned for Phil to pull him away and lowered the chair.

"That is not going to do us any good if the prince is going to have to hang up there," the gunnery sergeant grumbled. "He'll be in our way, not to mention the line of fire."

Hazard looked at his watch again. 0947. "No worries, folks. When the doors snap open, execute your plan."

He motioned for Phil to push him up against the door again, then raised the chair until he was at ground level with the floor and again pressed his head against the door. He still had a good connection. He accessed the system, promptly used his override, and began giving the computer that controlled everything in the palace its orders.

* * *

The Empire didn't maintain a large standing army. The few times in the past it had needed ground troops, the Imperial Marines had been utilized. Each warship in the fleet was assigned a marine contingent, ranging in size from "short platoons" of twenty men on the smaller ships to full-size battalions on the dreadnoughts. Three full-size regiments, a total of nine thousand marines, were stationed in the capital system along with assault transport ships which could move part or all of those marines anywhere in the Empire within ten days.

Four hundred and fifty years ago, as the Empire was expanding into a new sector, they had discovered a rogue human system, Mecca, which had initially been colonized by the Islamic Federation. Shortly after the colony was firmly established, an extremist faction had taken control of the government. What had started as a peaceful colony, established to ensure the Islamic faith survived, had turned into a modern-day Barbary State. Pirates sanctioned and supported by the Islamic Federation began raiding Imperial shipping and even nearby planets. Mining colonies were especially ravaged. The only solution was to put forces on the ground, so the Imperial Marines were sent in. Eventually, every marine contingent from almost every fleet ship was needed to put the moderates back in control of the planetary government.

During the post-conflict review of lessons learned, the lack of a well-trained, well-equipped army was mentioned. Even though they were far better equipped and trained, the marines had suffered severe casualties due to low numbers. It was also noted that the marines were trained and equipped for shipboard actions, space combat, and planetary assaults, not sustained ground combat. But this had been the first time in the Empire's history that a large force of ground troops had been needed. Training, equipping, and maintaining a force the size that was being discussed would be expensive.

Most planetary systems maintained small militias that were used to supplement planetary security or law-enforcement agencies. They were also used for rescue and recovery during natural disasters.

A military historian in the Pretoria system suggested that a system similar to the old United States National Guard be developed where each system would maintain a ground force based on the size of its population. Ten percent of that force would be full time, with the rest in reserve. The reserves would conduct regular training and annual certification. The Empire would provide all the equipment and pay for half the yearly maintenance costs of the full-time troops.

Private Gwayne Mordecai had been in the Palace Guard force for only six months but had spent ten years in the Royal Britannic Army and had risen to sergeant. Now he was beginning to rethink the decision to join the Guard. Sure, the pay was better. He was now getting more than a first sergeant in the RBA made. He also didn't have to participate in road marches or camp in cold bogs, but as a sergeant, he didn't stand boring guard watches and get every shitty little job that came up. He was back at the bottom rung of the ranking ladder, and he didn't like it, especially now.

When the empress fell sick, the crown prince decided it was a conspiracy. He had kicked the snooty Imperial Guard out of the palace, along with almost a quarter of the Palace Guards, including most of the senior officers. That left few Palace Guard to perform their regular duties *and* fill all the Imperial Guard's posts.

So here he was, standing guard in the tube security station. Mordecai had been here four hours. He still had two hours to go, and the armor was getting heavy. The Imperial Guard had only stood four-hour watches, and they had done it in power armor, so they didn't have to support the weight of the armor.

He was startled when the doors to the station snapped open. There had been no alert that a tube car was approaching. He felt a sharp pain in his chest and began to topple to the floor. The last thing he saw were two blurry shapes coming through the door.

* * *

"Are you sure about this?" Colonel Yvette Devereaux asked the guardsman at her side. The colonel was leading a group of forty Imperial Guardsmen in full combat armor through the corridor that connected the Imperial Guards' barracks to the palace.

"Yes, and yes again," Major Patrick O'Shaughnessy replied. "We've been over it. The message I received said 'Meet me at the seals and dress how I last saw you at 1000. Rabbit.' Phil and I have been friends for a long time, all the way back to the academy. He picked up the moniker Rabbit while running cross-country there. The last time I saw him was in the tube station and I was on duty in the booth, in full armor. The seal is obvious." He pointed ahead to the sealed security doors. On the left-hand door was the Imperial seal—on the right, the Imperial Guard's seal. It was the only place in the palace where they were side by side, and because of that they were often used as a location reference.

"I hope you're right. We'll have our asses hanging out if the crown prince or his flunkies see us on the security video," Yvette replied.

* * *

Even though he knew it would work, Hazard was surprised when the tube doors snapped open. Bummer and Corporal Gibson, another *Shinto* marine, activated their stealth armor. The technology still needed some work because the stealth features turned them into fuzzy blobs instead of armored marines. Bummer had explained they were designed to defeat sensors, not the human eye. Still, Hazard thought, you couldn't tell they were fully armored marines.

They rushed through the door, and it was like watching a well-orchestrated ballet. Hazard heard two pops, then the blobs were moving again. Two marines in guard uniforms quickly followed. Fifteen seconds later, Bummer, his stealth deactivated, stuck his head through the door and announced the all-clear. Hazard was jamming everything within twenty meters, so the sergeant had to make a direct report since the team couldn't use their internal comms.

"Phase two, people! Move!" the gunnery sergeant barked from his side.

The rest of the team rushed into the security station. Hazard saw five guardsmen, unconscious and bound, lying on the floor to one side. Now that he was out of the tunnel, Hazard could link into the network. He made a quick check of the systems.

"I just verified that there is no one else on this floor, Gunny, and no alarms. Phase one went as planned. I have deactivated the jamming," Hazard reported, and Sondheim nodded. "Let's move everyone to the elevator and get ready." They went through the corridor and down the short hall to the single elevator. Hazard checked the time. 0957.

"Assault team, load up," the gunnery sergeant said, announcing the start of the next phase, where the plan hit its first snag. The elevator wasn't big enough to hold Hazard in his grav-chair, two armored marines, and three more. The gunnery sergeant did what good marines did, he improvised on the fly. "Bummer, you and Gibson switch to your regular rifles and give your dart guns to me and Jerry. As soon as we clear the car, I'll send it back down and you come up."

Without the armored marines, there was just enough room for everyone else to enter the car. The gunnery sergeant pushed the Up button, and the doors closed.

Hazard maintained his link with the network and took control of the car. "There are two guards on the council room door. No others are nearby. We'll have about two minutes before a roving patrol approaches. I'll hold the doors closed until you give me the word, Gunny."

The old sergeant nodded. He and Jerry maneuvered until Jerry was standing on the right and Sondheim was on one knee to the left. Both had their weapons ready.

"Wait for the doors to fully open, Jerry, and take the one on the right. Your Highness: go!" the senior marine ordered.

Hazard released the hold and it felt a lifetime until the doors opened. The two marines moved almost as one, leaning out into the corridor and firing once. They disappeared into the hall, and Philip slowly pushed his chair off the elevator. Phil pushed the Down button to send it back for the two armored marines.

The team gathered around the doors to the council chambers. Hazard kept watch on the feeds.

"Two guards in the room. One against each side wall about halfway down," Hazard said in a low voice. "My brother hasn't arrived but everyone else is there. Phil will open the doors and move forward.

Gunny, you, and Jerry advance and take out the guards. We don't have time to wait for the others."

* * * * *

Chapter Twenty-Five
Empire Date: February 1033

Grand Duke Henry sat at the foot of the council table, which was unusual. His normal seat was to the left of the empress at the head of the table. However, today was anything but normal. His wife, Elizabeth, the empress, was lying in the Imperial apartments. Henry had found her in their bed three nights ago, pale and unresponsive. After an initial examination, the on-call palace physician had reported that she appeared stable but was in a coma. Henry immediately suspected something bigger was going on. What his son—their son—had done next had confirmed his suspicions.

When informed of his mother's state, Prince Edward immediately declared that she was unable to perform her Imperial duties, and he initiated the emergency powers of the Regency Council as laid out in the Imperial Charter. A council he was head of as the crown prince. These actions were done within an hour of the doctor's initial diagnosis. The empress wasn't moved to the Palace Infirmary or allowed to be examined by Imperial physicians. Instead, she was in the care of the crown prince's medical team. Henry hadn't been allowed to see her since that night. Something was definitely rotten in Denmark, as the old saying went. If only Henry could have delayed his trip to Honshu.

Today was the first official meeting of the Regency Council, where they would officially take up the emergency powers defined by the Charter. Henry also knew Edward would push to be granted full regency powers. He was sure that the crown prince had a medical diagnosis that would state that it was unlikely the empress would recover. The only card Henry could play was to insist on an independent medical exam. The grand duke hoped he could convince the lord chamberlain and the lord justice to support him in the request.

Except for the crown prince, the council members were present. Henry suspected Edward would be late, as usual, in an effort to affect a grand entrance and highlight his importance. That was why the duke was surprised when the doors to the council chambers opened. Edward would surely enter through the door at the other end of the room known as the Imperial Door.

A single guardsman opened the doors, entered the chamber, and walked straight toward Henry. Two more guardsmen followed, carrying wicked-looking rifles that were up and sweeping along the outside walls. The grand duke heard two soft *pffts* as both men fired the obviously silenced weapons, and then the sound of the two guards along the walls hitting the floor.

The older guardsman announced "Clear," and his partner answered with an identical "Clear."

The attack happened within three seconds. The rest of the council—hell, Henry himself—had no time to process what had happened. The older guard shifted his rifle toward the remaining men in the room.

"Gentlemen, please keep your seats and remain quiet." He turned to his partner and motioned to the Imperial Door. "Jerry, door."

Duke Henry hadn't seen the original guardsman leave the room. Now he returned pushing a gravity chair.

"Son!" the duke exclaimed. "How—"

* * *

Hazard raised a hand and cut off the duke.

"No time, Dad. Gunny, Jerry, the guest of honor is on his way; one minute out. If you would, Dad, push me to the head of the table. Phil, you'd better hustle if you're going to make that reunion." His personal armsman relinquished the chair to the duke, nodded to Henry, and rushed out of the room. The gunnery sergeant and Jerry took flanking positions on the Imperial Door.

"Gentlemen, once Prince Edward arrives I'll make everything clear to everyone." He produced a handgun, which he placed in his lap. "Dad, please take your normal council seat."

Using his right hand, he used the table to turn his gravity chair so he could face both the Imperial Door and the men on the left side of the table. He was not concerned about the two ministers, but Joseph Wells, the Senate majority leader, was a weasel. He was capable of almost anything.

"Gentlemen, I have taken the liberty of electronically isolating this room. There will be no communications in or out until we conclude our meeting."

The Imperial Door opened, and Prince Edward and his guard detail entered. Hazard shook his head. They walked right into the ambush.

Palace Guards were trained to be observant and stand guard duty or patrol. They were not trained in the protection of individuals. The lead guards didn't sweep the room before Edward entered, and the rest of the party hadn't waited for a sweep. The opened doors hid the gunnery sergeant and Jerry. When the two trailing guards stopped to close the doors, Hazard's marines promptly dispatched the entire guard force.

As the last guard tumbled to the floor, Hazard called out to the startled prince. "Edward, we've been waiting for you. Come and have a seat."

His brother approached the table, and Hazard checked his chrono. 1002.

So far, so good. Bummer and Gibson came through the main doors, each dragging a disabled guard. "Bummer, any word from Phil?"

"He was a bit late getting there, but everything is okay," Bummer said. "They're thirty seconds out from central security. Phil managed to get us linked into their network, so I have comms with Colonel Devereaux. She has ten armored Imperial Guards with her and has dispatched teams to the rest of the key posts."

"I love it when a plan comes together," Hazard said. "Bummer, take Gunny's sleepy gun and bring up the armored team and med folks. I want you personally to take that team and secure the Imperial apartments. Have the med team check out the empress. Gibson, stay here and secure that main door."

"You can count on me, sir." Bummer saluted, grabbed Gunny's rifle, and headed out.

"Edward, take a seat next to Dad," Hazard said.

"Henry, you are out of line here. Way out of line—"

"Edward shut it. The family has put up with your sniveling shit for far too long, and it ends now," Hazard barked. He paused and regained his composure. "Gentlemen, would you please direct your attention to the display panel." He used his neural link and had the computer play the Rightful Heir video.

When the clip ended, Hazard addressed the group.

"I am not sure what has happened to the empress, nor do I understand the conspiracy that is obviously taking place to rush Prince Edward into assuming full Imperial power, but I intend to find out. I am proposing to the council that the empress intended to replace Prince Edward as the heir based on this video evidence. That, in fact, in her mind, the empress had already replaced him. I ask for the council to approve my appointment as the Imperial heir."

Joseph Wells, the parliamentary weasel that he was, immediately spoke up. "Prince Henry, at this moment, you have no standing with this council and can't submit motions."

"You are correct, sir. You have manipulated votes in the Senate for most of your career. Do you really think I would put something to a vote that I was not sure of?" Hazard looked at his father.

Duke Henry announced, "Mr. Wells, I am a member of this council and I move that we accede to the empress' wishes and acknowledge Prince Henry as heir to the throne."

Before the duke spoke the last word, Kendrick Beckham barked, "Second!" The lord chamberlain looked around the table. "Now, I call for a vote. Those in favor of adopting the motion raise their right hand."

There was no hesitation by anyone. The lord chamberlain, the grand duke, and the lord justice promptly raised their hands. "Three yes votes have been submitted, which is sufficient to pass the motion. I'll not ask for nay votes. The motion is passed. Prince Henry is now *Crown* Prince Henry, heir to the throne."

Hazard took a moment, more for himself than for anyone else.

"Gentlemen. Those of you who know me know I never wanted this." Hazard looked at his father. "All I ever wanted was to be a fleet officer, like my father. And like him, I may have to put that aside for the good of the Empire. Like him, my love for the Empire comes before any consideration of my wants. The most important principle taught at the academy is duty. Now I have a new duty that means I'll take care of the Empire until the empress recovers. I intend to return the Empire into her capable hands better than when I received it and as soon as she is able to resume the crown."

Hazard stared at each council member individually. "I declare that under the succession clause of the Imperial Charter, the empress is incapable of performing her duties. Since that incapacitation has lasted seventy-two hours with no end in sight, the Regency Council has been convened. As the officially recognized heir and thus head of that council, I am empowering the council to act in the empress' stead. Said powers are in effect as of this moment. I see no reason for this council to meet regularly, but to meet as required by the Charter to vote on measures. If any three members agree that a council meeting is needed they should inform me and I'll promptly schedule one. Since numerous other items need to be accomplished by individuals on the council, I move that we adjourn until the next meeting is called."

Before Joseph Wells could respond, the lord chamberlain seconded the motion, and he, the lord justice, and Hazard's father verbally voted aye.

Hazard slapped his hand on the table. "As the motion has been made, seconded, and with four yes votes, the motion is passed. This meeting is adjourned."

Senator Wells rose from his chair, his face red and seething with anger. The overweight man practically roared. "This is preposterous.

Am I to have no say in these matters? You are insulting the democratically elected body of the realm. By ignoring me, their representative, you are ignoring them!"

"Mind your tone, Mr. Wells," Hazard said coldly. "This is not the floor of the Senate, where such bombastic speeches are mostly made for show. It is the Imperial Palace, the true center of power. If the empress were standing here, would you make such a stir?" Hazard waited a heartbeat and continued, "I think not. Remember, though I don't have the title of emperor, I am right now the head of the government."

Hazard thought for a moment. He had to do something with both Wells and his brother. He couldn't afford to release either of them. If the Council was going to get the information they needed about the conspiracy and detain the people involved, details of the morning's activities couldn't leave the palace. The prince realized he could use the same premise his brother had used, he would place them in "protective custody."

Hazard abandoned the use of the neural link. It was mentally tiring and since he was now in the palace proper the computer would easily pick up his voice commands.

"Computer, this is..." He paused and thought about what to call himself. "This is the prince regent."

From hidden speakers in the room, a distinctly electronic but feminine voice replied, "This unit recognizes you as Prince Henry, and also accepts that as of 1019 hours you are the prince regent, head of the Empire with emergency powers. This unit is ready to comply with your orders."

His brother's face turned scarlet. He was stunned by what he had just seen and heard.

Yes, brother, the computer is always listening.

"Computer, I want total emissions control in effect as of now. No messages are to leave the palace unless verbally authorized by myself or the grand duke. I want the tube system shut down until I authorize resumption." The system acknowledged both orders. "Computer, send a message to Colonel Devereaux that I want her, Captain Myerson, and six Imperial Guards to report to the council chambers ASAP."

The computer simply responded with, "Message sent."

Hazard motioned to the three remaining marines. "Mr. Wells, since there is obviously a plot afoot to change our form of government, members of the Regency Council might be in danger. Therefore, I am going to place you in protective custody until the Imperial Guard can provide adequate security for you." Before Wells could argue, Hazard continued, "I assure you that you will sleep in your own home tonight. Gibson." Hazard looked at the stealth-armored marines. "Please take Senator Wells to the tube security station. Since the tube system is shut down and we have a guard force there, he should be perfectly safe. Instruct our guard to make him as comfortable as possible, but he is not allowed to leave. Once he's settled, return here. I am sure I'll have more for you."

The corporal repeated the orders back and led the senator out of the room.

"Gunny, you and Jerry secure our sleeping guests. I know they'll be out for a while yet, but I would feel better knowing they were also secured." The gunnery sergeant gave a slight nod toward Hazard's brother. "Don't worry about him. You're not going to cause any trouble, are you, Edward?" The new prince regent looked at his brother while taking the pistol out of his lap and placing it on the council table.

The gunnery sergeant and Jerry had just finished binding the downed guards when the reinforcements arrived. The commander of the Imperial Guard entered the chamber still in full armor. Phil was close on her heels, along with eight more guardsmen. Some were in armor, while others were in their standard uniforms. Colonel Devereaux stopped to assess the situation, but Hazard's personal armsman approached and dropped to one knee in front of Hazard.

"Prince regent," Phil said loud enough for the room to hear. "I stand ready to serve."

A ripple ran through the room. The grand duke joined Phil, then the two cabinet ministers. Soon, all but one of the room's occupants were kneeling before Hazard. He looked at his father; the blue eyes, so like his own, stared back at him. Those eyes looked hopeful, and Hazard felt the hardness and anger flow from his body. Then he looked at his brother. The steely-gray, biologically engineered Kane eyes stared at him with hate and reminded Hazard that he still had things to do.

*****

Chapter Twenty-Six

Empire Date: February 1033

Hazard sat in his father's chair in the duke's office, meeting with those he considered his personal counsel: the lord chamberlain, the lord justice, Colonel Devereaux, Gunnery Sergeant Sondheim, Phil, and, of course, his father. They really should have been meeting in the empress' office, but Hazard didn't feel it was right. It would mean that she was not coming back anytime soon, and he was not prepared to accept that.

The palace was secure. All the Palace Guards who had remained in service under his brother were accounted for. They were being detained under the watchful eyes of four fully armed and armored marines in the Queen Anne Ballroom, the largest single room in the palace. They would stay there until they could be sorted. He knew only a few were active participants in whatever was going on.

His brother was being held in Hazard's old apartment. Edward would not be allowed back into his old suite until it had been thoroughly searched. Two armored Imperial Guards were keeping him company inside the room, with two more outside. Hazard had put Jerry in charge of the detail. No one would be admitted unless Hazard verbally authorized it.

Hazard thought about his mother. There'd been no time for him to visit her, though he knew his father was anxious to go to her side.

Phyllis Warren, the doctor he had borrowed from the *Shinto*, had performed an initial evaluation and verified the coma condition. They still didn't know what was happening inside her, but blood samples were taken and Phyllis was confident she was in no immediate danger. She had the empress moved to the palace's fully equipped infirmary. They were just waiting for his mother's personal physicians to arrive.

Hazard addressed the group. "Ladies and gentlemen, I don't want to get hung up in parliamentary procedures, titles, or anything that will slow down what really needs doing. I'm okay with you calling me Hazard. Don't call me Henry, because to me that's my father." He nodded to his dad. "If you aren't comfortable with that, call me sir. I'll not micromanage you. I'll give each of you tasks and turn you loose. If you run into obstacles, don't waste time, get me involved. Is that clear?" There were nods and murmurs of assent.

Hazard looked at the Imperial Guard's commander. "Colonel, I am placing you in charge of securing the palace. I know that's normally your job, but there are some added complications. So far, we've only accounted for some of the guard forces involved. That's why they're being detained. There may be servants involved as well. Start vetting both the guards and servants—no witch hunts. If we suspect a person, they will be comfortably detained for further investigation. If you need additional resources, I suggest the marines or the Fleet Investigative Service.

"Phil, I am placing you in charge of investigating Prince Edward. Use all the resources you have. I'll arrange for Snake to assist you. Start with his apartments and the security feeds. And don't forget his friend Sergey. Find and detain him."

Hazard turned next to the lord chamberlain. "Ken. I'm going to make a wild guess and say the Senate is going to be a problem."

Everyone chuckled. "I believe the Marxists are involved in some way. After they managed to force their membership bill through the Senate, only to have Mother veto it, I'm sure they were pissed. If they manage to get the bill resubmitted and passed again, we can't stop it. The Regency Council does not have veto power, and I could only do it if the council voted to give me full regency power. I don't want to use that option."

The prince regent said to the lord justice, "Dick, please work with Ken. I had time on the hyperspace journey back from Honshu and discovered an obscure law from many years ago. The Emergency Powers Act was passed during the Great Pandemic, and it gave the Crown special powers during an Empire-wide emergency. It turns out that the majority of the planets affected were strong supporters of the Imperial Charter. With those senators absent because of the quarantine, the anti-Imperials had a majority in the Senate and were prepared to start ramming their agendas through. The emperor at the time, Edward XVI, I think, submitted the Emergency Powers Act as the first item up for a vote. He cited that he needed the additional authority to control the spread of the disease and enforce the quarantine. Most of the senators were all for enforcing the quarantine, and in their rush to pass it they missed a key section buried in the appendices. It gives the Crown the authority to suspend the Senate during any Empire-wide crisis.

"Ken, draw up the document; cite the act. I intend to suspend the Senate. I want to sign the document tomorrow." He saw the lord justice was concerned. "Dick, I know as regent I may not have enough authority to do that. Let them file a petition with the justice department. If you ultimately rule that I don't, I'll abide by that and allow the Senate to resume. However, all that will take time." He laughed.

"When you are responsible for an entire Empire, you use your entire toolbox. That includes legal chicanery." The whole room chuckled again.

The regent checked the antique grandfather clock standing next to a bookcase on the far side of the room. 1145. Not even noon, yet so much had happened.

"Needless to say, it's been a rather eventful morning, and for my team and me an eventful three days, so I'm going to send you all off to start your tasks. My father and I'll check on the empress and see if the doctors have come up with anything. Then I intend to catch up on some administrative work this afternoon. I want to meet here again tomorrow to see where we stand. Does 1100 work for everyone?" Everyone nodded. *Then again,* Hazard thought, *if I had said 0400, they would have agreed.* "Good." He used the desk to propel himself in front of the seated men. Everyone stood and Hazard shook their hands as they left the study.

He motioned for Sondheim and his father to stay.

"Gunny, I would like to meet with you, Jerry, and Bummer this afternoon. Figure out a time and let me know," Hazard told the veteran marine. "Right after that, I want to meet with the entire team."

"Here in the grand duke's study? Might get a bit crowded," Sondheim.

"You are right, but gunnies are always right, aren't they?"

Sondheim and his father laughed.

"You, Jerry, and Bummer here. The whole team in the council room. Make it late in the afternoon. I need to make some arrangements before those meetings."

"Aye, aye, sir," Gunny responded.

"Now, I would appreciate it if you would escort my father and me to the infirmary."

* * *

Hazard and his father had dinner in the empress' private dining room, just the two of them. The afternoon, while less stressful, had been as hectic as the morning. He saw his mother and talked to the medical team; held vid meetings with the fleet commander, then the head of ImpSec; had a brief in-person meeting with Colonel Devereaux; and then the meetings with his team.

He felt better after seeing his mother. It was reassuring to know that whatever was going on inside her was not fatal. The rest of it was disturbing for several reasons. Whatever had been done was something unknown to them. If they couldn't identify the cause, they couldn't create a treatment. They also needed to determine how it had been introduced. All the initial test results showed nothing abnormal. Blood, urine, and various skin samples were sent to the Imperial Science Center and submitted to every test they knew.

Colonel Devereaux was unhappy when she left their meeting. Her ego had gotten a little dented when Hazard had informed her that Sondheim, Jerry, Gibson, and Bummer were now his personal security team, answerable only to him. To her, it said he didn't trust her or the Imperial Guard. He couldn't tell her the real reason that they had been made privy to Imperial-level secrets that even the head of the Imperial Guard didn't know.

Hazard realized he had made a lot of people unhappy. The head of ImpSec was unhappy her organization wasn't running the investigation into the empress' illness or Prince Edward's actions. Hazard had pointed out that Snake Atwater and a team of agents he was handpicking would spearhead the effort, but that didn't mollify her. In truth, Hazard had some suspicions about ImpSec, especially after being attacked on Central Station. It was clear someone had infiltrated them.

Doctor Warren had started off happy. She and the two corpsmen accompanying her were now the prince regent's personal medical team. Hazard would need a team to care for Hiroko anyway, so he decided to shanghai them. Phyllis and her team were on their way to King Manor to take up residence. The remaining *Shinto* marines had accompanied her and would become the manor's security force. She joined the "I'm pissed at the prince regent" club when he refused to rest and have his leg surgically repaired. Right now, that just wasn't going to happen.

Hazard looked at his father and knew the duke was the president of that exclusive club.

"Dad, it's something that I need to do, and I need to do it in person."

"What you need to do is be a ruler. You need to learn to put the Empire before your personal wants," the duke said. Hazard glared at him, and his father realize he had gone over the line. "I'm sorry, Henry. I know you're giving up a lot. What I said was uncalled for."

Hazard had decided they should go public about what was happening. The Empire's subjects needed to be reassured that nothing had or was going to change. "I don't intend to tell them everything, Dad, but I don't want us to have a bunker mentality. I need the people to see me."

"Why are Snake and his ImpSec team involved?" his father asked.

"Because I still want a chance, however slim, of going back to being Hazard King. ImpSec has disguise artists and I am going to take advantage of them. My scar—" he touched his cheek "—both helps and hurts that. With a change of hairstyle, a close-cropped beard, and covering my scar, most people won't connect Hazard King to Prince Regent Henry. I intend to make an Imperial address, then I'll make some public appearances. Dad, I believe the one thing that has always sustained the Empire is the people's belief in the Crown. I've been out among the people; I've seen it. The Kane Dynasty has always been at the forefront, leading the people and making each of them feel that the Crown cares about them. I can't do that hiding in the palace."

His father gave him a stern look. "You do realize that if something happens to you, Edward becomes the heir again? Is it worth that risk?"

"I know, and that segues into a touchy discussion. What do we do about Edward?" Hazard said, sorrow in his voice. "I am sure we'll turn up evidence that will be damning. How do you cut someone out of the line of succession?"

"That is an excellent question," his father said quietly. "I have arranged to meet with Richard and Ken before our meeting with you. I'll have them figure out a way to do that."

"About tomorrow's meeting, Dad," Hazard began, "I intend to ask for full regency powers." By his shocked look, Hazard knew he had surprised him. Hazard hurried to explain. "I know I have full support from the three of you, which basically means I can do anything that I want, within reason. I don't intend to be as heavy-handed as Edward was, but there may come a time in the investigation when quick action is necessary. If I have to wait for a formal consensus, we may miss an opportunity. Waiting for council approval may provide the legal loophole individuals need to escape justice."

His father nodded. "All solid justifications. Henry, the three of us believe in you. It shouldn't surprise you that most on the empress' council consider you not only a better choice than Edward as heir, but one of the best to ever sit on the throne. If we believe that, then we should trust you with the responsibility."

"I could not do this without you, Dad. You have always been my inspiration."

*****

Chapter Twenty-Seven
Empire Date: February 1033

Darrel "Snake" Atwater entered the suite of offices the Duke of Kara had made available to his team. Prince Regent Henry had assigned him to the team investigating what had happened to the empress. After his near abduction and assassination at Center Station, Snake could understand the prince's doubts about ImpSec. Hell, he had concerns about his organization. He was the ImpSec station chief, and two of his agents, agents he thought he knew and trusted, had been involved in the attempt. Which was why they were at Fleet Headquarters conducting their investigation. Prince Henry had total confidence in the fleet.

Imperial Security was formed during the early days of the Empire. It had started out as an intelligence gathering organization. As other Earth colonies were discovered, intelligence assets were dispatched to gather information on them. The Crown needed to know if a newly discovered planetary system was a threat or a potential ally. The AN-CUK colony fleet had been well organized and planned. Because of this, it didn't take long for the early Empire to become a thriving society.

Most of the early colonies they discovered quickly became friends and allies and eventually led to them becoming full members of the Empire. Others decided to try and go it alone. These colonies began their own intelligence operations aimed at the Empire, so a counterintelligence function was added to ImpSec. As the centuries passed, more functions were added, signal intelligence, espionage, and even black operations.

Snake always believed they had made a mistake having one person in charge of everything. There used to be separate entities in the old British Empire, MI5 and MI6 were responsible for counterintelligence and intelligence, respectively. Black ops had primarily been performed by specialized military units. With one organization responsible for all of it, the question of who watched the watchers raised its ugly head. There was doubt about the watchers, which was why he was at Fleet Headquarters instead of the ImpSec campus.

Michelle Montane spotted him when she looked up from her array of monitors. Michelle was one of the best—probably *the* best—analyst they had, and she thought she'd found something. Snake and Michelle went way back in the firm.

"Okay, M&M," Snake said, using her nickname based on the famous candy, "what've you found?"

"Right now, it is only a working idea, Snake. I have no proof. I've been sifting through any security footage we had of the empress on the day she became ill. She didn't drink or eat anything outside the palace. To cover our bases, I have a forensic team checking that angle, just in case. She only left the palace once the entire day, which is not unusual, and it was a trip that was scheduled well in advance, opening night of the Imperial Opera, which she has attended every year of her reign."

Michelle looked at Snake, making sure he was following along. "I've been reviewing the footage from the opera and discovered an interesting anomaly. You know how there's no such thing as an anomaly?" Snake grunted. "Guess who else was at the opera? Our old friend Sergey, with none other than Prince Edward. I backtracked and found them sitting together in a private box Sergey had reserved."

M&M motioned him around her desk so he could look at her largest monitor. "Look here. After the first intermission, Sergey and Edward appear at the Imperial Box. It seems obvious that Edward is introducing Sergey to his mother and his two sisters. Now observe." Michelle pressed play and the video moved forward at half speed. It showed Sergey, then the prince, taking and kissing the hands of the empress and the two princesses. Then they bowed and left. The whole thing took no more than two minutes.

"Did you catch it?" Michelle asked rewinding the video to the beginning of the exchange.

"No, I didn't see anything out of the ordinary. Don't mock me, M; you know I was always a poor analyst," Snake said.

"Watch his hands," Michelle said and she played the segment again. Snake shook his head; he still didn't see anything. "The prince takes and kisses each hand first, which is to be expected. Sergey is wearing formal white gloves that go with his tuxedo when he takes and kisses the empress' hand." Michelle paused the playback. "But notice, the gloves are missing when he kisses the princesses'." She advanced the recording. "I couldn't find it anywhere in the surveillance footage, but he obviously removed the gloves before kissing the other two's hands. I've even gone through all the videos from the opera house. I can find no occurrence of him wearing the gloves. In fact, they're not in any recording.

"Other than personal attendants, bodyguards, the chauffeur, etcetera, the empress didn't interact with anyone else. I also ran a background check on Prince Edward. This is the only occurrence I can find of him ever attending the opera. My analysis is that Sergey introduced some outside agent to the empress through his gloves, and Prince Edward facilitated that introduction. I am not prepared to implicate the prince directly, but Sergey definitely used him to gain access."

Snake continued looking at her display. Michelle had paused it at the point where Sergey was holding the empress' hand.

Bastard. I have you. Now, what can we do with it? "Michelle, this is compartmentalized at the highest level. No one at the campus is authorized to access it. You work for me and I answer to the prince. That is everyone in your chain as of right now."

Michelle nodded her understanding.

He went to his desk. He had messages to send.

* * *

Dr. Jayani Shamshaard, Empress Elizabeth's personal physician, sat at the medical research station in the palace medical facility. She had finally been allowed access to her charge the day before, and now she and her team were running every test they could think of. The fully equipped facility had all the resources of a major hospital, and they had used all of them. So far, they had found nothing. There was nothing that should be causing her coma like condition. The doctor's team was working in shifts so that testing and evaluation could run nonstop. Jayani had taken quick naps during the night, interrupted by the need to review results and give instructions. The middle-aged Hindi woman was bone tired and at wits' end.

An hour ago, she had received information from the investigation team that the empress' condition had been caused deliberately. They had determined a possible introduction method, and her team was researching it. The empress' right hand was thoroughly examined, swabs, skin samples, even a detailed MRI, but they'd found nothing.

Jayani called to her head assistant. "Gale, I don't see anything. I'm going to try something a little out of the box. I want you to carefully slice a skin sample from the palm-side, middle, and proximal faces of the middle and ring fingers of the right hand. The glove would have certainly contacted those areas. If we put the pads of those joints under the electron examiner, we may see something." Her assistant looked dubious, and she continued, "I know it's a long shot, but we have to start expanding our tests. Whatever is going on, it's something we've never seen before."

An hour later, the results were displayed on the enormous screens along one wall of the clinic. Again, both women scanned the images.

"This is odd." Gale pointed at four spots on the sample. "See the cell damage in these areas? I've seen images of old-style radiation therapies that caused damage like this."

"You are correct," Dr. Shamshaard confirmed. "But that kind of damage was widespread. This is extremely isolated; only one or two cells in each affected area. If I had to guess, I would say it was caused by something passing through them and blowing them out."

"What could cause that? We haven't found evidence of it anywhere else except in these small areas. A needle penetration could cause damage like that, but again, it would be wider," Gale said peering at the displays.

Jayani considered. She was the only person on her team who knew of all the medical augmentations the Imperials went through. The empress and her family had medical nanites in their systems. Each was injected as soon as they turned fourteen, any earlier and they might have interfered with childhood development. Medical nanites were designed to protect a person from viral diseases and even poisons; they also sped up the repair of physical damage. The nanites the Imperials used had been injected via an IV. She wondered if they could also be absorbed through the skin. The team leader spun on her heel and, without a word, walked across the room toward her private office and promptly closed the door.

Dr. Shamshaard powered up her comm terminal. Because of her clearance, she had access outside the palace. Jayani had only a limited knowledge of medical-nanite technology, but she knew someone well-versed in it. Carl Brougham was the empress' chief physician before her. He was involved in the initial research into the subject and was considered one of the top two or three scientists in the field of nanite technology. The empress herself had urged him to leave his post as her doctor and continue his research full time. He was now in charge of the ultra-secret medical-nanite research center, which was secretly housed within the Imperial Research Center.

A man in a lab coat appeared on her comm vidscreen. "Jayani, how good to see you."

"Carl, I have a problem, and I am hoping you can solve it. It's too sensitive to discuss over comms, even these comms. I believe your special expertise may help solve the issue."

"Of course," he said without hesitation. "I'll be there as quick as I can."

"I'll have the guards send an escort for you to cut through all the red tape," Jayani replied. "Be at the front entrance in ten minutes."

He nodded, and she disconnected before placing a call to Colonel Devereaux to arrange the needed transportation.

* * *

It took almost forty-five minutes for Carl Brougham to arrive at the clinic. He saw the microscopic slides projected on the vid screens as he entered the central lab area. The elderly scientist stopped in his tracks, then moved closer to the screens. Jayani had been waiting outside her office to greet him and joined him as he examined the displays.

"When did you start using topical nanite applications, Jayani?" Carl asked. "I'm sure you've already discerned that they're not nearly as effective as an intravenous injection."

"That's exactly what I called you in for, Carl. We're not experimenting. We had no idea what made those marks, but I had a suspicion." Her mentor turned to her and Jayani continued, "Those are samples from Elizabeth's right hand. Someone else has obviously developed nanites and managed to introduce them into the empress through surface contact. Come." She motioned for Carl to follow her into the empress' medical suite.

Like any doctor being asked for a consult, he immediately picked up the datapad in the holder at the foot of the bed and began reviewing the empress' condition. Jayani gave him a quick verbal rundown. "She was found like this on Tuesday evening. There has been no change in her condition. There is nothing in any of her bloodwork or other tests. Everything checks out perfectly, and she is in no danger of expiring."

"Except she's in a coma for some unknown reason," Carl finished for her. "Good catch on the surface nanites."

"We were just following up a lead the security forces fed us," Dr. Shamshaard stated. "I brought you in to help figure out how the nanites put her in a coma and how we can counteract that."

"I need some equipment from the research center," the nanite expert said. "I don't want to be constantly running back and forth to run samples. We've developed the ability to detect nanites in various samples. But first we need to find and collect some of them. If I can get enough of a sample, I'm reasonably certain I can break them down and figure out how they work. You've done well here, Doctor," Carl said to his former assistant. "We haven't solved anything yet, but like they say in baseball, we're on third base and about to score."

*****

Chapter Twenty-Eight
Empire Date: February 1033

Hazard King used a cane to hobble down the private corridor toward the cabinet room. He had reached an internal decision as to who he was. He would always think of himself as Hazard King, son of Henry King, captain Imperial Fleet retired, and Elizabeth Kane King. He was determined that sometime in the future, he would be that person again. But until then, he would be Henry Alexander Zebulon Arnaud Robert Dimitry Kane, prince of the Britannic Empire, to the rest of the universe.

Hazard entered the cabinet meeting room and saw the look of surprise on most of the Imperial ministers' faces. He had spent the morning with the disguise experts Snake Atwater had sent him. A complete, close-cropped beard now adorned his face. The scar from the wound he suffered during the Battle of the Echo System had been hidden. Scars were exceedingly rare since there were easy skin treatments to remove them, but he had decided to keep his. It was a reminder of what he had lost at Echo as well as a reminder of love. The scar would remain hidden for now. His new hair was the part of the disguise that bothered him most. It was long, nearly to his shoulders, and gathered into a single loose braid that hung down his back. He had never had long hair, but it was the current style at court.

This was a meeting of the entire Imperial Cabinet. Several of the senior members knew him personally and recognized him, even in disguise. The lord chamberlain and lord justice had been involved in his ascension and were also on the Regency Council. There were two other senior ministers—the lord exchequer of the Imperial Treasury and the defense minister. The remaining members were second-tier positions. The foreign minister handled relations with each of the Empire's client systems; the home secretary managed a variety of different agencies Hazard thought of as people-related, such as health, commerce, and education; and the science minister managed the numerous science and research projects the Crown funded.

All the ministers had stood at his entrance. He stood at his chair at the head of the table and motioned for everyone to take their seats. When no one moved, his father, who was to his right, leaned in.

"No one is going to sit until you do. Remember, to them, you are the emperor right now."

Hazard gave a slight nod and took his seat. The rest of the group then sat.

It's going to take some time to get used to being the grand poo-bah, Hazard thought. "Ladies and gentlemen, I thank you for attending this meeting," Hazard said. "For those of you who don't know me, I am Prince Henry, the second son of the empress. I don't intend to go into the details of my designation as the prince regent during this meeting. Suffice it to say, the majority of the Regency Council accepted the evidence presented that the empress had decided to name me as heir over my brother. If any of you have an issue with that, I ask that you speak with the lord chamberlain or the lord justice. If you still feel uneasy about the situation, I'll gladly release you from your obligation to the Crown without prejudice." He rose but motioned for the others to remain seated. "Pardon me, but I am a pacer and always think better on my feet. Hopefully, I'll stay at this end of the table and not have you craning back and forth as if you were at a tennis match." He got the desired laugh.

"I do want to emphasize one thing," Hazard continued. "The Regency Council has granted me full regency powers. Though my title is prince regent, we act with full Imperial power and we intend to wield that power." Hazard said a private prayer to the deities for all the command training he had received. And his use of the Imperial we had been noticed. "Last Tuesday, our empress fell gravely ill and is unable to fulfill her duties. There is little doubt in my mind that this was not an accident but a malicious act. During my return, an attempt was made on my life, an attempt that nearly succeeded.

"You—" he swept his hand around the table "—are my advisors. Investigations are underway into what happened and who did it." He sat. "I called this meeting so you all can hear what has already been discovered and can offer advice. Lord Chamberlain, if you would share with us what you know."

Hazard only half-listened as Kendrick briefed the rest of the cabinet on what they had discovered, how they had found foreign, previously unknown foreign bodies in the empress' bloodstream. The whole cabinet was not privy to the discoveries made in nanite technologies, so the "foreign body" description was used. Technically, they weren't lying. The foreign bodies were a type of nanite they hadn't seen before. He also described how investigators had pieced together the possible source of those nanites.

"We don't have a smoking gun, but compelling evidence points to Sergey Todorovich. The so-called count appears to have passed the agent to the empress during an introduction while attending the opera.

Naturally, we would love to question him—thoroughly question him, if you take my meaning—but he is an accredited diplomat of the Marxist delegation. He is now holed up in their embassy, beyond our grasp," Hazard added after the chamberlain finished.

Penny O'Higgin, the foreign secretary, spoke up. "Your Majesty."

Hazard was surprised, the tall matronly Irish woman was the last person he had expected to join the discussion.

"Penny—may I call you Penny?" Hazard asked. She nodded vigorously. "I'm a pretty simple person. When we're in meeting like this, I would prefer everyone either refer to me as sir or Prince Henry. I don't mind if you call me Henry, though I doubt many of you would." Quiet laughter ran around the table. "Now, Penny, go on."

"Sir, it is a minor point of law, but the Marxists don't rate diplomatic status."

Hazard straightened, and a low murmur started around the conference table. That simple fact could change everything. Before he could ask, she continued, "Under the Imperial Charter, the Crown has the sole authority to grant or reject embassies from outside groups. When the Marxists submitted their request, Empress Elizabeth had the foreign office investigate their federation. Due to their cruel form of government—their people are only a step above being slaves—the empress denied their application. As the foreign secretary, I informed them of the decision, and that while they could maintain a residence, they were foreigners in our Empire without any diplomatic status."

"So, if I wanted a company of marines to storm the place, there would be no legal issues?" Hazard said. She nodded. "Penny, right after this meeting, I would like you, Richard, Ken, and Edmund to stay. We have an operation we need to put together."

The rest of the meeting was mostly what Hazard considered housekeeping—letting each minister know that he was not changing any of the current policies. He adjourned the meeting and personally thanked each of the departing ministers for their support.

* * *

"Before we get started, I want to thank Penny for being on top of her duties. I believe the information she has shared will make an enormous difference," Hazard said. The older woman blushed, showing her Irish descent as dimples and freckles highlighted her face.

In the early days of the Empire, the foreign office was an important department. As exploration ships had moved out from the home system, they had encountered numerous other Earth colonies, and diplomatic relations with them were established. Unfortunately, most of the colonies were the results of hastily arranged expeditions during the last days and lacked the infrastructure to develop the way that the Britannia expedition had.

As decades became centuries, most, if not all, of those colonies had become part of the Empire. As the number of non-Imperial worlds had dwindled, so had the importance of the foreign office, sliding into the ranks of the second-tier ministries. Most of the surrounding space had been explored, and only three nations remained apart from the Empire. The Islamic Federation controlled five systems, three of them inhabited. They were a theocracy following the Islamic faith. They desired to remain apart from the rest of the human colonies to maintain their faith's purity. The Luddites had founded a settlement in a single system. True to their namesake, they were a totally anti-technological society. They wanted no contact with the outside.

The Empire had respected that. The Empire didn't have any formal relations with them but had designated the system a protectorate to shield it from outside interference. And then there were the Marxists.

"Hazard—" Edmund Randolph, grand admiral and Hazard's great-uncle, referred to him as Hazard since both he and his father were in the room "—we need to organize and plan a raid on the so-called Marxist Embassy. It's still early enough in the day that if I can get people working on it, we could launch a raid before first light."

"Edmund, if we go off half-cocked we could give them time to react and destroy evidence," Hazard's father said.

"I would normally agree with you, Henry. I prefer to spend at least a day gathering intel, preparing a plan, then rehearse it, etcetera," the admiral replied. "I don't think we have the luxury of that. I trust that every member of the cabinet is loyal. I don't trust that all of them will maintain security. All it takes is the wrong aide or secretary to overhear something, and the Marxists will find out."

Hazard looked at his chamberlain. "Kendrick?"

"I would like to take the time to make the operation as foolproof as possible. It pains me to say it, but the Marxists have managed to establish a sizable intelligence operation within the government. Until we root that out, I'm afraid Edmund is correct. We may have, at most, a day until the Marxists find out," the lord chamberlain said.

"And that brings up an ugly situation," Hazard said looking down the table at his foreign minister. Everyone at the table except for her was part of his inner circle. People in which he had the utmost trust. "Penny, we're about to touch on a particularly delicate and dangerous subject." Hazard gestured at the rest of the group. "These men have been a part of this from the beginning. I consider them my inner circle."

"So, we're finally going to discuss ImpSec," Penny jumped in. "I was afraid you wouldn't involve me. I am in."

Hazard chuckled. "Is it that obvious? Yes, ImpSec is a problem. I don't suspect; I *know* ImpSec has been penetrated. Two members of the team that attacked me at Central Station were security agents. The remaining members of the attack group were from a security contractor ImpSec routinely uses."

"Prince Henry," his head diplomat began, "there are already rumors floating around the Imperial Ministries that ImpSec is on the outs with you. There are also rumors that they've been totally cut out of the ongoing investigations. Add the fact that the ImpSec director wasn't at today's meeting says volumes."

"You are correct. I don't trust ImpSec. They have failed on multiple levels and have been penetrated, either by enemy agents or enemy sympathizers. They failed to detect and prevent an attack against the empress. I have been going through gathered intelligence about the Marxist Federation and it's next to useless; another failure on their part. Don't get me wrong, there are a lot of good agents—a lot of excellent ones—but I suspect that most of the senior leadership are professional bureaucrats who have gamed the system to get ahead. They are more concerned about themselves than actually protecting the Empire." Hazard paused. "I apologize for ranting, but if they had done their jobs, my mother wouldn't be in a coma down in the Palace Infirmary."

"Henry, there is not much we can do about it right now," his father said.

"Funny you should say that, Dad, because you're going to help me fix it. We have to do something about it right now. Portions of ImpSec are a part of this conspiracy. Surprisingly enough, Snake Atwater gave me the idea of what to do. Back on Old Earth, security organizations like we have eventually became entities unto themselves. They became kingmakers. Stable governments always made sure security functions were divided into multiple organizations. We need to divide ImpSec into its base parts. Foreign intelligence gathering will be folded into Fleet Intelligence. Counterintelligence would become a part of justice. Signals intelligence would be under the foreign secretary. Which would leave intelligence analysis as the only remaining piece, and they would be under a new Ministry of Intelligence. That minister would be responsible for coordinating the activities for the entire intelligence apparatus."

There were shocked looks all around the table. "Grand Duke Henry," Hazard said formally, "I am officially appointing you as the new minister of intelligence." His father nodded slowly, as if understanding the direction his son was going. "Work with the other ministers to flesh out a plan. Day after tomorrow, we're going to pay a visit to the ImpSec complex."

*****

Chapter Twenty-Nine
Empire Date: February 1033

Agnes Whitestone was as old school as you could get and had always had the pragmatism and stubbornness of her New Zealander heritage. She had entered the security service when she was eighteen and had worked as a clerk in the intelligence branch. The future director had steadily moved through the ranks, analysts' assistant, junior analyst, and finally analyst, within ten years. She always prided herself on being observant, and during those ten years she had discovered the skeletons several coworkers and superiors had hidden in their closets. She had leveraged that information to get transferred to the operation branch. No one in senior leadership at "the firm," as they referred to it, got there without spending time in field service.

Now, she was the director of ImpSec. She had scratched and clawed and blackmailed her way to the coveted position, and there were a lot of bruised and upset bodies scattered in her wake. She had spent the last five years solidifying her hold on the top spot. Enemies had either been forced out or moved into positions where they couldn't do any harm. Allies had been rewarded with critical posts. That was how she had become involved with Prince Edward. And now her position was in jeopardy because of it.

It had all started out so simply. A representative of the prince had put out feelers to the palace's ImpSec chief. After all the dancing around such feelers always created had settled down, the end result was that Prince Edward just wanted ImpSec to stay on the sidelines and not get involved in events about to take place. Of course, the prince would be personally grateful to the head of ImpSec if that were to happen. It was an easy request, and she had agreed. Having the future emperor owe you a favor was always a good thing.

When she had taken the top post in the firm, she'd replaced the palace chief, Darrel Atwater, with someone loyal to her. Atwater wasn't an enemy, but he was not her friend. Agnes wanted to have assets inside the palace. That meant arranging for ImpSec agents to be assigned to various staff roles inside the palace, including the guards. At the moment, she had five agents loyal to her in multiple positions around the palace. She would adhere to her agreement with the prince, but she would also gather information through her palace assets. That information would be her insurance policy.

Her intercom buzzed. "Director, Jimmy and Danny are here as you requested."

"Send them in, Doris," Director Whitestone replied and turned to the door to greet the two old friends. She motioned them to a sofa.

They couldn't have been more different. Inside the firm, staffers commonly referred to them as Laurel and Hardy. James "Jimmy" Gallagher was the brains of the two. Tall and gangly and pale. His methodical mind and keen eye never missed much, and he was a crack shot with both handguns and rifles. Daniel "Danny" Frasier had the look of a typical Irish street thug. He was of average height but a good four inches shorter than his partner. His broad, solid body was perfect for his personality. He was the brawler. If you needed intimidation or plain brute force, Danny was your man. They had been part of her personal team for twenty years. Technically, they were part of her personal guard detail. In reality they were her erasers. They got rid of mistakes.

"Before you ask, Director," Jimmy began, "I've gone through every resource I have, and no one saw this coming. Prince Henry has always been something of an enigma. By the time you took over and put your man inside the palace, he was gone. Best info has it that his sudden appearance to take over is the first time he's been in the palace in at least five years."

"What I don't understand is how he managed to get his hands on the assets he used to execute—successfully execute—his countercoup," the director stated. "And make no mistake, gentlemen, it *was* a countercoup, because Prince Edward was making a power play. Our problem now is that the new prince regent believes the firm may have been involved and doesn't trust us. Yes, the firm agreed to stay on the sidelines while Prince Edward took power. We have two other issues, though. At least two agents on Center Station were involved in an attack on Prince Henry and we had three assets in the Palace Guard who were directly involved in the original takeover. Neither I nor the firm knew of these actions."

"What do you need us to do?" Danny asked. "You have one of your special assignments for us?"

"Yes, Danny. Our biggest exposure is the three Palace Guards. They are being held and questioned by the Imperial Guard with help from Naval Intelligence. They have over forty guardsmen they are sifting through, so I don't know their status. If the Crown discovers that ImpSec had three agents hidden in the Palace Guard and actively colluded with Prince Edward, we will face serious repercussions. I need you two to do what you do best. Make that problem disappear. The operation will have to be totally black. No possible link to the two of you."

"If it were easy, you would have used one of your in-house weasels, Director." Jimmy chuckled. "I assume you need this soonest."

The director nodded. "The sooner, the better, but deniability is more important. We can't afford to rush in and botch things up even more."

Jimmy rose, quickly followed by his partner. "Then we'd best get to it. You won't hear from us until after it's resolved."

* * *

The director sat at the immaculately set table in her private dining room, angrily looking at the old-fashioned clock on the far wall. She was a creature of habit and always ate precisely at one in the afternoon, and it was already five past. There was a vacant setting to her right, which was the focus of her ire. She routinely dined with a senior member of ImpSec each day to keep up with goings-on and remind them who was in charge. Each and every one of them owed their positions to her, and they all knew it wasn't wise to be late.

Xavier Isaacson entered through a side door and practically ran to his seat. "Agnes, I know I'm late, but I received an intel note just as I was getting ready to join you." The apology and excuse rushed out of the spindly man. The director stared at him. Xavier was an old and close acquaintance. She had no friends. The director had enemies, acquaintances, and close acquaintances. Xavier had been her mentor in the operations department when she first transferred into that group. He had risen through the ranks in much the same way she had, but he was a novice compared to her. Agnes quickly passed him on her march up the bureaucracy ladder. She had rewarded his support for her by dragging him along.

"We've managed to arrange a method of drops to get information from our contacts in the palace," he explained. "They are only to be used for critical information. I was only going to glance at it, but what they sent is important to you and me specifically."

"That's all well and good, but I am sure it could have waited," Agnes said in a huff.

Her director of operations shook his head. "Were you aware there was a cabinet meeting this morning?"

Agnes set down the glass of wine she had just raised and stared at him, trying not to let her concern show.

The director of security was a cabinet-level post, and she hadn't been invited. Xavier knew that. Except for a few specially selected agents, their agency had been totally barred from investigating the happenings of the last several weeks. Now, the head of ImpSec had been excluded from a cabinet meeting.

"Were any other ministers missing from the meeting? Do we have any idea what they discussed?" Agnes asked.

"No other ministers were absent," he said. "I have no info about the meeting, but I have agents checking with their sources in the other ministries and should have something soon. I do know there was a follow-up meeting with only the chamberlain, justice, defense, and, surprisingly, the foreign secretary. Obviously, something that was brought up in the main meeting spurred the follow-up one."

"I need information, and I needed it five minutes ago, Xavier. Squeeze whoever you have to. We're blind, and the prince regent is keeping us in the dark." The director of the Empire's security thought back to the conversation she'd had earlier in the week with Prince Henry. "He's not as pliable as his brother was, and he's made it clear that he does not trust our organization. *We* may have to do something about that."

"You're not suggesting…" Xavier whimpered.

"I'm not suggesting anything! We just need to realize there are multiple options to ensure that the prince who is regent is a friend," she finished calmly.

Xavier Isaacson simply stared at his director.

*****

Chapter Thirty

Empire Date: February 1033

Hazard watched as his military commanders entered the room. He had finally broken down and moved into his mother's office. As regent, there really was no other choice. He had planned to deliver his live speech from this room later this evening, but because of the revelation about the Marxist Embassy, Hazard had pushed back the address by one night. News agencies were informed that the delay was because of new information the prince regent wanted to share with the Empire. It was an excuse that was entirely true.

Penny O'Higgin, the Duke of Kara, Phil, and Kendrick Beckham were present. Gunnery Sergeant Sondheim was also there, as well as a marine colonel Hazard hadn't met.

Hazard gestured for everyone to take a seat. Both his father and the lord justice were missing, but their absence had been planned. An evening meeting with such notable attendees would create suspicion. They hoped that if Marxist agents learned about this meeting, they wouldn't believe he would decide anything of importance without involving the grand duke.

"My Prince," his uncle said, "I would like to introduce Colonel Malcolm Lee. He is commander of the Ghost Force. The force was originally formed to infiltrate Swarm-controlled systems. As you know, there have never been any survivors found in any of those systems. All that we have learned has come from these recon missions. Colonel Lee was personally involved in two of them. The team members are all highly trained marines, specializing in small-group tactics, stealth, and recon. For tonight's op, I felt they would be the best choice for the assault."

Before Hazard could speak, Sondheim jumped in. "Sir, the colonel and I go way back. I was his team NCO on one of the insertions the duke is talking about. He's a good man to have in a tight spot."

"Colonel, I am glad to have you running this. Especially since the gunny thinks so highly of you. I know for a fact I've never heard him speak kindly of any officer, so you must be special." Hazard watched the colonel fidget in his seat. "You probably expected to deliver a detailed brief of your op and then discuss various parts of it with us, but that's not going to happen. You are the expert in this, not us. I *know* that any changes I might add would probably only get people killed."

Hazard looked around the table. "I want everyone here to understand that nothing we are doing tonight is worth a life. Certainly, we would like to grab everything intact, but not if it results in a marine death. Colonel, I want you to have forces available to provide any support you might need, and that includes gunships and indirect fire."

"Thank you, sir. It's nice to have leadership that gives us objectives and then gets out of the way," the colonel said. "I was wondering if—"

"No, Colonel, you can't have the gunny. Nice try, Gunny, but I need you in one piece so *I* can stay in one piece. Uncle, after the Ghosts secure the building, then what?"

"We'll have teams standing by to relieve the Ghosts and provide security in key areas," the admiral explained. "Then we'll sweep the building for traps and holdouts. When we're sure we have everything locked down, we'll have designated teams begin a sweep of everything in the building."

"As soon as the team assaults," Penny said, "I'll issue a prepared statement to our member world leaders through their embassies and to the other recognized representatives. The statement will contain an explanation of what we are doing and why. It will also have a copy of the search warrant the lord justice has issued."

Hazard rose and offered Colonel Lee his hand. "Good luck to you, and may the deities watch over you."

* * *

Hazard decided he wanted to follow the operation while it was in progress. The Duke of Alba had invited him to his own "War Room," where he and other senior officers would follow events. He had declined, deciding his presence in the control center would put an unnecessary kink in the chain of command. Someone might feel he needed a play-by-play, ask his opinion, or second-guess themselves. Things like that got good men killed. He just wanted to be a bystander and watch.

The palace had its own command center, a duplicate of the one at Fleet Headquarters. However, the crown seldom used it. In fact, Hazard's father told him it had been used only once by his mother, and that had been for coordinating disaster relief she had sent to a planet that had suffered a solar flare.

"This is way better than the last time I participated in an op like this," Sondheim said as he sipped his beer. He, Jerry, and Bummer sat around the conference table with Hazard and his father. Hazard had decided there was no reason for them not to be comfortable, so he'd arranged for sandwiches and refreshments. His father had pointed out a beverage cooler hidden behind a panel, into which stewards promptly placed a large variety of beer.

"I wanted you three—" Hazard pointed to the marines "—to educate me on what's going on. I understand what the fleet can do but not so much the marines. I definitely don't know anything about special or strike ops. For tonight, I relied on other people to develop the plan, but I'm sure that sometime in the future, I'll have to make a similar decision, and I need to understand what special operations can and can't do."

The three marines suddenly became serious, and Sondheim replied for all of them. "You're the first ruler in a long time, maybe ever, who's had a real military background. Someone who's put their life on the line as the rest of us do. We—" he nodded to his fellow warriors "—respect the hell out of that. Jerry and I saw you draw a weapon and use it and saw you get hit…" He paused, seemingly searching for the right words. "What I am trying to say is thank you. Thank you for caring about us grunts."

Hazard let the silence linger a moment. "Before we start singing 'Auld Lang Syne,' tell me what's going on." He gestured toward the displays showing the Marxist Embassy from various viewpoints.

"Colonel Lee and his infiltration team have been inside the compound for the last thirty minutes," Bummer said. "They have very tiny robots controlled by virtual-reality operators set up in a trailer about two blocks away. Stealth drones have been sweeping the area since dark, marking all the surveillance systems. The robots defeat the trip wires, video surveillance, etcetera, external to the building."

"The penetration team will go in next," Jerry said, picking up the conversation, "six two-person teams in grav-armor who will neutralize any guards outside the building—four teams on the ground and two on the roof. They use the drones to guide those teams right to their targets. That will take no more than two minutes."

Sondheim pointed to the main overhead display. "The pen teams are going in now. You can ID them on the IR display by their gravity packs." He used a laser pointer to indicate the teams. Then he highlighted the assault team. "The assault team has three components. The blocking force will neutralize these two outlying buildings. They house the off-duty guard force and most of the staff. The second ground team, consisting of four ten-man squads, will assault these doors and rapidly clear the main floor, then secure the basement and second floor." Gunny pointed to the doors. "The last team is the aerial assault. Four-person teams will assault through these windows and try to decapitate the leadership. Those are the bedrooms of the ambassador, his main assistant, the security chief, and our friend Sergey. There will also be an eight-man team which will cover the roof access."

"The nice part about the mission is that this is not a smash and grab," Bummer said. "All the teams have to do is secure the building as quickly as they can. Everyone will use sleepy darts and shoot everyone they come across. If they come across anyone in power armor, they'll do it the old-fashioned way." He grinned. "Once everyone is neutralized, they'll signal the intel weenies to come in and search. Easy peasy."

"It's starting," The gunnery sergeant said and they all turned to the monitor.

Almost simultaneously, eight bright flashes appeared and died out.

"That's the breaching charges for the windows and doors." Sondheim added. They saw more bright flashes through the ground-floor windows. "Flash-bangs."

The doors to one of the outer buildings opened. Men rushed out and promptly dropped to the ground as the blocking force did their part. Three more large forces proceeded onto the grounds from the main street. Two headed to the outer buildings and one to the embassy.

"It's over. Those are the mop-up forces, regular fleet marines."

Hazard checked the clock. It was only three minutes from the breach charges going off to declaring the building secure.

"That's damn impressive."

"Real life, sir, things don't normally go this well. We had all the advantages, and we were on our home turf. With a well-prepared enemy behind the lines, it's much different. I know; I've been there," Sondheim stated.

Hazard took a call from the Duke of Kara on his wrist comm. "Everything is secure, Henry. We only had one minor casualty, from the ground assault team who ran into a pair of armored sentries, but nothing else. The intelligence teams are already in the building."

"Thank you, Uncle. Please pass my thanks to Colonel Lee and his men for a job well done."

*****

Chapter Thirty-One
Empire Date: February 1033

Hazard decided to slack off and sleep late. He and his three marines had stayed in the command center for several hours after the operation had finished. Sondheim and Bummer had regaled him with stories of past operations, both real and training. He had enjoyed the camaraderie. It was something that he had always wanted to be part of, but growing up within the confines of the palace had made it impossible. He hadn't been on the *Shinto* long enough to develop many personal relationships before the ship went into battle and, of course, there had been Hiroko. After meeting her, he'd spent every free moment he had with her.

He was surprised when he walked into his mother's office, now his office. His father was there, along with Doctors Shamshaard and Brougham. His first thought was that something had changed for the worse if they were here.

"I apologize if you've been waiting long. I didn't have anything on my calendar, so I decided to play hooky this morning. I hope Mother's condition hasn't worsened."

"No, Henry, your mother is the same," his father said. "Since I didn't stay up late carousing with a bunch of marines, I was in my office at my normal time." The two doctors smiled at Hazard's embarrassment. "The doctors inform me they have new information they needed to share with us—and a possible treatment."

"Right now, it is more of an idea," Dr. Brougham said. He looked at his fellow physician. "Jayani, you should lay out what we have discovered since you're the empress' physician."

Hazard didn't know Jayani Shamshaard as well as he knew Carl Brougham. Carl had been responsible for the health of the entire family when Hazard was younger. Jayani had replaced him while Hazard had been away at the academy.

"Dr. Shamshaard, please enlighten us."

She nodded to Hazard. "Your Highness. I know you've followed our investigation from the reports we have been submitting. At first, we reached one dead end after another with our testing. Then we received the intel report from the team investigating how the empress might have been attacked. We observed some cell damage on the empress' hand that was inconsistent with anything my team had ever seen. On a hunch, I called Carl in to look at the evidence. He immediately recognized that the anomalies were from some type of medical nano that was introduced into the empress through her skin."

Dr. Brougham continued, "I was one of the early developers of nanomedical tech. It's still a very narrow and controlled field of medical science. We investigated delivery methods for the nanos and had tried skin absorption, which is why I recognized the skin cell damage; it was the result of nanobots passing through the skin cells."

"The next step was to find the bots," Jayani said. "We found none in her bloodstream, though we saw there was a significant reduction in the protective nanos in the empress' bloodstream. That was a sure sign there had been a fight between the protective nanos and the foreign ones. We took tissue samples from various organs and found no sign of the invaders. We eventually found them in a sample of spinal fluid."

"What the little buggers had done was attack the various synapses connecting the brain to the rest of the body," Carl Brougham explained. "The part of the brain controlling natural body functions was left to keep the body alive. Basically, they disconnected the empress from the rest of her body. It's a direction in medical nanites we hadn't explored. I wouldn't even call them medical nanites. The Marxists have developed those nanites to block neural impulses in certain parts of the brain. The medical nanites you have were grown to attack foreign bodies. This type of nanite research is beyond us at this point."

"That's because your focus is to help people, Carl," Grand Duke Henry said. "You would never think of weaponizing nanites. The Marxists would, though."

"Okay, Doctors, so we know the cause, and we know how," Hazard said. "What can we do about it?"

Jayani turned to the other doctor. "Carl, you're the expert in this field."

"We now have samples of the parasite nanos. We'll study them and develop a nanite to disable them. Our current generation of medical nanites will destroy them, but we have to ensure that in doing so, they don't cause the current condition to become permanent. We will find it, I have no doubt, Your Highness."

"We conducted a raid on the Marxist compound last night. I'll make sure any information that might help in your research is forwarded," Hazard said. "If there are any additional resources you need, contact my father and he'll make sure you get them." Hazard nodded to his dad.

"Computer processing power could speed things along. We use simulations to chart interactions as we develop the nanites. For normal research, the computers we have are adequate. But if I had access to the mega computer that the Ministry of Science has, we could cycle through the different scenarios significantly faster."

Hazard thought for a minute. The Imperial Fleet had a supercomputer, the largest and fastest in the Empire. The Fleet used it to simulate fleet actions to develop tactics. "Dad, get Carl access to the Grinder," Hazard said, using the nickname for the fleet's computer. "It's the fastest computer in known space."

Carl nodded. "That would help immensely."

"Keep me and my father in the loop. I have confidence in you and your teams. Carl, if you wouldn't mind, could I have a word with you?" Hazard asked.

* * *

Hazard's father and Dr. Shamshaard left the office. Carl looked at him inquisitively.

"Carl, the love of my life, the future empress consort, was severely wounded during the fleet action in the Echo System. Her mind is perfectly functional, but her body is horribly damaged. We managed to get her into stasis before she died, but doctors are certain she will expire before they can make enough repairs if they take her out of cryo." Hazard paused. "I know you're involved in cutting-edge research into medical nanites. What I'm asking if you have any nanites that can repair her while she is in cryo, and if you don't, can they be developed? I've already made arrangements for her to remain in stasis until we can heal her."

"Hazard, we don't have anything at this time, but my team has been busy since I left the palace. We've made some promising discoveries that we've been exploring, but nothing that will come to fruition soon." Hazard sighed, but his friend held up a hand. "But this new nanite may open doors for us. I promise nothing except that I'll try. I'll need to see the patient to understand what may be required."

"She's at King Manor. I converted a suite into a med center and have a team monitoring her. Go by there and see her. Use the cover that you used to be my doctor and I asked you to look in on her. I know how classified your work is."

"Well, you are the regent and will, eventually, be emperor. It's what I do, after all." He smiled. "And I wouldn't be lying. I *am* your old doctor, and you *have* asked me to take a look."

They stood and shook hands. "Thank you, Carl."

*****

Chapter Thirty-Two
Empire Date: February 1033

"Stand by for an announcement from the Imperial Palace."

The announcement was made as the Imperial seal appeared on every video and monitor screen across the planet. People stopped what they were doing in homes, offices, eateries, and bars, and waited. Naturally, there would be those who complained about the sporting event or entertainment that was interrupted, but most would be attentive. The empress rarely spoke to the Empire as a whole, and then only on special occasions. Moreover, the empress had never made a "live" address during her reign.

When they had planned this address, it was decided Hazard's father, the grand duke, would introduce him. While not as recognizable as the empress, his father was a notable public figure and sufficiently identifiable by the people so as not to thoroughly shock them. The population knew there was a Prince Henry but had rarely seen him. Hazard hadn't appeared in public since he was sixteen; after aging several years, and sporting a beard and long hair, he was unrecognizable.

"Citizens of the Empire," his father began, "for those of you who don't recognize me, I am Grand Duke Henry, consort to her Imperial Majesty, Empress Elizabeth. It saddens me to announce that the empress has been incapacitated by a grave illness and can't currently perform her duties. However, there are contingencies written into the Imperial Charter to ensure that leadership of the Empire is maintained. Those contingencies have been activated, and a Regency Council has been empowered. It is my duty to introduce my son, Prince Henry, who is now the prince regent."

The scene shifted to Hazard sitting at his mother's desk in her office. Behind him hung the coat of arms of the House of Kane, flanked by the Imperial flag on one side and the flag of the Britannia System on the other.

"My fellow subjects. I am Prince Henry, recognized by the Regency Council as the heir to the Imperial throne and the prince regent of the Empire. I am sure many of you are surprised that I am the regent instead of my older brother, Prince Edward. For reasons known only to herself, the empress changed the order of succession about a month ago and named me the heir. Following the Imperial Charter, the Regency Council has voted to grant me full regency powers. For those of you wondering what that means: I have the same powers as the empress and will retain them until the council decides that she can resume them. I wanted to inform you about what was going on and reassure you that the realm will continue as though nothing has changed. To facilitate that, using emergency powers granted to the Crown, I have suspended the Imperial Senate and sent them back to their home systems. Some may think this a removal of Crown oversight, however, this emergency power is to ensure that nothing changes while the empress is incapacitated."

Hazard took a breath, then continued, "Lastly, I wanted to share grave news with you. It was not a random illness that had afflicted my mother. We have discovered a conspiracy to attack her with a foreign agent that was introduced into her body. We are investigating leads into who did it and why." The camera zoomed in on Hazard and he stared hard into the camera. "People of the Empire, we will find the culprits and punish them. To those involved, I am coming for you. There is no escape and nowhere to hide."

The camera panned back and Hazard's expression softened. "I ask you, the people, to join me in prayers for my mother. Pray that we are successful in restoring her to full health. The best scientists and physicians are investigating the attack and working to cure her. And while you are doing that, say a quick prayer for me, that I rule in the empress' place with the wisdom and integrity she has always displayed. May the god you worship bless and protect each and every one of you."

The light on the camera blinked off, and Hazard sighed with relief.

*****

Chapter Thirty-Three
Empire Date: March 1033

Ivana Chernova settled behind her modest desk. She was in the middle of opening her modest but highly lucrative bookstore. New London was the second-largest city on the capital planet of Britannia, and her store was known as the best place to locate hard-to-find books, not only in the city but probably in the whole Empire. Though she did sell data chips with digital books or collections, she specialized in printed volumes. There was always a small niche market for such items, especially among the wealthy who liked to impress visitors with their libraries.

Many of the original colonists had brought printed books from Old Earth in their personal possessions. Most were family bibles, but there were others as well. There were less than ten thousand of these books, and they sold for exorbitant prices. She currently had seventeen such books in her shop. She also had several hundred books that were printed during the first century after landing. During the early days of colonization, when industry was restarting, the ability to manufacture personal comps or personal readers had been a low priority, however, the need to distribute information and learning within the colony had been great, so printing had made a brief resurgence. Digital copies of many books in the colonies' archives were printed out and sold in book form. Those books often came with a hefty price tag.

Ivana's checked her overnight messages. She could typically count on five to ten inquiries for specific books every night; most came from other star systems. One message caught her attention. The inquirer was Samuel Clemens, and he was asking if she had found a printed edition of *The Memoir of U.S. Grant.*

She supposed there probably was a Samuel Clemens somewhere in the Empire, but this was not him. Owning and running a bookstore was Ivana's passion, but her natural talent lay in other areas. Her alter ego, the Raven—another literary reference—was the leader of what was considered the best assassination team in the Empire. She was initially trained in wet work, as assassinations were referred to in intelligence circles by Imperial Security. However, after several years of such work inside the firm, she had decided to go her own way. People in her line of work were typically not allowed to do that, but she knew where many important bodies were buried. So, with the promise that she would provide the occasional service as needed, she was permitted to leave.

In the early days of Ivana's career, her jobs had made sense to her. She had taken out some evil individuals, people who would never see justice through normal processes. Then things changed. She realized her targets were individuals who were a threat to ImpSec rather than the Empire. As an agent, she had no choice but to accept her orders, which was why she had gone freelance. The book request was the code to contact her "handler" inside the firm about a job. Of the six previous times, she had accepted only four jobs.

Ivana typed in the special commands on her desk terminal. They activated both a privacy shield around her office and an encoded connection request to Mr. Clemens. Both systems were the best ImpSec had. Now she just had to wait.

"Good morning, Raven," the terminal responded almost ten minutes later. "Thank you for responding."

Ivana knew part of the encryption protocol was voice synthesizing, but she could tell this was not the Samuel Clemens she had spoken to in the past. People in her line of work didn't like change.

"Good morning," she replied. "Might I ask what happened to Samuel?"

"You can ask." The voice chuckled. "But that's not important. What is important is that we have a very special job for you, and once completed, we will never contact you again."

Ivana laughed herself. "I doubt that. You probably also have prime real estate on Old Earth you'd like to sell me. What's the target?" She never asked who, only what. It helped her depersonalize the operation. The mysterious voice told her and she instantly said, "No."

"You don't have an option on this one, Ivana," the voice said. "Yes, I'm well aware of all the evidence you have against the firm and, frankly, I don't care. Release it if you want. The firm and I have nothing to lose. The most that could happen is we'd be dismantled or replaced. You, however, have much more to lose. What would happen if we leaked information about *your* past deeds to the various news organizations? How long do you think you would remain alive?" The mysterious voice waited for that to sink in, then continued, "You need to be aware that there will be another operation running at the same time." The Raven grimaced at the complications that could cause. "It has nothing to do with your op and should create no interference. It will occur thirty minutes after your start time."

Ivana scowled at the terminal. She felt like a cornered rat with the hawks circling her. They had her, and Raven knew it. She was also sure they had their own teams watching her.

One last job, the elite assassin decided, though Raven didn't like it. She would do it and then disappear completely.

* * * * *

Chapter Thirty-Four
Empire Date: March 1033

The Raven floated silently through the darkened night. The heads-up display inside her helmet showed her projected path. So far, she was right on course. She was using a special glider parasail and was wearing a special suit based on the gliding skills of an ancient Earth mammal known as the flying squirrel. Skydiving and parasailing were popular sports among thrill-seekers in the Empire, but few had ever heard of the original forms of the sports. This form didn't use gravity units or power assists but silk and synthetics. With no detectable power sources and the small profile of her flying squirrel suit, she should stay undetected until touchdown.

This is the easy part, she thought, and adjusted her flight path by changing the position of her arms. She banked slightly to the right and steadily maneuvered back on course.

Ivana was soaring through one of the most heavily defended areas of the Empire. Any number of laser batteries would fire on her if she were detected, leaving only a cloud of ash in the sky above the Imperial District. She had to rely on her skill, and a bit of luck, to land silently on the balcony of her target.

Now! And she spread her arms wide to stop her forward motion and pushed the control button in her right hand. The wings of the parasail instantly folded in on themselves and she lost all lift. She pulled her arms in and dropped—gracefully, she thought—onto the balcony. She took two steps and dropped to one knee.

No alarms so far. Now for the hard part. She needed to penetrate and eliminate with little or no idea of what might be waiting for her.

There were no lights on inside the suite, which wasn't surprising since it was three in the morning. There were two sets of doors that opened onto the rather large terrace, and Raven chose the set that most likely led to the bedroom. It wasn't locked. She smirked as she entered the chamber. The operation might be more straightforward than she'd thought.

She brought her right hand up, holding a silenced, old-fashioned projectile weapon. The pistol would fire a 5 mm slug with almost no noise and no flash. In her hands, it was lethal. She scanned the room and looked for her target.

Nothing. Damn.

There wasn't even a residual heat signature on the bed. The target hadn't been in here recently. She was on the clock, and she didn't have much time left. After a quick check of the sitting room she would go.

* * *

Prince Edward stepped onto the balcony off his sleeping chamber carrying a flat package. He had been allowed to return to his private rooms earlier in the week after they had been thoroughly searched. He'd also been allowed to have his regular staff back to take care of him.

He'd found the package, as well as the strange one-piece bodysuit he was wearing, under his bedding on the second night back in his familiar surroundings.

The instructions were both concise and straightforward, even if they made no sense to him. If he wanted to be free and regain the throne that had been stolen from him, he would follow the directions exactly. Any deviation could result in failure. So, he had stepped onto the balcony, dressed in the suit along with the strange belt that accompanied it. The time was 0215.

All of that had been simple enough. It was the next part that made no sense to him. He was to unfold the package and place it on the balcony floor. The X on the box needed to be face up. He was to sit on the X, knees pulled up to his chest, and wait. It all seemed ludicrous to him, but if there were even a remote chance for him to regain power, he would do it.

Suddenly, he heard alarms within the palace. The directions warned him of that possibility and emphasized he was to remain in position until the signal was given.

The buckle of the strange belt began vibrating. The signal. This was it. He lifted the cover from the front of the belt fastener and pressed the button inside. Everything went dark as a sphere of unknown material enveloped him. Edward took several long, slow, calming breaths to fight back the panic. He sensed movement, but he couldn't tell speed or direction.

Edward noticed a change in the motion of the sphere. He had lost all sense of time and didn't know how long he'd been in the bubble. The slow, constant movement changed, becoming abrupt and jarring.

As quickly as the sphere had formed around him, it now disappeared and he found himself sitting once again on the mat but in an air vehicle, the kind used to ferry cargo around the city. He then spotted the men who had rescued him, and one was an old friend.

"Sergey!"

* * *

Hazard didn't know what had stirred him out of a sound sleep. It had been a long day and he had relaxed into what was becoming his favorite armchair, one of two facing the fireplace. He had fallen asleep there. Sometime during the night, a servant had draped a blanket over him, and the fire had dwindled to a few glowing embers.

He sat for a moment, deciding whether it was worth getting up and going to bed, when he heard the noise, the soft sound of a door latch. He assumed it was a servant checking on him, so he looked to the door on that led to the dining area and, beyond that, the servants' area. The door was shut.

Hazard was instantly alert. There were four doors into this room, and he could see three of them from his position: the main entrance from the outer hallway, the one to his private study, and the dining-room door. All were shut.

Hazard quickly analyzed the situation and ran through his options. The door behind him led to the bedroom, and no one should be coming from there. At least no one with good intentions. If he used his neural link to sound the alarm, he would probably be dead before a guard could arrive. He broke it down into advantages.

It was dark inside the room, but any professional would be using thermal and infrared. The heat of the stone fireplace would provide him some protection from thermal scanning as long as he stayed between it and the assailant

He needed a weapon. There was the fireplace poker. *But I doubt I could get close enough before getting shot,* Hazard thought. These were his chambers since before leaving for the academy. There had to be something close he could use. He remembered his baseball on the mantel, an award after pitching his team to a planet championship. It would have to do. He put together his plan.

* * *

Ivana swore silently to herself. She had been here too long, it was time to go. The firm would just have to understand. She began her silent retreat toward the bedroom and heard a faint noise to her left. A red blob indicating a fireplace blazed on her HUD. There was another sound to her right and she immediately swung the gun in that direction as the room lights snapped on, suddenly blinding her. Her instincts took over. Her left hand deactivated the imaging system and her eyes adjusted to the now-lit room. She continued moving left and saw her target a moment before she was struck squarely in the left temple. Then darkness.

* * * * *

Chapter Thirty-Five

Empire Date: March 1033

"Well done, My Prince!" Phil exclaimed as he checked the bindings of the prisoner. "I was never able to see you pitch but heard the stories. It seems like you still have it."

Hazard had concentrated on the throw, so hadn't called for his guards until afterward. They had burst into the room, weapons drawn. His assailant, still standing despite the blow, was dazed and wobbly, gun in hand. She had promptly been hit with five or six sleepy darts. She dropped like a puppet with its strings cut. Hazard was somewhat concerned about how much of the chemical was in her. Not because of concern for her physical being, but because he wanted to interrogate her.

"Phil, I want our friend here—" Hazard motioned to the assassin "—moved somewhere secure. I want medical to look at her; not only for overuse of sleepy juice but for any hidden suicide implants." Phil spoke into his wrist comm. "And, Phil, I want this kept close." His armsman nodded and continued his conversation.

Hazard spotted Colonel Devereaux and motioned for her to approach. "Colonel, I want this floor locked down and swept. Additionally, I want guards on all the family suites' doors and balconies. I also want a two-person roving patrol on each floor of the palace." Hazard looked at his wrist comm. "It is 0240. I want an initial report on tonight's events at 0900."

"Yes, Prince Henry," the colonel replied, then held up a hand. Hazard saw she was receiving a message through her earbud. From her grimace, he was sure it was more unwelcome news. "Your Majesty, Prince Edward is missing. His guard team went in to check on him, and he was just gone. They performed a thorough search but found nothing." A stormy night for the guard commander had just turned into a disaster.

"Well, this just keeps getting better and better," Hazard muttered angrily. "This was no coincidence. I'm not going to tell you how to do your job, Colonel. At least not yet." He could see the last arrow had hit home. "Figure it out. Be ready to report what you have in the morning."

Hazard looked back to Phil, who had finished issuing his instructions. "Phil, once medical finishes examining her, I want the prisoner isolated. I want whatever room she's in stripped bare. Leave her a bottle of water." Hazard thought a moment. "And I want Snake involved. This attack has the firm, or at least some of their cronies, written all over it."

***

It was an odd group that crowded into the empress' study: Grand Duke Henry, the lord chamberlain, the lord justice, and the Duke of Kara on the nobility side, Yvette Devereaux and Phil Myerson representing the Imperial Guard, and Gunnery Sergeant Michael Sondheim and Sergeant Bummer Baumgardner representing the marines. Then there was Snake Atwater, who Hazard hoped represented the loyal side of Imperial Security. They all stood as Hazard entered through a side door.

"Sit down, sit down." Hazard motioned as he took his seat at the desk. "We have a lot to discuss, and we don't have time for pleasantries. Some hard choices will be made, and there will be some hard feelings, but we will make them, rest assured." Hazard let that sink in. He saw understanding circle the room at his use of the Imperial we. "Colonel Devereaux, you're up first."

The colonel's report was short and to the point. There was not much more in it than Hazard had known when he'd gone to bed. Interestingly, they caught his assailant on surveillance footage and used it to track her penetration of Hazard's balcony. "Were you able to cross-reference the video to the rest of the surveillance system, Colonel?"

"We did, Your Highness. But both her skinsuit and the hang glider were very stealthy. When we checked the radar and lidar recordings, all it showed was what appeared to be a medium-size bird flying through the palace grounds," the colonel said.

"And my brother?" the regent asked with a raised eyebrow.

"We are tracking him through his implant. We acquired his ping within thirty minutes and have maintained surveillance on him. We've deployed four teams, and at least one team has eyes on him or his location at all times."

"When you say eyes on him, I hope that means that someone has positively identified him?"

"Yes, Your Highness. We got a positive ID from three sources as they transferred him from an air lorry to an apartment building on the north side of Aberdeen." The guard commander looked tired as she made the report. "One final piece of information. While reviewing sensor data, we found another anomaly similar to the one caused by your assailant. Technicians spotted another small lidar signal that moved very slowly. They picked it up because it moved in a straight line and did so for almost twenty minutes. Then it merged with an air lorry, which was waiting in a parking circle well outside the palace's no-fly zone. This turned out to be the same lorry to which Prince Edward was tracked. Some stealth system and probably a counter-gravity unit was smuggled in and used to spirit him out."

"Some of the conspirators still have operatives inside the palace," Snake Atwater commented. "They also have details on the palace's security systems. They knew exactly how small an object had to be and how slow it had to move to avoid raising alarms."

"And they know that most of the palace systems are automated," Hazard added. "A technician straight out of school monitoring the sensor feeds would have picked up on my brother's escape." Finally, Hazard asked, "Snake, what do you think about my brother?"

"It is a risk-reward situation, Henry. I think the risks outweigh any possible reward. Sure, if we wait it might lead to more information about the overall conspiracy, but if he slips away..." Darrel Atwater didn't finish his sentence.

"Who's in charge of your surveillance teams, Colonel?" Hazard was very formal with the commander.

"Daniel Shipwright," she replied. "He was Edward's personal armsman before the recent problems. We thought he'd be best for the job."

Hazard nodded and turned back to Snake. "What about our guest?"

"Thanks to the fleet and the Duke of Kara—" Darrel Atwater nodded to Hazard's uncle "—I managed to pull a complete download of the ImpSec data files before they decided to cut off an out-of-control but extraordinarily good-looking agent." A few people chuckled. "Our guest is Ivana Chernova—and yes, that is her real name—who for the last ten years or so has been a rare-book dealer in New London. Before that, she spent twelve years with the firm. Her personnel file is heavily encrypted. My codes won't open it, and I've had Fleet intel running the code crackers, with no luck. I made a few discreet inquiries with some retired agents, ones with no connections with the current leadership, and discovered that while at the firm she was considered the best problem solver they had."

"A problem solver?" the lord justice asked.

"My Lord," Atwater responded. "That's firm-speak for an assassin. They believe such phrases make inhumane concepts more acceptable. Don't mistake me: for the safety of the Empire, there are times when such measures are required. Unfortunately, they have begun to be used as a means of acquiring power within the firm."

"Such is the state of our security forces." The lord chamberlain sighed.

"Indeed," Hazard said and sank back into his chair and thought. Everyone watched him as the silence grew. Still leaning back he said, "Last night pointed out several issues that need to be resolved." Hazard nodded to the Duke of Kara. "At heart, I am a fleet officer, and thus I'll always tend to solve problems that way. However, before I begin laying out what I want to do, I want everyone in this room to understand that I hold no one at fault for what happened. Our system and processes failed, not you or your people."

Hazard saw his guard commander visibly relax. "First, the easy decisions. Colonel Devereaux, order the surveillance teams to use whatever means necessary to recover my brother." The "whatever means" statement startled some of the advisors. *Well, this will scare them even more.* "The governance of the Empire is being assaulted, people, by enemies either foreign or domestic. My brother, either willingly or coerced, has abetted those enemies. We need to recover Edward, whether alive, injured… or dead."

Hazard saw sorrow fill his father's face, but he nodded to Hazard.

"My Prince, you can't mean that. You must attempt to save him," Kendrick Beckham, the lord chamberlain, exclaimed. "He is your brother."

"Ken," Hazard said softly, "I must protect the Empire. Yes, I want him back alive, but our enemies will use him against us if he can escape us again. As long as he remains in their control, the rest of the Imperial line is at risk. The Regency Council accepted the evidence of the empress' wish that I am the heir and named me prince regent. Unfortunately, the Charter is specific. If something happens to me, the next male would become regent, and that's Edward. Even if he's killed in the recovery attempt, his body must be recovered so we have documented evidence of his demise. I worry. Not about my own safety but the Empire's." Hazard stared at his old friend and saw him nod slowly with reluctant understanding.

"As emphasized before, I hold no one at fault, but it is obvious that palace security is woefully inadequate. Part of this is due to complacency. There have been no direct threats against the Crown in centuries. ImpSec is also to blame. Their charter is for the defense of the Empire, not the creation of their own. If they had discovered the plots that are in play and advised the Crown, then I'm sure adequate precautions would have been in place." Hazard explained his plan. "This morning, I did a little research and found that there has not been an evaluation of security effectiveness in more than fifty years."

"Colonel Devereaux, as of this moment, you are relieved of your duties as head of the Imperial Guard." Hazard held up a hand at the distress on the guard commander's face. "One of our problems was that there was no single person in charge of palace security. We had the Imperial Guard and the separate Palace Guard, as well as a Marine force on external security. Colonel, you are now head of palace security. You will retain your title, of course. The new Palace Guard force will be responsible for all security measures for the entire complex. Physical security of the walls, grounds, the palace itself, and electronic and other surveillance. This plan means we'll do away with the Marine force, though I am sure some of them may be rolled into the new force. Will you accept this new charge?"

Colonel Devereaux stood and bowed. "It would be my honor, Your Highness."

"Thank you, Yvette," Hazard said. "I want security to be as airtight as possible. Therefore, the Imperial Guard will revert to how it was originally envisioned: the Crown's private military force. The force will be a two-company unit of fully equipped armored troops. The best of these troops will have additional training to become the Crown's personal security details. I believe Major O'Shaughnessy would be an excellent choice to lead this force. Do you agree, Colonel?"

"Patrick would be an excellent choice, sir. This arrangement will do away with the conflicts of opinions and turf wars between the different guard units," Devereaux said.

Hazard nodded. "Precisely." Hazard shifted the conversation. "Father, I believe we need to move sooner rather than later on the ImpSec reorganization. When will you and your group be prepared to present a workable plan?"

"Give us three more days, and we'll present it to you," Duke Henry said. "No doubt it is now obvious to everyone that it is required. I'll call a meeting of the group for this afternoon to escalate the timeline."

"Great. Now for one last item, which I am sure will upset a lot of people." Hazard glanced around the table. "To minimize the risk that a single attack at the palace could decapitate Crown authority, I am going to relocate to King Manor." Everyone started talking at once. Hazard broke into the din. "I know, I know. On the surface, it would appear that security there is weaker there than here in the palace, but that is not the case." Hazard paused until everyone was quiet. "There is no question in my mind about the loyalty of the staff there, so that dispels any internal threat. Our major threat then becomes external. I believe that what many of you refer to as 'the prince's Marine force,' led by the gunny here, supplemented with some of Colonel Lee's special operations troops, could easily defeat any outside threat it encountered." Hazard saw Sondheim nod in agreement. *He should agree; it was his idea.* "Remember, they don't have a whole palace to defend, just a small manor." His father and both cabinet members continued to voice their displeasure. Hazard stood, and the room quieted again. "Gentlemen, it has been decided; accept it. Now, we have much to do, so let us be about it."

* * * * *

Chapter Thirty-Six
Empire Date: March 1033

Hazard stared at the large monitor on the far wall, lost in thought. The monitor showed a split-screen image of two stasis pods in the palace's medical suite. The two doctors seated in front of his desk were droning on about matters, but he didn't hear them. They were simply background noise. Had it only been less than a month since he had first heard of his mother's supposed illness? So much had happened. So much turmoil. His dash back to the capital, assassination attempts, and wresting the regency from his older brother.

Now his brother, Prince Edward, was lying near death. The medical stasis pod was the only reason he still lived. And Hazard was second-guessing himself.

No, I'm blaming *myself.*

He had ordered the assault to recover Edward and had defined the mission parameters. His brother was under the control of outside influences and that placed the Imperial Crown and the Imperial lineage in danger, so Hazard had given the execution orders to recover the prince, either dead or alive.

The operation hadn't gone as well as they'd hoped. Edward had been recovered but severely wounded. Whether the Imperial forces or his friends had injured him during the firefight that had occurred would never be known. Count Sergey, the elusive emissary of the Marxist System, was also killed, along with numerous conspirators and guardsmen. Nevertheless, substantial evidence had been obtained directly linking the Marxists to both Edward and the attempted coup.

If only he had waited. The guardsmen were not the ideal troops to use in such an operation. Colonel Lee's special operations teams would have been a much better choice. Lee would have insisted on more planning, but that would have taken time. Darrel Atwater had sized it up well: take time to better prepare and they run the risk of Edward and his friends eluding them, or run a higher risk while Edward was still within reach.

"Your Highness, your brother can recover. I am close to developing the medical repair nanites you previously asked me about." Doctor Carl Brougham's words suddenly broke through his haze.

Hazard snapped fully back into reality. This was important news. It would be a huge medical breakthrough—a boon to all of the people of the Empire—but what mattered to him was that it might restore Hiroko to him.

"You're that close?"

"Well, they won't be ready in the next several days," the doctor replied, backtracking his statement slightly. "But I believe I'll have a prototype ready by the end of the month. Of course, the initial nanites will only have the ability to perform basic repairs. Still, the ability to inject them into a person in stasis means that even basic trauma repairs can be performed without having to revive that patient. That means surgeons don't have to race the clock to perform corrective surgeries before a patient dies."

Hazard thought about that. "What kind of testing can we perform to ensure they're safe?"

"It may sound gruesome," Carl said, "but we have been injecting the test nanites into recently deceased bodies that we put in stasis. First, we thoroughly examine the body before they go into stasis, then we inject the test nanites. After twenty-four hours, we thaw the body, perform a second examination, and note any changes. The current generation has shown a small amount of internal repair. The drawback of this testing is that the nanites depend on the host body as an energy source to recharge and since a dead body has no energy, most of the nanites stop working well before the twenty-four-hour time limit. Therefore, the next phase will use test animals."

"That all sounds promising, Carl. And you're right, it does sound gruesome." Hazard chuckled. "Now, what about the empress?"

Doctor Jayani Shamshaard looked at her mentor and answered, "As I already said, we have the special nanites prepared to eliminate the blocking ones in the empress' nervous system." They realized Hazard hadn't been paying attention. "Carl and I have agreed that we should wait until his nanites are ready so we can use them to aid against any unknown results."

"An innovative idea, Jayani. Forgive me for being distracted earlier," Hazard apologized. "You caught me wool-gathering. I feel personally responsible for my brother's condition, and it weighs on me. But that's why they pay me the big bucks—to make decisions that cause dilemmas like this. I want to thank both of you for your efforts. The Crown will not forget what you have done." Hazard's mood was lightened by their smiles at his praise. "I want to emphasize one thing, though. We will not move forward with these treatments unless I give my personal permission." Both doctors nodded, agreeing.

Hazard looked back at the monitor, the kernels of a plan forming in his mind. It was not a plan he would enjoy implementing.

*****

Chapter Thirty-Seven
Empire Date: March 1033

Two weeks had passed since Hazard's Imperial address. He had received messages from each of the Empire's system governments, and they were overwhelmingly supportive. Since the notes had been personal, from vassals to their monarch, most of the messages were also very frank. Those who had offered opinions suspected the Marxists were behind it. Those rulers essentially gave Hazard a blank check to deal with the Marxists as he deemed appropriate. He had sent each a personalized reply, thanking them for their support. He also informed them that he would set up regional meetings so he could see each individually. He didn't have the time to visit each of the systems separately and bringing all of them to the capital system didn't seem wise, so he had asked the home secretary to arrange a series of four or five regional meetings.

In the days since the disastrous recovery of his brother, Darrel Atwater's team of agents had pored over the information they'd gained. They now had a more precise picture of what was going on. There was specific evidence that the Marxist System's government had been behind the plot to disrupt the Imperial throne. Count Sergey Todorovich had been their point man. He was a senior man in the People's Security Force or PSF, the Marxist's state security, and was in charge of all that agency's activities on Britannia. The lack of information recovered from the Marxist Embassy was due to the ambassador not being in the loop.

The evidence also named several Imperial senators, most notably Joseph Wells, as well as minor bureaucrats in several Imperial departments and members of the palace staff. All the exposed individuals were being closely watched rather than taken into custody. They'd decided to wait to avoid warning any others who they hadn't yet discovered.

There was no indication his brother had been a knowing accomplice, but that he had conspired with them in some way there was no doubt. The late count had kept a detailed account of his conversations with Prince Edward. Edward's promise to get the Marxist System admitted to the Empire when he was emperor was the catalyst that drove the entire conspiracy.

The part ImpSec played was more vague. There was ample evidence of the involvement of ImpSec, but they only had the names of a few junior agents. They only had code names of the higher-ranked officials in the agency. The evidence suggested that at least one of these officials was at the highest level of the spy system.

Hazard had to address both issues they had discovered. First, he needed to deal with the Marxist Federation. He had been hesitant to exercise any more Imperial authority than required, but it was necessary in this case. He had already directed the Duke of Kara to assemble a fleet and plan a punitive expedition to the Marxist System. Second, he was not going to declare war; in fact, he could not. One of the few restrictions of the regent's Imperial power was the ability to declare war. The Crown could declare war only with the consent of the Imperial Senate, and Hazard wasn't going to call them back into session. A military expedition would sidestep that restriction. He didn't plan to conquer them, only isolate them.

The other issue, the involvement of ImpSec, was more immediate.

* * *

Jimmy Gallagher and Daniel Frasier stood side by side in the dimly lit room. They seldom met in person with the man who was sitting at the desk in front of them. To the rest of ImpSec, they were the private agents who answered directly to Director Whitestone. In reality, they served the seated figure before them and had done so for over fifteen years.

"We just received word from our sources in the palace. It took them some time to get the information to us," Jimmy reported. "Our street sources were correct; the palace source confirmed that Prince Edward managed to execute his part of the plan and did manage to escape the palace and rendezvous with the air lorry. The palace source also corroborated that Prince Edward is back in the palace, but is seriously wounded and near death."

"I canvased the area around the safe house," Danny added. "People in the area confirmed that some type of officially sanctioned event took place. There were shots fired and some explosions. The witnesses observed several official vehicles, including ambulances, arriving at the scene. Many bodies were brought out on stretchers and loaded into the ambulances. I managed to slip inside and do a quick recon. There were intense firefights in several locations in the building. I can also report that the place has been stripped bare."

"What about survivors among our people?" the shadowed figure asked.

"Other than the prince, we don't have any information. However, I did confirm that the count was there when the attack took place," Jimmy said. "I would expect that at least some were taken alive."

"And what of the Raven?" their boss asked.

"She failed in her attempt, sir," Jimmy responded quickly. "Even more important, the evidence seems to indicate that she may have been taken alive. After the attack, Atwater and some of his agents were called to the palace; those agents have not left. That leads me to believe she is being interviewed."

"It seems we only have one card left to play," Xavier Isaacson said from behind his desk. "To think one single person could derail all of our carefully laid plans," the ImpSec director of operations lamented. "Prince Henry returning to the home system so quickly, then avoiding the assassination, on top of the empress deciding to switch heirs and having a record of it. It seems circumstances broke just right for the regent and led to our defeat. Now we need to see to our own safe exit. I want to execute the Trojan Horse Plan in thirty minutes. Can you be ready?"

Both men nodded and left the room.

* * *

Director Whitestone spent her morning trying to piece together what was happening in the palace. What sources she still had access to were next to useless. All she knew was that there had been an attempt on the regent's life. Several inquiries to Xavier had gone unanswered, which only deepened her concern. Had the sniveling coward bailed on her? The intercom chime interrupted further thoughts.

"Director, Jimmy and Danny are here to see you," her assistant announced.

"Excellent. Send them right in," Agnes said. Excellent indeed. If any person had up-to-date info from inside the palace, it would be one of those two.

She stood as the two men entered her office and stepped up to her desk. "I am glad to see you two."

She stopped abruptly when both men produced silenced handguns.

"You see, Director," Danny said, "we've decided you will be the sacrificial lamb. Mr. Isaacson has decided to eliminate you to cover our tracks." At her wide-eyed look, he continued, "Oh yes, we've been his men from the beginning. He knew he would never be acceptable as director, so Mr. Isaacson allowed you to obtain that title while he ran the firm the way he wanted behind the scenes."

* * *

The three people at the desk didn't observe Xavier Isaacson slip into the room. He hated killing Beverly, the director's assistant, but she could identify him. This was the way things had to be. No witnesses. He had already scrubbed his computer. He had known the director always used her override to shut down all the monitoring systems whenever she met with Jimmy and Danny, so there would be no visual record of what happened in her office, and soon there would be no people to worry about, either.

There was a faint stutter as both men fired their weapons. One round struck the director in the middle of her forehead, the other in the center of her chest. She slumped over her desk, the pool of blood partially absorbed by the old-fashioned blotter.

Xavier had been a field agent years ago and had always prided himself in his marksmanship. He had maintained his skill over the years through weekly visits to the shooting range in the basement of the operations building. Before the two men in front of the desk could turn, Isaacson fired twice, the rounds of his large-caliber pistol striking each man in the back of the head. The front of their heads exploded, blood and brain matter mingling with that of the former director of ImpSec.

* * *

Hazard's thoughts were interrupted by his intercom. His vid display said the director of operations for ImpSec, Mr. Isaacson, was calling with important news. He accepted the call. The image of a mousy ImpSec bureaucrat filled the screen.

"Mr. Isaacson, what can I do for you?" the regent asked.

"Your Highness, Director Whitestone has been assassinated. It happened about an hour ago. We—I should say I—delayed in screening you this long to secure the scene and do some preliminary investigation," Isaacson told him. "Two of her personal agents were the perpetrators. Both men served her for years. I came upon them as they were shooting Agnes and drew my own weapon in an attempt to save her. I managed to take down both men, but the director was already dead."

Hazard was suspicious of the circumstances. He suspected Isaacson was somehow involved. However, he also suspected that there would never be any proof. "It was a good thing you arrived when you did," Hazard said. "Do we have any idea why they did this?"

"Only theories at this point, sir," the ops director said. "Speculation is that all three were involved with the Marxists. However, with the failed attempts to secure the crown for Edward and your assassination attempt, we believe that whoever was in charge was tidying up loose ends. We will, of course, continue to investigate this and dig into all three individuals' records."

"Very well, Mr. Isaacson. Continue your investigation. For the time being, you will be the acting director." *Which will be a truly brief time,* Hazard thought as he terminated the call.

Time to get my father involved.

*****

Chapter Thirty-Eight
Empire Date: April 1033

Admiral Winfred Mason sat in the fleet commander's chair on the flag bridge of the dreadnought *Indomitable.* He stared at the holographic tactical display, which took up most of the right side of the compartment, watching as the remaining units of his command, First Fleet, appeared as they exited hyperspace. The expansive display dominating the forward bulkhead showed a real-time image of their surroundings. The planners had decided to have the fleet exit hyper well away from the system's primary and its two inhabited planets. The exit would allow sensors to update the location of forces and defenses well before they became a threat.

They were in the home system of the Marxist Federation. It was not much of an empire. Two systems, three habitable planets, of which only one was in the Goldilocks Zone.

Winfred smiled to himself. What they lacked as an empire, they certainly made up for in stupidity. Through hook or crook, they had almost become a member of the Britannic Empire. The den of sharks and snakes they called the Imperial Senate had approved their membership application, but the empress had said no. An Imperial veto was a challenge to override, and the supporters had decided not to try. Instead, they had attempted to remove the empress and replace her with someone more sympathetic to their cause.

Winfred didn't know the details; in fact, he knew very little about what had occurred. Like everyone else in the kingdom, he was surprised when Prince Henry was named regent. Prince Edward had been named heir on his fifth birthday, and how and why he had been passed over was a mystery. What he did know was that the new prince regent was no friend to the Marxist Federation. The attack on the empress and an assassination attempt on the regent himself had been linked directly to them. Which was why his fleet was here.

First Fleet was composed of one squadron of dreadnoughts, two battleships, and two heavy cruisers. Thirty light cruisers and destroyers provided a security screen around the major fleet units. The fleet mission was simple: they were to punish the Marxists. More importantly, the Marxist Federation was to be isolated so they would never pose a risk to the Empire again.

The fleet had been in the system for thirty minutes and was moving at a relatively sedate pace. They were in no hurry. In fact, Admiral Mason wanted to make them sweat. He had invoked a total communications blackout, but they weren't hiding. On the contrary, recon drones preceded the force, locating and logging targets. Additionally, the forward screening ships were using active sensors to search the entire system. That way he would know where everything was long before they were anywhere close to the planet.

"Admiral, we're getting official hails from their fleet units," the comm officer reported.

"Give them silence, Betty," he informed Lieutenant Betty Anderson. The admiral turned to his chief of staff. "Anything on their fleet units?"

Rear Admiral George "Ace" Armstrong turned from the tactical display. "We've accounted for all the units known to fleet intel. One light cruiser, four destroyer-size units, and sixteen of what they call corvettes. Only one of the destroyers and eight of the corvettes show active power levels, but the rest of the units are lighting off."

"Thank you. It's time to rouse our new friends a bit. Betty, to all ships: energize navigation transponders. Let them see who's come calling," the admiral ordered. "George, what do they have for orbital infrastructure?"

"Around the principal planet, Lenin, there is one large space station which appears to be their fleet base as well as a shipyard. One other sizable station, with no clear purpose, is likely a shipping terminal," his chief of staff said. "There are twenty large satellites in geo orbits, which I would guess are defensive units. Around the smaller planet, Putin, I see only ten of the defensive satellites."

"Thank you." The fleet commander nodded. "We need to get the execution plan updated to account for those defense satellites." He looked at the tactical plot. "So far, we seem to be on schedule for arrival at Point Bravo. Signal all ships to go to Condition Two. We'll stay that way until it's time to execute the plan."

Condition One was a ship at battle stations, meaning the vessel was sealed, all weapons were ready, and the remaining crew was at damage-control stations. Condition Two meant the ship was sealed, but only half of the crew were at their weapons stations and other support teams. Condition Three was normal peacetime operations. The internal hatches separating compartments were open, and the ship's company operated in a four-section watch schedule.

* * *

Thirty-six hours after arrival, the majority of First Fleet reached Point Bravo. They were eighty thousand kilometers from the planet and still slowing to enter orbit around Lenin in twenty minutes. During the approach, Rear Admiral Armstrong had detached a single squadron of destroyers to Putin and they were already in a high orbit above the minor planet.

The primary purpose of their slow approach was reconnaissance. The long-range probes had performed a detailed scan on each planet. Every military facility, communication center, and spaceport had been located and fed into the master fire-control system. A targeting package had been developed, and each ship now had a fire plan. Now it was time to talk to the Marxists. Talk at, not speak to. There would be no discussions or negotiations.

"All right, Betty." Admiral Mason turned to his comm officer. "It's time to send message number one."

Lieutenant Anderson had loaded the message into the system hours ago in preparation. She pushed the activate icon on her display. "Message one broadcasting, sir. All frequencies and bands at max power," she said watching the display. No one in the fleet had seen the message; it had been held under a tight security protocol. When she saw the image of the speaker, she immediately sent the message to the main display.

Prince Regent Henry sat behind a desk. "I am Prince Henry, the prince regent of the Britannic Empire. This message is for the government of the Marxist Federation, however, the people of the federation need to be aware of what is going to happen. The federation government has orchestrated attacks against the crown of the Britannic Empire. Specifically, assassination attempts against the empress and me. These attacks were to initiate a regime change that would place a ruler more sympathetic to the Marxist Federation in power. We have all the evidence we need to support this claim."

The prince looked straight into the camera and continued. "Attacks such as these could be considered an act of war, but we have no desire to go to war with the federation. The Empire does not wish to kill millions of individuals for the crimes of a select few. At the same time, we can't idly sit by and allow the federation government to continue to plot against us. Thus, we have selected a third course of action: You will be isolated. The Empire has named you a rogue state, a pariah. What this means is that you will be separated from the rest of society. As of now, you are confined to your planets. No Marxist citizen will be allowed to leave the surface of the three worlds you inhabit. To accomplish this, we will eliminate your space-faring capabilities.

"You have two hours from the end of this message to evacuate every spaceport, communication center, military installation, and any space-related manufacturing facility. Within six hours, all ships, whether they are military or civilian, will dock with an orbital facility and evacuate. Any ship that can't dock within that time period will abandon ship. Imperial units will promptly retrieve rescue pods and the individuals will be returned to the planet. You have twenty-four hours to evacuate all space platforms. When the indicated time limits expire, Imperial Fleet units will target and destroy the indicated sites. There will be no appeal, no extensions. After the elimination of your space infrastructure, additional fleet units will arrive to establish a quarantine zone. A special ambassador will accompany those units to institute the additional guidelines necessary to enact the quarantine.

"I have no quarrel with the people of the Marxist Federation, only with a few select leaders, but I must protect the Empire from those leaders and what they might do. I hope this will not be forever, and that a proper government of the people can be created to correct these wrongs.

"We look forward to that day."

*****

Chapter Thirty-Nine
Empire Date: April 1033

Hazard sat in his study at King Manor reviewing the reports concerning the two security operations he had commissioned. Both operations had been successful but not nearly as complete as he had hoped. Two glaring problems, one from each, quickly became apparent.

Admiral Mason had successfully emplaced a quarantine zone around the two systems of the Marxist Federation. The Marxist government was furious and had rained threats down on the admiral, but had eventually complied with the officer's demands. The Imperial Fleet captured all the Marxist ships. After a thorough examination by intelligence experts, they were destroyed. All the cargo and other miscellaneous vessels in the system had been captured and now sported Imperial registry. They were part of the plan to maintain controlled trade between the different Marxists planets and allow trade between the federation and the Empire.

A spaceport on Lenin, the federation's homeworld, had been repurposed as a trade port. Cargo pods could be delivered there and dropped. After a thorough search, the pods were shipped to the former federation fleet base, which was now the headquarters of the interdiction force. The spaceport and the fleet orbital were now manned entirely by Imperial Fleet personnel. The cargoes would be inspected again before being loaded onto a freighter for delivery. No federation citizen would ever be allowed to leave the planet.

The Marxists had been incredibly careful about erasing all captured computers. However, to obtain the intelligence he desired, Mason had launched a surprise raid on the fleet orbital using the special operations teams that had deployed with him. Colonel Lee's troopers had successfully captured the central computer core, providing a wealth of information. Most of what they already knew of the plot was confirmed by what they recovered. More importantly, a new danger had been discovered. The federation had created its own "pirate" fleet that was now operating inside Imperial space. It had started as a collaboration with various pirate associations within that sector but had grown, and the Marxists had melded the groups into a single entity controlled by them. The actual number of ships involved was unknown, but evidence indicated at least one light cruiser and four destroyer-size units had been built and were a part of that force.

When Hazard had been aboard the *Avon* during his return to the home system, Captain Kong had mentioned the increase in pirate activity. At the time, he hadn't paid any attention to it. Now it was evident that this had been going on for a while. The prince was sure the pirates were not targeting merely cargo but technology. Advances, specifically in any area that could be militarized, had been denied to the Marxists, so they had stolen it. Though still inferior to the technology of the Empire, a combination of the heavier pirate units could easily overwhelm the older destroyers the fleet used to patrol the inner systems. The grand admiral of the fleet requested a meeting to discuss responses.

The situation with the security forces had been resolved. Hazard's father had the situation well in hand, but there were still problems.

The former operations director Xavier Isaacson had disappeared after the assassination of ImpSec's previous director. Isaacson had erased all his computer records, but the late Director Whitestone's were primarily intact. It showed she had been involved in numerous distasteful operations throughout her career, but none of it was connected with the Marxists. The working theory Snake Atwater had developed was that she had been set up as a patsy by Isaacson. To infiltrate the security agency to the extent the Marxists had they needed support at a high level. The director of operations would have been in the perfect position.

Unfortunately, Isaacson was not the only security officer or agent to disappear. So far, over one hundred former ImpSec operators had dropped out of sight, with more going missing every day. While Hazard was sure that some of them had disappeared for other reasons, like abusing their offices, he was now confident many were Marxist agents. ImpSec had ultimately failed in its primary responsibility: protecting the Empire from foreign espionage. His father couldn't move fast enough to dismantle the agency.

Hazard recalled his father's briefing. "First, foreign intelligence. It should be exactly that. Intelligence gathering outside the Empire. What better department to oversee that than the foreign office? They already have their own intelligence assets, so we simply combine them with the foreign assets of ImpSec. Second, domestic intelligence. During our research, we discovered that ImpSec spent most of its assets spying on our system and planetary governments," Hazard's father had said, disgusted. "Needless to say, we found that distasteful. True, we need to keep a finger on the pulse of each system and remain wary of any anti-Imperial foment that's going on, but that's why we have Imperial governors. The new domestic intelligence branch will be under the home secretary, responsible for antiterrorism and counterintelligence operations in each system. It will also be responsible for counterintelligence at the Imperial level. Third, analysis. All the data gathered by the first two groups and the inputs from other organizations, such as Fleet Intelligence, will be sifted and evaluated. This will be Imperial Intelligence or, as we've begun calling it, I2. They'll answer to the new minister of intelligence, me. We're also establishing a security inspector general's office, which will be a part of the justice department. They'll be set up similarly to the fleet inspector general's office and will be responsible for routine checks of the branches to make sure they're performing as required. The final piece is black or special operations. As distasteful as it might be, there are times when espionage or even assassinations are required to protect the realm. Such operations would be enacted only with Imperial approval. Since most of these operations are military, we're creating a small clandestine group within the fleet's Special Warfare group. They'll be similar to the old Special Air Service, or SAS, on Old Earth," his father concluded.

Hazard was pondering how to deal with the Marxist spy network when his intercom chimed.

"Yes, Amanda," he answered. Amanda Barnes was his mother's private secretary. When he started getting further and further behind with his correspondence, Hazard had agreed to his father's suggestion to use her to manage his workload and act as a gatekeeper. The grand duke had pointed out that senior fleet officers had flag secretaries, personal aides, and chiefs of staff to handle much of the administrative load; that left them time to make the more significant decisions.

"A message just arrived in your Hazard King account that I believe you need to see," she replied.

"Thank you, Amanda. Send it to my private terminal," Hazard said and waited for the message to arrive.

He saw the message header and thought, *Finally.*

It was from Hiroko's parents. After much deliberation, they had decided to accept Hazard's offer and had already arranged passage to Britannia. Their itinerary was attached to the message and they were arriving late next week. Once again, Hazard's two identities were colliding, but at least he had a few days to figure it out.

He keyed his intercom. "Amanda, I assume you read the message since you brought it to my attention." There were very few secrets that Amanda was not privy to, and Hazard had given her carte blanche to go through his message traffic. "We need to make arrangements for Hiroko's parents. I want them met at Central and brought to King Manor by private shuttle. Please inform the rest of the staff to prepare for their arrival."

*****

Chapter Forty
Empire Date: April 1033

Friday morning, Amanda dispatched a limo to the spaceport to meet Hiroko's parents. Hazard had been grappling with how to broach the subject of his true identity since he'd received the Ogowa's message. They had been lukewarm about his involvement with their daughter, and he knew it hadn't had a thing to do with bigotry. They didn't care that he was black, and she was Asian. It was about culture. The descendants of the original Japanese colonists had carried that culture and embedded it into their new society—a culture of shunning outsiders and relying on themselves.

Hazard thought back to their lunch meeting. It seemed a lifetime ago, though it was little more than two months ago. So much had happened. In a way, it was a lifetime. His time on Honshu was the last time he had truly been Hazard King. He could never be that person again. Even after his mother recovered and resumed her duties, he would still be the heir. There was still a chance, slim though it was, that he could be both, and he was working on a plan that would allow that.

A notice popped up on his terminal informing him that the Ogowas had arrived and he left his office to wait in the entry foyer. He had asked his father to join him, hoping his presence might make the revelation easier. The grand duke had agreed but not yet arrived.

The front door opened, and Mr. and Mrs. Ogowa entered, escorted by one of his marines. Hazard approached them and gave a short bow.

"Welcome to my home, Mr. and Mrs. Ogowa," Hazard said. "Your presence honors me and my house."

Daizen Ogowa returned Hazard's bow. "You honored us in the invitation, Mr. King."

Hazard turned to Hiroka Ogawa. With another slight bow, he remarked, "Your beauty is a welcome addition to this humble abode, Mrs. Ogowa."

She laughed softly. "Is your intention to woo me instead of my daughter, Master King? I can see why my daughter became attached to you."

"One needs to be charming when confronting the parents of the woman he loves," Hazard replied earnestly. "I assure you that when she is able, Hiroko will tell you that I was never like this with her on board the *Shinto.* If the two of you would join me in the library for some refreshments before we go to see Hiroko, there is something important we need to discuss."

Mr. Ogowa nodded, and they followed him into the library. Cecile Kendrick, the housekeeper, had arranged various snacks, sandwiches, and refreshments on a side table.

Hazard waved at the arrangement. "Please help yourselves. I would prefer this be a family conversation."

He waited as his guests poured cups of tea and sat on the sofa. Finally, he got himself a cup of coffee and settled in an armchair facing them.

They sat in silence as the Ogowas looked at him expectantly. Finally, Daizen Ogowa broke the silence.

"Since you said this is to be a familiar conversation, I am going to call you Hazard. I must admit your manor is impressive, and the level of security is surprising. Both confirm our previous belief that there is more than you have previously revealed to us."

"Sir—" Hiroko's father raised an eyebrow and Hazard chuckled. "I find it hard to call my future bride's father by his given name." The elder Ogowa nodded, and he continued. "Yes, there is more to me than you saw on Honshu. At that time, I was a second son, so to some extent, I was allowed to be who I wanted to be. Since I was a child, all I ever wanted was to be a fleet officer. But events have occurred that have changed that. And while I still yearn and hope to return to that life, I understand my family responsibilities will force me to change."

"Hazard, the quality of you as a person has just risen, and risen exponentially, with your obvious devotion to those responsibilities," Daizen Ogowa stated. "To know someone with such values is the man our daughter intends to marry alleviates most of our fears."

Before Hazard could reply, the library doors slid open, and his father walked in. He walked to Hazard and shook his hand. "I am sorry to be so late. I was held up at the—" his father almost said "palace" "—office."

They turned to the seated couple. "Mr. and Mrs. Ogowa, may I introduce my father, Henry King. Dad, this is Daizen and Hiroka Ogowa, Hiroko's parents." He shook Hiroko's father's hand and offered a small bow to Hiroka. "My father went through a similar issue of family responsibilities, where he had to choose between a fleet career and what the family needed."

"Hazard, it was an easy decision for me. I could choose your mother or the fleet. I could never have both. I made the correct choice," the senior King said to the group. Hazard saw the looks the

Ogowas gave each other. Hiroka clearly admired the man for giving up his future for his bride. "You, on the other hand," his father continued, "never had a choice, even though you have more control over the situation."

"Mr. and Mrs. Ogowa, when I introduced my father, I left out a bit." At their confused looks, he said, "He is indeed Captain Henry King, Imperial Fleet retired, but he is also His Grace, Grand Duke Henry, consort of Empress Elizabeth V." The Ogawas were surprised and amazed, and clearly a little awestruck. Then the realization hit them. If Hazard was the son of Grand Duke Henry and the empress, then he was… Hazard confirmed it for them. "Yes, I am Prince Henry, second son of the empress, and because of circumstances that we can discuss later, I am now the prince regent and heir to the Imperial throne. It is not what I wanted, but it is what duty requires of me. And yes, it means your daughter will be Empress Hiroko."

The people of Honshu were instilled with a deep respect for tradition. That culture caused the Ogowas to rise and begin bowing in homage to their sovereign. Hazard held up a hand, forestalling them. "I told both of you that I wanted this to be familiar. Family does not bow to each other in private. Besides," Hazard said wryly, "I am in charge, and I make the rules. One thing I insist on is that you call me Hazard."

* * *

After finishing an excellent meal, they were joined by Phyllis Warren and Carl Brougham. After the initial meeting in the library, Hazard had taken the Ogowas up to Hiroko's suite. Phyllis had explained Hiroko's medical condition to the couple, how they had set up the medical suite, and how Hiroko was constantly monitored. They were allowed as much time alone with Hiroko as they wanted. Daizen and Hiroka had spent almost an hour in the suite before joining them for an evening meal.

"Daizen and Hiroka," Hazard began, "I invited Doctor Brougham to join us so he can discuss a possible course of treatment for Hiroko. I introduced Carl as an old family friend, and he certainly is that, but while I was growing up, he was not only my physician, he was also the empress' personal physician. He left that position to become head of a secret research project specializing in nanites and how they can be used for medical purposes. Carl, if you would, please."

Carl, with the tone of a college professor, which Hazard thought he was, said, "Mr. and Mrs. Ogowa, several years ago, I became aware of research being done in the field of nanites. These fascinating devices are tiny robots that can be designed to perform a variety of tasks. The earliest versions were created to assist with shipbuilding and repair. Those versions were crude, the size of small ants and only had one skill, such as welding—they could find cracks or holes and weld them closed. They were extremely useful during a space battle. I believed that they could be adapted for medical purposes. Over the next several years, researchers continued to improve the technology. We developed smaller and smaller versions and expanded the tasks which they could perform. About eight years ago, we developed the first practical blood-borne version capable of combating diseases as well as mending minor damage." Carl paused and looked around the table. "This next part is highly classified. After significant testing, we decided to inject certain members of the Imperial family with the medical nanites."

The Ogowas and Phyllis Warren look at Hazard and his father. He nodded. "Yes, I have been injected with the nanites, though my father was not. Only the empress, my brother, and I were. I can attest that I have seen no ill effects. In fact, since the injection seven years ago, I have never been sick. No colds, flu, nothing. They will heal cuts and broken bones faster, as well."

"Only the direct royal line and a few test subjects were ever injected with the treatment. Developing and producing the nanites is prohibitively expensive as far as mass use is concerned," Carl said answering the obvious question. "And no, injecting Hiroko with that type of nanite would not help. That version of the medical nanite would not be robust enough to repair her injuries. I did this work while I was the Imperial physician. The empress has a dream of making this technology available to everyone, so she established a Nanite Research Center and put me in charge of it. That's what I've been doing for the last six years. Constantly trying to improve and expand the technology. It's nowhere close to being economical yet, but we have improved our production process to make more available. We have also started development of special nanites to treat more serious injuries."

"Which is why I've asked him to be here to discuss it," Hazard said. "Dr. Brougham has developed a surgical nanite which he, or I should say we, believe can help Hiroko. So far, two test patients with horrific injuries have been successfully restored to full health. The nanites have been used on me to repair my injured leg." Hazard saw the shock on everyone's faces. "Carl wasn't happy about it, but he followed orders and gave them to me." Hazard looked at his father. "I wasn't going to have them tried on my mother or my future wife without satisfying my own concerns."

Hazard sipped his coffee, which he noted had gone cold, and continued. "Mr. and Mrs. Ogowa, Carl and I would like your permission to use these surgical nanites on Hiroko. Neither of us believes that they can heal her by themselves. We just need them to repair her body enough so we can bring her out of stasis without her dying, then a surgical team can fix the rest." The Ogowas looked at each other, and Hazard held up his hand. "Take your time. We don't need an answer now. Hiroko is stable for now, and it will be some months before the stasis field begins to diminish."

Daizen Ogowa looked at his wife and back. "Hazard, if you're willing to put the entire Empire at risk by taking the treatment to prove to us it's safe, how can we not agree? The only question we have is whether Dr. Brougham has any of these nanites with him?"

* * * * *

Chapter Forty-One
Empire Date: April 1033

Hazard loathed reports. It hadn't started when he'd accepted the mantle of regent, either. No, it had begun with his first actual assignment to a ship, the *Shinto*. There, as a junior officer, he had spent more time creating reports for his various superiors in the chain of command than reading them. Now that he was at the top of the food chain, it was the opposite. Every morning, people filled his inbox with the daily and other scheduled reports people in the government thought he should read.

He soon discovered that various bureaucrats had devised the majority of the reports not to keep him informed but as a reminder of the originator's presence and importance to the Crown. He decided to change that. A ship's captain, or an admiral in a fleet, didn't get daily reports concerning routine operational information from numerous sources. Those reports went to a ship's executive officer or an admiral's chief of staff. Now the lord chamberlain would be responsible for handling all of those types of reports for Hazard. That was the original purpose of the position anyway: to manage everyday affairs while the Crown tackled the significant issues.

Hazard had learned to trust Kendrick Beckham and they had quickly established a rhythm for handling the matters of the Empire. Both the chamberlain and the regent were early risers, so they had breakfast together each day to discuss issues and events. Since relocating to King Manor, these sessions were virtual since Hazard didn't want to pull Beckham away from his duties any longer than necessary.

Hazard sat at his desk drinking his coffee and conversing with his chamberlain, whose image was displayed on the monitor on the wall. "Henry, I'm sure you've lost track of the fact that next week you are scheduled to depart for the first of the meetings with system leadership." Since Hazard's preadolescence, Kendrick Beckham was one of the few people comfortable calling him Henry, though only when they were alone. "Both Penny O'Higgin and the Duke of Kara have sent me notes complaining that you haven't given them any feedback on the plans for the trip."

"I'm beginning to regret that I ever suggested that in my regency speech." Hazard laughed. "Truth is, I was hoping that if I ignored it long enough the trip would go away."

"My Prince, it was and still is an excellent idea. No head of state has met with the individual system leaders in over three hundred years. Your mother has only met with about a quarter of them, most of whom traveled here. There is no dispute that you are the regent, but in those first few dark days, the support of the individual system leaders was crucial in validating your position."

"I know, Ken. Okay, I'll review the plans and will schedule a meeting with the three of you tomorrow to finalize the trip," Hazard relented.

* * *

The night before leaving on the diplomatic trip, Hazard had dinner with his father at King Manor. He had decided to name his father as his regent while he was away from the capital. Although Hazard would be in communication with the palace, there would be a severe time delay. He trusted his father and Ken Beckham to make good decisions if they were needed. Fortunately, there would be no constitutional crisis in this appointment because the Charter never defined who should be in charge during such a circumstance. It only mentioned the Crown could appoint an individual to act in their stead if the need arose.

"Have you gotten a final count on how many will be attending?" his father asked.

"Seventeen for sure. Three system rulers are deciding between this one meeting or one of the later ones. The feedback I've received via private messages indicates all the rulers are excited by the opportunity, so barring an unforeseen incident, they will all attend one of the meetings. So many have never met the crowned ruler. I'm going to suggest to Mother that this become a regular event; have an annual meeting at a convenient location for twenty or so of her vassals and rotate it every year so the system rulers gets the chance to see the leader of the Empire at least every four or five years."

His father laughed, and Hazard raised an eyebrow. "For someone who didn't want the job, you certainly have taken to it," his father said. "Let's see: reorganized Imperial Security, reorganized palace security, neutered the Imperial Senate, and now a diplomatic trip that has all the system leaders eating out of your hand."

"But that was easy," Hazard said. "They all needed to be done."

"Henry, your mother wanted to do some of those same things. You have succeeded where she failed." His father looked him in the eye. "I love your mother, but she was not prepared to be empress. Because of that lack of knowledge and training, she has ruled the same way her ancestors did. I have to be careful offering advice to her for fear that me doing so may make her appear weak. Also, there has been the fear of system revolts. This fear has existed for several hundred years. Some feel the Empire is too large for a single ruler to reign over, which may be true. Using the fastest courier ship, it can take up to eight days for messages to reach the capital of the farthest Imperial system. If systems feel they aren't part of the Empire, why should they send money or their sons and daughters to support the Crown? These meetings of yours will go a long way to alleviate those feelings."

"I am just doing what feels right, Dad."

"Yes, you are, but you are doing them. I believe your military training is influencing you. Just like you were trained at the academy, you see a problem, analyze it, and implement a solution. You don't get bogged down in politics because you weren't brought up in politics. That's why you can accomplish things, and why your mother does not. She grew up inside the political beast, and she gets bogged down in it."

"Well, when she returns to her duties, we'll just have to help her change. If we need to, we can blame it on my mulish impulses." Changing the subject he asked, "With the improvement Hiroko is showing after her nanite injections, have there been any discussions about starting Mother's treatment?"

"I spoke with Carl and Jayani this morning. Carl is all for beginning, but Jayani is your mother's doctor, and she wants to wait for at least another week."

"That means the decision would be made after I leave for the summit. The time delay will affect how soon the treatment is started. I think that's unacceptable, so I'll authorize you as my regent to make that decision. I'll have Amanda create a formal document for me to sign."

*****

Chapter Forty-Two
Empire Date: April 1033

Hazard and his personal guard, Sondheim, Bummer, and Jerry, sat on the observation deck of the Imperial yacht, *King Wilhelm*. Well, the gunnery sergeant was sitting, Bummer and Jerry were standing on either side of the access door. Two more of his marines guarded the outside of the door. The room had initially been designed as a flag bridge since *King Wilhelm* was a modified light cruiser. The flag officer's chair, now somewhat more ornate than its original design, was flanked by three additional chairs on either side and formed into a half circle facing the view screen on the forward bulkhead. The rest of the former combat stations had been removed. The original communication station had been expanded to allow the empress to stay in touch with the rest of the Empire.

King Wilhelm was also heavily modified. The four missile tubes in each broadside, as well as their magazines, had been removed. The tubes were replaced with additional rail gun missile-defense batteries, while additional staterooms and storage replaced the missile magazines. The Duke of Kara, knowing Hazard would need the yacht, had all the missile-defense batteries replaced with the new quad rail gun systems, which incorporated the barrage-defense system. The ship retained the original four forward-firing medium lasers.

Hazard watched the four escort destroyers take their positions around the yacht as they proceeded toward the hyper limit. All the destroyers were new designs and new construction. The *Longbow*-class was the next-generation destroyer, designed using the lessons learned during the Swarm war. Missiles had long been abandoned by the Empire since, with current technology, they had neither the speed nor the guidance systems to effectively engage Swarm attack ships. Those were replaced with additional rail guns. The *Longbows* had done away with the beam weapons, as well. Even with advanced fusion power plants, destroyer-sized ships couldn't generate enough power to enable beam weapons that could consistently penetrate Swarm attack ship shields.

The *Longbows* mounted the new 40 mm rail guns along the ship's sides, four dual mounts along each axis. The hammerhead design, which included the turrets most fleet ships incorporated, had been replaced with a bulbous bow. Instead of lasers, the *Longbows* mounted two 100 mm rail guns. They were not spinal mounts, but they did have extended rails, and their fixed rails could propel a slug at 0.3 *c*. Fleet design experts had borrowed an idea from the age of sail and adapted it for modern space warfare: the large rail guns could fire what was once called canister and grapeshot rounds. A canister round was a cylindrical canister whose center was a bursting charge surrounded by thousands of 5 mm projectiles. The shaped charge would explode at a set distance and the projectiles spread out in a cone across the front of the ship. Grapeshot did the same thing but contained 40 mm projectiles. Similar to the barrage attack Hazard had developed, the idea was to create a cloud of debris the Swarm attack ships had to fly through. Full-sized solid projectiles were also available to allow the destroyers to engage other types of targets as needed.

Sondheim broke the silence. "I've never seen a ship transition into hyperspace, at least not in person. Sure, I've seen recordings, but I was always busy doing other things when ships jumped."

"When I was on the *Shinto*, I was able to watch other ships generate a portal and enter hyper, but never the ship I was on," Hazard said. "I think we should both take the opportunity to watch this one."

* * *

Commander Jordan Ramsey sat in the command chair of *Prince Wilhelm*. He was relatively new to the ship and had just qualified as a ship's duty officer. As the ship's tactical officer, he was in charge of the first watch team. Imperial Fleet ships used a three-watch-team rotation, each team standing a six-hour watch. Thus, over three days, a watch team would stand four watches, one on each of the ship's cycles—mid, morning, afternoon, and evening watches.

By tradition, the Imperial yacht, a modified light cruiser, was only crewed by experienced combat officers and crew. He was the assistant tactical officer aboard the cruiser *Achilles* during the battle in the Echo System before being transferred to the "Willy" to become the tactical officer. The *Achilles* had received minor damage and destroyed six attackers, but he had been in battle, and the previous TO was due for relief, so he had been assigned.

It was the evening watch on the second day of a five-day hyper trip to Delphi, a routine run carrying VIPs, so Jordan was taking advantage of the time and reviewing any message traffic that affected him. Unfortunately, there never seemed to be enough time for all the paperwork handled by a department head.

"Commander," his sensor officer called out, "just picked up a small sensor contact thirty million kilometers out. It's small and fast and on a reciprocal course."

The ship was in a standard hyper transit lane, so a vessel on such a course would be on its way to the capital system. But when you had the prince regent on board, nothing was normal.

"Tactical, start a plot until we can get a good ID on this fellow. Guns, get the on-duty laser and rail gun teams spun up. Comms, holler out when you get a transponder."

The crew repeated and acknowledged their orders. Jordan debated calling the captain, but he glanced at the tactical display and saw they should be getting a transponder report in two minutes. He decided to wait.

"Commander Ramsey, I have a solid Imperial transponder," the comm officer announced. "She's a system courier, designated *Haven Two*."

The Imperial Courier Service maintained a fleet of ships in each of the Empire's client systems. The number of couriers varied depending on the number of nearby hyper lanes. The Haven System had one lane that transited near the system. They would typically keep one courier near the jump toward Britannia and another near the one for Delphi. After being dispatched along one of the routes, the planet would send a replacement to the station. Until some means of faster-than-light communications was developed, this was the best they could do.

"Commander, the courier is now flashing a code Xray," comms said. A code Xray indicated that a system was under attack.

"Signal *Haven Two* that we will execute a zero-zero intercept and be ready to receive a data dump. Helm, coordinate with the courier to execute the rendezvous," Jordan ordered. *So much for a quiet watch,* he thought. Jordan pushed the CO's call button on the left arm of the command chair and the ship's computer the call to wherever the CO was.

Captain Doris Winters' soft soprano came through the speaker in the chair. "What is it, Commander?"

"Sorry to disturb you, ma'am. We have encountered a courier from the Haven System, and it's squawking a code Xray. I have ordered a zero-zero intercept to receive their data dump. Rendezvous time sixty-eight minutes."

"Very well, Jordan. Excellent job. There is no reason to do anything until we get that data dump. I'll hold a senior officers' meeting in the bridge briefing room at 2115 to discuss the data and next actions."

* * *

Lieutenant Commander Kristen Jurgenson sat in the well-appointed sitting area of her cabin on *King Wilhelm*. She couldn't believe she had lucked out in this assignment. After being wounded in the Echo System, she'd been assigned to Fleet Headquarters until she healed enough to return to full duty. When the comm officer assigned to the yacht suddenly needed a leave of absence due to a family emergency, the Fleet Manning Office had scrambled to find a replacement who could report before its departure. Kristen had been one of the few officers available with both the security clearances and seniority to fill the position, so even though she was still on restricted duty, here she was.

The communications group that supported the Imperials on board consisted of three communication ratings and an officer, so there wasn't much to the job. They handled any message traffic coming from or going to the Imperial passengers on board. It wasn't necessary to have multiple officers for this. The three enlisted spacers stood a regular watch rotation at the communication station on the observation deck and they monitored traffic coming in and directed the messages to her for decoding and review before delivery. Outbound traffic was the reverse.

A soft chime announced an incoming comm request. The green light indicated it was from the on-watch communication tech.

That's odd, she thought. Unless a courier had intercepted them, her section should have nothing to do. If a courier had rendezvoused with important dispatches for the regent, the ship's duty officer would have informed her of it. She opened the channel. "Commander Jurgenson here. What's up?"

"Commander, the ship is in the process of rendezvousing with a Haven System courier ship," the technician said. "It popped up about twenty minutes ago, and ma'am…" The tech paused. "Its transponder is flashing a code Xray."

"Do we know anything about the reason for the code?" Kristen asked.

"No, ma'am. They're far enough out that the time delay is noticeable. That's why Captain Winters set up for the rendezvous at 2100. *King Wilhelm* will receive a data dump at that point. The captain has scheduled a senior staff meeting, including the rest of the escort force, at 2115."

"Does His Highness know about this?" she asked.

"No one has asked to communicate with the prince regent, at least not through me. I suppose Captain Winters could have spoken directly to him, but that would be against protocol."

Yes, definitely against protocol. Communication requests were supposed to pass through the comm department. "Thank you, Hansen. Excellent work. Be prepared to copy the data packet when the courier transmits it."

Jurgenson contemplated what her course of action should be. Captain Winters seemed to be keeping the prince in the dark. Pissing off a senior officer was never a good idea, but then again, she didn't work for the captain. She pushed the blue comm button on her console to call the prince.

* * *

Jurgenson arrived on the observation deck five minutes before the rendezvous time and found Prince Henry and his marine bodyguards already there. Penny O'Higgin, the foreign secretary, the prince's diplomatic advisor for this trip, was also on the former flag bridge.

Communication Tech First Class Hansen looked up from his console when she came in. "We're receiving the data dump, Commander. It is a combination of data, video, and audio." He paused then said, "Download complete. Give me a moment to decode it, then I'll display it on the screens."

The rest of the group took their seats and a recording of a tactical display appeared on the main screen. It showed a force of thirteen ships moving through the system toward the planet Haven. A screen on the left displayed an analysis of the ships in the force. A cruiser-sized ship with four destroyers or large frigates and eight smaller craft the system couldn't identify.

Hazard immediately knew what he was seeing. "That's the pirate fleet our Marxist friends created. That force originally fanned out across our central systems and gathered technology by whatever means they could. That they're here, with the whole force, indicates the game has changed."

"Why do you say that, Your Highness?" Penny O'Higgin asked.

Hazard gestured toward the screen. "That's their entire force. True, it's more than a match for the system defense force, but they don't stand a chance of taking the main orbital stations. They don't have enough ground troops to do that. To get the technology or plans they want, they would have to go after one of the large orbitals or, even better, land a force on the planet for a snatch-and-grab. The real indicator is the eight smaller ships. They are next to useless for a mission like this. They're just small missile boats with eight-men crews and four missile tubes with no reload. Small, fast, but only useful against unarmed merchant ships. We need to figure out what they are doing."

For several long moments, the group stared at the displays, analyzing the data. The quiet voice of the foreign secretary broke the silence. "Hostages. They're going to take the entire system hostage."

"What could they accomplish by doing that?" Sondheim asked.

"We Irish are proud of our history, but there's a part of our past which we seldom talk about. During the troubles, when we were trying to gain our independence back on Old Earth, we did some horrible things under the umbrella of patriotism. Assassination, wholesale murder, and the taking of large numbers of hostages in an attempt to force our oppressors to give us our freedom. It never worked. All it did was escalate the cycle of violence. In the end, we gained our freedom, not because we forced the English to give it to us but because we showed them we deserved it."

"And this group knows that we now control their federation," Hazard said. "Yes, the plan is farfetched by our way of thinking, but they come from a society that was isolated from the rest of humanity for a long time. A society that originated from an Old Earth regime that incorporated similar ideas. They may believe they can pull it off."

"If that's the case," Commander Jurgenson said, "what can we do about it? The nearest major fleet units are in the home system, and that's two days behind us. Even if they can quickly assemble a task force, it would still take five days for them to arrive."

"Your Highness, if they have five days to get established, I hate to think what they could do," the foreign minister said somberly.

They saw a gleam in the prince's eye.

"You're right, Penny," Hazard said. "However, Kristen, you are slightly mistaken. There is a capable fleet force much closer to Haven than the Marxists know." The young prince turned to look at his communication officer. "Kristen, I need you to use the hyperspace comms to connect me with the Duke of Kara."

* * *

Captain Winters looked around the conference table and then at the images of the four destroyer captains on the forward display screen.

"Then we are all agreed. The priority of protecting the regent overrides the required actions of the Xray protocols." The officers nodded their agreement. "I've already sent a hyperspace comm to Fleet HQ about the situation and our intentions. We'll send the courier on to the home system, and we'll continue as scheduled to Delphi. We'll transfer the prince and his party to a secure facility and return to Haven. I suspect by then the pirates will be long gone, but we'll render what assistance we can."

Captain Winters finished outlining her plan with her back to the display when a new voice entered the conversation. "I don't believe that is the best course of action." The captain turned and saw there was now a fifth image on the screen: Prince Henry.

"I appreciate the concern for my safety, but there is much more at stake here than you know. These are not simple pirates who are mounting a large raid. They are privateers supported by the Marxist Federation. There are no transports accompanying the force. How are they going to carry off their loot?"

* * *

Hazard sat in the command chair on the observation deck. He looked at the faces on his display. "This is a terror raid. My belief, supported by my staff, is that they intend to take the system hostage with the expectation that they can force us to negotiate about our actions against their federation."

Doris Winters turned to fully face the display screen and responded to the prince regent. "Your safety is our utmost priority, My Prince. Our oaths demand this of us."

"I swear to defend the Empire against all enemies, both foreign and domestic, and to obey the lawful orders of those officers and civilian administrators appointed over me," Hazard recited calmly. "That is the oath every person in this meeting took, including me. Nowhere does it mention me as the regent, nor the empress herself. The Empire is not my mother, me, or even the star systems that make up the Empire. The Empire is its people. They are its true wealth, and it is they who we swore to protect. Therefore, any decision made here that does not involve going to the defense of the Haven System is a violation of that oath."

Captain Winters stiffened at his veiled rebuke. Hazard saw he had angered his flag captain.

Good, Hazard thought. He also saw three of the destroyer captains nodding in agreement. Hazard decided it was time to seal the deal. "The oath states that we will obey the lawful orders of the officers and civilian administrators appointed over us. I do believe that makes me the senior authority." Hazard let that sink in. "It is *our* decision—" Hazard invoked the Imperial plural and hoped no one missed it "—that we proceed to Haven at best speed to at least evaluate the situation. I would think that a modified light cruiser and four of our newest destroyers could handle the force of severely outdated ships the Marxist pirates are employing. I have already discussed the situation with the grand admiral and a sizable force, including the fleet flagship, should be departing the home system within the hour. We will enter the Haven System and evaluate the situation."

The destroyer captains nodded in assent. Doris Winters looked around the conference room, making an obvious effort to become calm herself before responding to the prince. "What are your orders, Your Highness?"

"We need to get the courier on its way to Britannia. I have a special packet I need to send to the council via courier that I already have prepared. The courier will depart in ten minutes on a best speed course to Britannia. As soon as the courier is away, we will depart for Haven at our best speed possible. I expect ship status updates within thirty minutes as well as our ETA to Haven."

Captain Winters took charge. "We need to make this happen, people. The prince has issued his orders." With that, the *Willy's* officers left the room.

Captain Clarice Larue, the commander of the *Longbow* said. "What will be our command structure?"

Larue was senior to Doris Winters, but Winters held the position of flag captain, as the commander of the Imperial yacht. Before anyone else could speak, Hazard said, "I'll be sending out the task force organization and command structure within the hour." Shock was apparent on everyone's faces. They were uncomfortable with him exerting this much control—an amateur interfering with the professionals. "For now, we have things we need to do, so let us be about it."

* * * * *

Chapter Forty-Three
Empire Date: April 1033

Hazard reviewed the message he had recorded for his father. In fleet jargon, it was the last message. The message a spacer would dictate to loved ones to be delivered upon their death. Most were written, though nowadays some were audio or even video. They were kept in a fleet member's personnel file to be delivered when fleet command officially recognized their death. In Hazard's case, he was sending it directly to his father.

"Dad, if you are reading this, something must have happened to me in the Haven System. I don't want you to blame the officers commanding the ships in the force with me. They tried to get me to go on to Delphi, but I pulled rank on them. There was no way I was going to leave the people of Haven, my people, in the clutches of the Marxist bastards a moment longer than necessary. With an older modified light cruiser and four state-of-the-art destroyers, we should be able to handle anything.

"I would like you to do two things for me. Take care of Hiri. In my will, I have left everything to her. Help her become the princess she was meant to be. Second, I have a secret program on my laptop, the one on my office desk. The password is hazard-revelation. When it asks if you are sure, type in Henry-V. When you see the accepted prompt it means the program is running. Turn off the computer and leave King Manor. Take care of Mother and the girls. Let them all know I was thinking of them and the Empire. I love all of you."

Hazard closed the file and sent it to comms to be transmitted to the courier ship. He stood and decided it was time to be on the bridge. He exited the cabin and nearly ran into the gunnery sergeant, who had been waiting outside his door.

"Gunny, trying to ambush me?"

The rumble of what had to be a laugh erupted from the barrel-chested man. "No, sir, but I would like to know if you've thought everything through. You're taking a big chance. If something happens to you, there would be a vacuum in the leadership chain. That would be bad right now."

Hazard thought about the message he had sent his father. "I believe I've made allowances for that, Gunny. No person is indispensable. I would not have suggested this if I thought we couldn't do it." He looked intently at the grizzled veteran. "You saw the reports from the Federation's homeworld; their ships are three or four generations behind us. The destroyers alone could probably take them, and that is the plan. We're going along just in case." He could tell the marine was not convinced. Hazard gestured toward the bridge, "Come on. Join me on the bridge. Listen to what I intend to do."

The two men walked onto the bridge. Hazard sat in the command chair and motioned for Sondheim to take one of the adjacent observer seats. Hazard noted that the commanding officers of the task force were already on the video link.

Hazard nodded to his comm officer. "Okay, Kristen, tie me in."

A green light on the screen told Hazard he was live. "Gentlemen, I want to start by giving you some background on the enemy force. When we neutralized the Marxist Federation, we encountered the same types of ships we'll face here. They are using an early-generation grav-drive with a two-hundred-gravity-acceleration limit, so we can out-accelerate them, outrun them, and out turn them. The light cruiser has four dual-turret medium lasers; two mounted on the dorsal and two on the ventral side. She also mounts eight missile tubes in each broadside. The missiles are single-stage, fusion drive with fusion warheads. Our tests showed they have a five-minute powered endurance at two hundred fifty Gs for an active envelope of one hundred ten thousand kilometers." Hazard looked at each officer. "That's their long-range weapon. That range and speed is the reason why we don't use missiles any longer. The technology can't be improved to make them more effective. The destroyers are effectively smaller versions of the light cruiser. One dual-mount medium laser in a dorsal position with four missile tubes in each broadside. The cruiser has four reloads for each missile tube, and the destroyers have two.

"The small ships, which we refer to as corvettes, are a bit of a wild card. They are essentially missile boats with four missiles mounted on external racks. No other weapons, shields, or armor. One big fusion engine and a fuel tank. Examination of data showed that they still use drugs to allow the crews to endure high G-forces up to four hundred fifty Gs. That will allow them to fire missiles that reach a much higher velocity and have a bigger envelope."

Hazard looked at the officers. "Comments, gentlemen?"

Clarice Larue, the captain of the *Longbow*, spoke up immediately, "None of the ships should be an issue. We have both a range and speed advantage over them. True, the small ships will be a bit harder, but we can use our main rail guns as big shotguns. It won't take many forty mm hunks of metal flying at partial *c* to take them out." The other destroyer captains nodded in agreement.

Hazard looked at Captain Winters. "My one concern is that the only ship we have with beam weapons is *King Wilhelm*. Captain Larue, the *Longbows* were specifically designed to fight one kind of ship; that may have been shortsighted of us."

Larue replied, "Your Highness, we can handle this mission with no problem. I do see your point, though. If I had a couple of heavy beam weapons on *Longbow*, I would approach the battle differently."

"Well, we have to dance with the girl we brought to the ball, gentlemen." Hazard chuckled. "And I certainly like the look of *Longbow* and her sisters. Captain Larue, the four destroyers will constitute First Division, and you will be in command. The *Willy* will constitute Second Division. We will jump to a distance of thirty light-minutes from Haven actual. We'll come in at one hundred gravities acceleration and evaluate sensor data. Based on that information, First Division will proceed into the system to engage the enemy. Second Division will maintain its position outside the hyper limit until it's needed. Any questions?"

"It appears you have appointed yourself as overall commander, Your Highness," Captain Winters stated, a hard look on her sharp face.

Hazard looked directly at her for a long moment before pulling back to view the ship captains. "I prefer to think of it as organizing things. I have no intentions of taking control of this ship or jiggling the elbows of the other captains." Hazard gave each captain a stern look. "Each of you is a trained ship's captain and an experienced officer, and I wouldn't presume to know more than you do. However, I am the regent. If I should give an order, I don't expect an argument, I expect you to obey the order." He paused and looked at the chronometer. "We're about six hours until transit. Until then, I leave it to you to get your ships and crews ready for what's to come. Good luck, Captains." Hazard motioned for the comm officer to drop the circuit.

"I don't think you're on Captain Winter's Christmas card list." Sondheim chuckled. "She was pissed."

"Can't be helped," Hazard said. "She doesn't understand the capabilities of the new destroyers, and they are the true striking force.

She also doesn't have recent combat experience. I checked Captain Larue's service record, and she was an XO on one of the destroyers in Task Force Twenty-Three and was part of the last stand with the *Shinto*. She saw firsthand what the new systems can do if properly utilized."

"Don't expect her to be cooperative," Sondheim said somberly. "I've seen officers with that look. She feels usurped. It could be a problem."

"It will only be a problem for however long it takes me to relieve her. Think about it, Gunny. If she was that good, she would have been commanding a cruiser in the Echo System, not the Imperial yacht."

"You have a point there, sir. The Corps is the same. The best officers are out in the real fleet, not commanding training battalions or pushing papers around a desk."

"Now, I'm going to follow the example Captain, now Commodore, O'Riley showed before the battle at Echo and take a nap. I suspect there will be a lot to do when we get to Haven. I need you to do something for me in the meantime, Mike."

Gunnery Sergeant Mike Sondheim, Imperial marine, looked up sharply. His Prince had never called him by his first name. "Sir?"

"I need you to get me a fleet uniform that comes close to fitting. Just the uniform, no insignia or anything else." At Sondheim's raised eyebrows, Hazard said. "It doesn't feel right going into battle and not being in uniform."

*****

Chapter Forty-Four
Empire Date: April 1033

The tiny task force flashed out of hyperspace into the Haven System. The astrogation had been impressive, and they arrived three light-hours out from the primary planet of the system, also named Haven, as planned. Hazard sat quietly in the command chair on the observation bridge, patiently waiting for the tactical display to update. It took twenty seconds for the sensors to stabilize after the transition.

No system traffic was visible. Nothing. A system that typically had freighters moving through the system, mining ships scattered through the asteroid belt, shuttles—all were missing. Hazard couldn't detect any damage to the outer facilities in the system.

Hostile icons began appearing around Haven. There were two formations in orbit. One about one light-second out consisted of all the small corvettes. The other formation, containing the light cruiser and destroyers, was another light-minute out.

Hazard looked at the chronometer. They had been in the system for only two minutes. It would be almost three hours before the hostile forces saw them and six hours before his task force saw a reaction. One really could not appreciate the vastness of space until they were in a space battle. If they stormed in at full speed for a fly-by, it would take six hours. For a battle intercept, it would take over twelve

"Kristen, connect me with Captain Larue." A moment later, the face of *Longbow's* commanding officer appeared. "Captain, they are much deeper in the system than we anticipated, and their setup is different than I suspected. I figured they'd have the corvettes pushed out as a picket, not in a close orbit over the planet."

"Yes, sir. I find the setup odd. I recommend sending First Division in at max acceleration to close the range. We'll still have plenty of time to adjust after they react to our arrival."

Hazard chuckled. "I told you I was going to leave things up to you and I meant it. I agree, we need to get you moving in the system. One thing, though, at the distances we're seeing, *King Wilhelm* will not be able to support you."

"I don't see that as a problem, sir," the red-haired captain replied.

"On your way, then. Good luck, and good shooting."

Captain Larue nodded, and the screen blanked out.

* * *

It took hours before there was any visible movement by the Marxist forces. Hostile Force A, which consisted of the enemy cruiser and its accompanying destroyers, began moving out toward the Imperials. They accelerated at a leisurely one hundred gravities. At that rate, First Division would be within weapons range in just over three hours. The small corvettes, in close orbit over the planet, still hadn't moved.

"Prince Henry," Commander Jurgenson said, getting his attention. "We finally received an answer to our previous tight beam message to the system government."

"Thank you, Commander. Throw it on the screen."

The main screen display was suddenly replaced by the image of an older man of apparent Hindu descent. Hazard saw bags under his eyes and stress lines on his face.

He bowed his head and said, "Your Highness, I am Veer Sanyal, the deputy prime minister. Chunder Sarkar, the prime minister, was on his way to Delphi when the pirate forces attacked. His transport barely managed to escape the system. My last message from him was that he was going to obtain whatever forces he could at Delphi and return to help us." The deputy PM paused to gather his thoughts. "Planetary defense forces didn't detect the arrival of the enemy force. They must have exited hyperspace behind our largest gas giant and used it to prevent observation. They destroyed any communication or defense orbital they encountered as they proceeded into the system. They also rounded up any ship they could run down and destroyed the ones they could not. The force then destroyed any orbital around Haven they thought might be a threat. Even though we continually tried to communicate with them, they didn't reply until they were in orbit around the planet. It was only then that they revealed their intent. There has been no two-way communication with them, even though they are close enough for a real-time conversation. They sent a wideband message on all channels. I have attached a copy of their transmission. In short, they call themselves the Marxist Liberation Fleet. They intend to place us in interdiction, just as the Empire has interdicted their federation. They claim all the small craft in orbit are loaded with missiles containing biological warheads. We can't confirm whether the claim is true or not. Your Highness, we recognize the risk you are taking by becoming involved in this conflict. Any help we can render in resolving this is obviously at your disposal. We await any requests and pray for a peaceful solution to this situation."

Hazard contemplated the message. *Well,* he thought, *now we know why the small ships are hanging around in low orbit.* "Kristen, play our friend's message."

The brutish face of a man, obviously of some Slavic descent, filled the screen. Hazard had always been fascinated by history, especially Old Earth militaries. The all-black uniform with the high-peaked hat reminded him of the ones Russian Security Forces wore before the Exodus.

"People of Haven. I am General Kanadin Vasil Aleskeevich, commander of the Marxist Liberation Fleet. We have only the most peaceful of intentions. The corrupt leadership of your Empire has taken control of our federation in a gross miscarriage of justice. They claim that we support terrorism and have attempted to usurp the rule of your decadent empress. We have done nothing of the sort. We have only attempted to become a part of your society and share in its vast resources. We have only protected our rights.

"In orbit around your planet are numerous ships that contain missiles with special warheads. These weapons, if dispersed, will destroy all plant-based life on Haven; it will not affect humans. These ships will remain in orbit until the Empire agrees to lift the interdiction of our home worlds. Any non-Liberation ship that approaches within thirty light-minutes of Haven will cause my ships to deliver their payload. If any ship engages a Liberation Fleet ship, the missiles will be fired. If any Empire fleet enters the system and threatens my forces, the missiles will fire. I have sent a freighter we captured in this system to the Britannia System to deliver this message. The missiles will fire if I don't receive a coded message from the Marxist Politburo within forty days. You have your warning and our demands. There will be no negotiations." The message, thankfully, faded out.

An entire system held hostage, Hazard thought. It wasn't much different from what he had ordered done to the federation if he thought about it. Sure, the Marxists had threatened to use biological weapons, but the Empire had threatened them with systematic bombardment.

He needed to come up with a plan. They had time, but coordinating it was going to be a bitch. There were things that needed to be done now, though.

"Kristen, I need to send a message to Captain Larue."

"You are live, sir."

"Captain Larue. I am sure you have already viewed the message from our federation friends. For the time being, we need to start looking at options. I need you to take action to avoid direct contact with the enemy's main force, which is moving toward you. Regardless of what we eventually decide to do, having forces as close to the planet as possible can only help us. Let me know what your plan is. Henry out."

Kristen checked the recording. "Good copy."

"Send it on a tight beam, Commander."

Hazard pushed a comm button on his armrest, and the stern visage of Captain Winters appeared.

"Yes, sir," the flag captain said, barely concealing her irritation.

"What do you think, Captain?"

She looked surprised. "You want my opinion?"

"You are a trained fleet captain. The captain of what is essentially a light cruiser. Of course, I want your opinion."

"Well, sir, they have us over a barrel. With the weapons we have and the distances involved, we can't take out those ships." She paused for a moment. "It could be a bluff, but we can't take that chance. Biological weapons were always a part of the old Russian arsenal."

"Doris, do you think their sensors are good enough to get a good return on us?"

"Your Highness, based on what our sensors indicate of their capabilities, we're just a blip on their screens. I doubt they have any idea what we are. Why do you ask?"

"Eventually, I'll need to visit with Duke Kara when he arrives with his task force. I want to sneak a shuttle behind us, so I can transfer to a ship that can jump into hyper. They need to travel far enough so the Marxists won't spot their transition."

"We can do that. We can use the Oort cloud and the outer planets to screen them."

"Great. I'll also need a ship that will warn other ships from entering the system. I'll let you take charge of that. Go ahead and get them moving."

Winters nodded, and Hazard broke the connection. He turned to Sondheim. "I saw the shuttles Colonel Lee used in the embassy raid. Based on what we know, are they stealthy enough to get close to those corvettes?"

"Sure, their sensors are for shit," the gunnery sergeant replied. "But those shuttles have limited range and no hyper capability. Sure, another ship could open a hyper portal for them, but they wouldn't have the endurance to make the flight from where a translation wouldn't be observed."

Hazard nodded. He looked at the system display and a plan began to take shape.

*****

Chapter Forty-Five
Empire Date: May 1033

It was three days before Hazard received the summons he'd been expecting. A courier ship transitioned into the system to deliver a message that the Duke of Kara needed him aboard the fleet flagship for planning sessions. He was to take a shuttle to the secure transition point and transfer to the courier that would carry him into hyperspace. There was no other information in the message, but Hazard knew his uncle, the duke, would only have called for him if the resources were available for his plan.

It had been three long days. The captains of his small task force drilled their crews, making sure they were as ready as they could be. Since he was not a part of the crew, Hazard didn't take part, and he found he missed it. Without it, he literally hadn't had a thing to do. When he had asked Captain Winters about participating in officer-of-the-deck training, she had politely informed him that she needed to dedicate the available training time to converting a crew of cruise ship sailors into warriors.

So Hazard read. A lot.

When the small courier translated out of hyper, it jumped into the midst of an extensive collection of Imperial Fleet ships. The fleet flagship *Devastator*, along with the other dreadnoughts of the First Dreadnought Division, was there, along with their smaller escorts. There were also eight of the enormous monitors that had been built for the last Swarm battle. Unfortunately, their discovered shortcomings made them of little use in any future engagements against the Swarm, and Fleet Command was still deciding what to do with them. But, in a worst-case scenario, they could help with the evacuation of Haven. With a minimum operating crew on board, they predicted each could hold almost forty thousand Havenites.

Rather than use one of the *Devastator's* landing bays, the courier proceeded to a docking port adjacent to the central bay. Tradition and protocol were essential to the fleet and the docking port was the one used when receiving high-ranking visitors. Hazard had learned about all of this at the academy, but he had expected it to be years before it affected him. It required years of service and training to become the captain of a starship, the usual position where ship's crews observed these types of protocols. He knew he was the regent and heir now, but a part of him still felt like he was a mere lieutenant.

After the courier crew opened the docking connections, he rose, started to leave the ship, and stopped. He realized he was still in a fleet officer's uniform, sans insignia, and no cover. The ever-present and ever resourceful Gunnery Sergeant Sondheim handed him an officer's brimmed uniform cap. The brim was adorned with the double "scrambled egg" flourishes of a flag-ranked officer. Hazard smiled at his bodyguard and friend and donned the hat.

Hazard passed through the docking hatch and paused to examine the spectacle in front of him. When he appeared, an entire company of Imperial Marines in full-dress uniform came to attention. The rifles of two hundred men were snapped up in unison to a vertical position in front of each marine. Since he was almost in uniform, Hazard turned to face the aft bulkhead of the shuttle bay, where the flag of the Empire hung, and saluted. He dropped the salute, turned, and moved between the double rank of marines toward the awaiting senior officers. At his first step, the dreadnought's PA system blasted, "Britannia Arriving." A bosun's pipe whistled the ceremonial arrival salute, and Hazard saluted again as he continued down the path formed by the marines. He stopped in front of the commanding officer of the *Devastator* and the piping stopped.

"Permission to come aboard, sir?" Hazard barked with parade-ground precision.

Renee Giraud, the *Devastator's* captain, saluted and replied, "Permission granted, sir."

Both men dropped their salutes. The ritual was over.

* * *

It took an hour for the rest of the welcome to wind down before Hazard was able to talk to his uncle in the flag briefing room.

"I could have done without all of that, Your Grace," Hazard said irritably. "We have things to do."

"Hazard, my boy, eventually you will see the purpose behind such pomp," Edmund Randolph replied. "The crew of the *Devastator* didn't render honors because they were expected to; they did so because they wanted to. You know how fast word spreads through the fleet. It didn't take long for everyone to know the prince regent had taken personal command of his little task force and proceeded to Haven to fight. The crew of *Devastator* respects the hell out of that. I did a little research. That has never happened in our Empire."

"Okay, Uncle Ed. Bring in the experts and dazzle me with your proposed plan."

The Duke of Kara typed in a quick message on his data link and his staff and advisors filtered into the briefing room. Hazard was glad to see that Colonel Lee, the Special Operations Marine, was included. They settled into seats, with Hazard at the head of the table and the admiral opposite him. Sondheim's presence drew some stares from some of the other attendees, but he didn't care.

Rear Admiral Dustin Conyers, who was still the admiral's chief of staff, began the briefing.

"We are going to call this Operation William Tell, because like the famous archer we are going to perform a precision strike on a target." That immediately bothered Hazard because, as a weapons officer, he knew the fleet didn't have any precision-strike weapons.

The admiral gestured to the holographic display of the Haven System. "The marine transport *Lovat* will exit hyperspace here at Point Luck, which is ten light-hours out and above the ecliptic from Haven." A silver icon appeared on the hologram, far out from the system primary. "She will then accelerate at max G until she reaches 0.6*c*. That should take approximately eleven hours. At the 2.5 light hour point from Haven, the *Lovat* will release her squadron of twelve stealth shuttles." A gold icon appeared. "From that point, the shuttles will fly, dead stick, at 0.6 *c* toward the hostile formation in close orbit. It should take 4.2 hours to reach the optimal firing range of the ships. At one light-minute out, the mission commander will use tight-beam comms to coordinate targets. Then it is just a matter of closing and engaging. Any comments or questions?"

Hazard studied the hologram and various other displays. "Your Grace, this is a bold plan. I need to examine it for a bit." Some of the officers shifted in their seats. They weren't used to civilians questioning military plans. "Before I do that, though, I have some questions for the experts. Colonel Lee, have we evaluated whether our stealth fields will be effective against the almost archaic sensors the federation uses? They use old-fashioned radar waves instead of lidar. I seem to remember reading that our stealth coating bends the laser light instead of reflecting it, somewhat similar to a mirror reflecting light. Will it do the same to electromagnetic waves?"

Hazard could tell by the colonel's expression that he either didn't know or else the stealth material was not as good as they hoped. "I don't expect an answer now, Colonel, but I would like it by the end of the day.

"Next question, time distortion on targeting. Has that been factored in? Remember, we're talking about precision strikes. What about the zone of engagement? The window has to be in milliseconds. Can the firing computer and the shuttle rail guns adequately fire in that window?" Hazard paused for emphasis. "This is not like engaging Swarm attack ships. I have seen the results of our rail gun performances under automatic fire. From an Imperial ship sitting almost stationary, a normal lidar-controlled rail gun will only hit one time in ten against a Swarm ship traveling at only 0.2 *c*."

Admiral Conyers looked at Hazard. "Your Highness. You have brought up some valid points, some we haven't considered. We'll go back and see if we can adjust for the issues you've raised. We have looked at a variety of proposals, and this was the one that seemed to have the best chance of success."

Hazard stared right back. "Tell me, Admiral, what were your odds of success for this plan?"

"Seventy-thirty, Your Highness."

"And now, Admiral?"

"Less than fifty percent, sir."

"Then we have some work to do." Hazard let that remark lie for a bit. "Ladies and gentlemen, something that needs to be said is that we will not give in to those people. I have already directed the preparation of a plan for evacuating the planet after the strike. Fleet Headquarters is preparing transports to bring in food to support the planet and take people out if necessary. I don't want that to happen. We need a workable plan that has at least a moderate chance of success. Think out of the box, people. I am." Hazard looked at his uncle. "Your Grace, I believe we need to adjourn and reevaluate. Do you agree?"

"I certainly do, Your Highness." The admiral turned to the rest of the team. "Okay, people, get to it. Admiral Conyers, take charge of the team and dig back into it. I want an update by 0800 tomorrow. Dismissed."

Once the last of the attendees had left, Hazard turned to the old admiral. "Uncle Ed, are the experts I asked for available?" The admiral nodded. "Then arrange to have them here at 1800 for a discussion."

* * *

Hazard entered the conference room five minutes before the appointed time and found it already crowded with people. There were more than he had expected. He made his way to the head of the table, and Sondheim followed him.

There were three distinct groups of people that Hazard broke down into the scientists, the explorers, and the warriors. He had asked for an expert in hyperspace portals, and his uncle had corralled three of them. Dr. Dundi Dempsey was the youngest ,and probably brightest, of the group. Her team at the Imperial Science Academy had created the current generation of tachyon generators the fleet was using.

They had also made the most precise and stable hyperspace portals to date. She had brought two of her team members with her.

The explorers were an eclectic group. Led by Leonard "Daniel" Boone, they had the laid-back characteristics of people who spent prolonged periods of time in hyperspace. The Exploration Corps was created to help explore, navigate, and develop an understanding of humanity's only means of faster-than-light travel. Over a thousand years later, the Corps still operated science-and-exploration ships, continuing the legacy. They were also responsible for establishing and maintaining the hyperspace buoy system. This system marked the safe travel lanes between systems and provided safe exit-point locations at all explored systems.

The warriors were the group most familiar to Hazard. Colonel Lee was present, along with his lead shuttle pilot and team master sergeant. The shuttle pilot was an ancient warrant officer wearing the traditional gear of a Gurkha warrior, including a kukri.

"Ladies, gentlemen, if you would please take your seats."

Hazard brought up a holographic display of Haven. The holo was large enough to include Haven's moon as well as the two closest planets. It also showed the locations of the Marxists' ships.

"Here's the current situation. These eight small ships are in low orbit around Haven and supposedly are equipped with biological weapons capable of destroying the planet's ecosystem. We can't confirm whether any of that is true, but they are using these ships to hold Haven hostage against the Empire. They hope to force us to lift the interdiction I ordered against the Marxist Federation. I'll tell you that I have no intention of doing that." Hazard looked at the timer running on a panel display on the wall. "So, in a little under twenty-seven days, they will fire the missiles.

"We need to develop a plan that has the greatest chance of success in stopping these missiles. The fleet has put together a plan that I find unacceptable, and they are working to improve it. That plan only has a seventy percent chance of success under the best conditions, meaning one or two ships could still launch their missiles. Since we don't understand the scope of the weapon, we don't know what the consequences of eight missiles detonating in the atmosphere would be. I consider that a plan of last resort.

"While waiting for all of you to arrive, I had a lot of time to consider the issues we are facing. I don't think there is a captain in space that hasn't wished for his ship to fly faster or be able to jump closer to a planet. If we could do that, there would be many easy solutions. Doctor Dempsey, my understanding of hyperspace is that nothing scientifically prevents us from opening portals deep in a gravity well, we simply haven't developed the emitters or power sources capable of doing that, correct?"

"That is correct, Your Highness," Doctor Dempsey said. "The higher the gravitational effect at the portal location, the higher the graviton density needs to be. This means pushing more energy through the emitters. Our emitters today can handle almost twice the power as those used a century ago, but it still isn't enough to get us close enough to Haven."

"It seems I didn't sleep through all my astrophysics classes," Hazard quipped and received laughs from around the table. "I also seem to remember that it takes less energy to return to normal space than it does to enter hyperspace."

Dr. Dempsey nodded. "You were paying attention. It takes only one-third the energy to open an exit portal compared to an entry portal at the same location in space. One other point—which is obvious, but

I'll say it anyway—the size of the portal also affects the number of gravitons needed. We are currently developing a prototype probe that can open a half-meter portal deep inside a gravity well. My team successfully launched this probe from close orbit around Britannia into hyperspace and returned it safely. We see this as an improvement in our ability to transmit messages between systems."

"Congratulations, Doctor. That will be a significant achievement and may be of use to us here." Hazard manipulated some controls and the holographic display changed. "What you are now seeing is how the Haven inner system will look like eight days from now. The alignment of the planets affords us a unique opportunity. The missile ships are one light-second out from Haven. To stay in comms range, they maintain position facing their main force, covering a one-hundred-twenty-degree arc around the planet. In addition, they have numerous surveillance satellites deployed to watch the backside of the planet." Hazard highlighted the largest of Haven's two moons. "This is Idal. It is two light seconds out from the planet." He then highlighted the second smaller moon. "This is Mirror, the smaller moon. Scientists don't believe it's a true moon, but rather an asteroid captured by Haven's gravitational forces. It's three-quarters of a light-second out from the planet and passes between the missile ships and Haven."

Hazard looked at the assembled group. "I'm going to give you a problem and ask you to develop a way to address it." He pointed to a spot on the leading edge of Idal. "I want to deliver a force of stealth shuttles to this location. The bulk of Idal would block the enemy forces. As Idal passes behind the planet and Mirror overtakes it, the stealth shuttles would proceed to Mirror and land on that moon. Once Mirror passes behind the missile ships, the stealth shuttles would engage them with their rail guns. Positioning and surprise should allow a complete sweep, but this would also give us the ability to use the shuttles to intercept the missiles if necessary."

The young prince focused on the exploration team. "Captain Boone, you're probably wondering why you and your team are here. You are the best hyperspace navigators in known space. It's not just enough to open the portal, we need to be able to do it in the right location. You and your team are here to tell us where to do that.

"All right, I'm going to leave you alone. Work it out. You have six days to come up with a plan. If you need anything, contact Gunny Sondheim here. Since he's my official keeper, he has access to me."

The group laughed and smiled as Hazard nodded and left the room.

*****

Chapter Forty-Six
Empire Date: May 1033

Hazard waited in the flag conference room for the rest of the meeting attendees to arrive. His team took a little over two days to formulate the first draft of their plan. While they worked, Admiral Conyers' team made changes to their plan and resubmitted it for review. Hazard deemed it only marginally better than the original version. The chief of staff had stated the odds at 65 percent. Hazard rated it much lower than that; it was still traditional thinking, using the same old equipment in the same old ways.

As a very junior officer in the fleet, Hazard hadn't realized the problems with that type of thinking. Now, sitting in a much more elevated position, he saw how the fleet had become trapped in such thinking. Since the Swarm began attacking, it seemed the only recent innovations were making existing systems better. The barrage firing plan he had developed on the *Shinto* was a perfect example. It was such an obvious solution to improve their kill ratio against Swarm attack ships, but the fleet's entire focus had been on improving firing rates and targeting computers, when all it took was a simple change in doctrine.

Examining the Haven problem showed that. They had no practical way of engaging the missile ships with the current available systems. It would take hours for the fastest ship to close and engage the missile ships, giving them ample time to launch the deadly warheads. Hazard thought of two weapons systems that had once been part of the Empire's arsenal that he wished he had.

Before the Swarm war, missiles had been part of every warship's arsenal. Yes, they were slow and capable of being intercepted, but they also allowed for long-range precision strikes. If he had forty missiles, he could launch them from their current position in the system and let them fly inward on a ballistic course. Their small size would have made detection unlikely, and with a prearranged targeting plan, they could have closed within point-blank range before engaging their drives and striking. And missiles didn't require a direct hit. Multi-megaton warheads detonating nearby would be enough to kill one or more of the missile ships. However, missiles were inadequate to engage Swarm ships, and even if they had been, a ship could carry only so many.

The other thing Hazard wished he had was fighters. When the early colonists had arrived in this part of space, small attack craft had been an integral part of the fleet. The original fighters were armed with two small missiles and an old-fashioned slug thrower. Propulsion was provided by a fusion drive, with plasma provided by a fusion bottle. When starship technology shifted from fusion propulsion to gravity drive, fighters had fallen out of favor and were eventually abandoned. Gravity-drive technology was bulky and wouldn't fit in a fighter.

That was more than a thousand years ago.

With their gravity drives and small fusion reactors, the stealth shuttles they were using to attack the missile ships were about five times larger than the last generation of fighters. Strip out the space for carrying marines, the extra life support, and the additional crew and you would have a ship that was the same weight as the last generation of fighter, capable of more than five hundred gravities of acceleration and two 40 mm rail guns. That would have an even better solution than the missiles, and they could be used to take on Swarm attack ships.

The last of the attendees finally found seats, and Hazard addressed the group.

"I'm sure it will be of no surprise to anyone if I stated I am not happy with our plan to eliminate the missile ships before they can launch their payload." Hazard raised a hand. "I assure you, I appreciate the effort, and you've done what you can with available assets. One thing that has become evident in this crisis is that we've allowed ourselves to become stagnant in our thinking, both with tactics and weapon development.

"I am also sure most of you are wondering about the additions to today's briefing. I'd like to introduce Captain Leonard 'Daniel' Boone of the Exploration Corps Ship *Polaris* and his senior staff. Captain Boone is an expert in hyperspace navigation, and *Polaris* has cutting-edge hyperspace emitters, sensors, and engines."

Captain Boone nodded to the rest of the team.

"Next, Dr. Dundi Dempsey heads Imperial research into hyperspace and hyperdrives. No one in known space knows more about how hyperspace works. The last part of the team is Colonel Lee's marines. His group advised us on the capabilities of his stealth shuttles and the military aspects of the operation.

"Captain Boone, please brief the rest of us on your plan?"

Boone rose and cleared his throat. "Before I get started, Dr. Dempsey will give a short briefing on hyperspace travel and creating portals."

What followed was an introductory lecture on hyperspace mechanics. It took her ten minutes, after which the exploration captain continued, "As Dr. Dempsey just explained, the higher the gravitational force, the more gravitons it takes to open a portal. Opening a portal into normal space takes one-third less energy compared to the reverse."

Boone's hands swept across his datapad and a holographic display appeared above the conference table. "This is the area around Haven as it will appear in ninety-two hours.

"At H-Hour, the *Polaris* will open a portal at this location and jump into the system." He pointed to a spot on the forward side of the moon Idal. "Using special hyper probes which Dempsey's team has designed and brought along, we have already determined and marked the point in hyperspace where we'll make the jump. Her team has also adjusted our emitters and navigation computer to minimize the size of the portal we will generate. Thirty minutes before we jump in, Captain Larue's destroyer group will create a disturbance to hold the attention of the Marxist attack group. With their attention directed away from Haven and with the moon's bulk in the way, we are ninety-nine percent confident we won't be detected. Idal will also shield us from the missile ships and—based on intelligence data—their sensors won't be able to detect us.

"*Polaris* will have eight stealth shuttles magnetically attached to the outer hull. Once in the system, we'll use thrusters to maneuver close to the moon and detach the shuttles. Once we launch the shuttles, we'll remain hidden behind the moon until it passes behind Haven. Then we'll perform a short burn to initiate a ballistic course out of the system to remove ourselves from the battlespace. Colonel Lee, if you would continue."

"Once detached, the shuttles will maintain position behind the moon and wait for it to pass behind Haven." He advanced the simulation. "At this point, we'll perform a posigrade acceleration, and yes, I had to look up what posigrade meant; we accelerate in the same direction as the moon's rotation. That will allow us to perform a slingshot to boost the speeds of our shuttles. Just before emerging from behind the moon we shut down the drives and go full stealth. We'll follow a ballistic course to the inner moon." Lee slowed the simulation. "This is where we run the highest risk of detection, but compared to the other plan, the risk is extremely low. We'll only be in the range of three sensors, at most, and for most of the time only one platform will be able to detect us. The other plan had all the shuttles exposed to numerous sensors for extended periods of time. I am confident our stealth systems will keep us hidden."

He pointed to the holo. "We'll intercept the inner moon here. Since the inner moon is tidally locked, we'll land on the side away from the planet. We proceed around the planet and end up here." Colonel Lee stopped the simulation. "This is almost central to the missile force. The shuttles, still under stealth, will perform a silent dust-off—that's a liftoff using only anti-grav and oriented to present their rail guns. We'll be well within the range of all the targets. On my command, the shuttles will engage their designated targets and go to maximum acceleration. If the enemy launches missiles before being destroyed, the shuttles can shift targeting to the missiles. That's one of the advantages with this plan." Colonel Lee turned off the holo and sat.

"That's the plan we've developed," Hazard said. "Once the assault shuttles engage with the missile force, Captain Larue's destroyers will go to max acceleration to engage the main enemy and the rest of the fleet will jump in." Hazard waited to judge the response to the plan.

Aside from his team, there were only blank expressions. "I realize our plan uses the science and technology in new ways. It's just never been applied to military planning before.

"It certainly is a bold and unusual plan," said the grand admiral, standing. "Despite that, I'm inclined to go with it. And we have time to evaluate it before committing to it. If you have questions or concerns, bring them to the chief of staff or His Highness. I'll not convene another meeting to discuss this. Unless we discover serious issues, we'll go with this plan."

*****

Chapter Forty-Seven
Empire Date: May 1033

In the end, it was decided to proceed with the plan. Hazard returned to *King Wilhelm* to be closer to the action, but he felt helpless waiting on the observation deck. All he could do was wait and watch, which was even more challenging with the time delays involved. He'd been sitting in the command chair for the last six hours waiting for any response from the Marxist forces.

He had received the execute message a little over five hours ago, but because of the daisy-chained communication setup, it came in an hour after the *Polaris* opened its portal behind Idal. That moon and its trailing sister, Mirror, were now behind Haven.

Hazard checked the chronometer. If everything was on schedule, the assault shuttles would be landing on the surface of the smaller moon. It would be another three hours until the smaller moon moved out of the planet's shadow and was again visible. Three hours after that, the assault would begin.

Hazard decided it served no purpose for him to sit and wait for something to happen. At three light-hours out, they couldn't affect anything. He told the bridge he was going to rest, but they were to inform him of any activity, then he went to his stateroom.

* * *

Hazard returned to the bridge an hour before they would be able to see anything. He hadn't rested much. His brain wouldn't let him as it ran and reran the plan in his mind. While not exactly *his* plan, it couldn't have been created without his influence. Before this mission, he had never fully grasped the weight of his responsibilities. A whole planet was at risk and depended on a plan he had backed to survive.

Haven wouldn't be in danger in the first place if he hadn't authorized action against the Marxist Federation. That thought made him even more tired.

"Aspect change on our destroyers. They've turned and gone to maximum acceleration toward the enemy." *King Wilhelm's* tactical officer's announcement blared through the observation bridge speakers. The comm officer had tied the bridge voice comms through them.

Hazard looked at his flag captain, Doris Winters, displayed on the small screen in the right arm of his command chair. "Any enemy movement?"

"Nothing we can see, Your Highness. Captain Larue has seen the light from the attack and executed her orders. I've sent a message to the grand admiral indicating the attack has begun. The Marxists probably aren't looking toward the planet. If we're lucky, they'll stay dumb for a while longer."

"We should see that light in a few minutes, but it'll be longer before we get anything verbal from the shuttles, Doris. I'll stay up here and watch what's happening. Keep me informed."

* * *

It took the Marxist commander only thirty minutes to decide on a course of action. His force was heading back toward Haven under max acceleration. Captain Larue's destroyers were still accelerating through the system and had closed the distance to the Marxist units from one light-hour to twenty light-minutes. The destroyers would soon have to turn over to begin decelerating into Haven's orbit. The rest of the fleet had jumped in around *King Wilhelm* and were now accelerating into the system.

The flag captain appeared on his chair's arm display. "Prince Henry, we just received the action report from Colonel Lee. All enemy corvettes and all missiles fired were intercepted and destroyed." Captain Winters paused to read the message on another display. "He lost three shuttles. The Marxists rammed them in an attempt to prevent the missiles from being destroyed. Fortunately, all the shuttle crews were able to evacuate and were recovered. Colonel Lee also reports that two of his remaining five shuttles are winchester." Winchester was fleet slang for "out of ammunition."

Well, this is not good, Hazard thought.

After eliminating the corvettes, the assault shuttles were their backstop against the main force if it launched missiles against Haven. Now there were only three shuttles capable of doing that, and were probably low on ammunition, as well.

"What do you think, Captain?"

Winters held up a finger to ask for a moment and went mute. He watched her consult with her bridge crew.

The speaker came on and she reported, "Technically, our destroyers could engage, but at their current range, they would have to be incredibly lucky. Even at max acceleration, our destroyers wouldn't close to optimal range to engage until they were past the planet. Based on what we're seeing, the Marxists are going for a passing engagement against the planet. And based on our intel, they'll have plenty of time to launch all one hundred fourteen missiles we think they have on board. Based on what we saw in their home system, they'll be thermonuclear warheads. That kind of salvo would not only destroy the planet but instantly vaporize a good chunk of the population. Even if he had adequate ammunition and all eight of the original shuttles, it's doubtful Colonel Lee could stop that kind of volley. He definitely can't with only three shuttles."

They had done everything right, and Haven was still going to die unless they could get one modern warship between the enemy force and the planet.

Hazard suddenly realized there was a ship that could do it, but a lot of people were going to be unhappy about it. He'd never been happy about using the *Polaris* to insert the assault shuttles into the system, he had ordered all available ships to be evaluated for the mission. Besides *Polaris,* only one other available vessel had enough power and sufficiently strong emitters to open the portal they needed: *King Wilhelm.*

Yeah, a lot of people were going to be very *unhappy.*

"Captain Winters, the *Wilhelm's* hyper generators are just within the margin of the capability for opening the entry portal, making us the only combat ship available that can make that jump. We have to cut those hostiles off. Spin up the standby fusion core to full power and prepare to make a hyperjump. Have your navigator prepare for a micro-jump to the location the *Polaris* used to insert the assault shuttles; that location is well marked."

The captain of *King Wilhelm* understood what was being asked of her ship and crew. She nodded.

*****

Chapter Forty-Eight
Empire Date: May 1033

The modified light cruiser *King Wilhelm* had been making slow circles in space at 0.05 *c*. When Hazard ordered the jump, the ship accelerated to its maximum of four hundred gravities and accelerated into the hyperspace portal. She carried that speed and acceleration through hyperspace. It took only twenty seconds to reach the hyper buoy marking their exit and the ship's emitters began the process of opening a portal back into normal space.

During standard hyperspace jumps, procedure recommended that generators complete a five-minute cool down before being reenergized. Ship captains seldom gave any thought to the requirement since micro jumps were rarely used. Additionally, the hyperspace generators used on military ships were designed and manufactured to be significantly more robust than civilian versions. *King Wilhelm* had six generators positioned in pairs along the length of the ship. The forward, most powerful set, was designed to open the hyper-portal. The remaining two pairs were designed to ensure the portal stayed open as the ship passed through. The ship could enter hyperspace with some of the generators damaged and out of service, but at least one generator on each side of the ship had to be in order to open a portal. The size of the tear in space and how long it would stay open, would be severely reduced with only two generators in service.

Hazard, like the command crew, usually disregarded the warning. In this case, it made a difference. All the operational specifications were based on opening portals outside a gravity well. The radically increased forces needed to open a portal *inside* a gravity well overstressed the generators. The increased power passing through the generators in a brute-force attempt to open the portal didn't help.

The portal opened, the *Wilhelm* passed through, and all hell seemed to explode around them.

The ship shook violently, and Hazard saw red icons appear on his display of the light cruiser. He saw they had suffered some type of casualty but could glean nothing else from his simple display. Hazard looked at the screen that connected him directly to Captain Winters and saw it was blank. He pushed the button to connect directly to the bridge circuit.

"Bridge, this is the prince. Report!"

It was several moments before there was a response, during which time the vibrations ended. "Sir, this is Ramsey, the tac officer. CO and XO are injured, along with several other members of the bridge crew. Both forward portal generators failed as we entered normal space. They are located outboard of the main bridge. We suffered a lot of damage down here."

"What's the status of the ship, Commander Ramsey?"

"No holes in the ship, sir. Engineering and life support are in the green."

"Are we still combat-capable?"

"The ship is, sir, but not the people. I had to move over to flight control and we don't have anyone to man the tactical station."

"Put us on a course that puts us between the bad guys and the planet, Commander. Maximum acceleration. I'll get you some help. Flag out."

Hazard turned to the people on the observation bridge. "Everyone, with me. We need to get to the main bridge, clean this mess up, and protect the planet."

* * *

The doors to *King Wilhelm's* bridge swished open, and Hazard and everyone who had been on the observation deck rushed onto the bridge. What greeted them was not as bad as the prince had feared. Standard routine while transiting a portal into a warzone required the crew be strapped into their seat. Bodies were strewn around the deck, indicating that many of the bridge crew hadn't been in combat in a long time. Hazard was sure some had even been standing.

Hazard quickly assessed the situation. "Gunny, take over the damage-control station." The marine gave him a sour look and he said, "I know, but you're familiar with assault shuttle controls, so figure it out. Kristen, take over comms and get medical up here. Bummer, Jerry, take care of the wounded." Hazard slid into the tactical station and worked through the displays to determine the status of weapons and sensors. He noticed the odd look from Commander Ramsey, the ship's tactical officer now flying the ship from the pilot's seat. "Yes, I know how to run a tactical station. It is a long story that we don't have time for now. Where are we and what is our status?"

"We exited right where we were supposed to, but the hyperspace generators started blowing due to overload. Fortunately, we had enough speed built up with us running at max acceleration, that we managed to clear the portal before it collapsed. The XO was standing behind the pilot and got thrown across the bridge. The CO, likewise, was thrown out of her seat. The explosions threw the remaining crew against their panels. We are now accelerating toward the planet at three hundred gravities and will beat the Marxist forces there. We had one fusion reactor crash due to the power cascade when the emitters blew but the other is stable. Engineering is fine but, like the bridge, has numerous casualties due, to the vibrations when the generators blew."

Hazard finished going through his displays and assessing the damage. "We still have the four main lasers and the forward sensors. We lost the forward rail guns in all four defense batteries and the starboard battery lost its midship gun. Shields and side sensors are worse. Same losses as for the rail guns, which makes sense since they're clustered together, but the starboard side is completely gone—no shields or sensors. I can extend coverage on the remaining shield generators to cover their respective sides, but only at fifty percent capacity."

"Not much to defend with," Ramsey stated flatly. "You're controlling the weapons, sir. Far as I am concerned, that makes you tactically in command."

Hazard updated the tactical display and overlaid the range of *Wilhelm's* lasers onto the plot.

"The hostiles can launch their missiles on a ballistic course from where they are now, but that would give them a long flight time and make it easy for us to shoot them down. So, they're hauling ass toward the planet to reduce the flight time of their birds. They'll try to get in close and swamp us with their barrage." Hazard made some inputs into the console and a course for the *Wilhelm* appeared. "Jordan, I need you to fly this course for the time being. It's a compromise to get us closer to the planet and allow us to close on the enemy."

Jordan Ramsey nodded his agreement. "You do realize this could be a suicide run? They have no intention of slowing down."

"I know," Hazard said in a soft voice. "Larue's destroyers will catch them before that and eliminate the ships, but she'll never get close enough in time to prevent launches. That's our job. We have to make them launch sooner than they want to, and I only know one way to do that."

Hazard noted a change in the tactical display. "Seems Captain Aleskeevich has realized it as well." Hazard gestured toward the display. The enemy cruiser had altered course and was now on a vector to intercept the *Wilhelm*. "He's maneuvering to engage us with the cruiser. It's a good plan but poorly executed. He should have used a destroyer. His cruiser has over half the total missiles of the entire force, and he's potentially removing them from the attack. If we take the cruiser out, we also take him out."

"And if we make him believe he's in danger, he may order the destroyers to launch. Hell, he may launch himself!"

"Exactly! Lay in a reciprocal course. I know our sensors are better; I can hit him with lasers well before he can engage us."

Hazard looked at the tactical plot. They had accelerated up to 0.07 *c* and were still accelerating at three hundred gravities. The enemy cruiser was only up to 0.02 *c* and was accelerating at their max of two hundred gravities. The enemy force had started their acceleration well before the *Wilhelm* had started their jump maneuver but had been one light-minute out from the planet. They were currently thirty-one light seconds apart, and with their current accelerations, it would only take them six minutes to achieve the optimal laser range of the cruiser. Then, unfortunately, they would have to begin braking to reduce speed to engage them. That would leave them too far out at too low a speed to engage the destroyers.

"We'll be within optimal range in five minutes and forty seconds. Once we engage, we'll only be in firing position for—" he checked his displays "—four seconds. I want to blow right past and rake him with our rail guns. No deceleration. We need to pass inside of him and continue toward the destroyers. A standard passing engagement, just like they teach at the academy."

Jordan nodded and gave him another look.

"Yeah, I went to the academy. It is part of the long story. Kristen, patch me into the ship's announcing system."

There was a tone. "You are live on the 1MC, sir."

"Everyone, listen up. This is Prince Henry. We are right at five minutes from engaging the first of the enemy warships. I realize some of you didn't anticipate being involved in anything quite so dangerous when you were assigned to *King Wilhelm*; however, we are members of the fleet, and our oaths require us to defend the Empire. The inhabitants of Haven are part of that Empire. I am proud that all of you are my shipmates, and I want you to know that the House of Kane stands with you as we defend those who can't defend themselves. The deities be with all of you." Hazard signaled for the comm officer to cut the channel.

"Does it seem like this is taking forever?" Hazard asked with a soft laugh. "I know it's only been two minutes." There were laughs around the control room. Eight red icons suddenly appeared on the tactical display. "Looks like they've decided to launch missiles on us. The cruiser is trying to turn inside of us."

"He's trying to expose his starboard side missiles. Our dear Captain Aleskeevich is only thinking in two dimensions. He doesn't realize that all he needs to do is roll his ship," Jordan Ramsey said.

Hazard surveyed the missile tracks. "The rail gun batteries can handle the missiles, no problem. But, Commander, we need to keep our nose toward him so we can engage with the main lasers."

Ramsey adjusted *Wilhelm's* course to maintain the intercept. *King Wilhelm* turned to starboard and continued to close on the enemy ship.

"One minute to firing range," Hazard said. The Imperial cruiser had turned sufficiently for the rail guns to see the missiles. "Portside rail guns, engaging incoming missiles. I have the enemy's laser turrets targeted. Forward lasers are in automatic."

Everyone on the bridge knew when the rail guns began firing. There was a steady *thump* as the eight 40 mm guns spit out their slugs every ten seconds. The lights dimmed when the bow-mounted lasers began firing.

"Ramsey, bow up hard," Hazard called out. As they passed above the enemy, Hazard took remote control of the dorsal rail guns and initiated the bombardment fire pattern. Eight guns spat out solid chunks of metal, one every five seconds. The Marxist cruiser flew right through the rain of projectiles and suffered severe damage. Atmosphere streamed out of holes made by the slugs. Secondary explosions rippled along the hull and the ship erupted into a cloud of exploding wreckage.

Suddenly, the entire ship shook as it streaked away from the stricken cruiser. "Looks like the cruiser gave us a parting gift," Commander Ramsey announced calmly. "Several pieces of debris struck aft near the drive units. We've lost at least half of our acceleration." Ramsey worked his navigation controls and their course updated on the main screen. Now, unless something changed, they couldn't get between the planet and the farthest destroyer.

"Engineering reports that number two fusion plant is offline. Thirty minutes to bring it back up," Commander Jurgenson announced. "The chief also reports that number four gravity drive is out of commission. Repair time for that is unknown."

Hazard had turned to take the report from Jurgenson and wasn't looking at the tactical display.

"Sir, the enemy destroyers are turning to fire!" Ramsey called out.

Hazard turned back to his display. Sure enough, the enemy was beginning the final phase of the battle. Sixteen missile icons appeared on the tactical display and sped toward Haven.

"Adjust our course the best you can, Jordan. We have to try to knock down as many as we can," Hazard said sadly. They had nearly succeeded.

Hazard shifted all the rail guns to automatic missile-defense mode. It was useless against Swarm attack ships but would be more than sufficient against the older Marxist technology.

They could feel the vibration of the rail guns as they began firing again. The *Wilhelm* streaked in front of the missile barrage only one light-second, or three hundred thousand kilometers, above the planet. Missiles exploded as 40 mm chunks of metal tore through their thin metal casings. The destroyers finished turning, fired their remaining broadside, and then turned to flee the system. The second volley of missiles fared no better. The Imperial ship destroyed every missile it could reach. Four missiles rocketed across the path of the *Wilhelm*, toward the planet.

Commander Ramsey turned the Imperial cruiser so the rail guns could engage the last of the missiles. The odds were not good since the distance was rapidly increasing. Suddenly one, then two more, missiles exploded. Finally, the fourth missile disintegrated in a ball of nuclear fire, just short of the planet's atmosphere. Hazard and Ramsey looked at each other, confused. Neither had fired a shot.

Commander Jurgenson said, "Prince Henry, I have incoming from Colonel Lee. Audio only."

"Put him on, Commander."

Three stealth shuttles suddenly appeared on the tactical display as they fired up their engines. "Prince Henry, we thought you might need some help, so we've been here waiting for our shot."

"Thank you, Colonel. We appreciate the help. It seems like we failed to anticipate what they would do when we took out the missile ships."

"That is what marines do, sir. We adapt and overcome."

"Oohrah, Colonel," Hazard responded sincerely.

* * * * *

Chapter Forty-Nine
Empire Date: May 1033

Hazard sat in the VIP quarters of the fleet flagship, IFS *Devastator*. It had been two days since *King Wilhelm* had battled above Haven. The *Wilhelm's* captain, Doris Winters, had recovered enough to sit in her captain's chair again, but her exec was still confined to the sick bay with multiple fractures. The ship itself was space-worthy but limping along on only one gravity drive. She would leave before the end of the day to return to Britannia and enter space dock for repairs.

The remaining Marxist ships, the four destroyers that had launched their nuclear missiles at the planet, had been tracked down by Captain Clarice Larue and her destroyer force. When a squadron of Imperial cruisers exited hyperspace to block their escape, the federation ships turned to engage the destroyers. It hadn't been much of a fight. The Imperial destroyers' shields easily shrugged off the inferior lasers of the enemy destroyers, and Larue's destroyers pounded them to scrap with their spinal rail guns. Since the enemy had known what their fate would be, there had been no surrender, and one by one they had self-destructed. Hazard doubted Larue's ships even made an offer of surrender.

Colonel Lee's shuttle force was also recovered. The fleet commander dispatched a battleship into the system to pick them up.

Hazard had to correct himself, not Colonel Lee, he was now Brigadier Lee. Hazard had promoted him by Imperial decree for his actions in defending the planet. There would be numerous awards and promotions for key contributors.

"We'll be starting our return to Britannia before the end of second watch," the Duke of Kara informed Hazard.

Hazard started. He'd forgotten he wasn't alone. "I wish I could say that I was looking forward to a relaxing three days, Uncle. Unfortunately, I seem to have at least two weeks of correspondence to get through. No rest for the weary."

"Or the wicked." His uncle chuckled.

"Uncle, it's just the two of us right now. Would you mind if I made some observations?"

Edmund Randolph, the Duke of Kara and grand admiral of the Imperial Fleet, gestured for him to go ahead.

"First, we have several less well-off systems which have little or no defensive capability. What was basically a pirate force of severely outdated ships tried to hold an entire empire hostage. The system defense forces would have easily handled it if they had tried this at Delphi or Honshu. Second, we have a small force of older-generation destroyers patrolling along shipping lanes. Most of them are alone. If we'd had a four-ship group of those destroyers guarding Haven, the Marxist attack would have failed."

"What are you suggesting, Henry?"

"It's the Empire's responsibility to protect its subjects. Instead, we have destroyers running around protecting shipping when they should be protecting systems." Hazard pointed to the display showing one of the enormous monitor ships. "There's another example. The monitors are useless in a fight against the Swarm, but they would be a perfect system-defense platforms." Hazard stopped to gather his thoughts. "I want a detailed analysis of each and every systems' defensive capability. Any system which does not have the equivalent defensive capability of four of our patrol destroyers will be reinforced to meet that defined capability."

"It shall be as you command, My Prince, but this could be expensive."

"Not necessarily. We have the grand fleet split between several systems, facing toward the Swarm incursion. Looking at history, we have always had at least three weeks of warning when the Swarm is on their way." Hazard looked at his notes. "Right now, the fleet has over one hundred eighty destroyers assigned to the grand fleet. Form them into ten-ship flotillas and assign them to planets within two weeks' hyperspace-drive distance from the front, and with them, the eight remaining monitors. By splitting the patrol fleet into nine four-ship groups, you can now cover twenty-seven-star systems."

"I'll make it happen, Henry. What else are you thinking?"

"We have become too one-dimensional in our thinking. The four new destroyers have nothing but rail gun weapons, no beam weapons. We were limited in our options when we jumped into the system. We've been concentrating on what we think will work against the Swarm. We're not looking at how recent technology may allow us to develop new strategies. Did you know that engineers have scaled down the newest generation of fusion reactors to fit into an assault shuttle?"

"We don't need a shuttle that has a lot of power but little carry capacity," his uncle replied.

"It wouldn't be a shuttle. It would be our version of a Swarm attack ship. Improved rail guns paired with new and improved gravity drives and enough power on board to support it all. We'd have a small craft capable of five hundred Gs of acceleration and the stopping power of rail guns. Create a carrier to transport them through hyperspace and you suddenly have a force multiplier."

The old admiral looked thoughtful. "That could definitely work. Many years ago, the fleet tinkered with the idea of small attack ships or fighters, but power sources and gravity drives were always the issues. If the power-generation issue can be overcome, it could be a game changer. All right, Henry, I'll get people on it."

Before he could continue, they were interrupted by the admittance chime. He opened the door via a button on his desktop. The newly promoted Commander Kristen Jurgenson stepped into the office holding a memo pad.

"Your Grace."

"Admiral, I don't believe you've met my new personal comms officer. May I introduce Commander Kristen Jurgenson? She was attached to *King Wilhelm* as a communication liaison to any VIPs embarked. I felt since *Willy* is so infrequently used, her talents were wasted there. Numerous wise individuals, including yourself, Uncle, have been telling me I needed more assistants to handle my day-to-day schedule, so it made sense to assign her to my staff."

The Duke of Kara rose and shook the nervous commander's hand. "Commander, welcome to the zoo that is the world of our beloved prince regent. I don't envy you in trying to manage the prince's schedule." The old admiral paused and winked. "Scheduling is easy; keeping him *on* schedule will be a chore."

"Stop it, Uncle," Hazard chided. "The commander is, in fact, more terrified of you than she is of me. I must work on my scowl. What do you have for me, Kris?"

"A courier boat just arrived with the latest round of messages. I already have them highlighted by priority on your terminal." She handed him the comm tablet. "This is from the grand duke, your eyes only, sir."

Hazard took the pad and glanced at the chronometer. "It's late, Commander. I won't need anything else today. Go get some rest. We've been running nonstop for the last few days, and I'm sure things will be hectic once we get back to Britannia. Take advantage of this quiet time."

The comms officer looked nervously at the grand admiral. Hazard sensed she was contemplating her words. "You need rest too, Your Highness. You've worked harder than the rest of us. Take some time for yourself."

"Thank you, Kris; I will," Hazard said warmly. "I promise I'll take the rest of the day off right after I look at my father's message."

With that, she nodded and left the office.

"I also need to be on my way." The admiral gave Hazard a slight bow and headed toward the door. "I'm sure my flag lieutenant has a stack of work for me the courier just dropped off. On top of that, my boss just gave me two new assignments." Hazard's uncle winked at him and strode out the door.

Hazard watched the door close behind his uncle. He was grateful to have someone he could trust by his side. Somehow, Hazard had managed to acquire several: Sondheim, Snake Atwater, Phil Myerson, and his father, most of all. He synced the tablet to the office's wall screen and played the message.

The image of Henry King, Grand Duke of the Empire, sitting behind his office desk appeared. "Hazard, I am sure by now the final battle in the Haven System is over. It is too soon for word to have reached us as to the final outcome, but I know you did everything you could to achieve success. I originally wanted to wait until we had word, but my news is too important to wait.

"Your mother has come out of the coma; it's been almost two days now. We wanted to wait until we were sure she would remain awake before notifying you. Dr. Brougham's nanobots worked just as he anticipated. They destroyed the nanites which were blocking nerve impulses and repaired any damage they found. Your mother is a little disoriented and weak, but she has already had several long conversations with me."

His father's face broke into a lopsided grin. "You're not off the hook yet, son. Your mother and I agree that it will be some time before she is ready to resume her duties. She is aware you were named regent per her wishes." Henry King became sad. "I have not given her any information about Edward or the plots against her. I have sworn the staff to secrecy and we are screening any material we give to her. I have no idea how long it will take her to convalesce enough to take back her crown. By the time you get back, we should know more. Remember, your situation will not change much. You will still be the heir.

"I'll never convince you of how proud I am of you, of what you have done in the Haven System. I believe that, like your mother, you were meant to wear the crown. Know that both your mother and I love you very much."

Hazard stared at the fading image of his father with tear-filled eyes.

*****

Epilogue

Empire Date: May 1033

It took *Devastator* four days to make the hyperspace journey back to Britannia. Well before the fleet flagship docked, Hazard and his uncle took the fleet admiral's shuttle groundside. Hazard wasted no time traveling to King Manor to visit Hiro. Phyllis Warren, formerly the chief medical officer of the cruiser *Shinto* and now Hazard and Hiro's personal physician, gave him an update on her condition. The nanobots designed to repair the empress' medical issues were also used on his fiancée. Phyllis informed him Hiro would be brought out of stasis the following week and the first of several surgeries performed.

News of the final events in the Haven System arrived two days earlier. The palace did all it could to minimize Prince Henry's involvement, to little avail. Several celebrations were planned, and Hazard was expected to be at every one of them. Unfortunately, due to the lateness of their arrival, Hazard wouldn't be able to see his mother until the following morning.

And there was one last thing he had to do. He had put it off as long as he could. The incident in the Haven System had shined a bright light on the issue of succession. The Imperial Charter was quite clear. If a male offspring existed, succession must pass to them before a female. It could be changed by amending the Charter, but that would create a political firestorm. Every political party would be pushing for their own amendments to the Charter and undoubtedly weaken the Crown.

No, there was only one sure way to make sure Edward didn't inherit the crown.

Hazard sat behind his desk and opened his personal laptop. He logged in, accessed a hidden folder, and entered a coded sequence. He had spent quite a lot of time working on the program in question. He had never been great with computers, but he had improved while creating the test scenarios for his barrage firing pattern. It also helped that the palace's central computer was his to command. The virus he was activating was an old one stored in the palace computer's archives. The program was timed to wait an hour before executing, then the virus would be introduced into the system. The program would erase all actions from memory.

When the entry was accepted, he logged off and closed the lid on the computer.

The prince regent of the Britannia Empire opened a video feed on the office's main display, and an image of Prince Edward, visible through the opaque cover of his stasis chamber, appeared.

Hazard was not proud or happy about what he had done, but he'd taken an oath to defend and protect the Empire against all enemies, foreign or domestic. He would do that now and always, even if that enemy was his own brother.

# # # # #

Appendix
Exodus Timeline

November 15, 2141: Exodus fleet of eleven colony ships and two escorts leave Sol System.

December 20, 2142: Exodus fleet exits hyperspace after a four-hundred-day journey into the Orion Cluster, eight hundred light-years from Earth.

March 17, 2143: Exploration party lands on the fourth planet in a binary star system. System and planet are christened Britannia.

April 1, 2143: Landing Day. Initial five thousand colonists land on Britannia and begin construction of colony infrastructure. Captain Isaac Kane of the colony ship *Drake* assumes the role of governor.

January 1, 2144: Britannia Colony population passes twenty thousand. The first ruling council is elected in a general election. Council confirms Isaac Kane as governor. With a planetary rotation of 1,562 minutes, the official clock is changed to sixty-five minutes per hour while still reflecting twenty-four hours in a day.

Feb. 19, 2146: Final remaining colonists on HMS *Drake* land on Britannia. Conversion of colony ship into orbital station begins.

April 1, 2153: Ten-year celebration of Landing Day. All "British" colonists have landed. The population of Britannia stands at 417,000. Landing City boasts a population of 105,000. A new calendar is created based on Britannia's 384-day orbit around Britannia A. Each month now has thirty-two days except for February and August, which have thirty-one. To position the summer and winter solstices in the appropriate months, January 2, 2154, becomes January 18, 0011E. The year date is counted from the year of landing.

January 1, 2154: Ruling Council has expanded to twenty and the planet is divided into representative districts. Generally lauded as the man who made it happen, Isaac Kane is again confirmed as governor.

May 1, 0011E: Leadership teams from the remaining colony ships are woken. The consensus among non-British leaders is that the remaining colonists would become second-class citizens.

June 1, 0011E: The Long Council as it later becomes known, begins. The remaining colony ships will establish colonies on habitable worlds in the surrounding systems. A commonwealth of colonies is established. Each colony will have one delegate on a commonwealth council. Isaac Kane is elected governor-general of the Commonwealth.

April 1, 0025E: Twenty-fifth Anniversary of Landing Day. The Commonwealth government is transformed into a constitutional monarchy. The eight star systems of the Commonwealth—Britannia, Eire, Highland, Outback, Zion, Cape, Dominion, Viking—will have self-governance within their systems. Each system will select two senators for a Crown Senate. Isaac Kane is elected Isaac I, and the House of Kane is established.

January 1, 0046E: Population of Commonwealth surpasses five million.

January 1, 0200E: Population of Commonwealth exceeds one billion.

January 1, 0475E: Britannia Commonwealth evolves into the Britannia Empire as four discovered colony systems join.

January 1, 1000E: Empire population exceeds fifty-one trillion. Empire encompasses ninety-three system governments and twenty-three colonies.

February 14, 1007: Princess Elizabeth, daughter of Emperor Wilhelm X, marries Captain Henry King, Imperial Fleet.

March 7, 1008: Prince Edward, son of Princess Elizabeth and Captain King, is born.

January 11, 1009: Crown Prince Michael dies in a mountain-climbing accident. Elizabeth is named crown princess.

February 30, 1012: Wilhelm X dies due to natural causes. Elizabeth assumes the crown as Elizabeth V.

April 28, 1012: Prince Henry, son of Crown Princess Elizabeth and Captain King, is born.

May 5, 1032: Prince Henry, under the guise of Hazard King, graduates from Fleet Academy.

January 1033: Battle of Echo System

February 1033: Hazard successfully leads a countercoup against his brother Edward. Prince Henry (Hazard) is named Crown Prince and Heir. Due to the Empress' coma, he is named Regent.

May 1033: Battle of Haven

June 1033: Prince Edward dies from wounds suffered during a failed kidnapping.

# # # # #

About the Author

During my 20 years in the US Navy, I spent long periods of time away from home, most of it on submarines, where I developed a great appreciation for the written word. Naval service also gave me an understanding for organization and processes. Following my first retirement, I spent the next 20 years in manufacturing as a manager until ultimately retiring. I have always had a busy mind, and to relax, I began creating what was to become the Britannia Empire in my head. I am now retired and living with my loving wife, Dundi, in the Dallas area of Texas. Our four children, Danielle, Kyle, Allison and Holly have been the inspiration for me to put my thoughts into words.

Ultimately my books are about personalities. I have tried to create characters people care about, and yes, that does mean that characters you get attached to die. Sorry—it cannot be helped; war sucks. The books include numerous space battles, and I tried to make them as realistic as possible. During my research, I discovered that space battles will likely be similar to battles fought during the age of sail. Two sailing ships sail past each other and blaze away at each other for two or three minutes, then spend the next hour getting turned around and headed back toward each other.

Finally, I am new at this and learning as I go. You can find me on Facebook at Fred Hughes Publishing. Drop me a line there, and I will get back to you.

* * * * *

The following is an

Excerpt from Book One of the Lunar Free State:

The Moon and Beyond

John E. Siers

Available from Theogony Books

eBook, Audio, and Paperback

Excerpt from "The Moon and Beyond:"

"So, what have we got?" The chief had no patience for inter-agency squabbles.

The FBI man turned to him with a scowl. "We've got some abandoned buildings, a lot of abandoned stuff—none of which has anything to do with spaceships—and about a hundred and sixty scientists, maintenance people, and dependents left behind, all of whom claim they knew nothing at all about what was really going on until today. Oh, yeah, and we have some stripped computer hardware with all memory and processor sections removed. I mean physically taken out, not a chip left, nothing for the techies to work with. And not a scrap of paper around that will give us any more information…at least, not that we've found so far. My people are still looking."

"What about that underground complex on the other side of the hill?"

"That place is wiped out. It looks like somebody set off a *nuke* in there. The concrete walls are partly fused! The floor is still too hot to walk on. Our people say they aren't sure how you could even *do* something like that. They're working on it, but I doubt they're going to find anything."

"What about our man inside, the guy who set up the computer tap?"

"Not a trace, chief," one of the NSA men said. "Either he managed to keep his cover and stayed with them, or they're holding him prisoner, or else…" The agent shrugged.

"You think they terminated him?" The chief lifted an eyebrow. "A bunch of rocket scientists?"

"Wouldn't put it past them. Look at what Homeland Security ran into. Those motion-sensing chain guns are *nasty*, and the area between the inner and outer perimeter fence is mined! Of course, they posted warning signs, even marked the fire zones for the guns. Nobody would have gotten hurt if the troops had taken the signs seriously."

The Homeland Security colonel favored the NSA man with an icy look. "That's bullshit. How did we know they weren't bluffing? You'd feel pretty stupid if we'd played it safe and then found out there were no defenses, just a bunch of signs!"

"Forget it!" snarled the chief. "Their whole purpose was to delay us, and it worked. What about the Air Force?"

"It might as well have been a UFO sighting as far as they're concerned. Two of their F-25s went after that spaceship, or whatever it was we saw leaving. The damned thing went straight up, over eighty thousand meters per minute, they say. That's nearly Mach Two, in a *vertical climb*. No aircraft in *anybody's* arsenal can sustain a climb like that. Thirty seconds after they picked it up, it was well above their service ceiling and still accelerating. Ordinary ground radar couldn't find it, but NORAD *thinks* they might have caught a short glimpse with one of their satellite-watch systems, a hundred miles up and still going."

"So where did they go?"

"Well, chief, if we believe what those leftover scientists are telling us, I guess they went to the Moon."

*****

*****

The following is an

Excerpt from Book One of Abner Fortis, ISMC:

Cherry Drop

P.A. Piatt

Available from Theogony Books

eBook, Audio, and Paperback

Excerpt from "Cherry Drop:"

"Here they come!"

A low, throbbing buzz rose from the trees and the undergrowth shook. Thousands of bugs exploded out of the jungle, and Fortis' breath caught in his throat. The insects tumbled over each other in a rolling, skittering mass that engulfed everything in its path.

The Space Marines didn't need an order to open fire. Rifles cracked and the grenade launcher thumped over and over as they tried to stem the tide of bugs. Grenades tore holes in the ranks of the bugs and well-aimed rifle fire dropped many more. Still, the bugs advanced.

Hawkins' voice boomed in Fortis' ear. "LT, fall back behind the fighting position, clear the way for the heavy weapons."

Fortis looked over his shoulder and saw the fighting holes bristling with Marines who couldn't fire for fear of hitting their own comrades. He thumped Thorsen on the shoulder.

"Fall back!" he ordered. "Take up positions behind the fighting holes."

Thorsen stopped firing and moved among the other Marines, relaying Fortis' order. One by one, the Marines stopped firing and made for the rear. As the gunfire slacked off, the bugs closed ranks and continued forward.

After the last Marine had fallen back, Fortis motioned to Thorsen. "Let's go!"

Thorsen turned and let out a blood-chilling scream. A bug had approached unnoticed and buried its stinger deep in Thorsen's calf. The stricken Marine fell to the ground and began to convulse as the neurotoxin entered his bloodstream.

"Holy shit!" Fortis drew his kukri, ran over, and chopped at the insect stinger. The injured bug made a high-pitched shrieking noise, which Fortis cut short with another stroke of his knife.

Viscous, black goo oozed from the hole in Thorsen's armor and his convulsions ceased.

"Get the hell out of there!"

Hawkins was shouting in his ear, and Abner looked up. The line of bugs was ten meters away. For a split second he almost turned and ran, but the urge vanished as quickly as it appeared. He grabbed Thorsen under the arms and dragged the injured Marine along with him, pursued by the inexorable tide of gaping pincers and dripping stingers.

Fortis pulled Thorsen as fast as he could, straining with all his might against the substantial Pada-Pada gravity. Thorsen convulsed and slipped from Abner's grip and the young officer fell backward. When he sat up, he saw the bugs were almost on them.

*****

*****

The following is an

Excerpt from Book One of The Last Marines:

Gods of War

William S. Frisbee, Jr.

Available from Theogony Books

eBook and Paperback

Excerpt from "Gods of War:"

"Yes, sir," Mathison said. Sometimes it was worth arguing, sometimes it wasn't. Stevenson wasn't a butter bar. He was a veteran from a line infantry platoon that had made it through Critical Skills Operator School and earned his Raider pin. He was also on the short list for captain. Major Beckett might pin the railroad tracks on Stevenson's collar before they left for space.

"Well, enough chatting," Stevenson said, the smile in his voice grating on Mathison's nerves. "Gotta go check our boys."

"Yes, sir," Mathison said, and later he would check on the men while the lieutenant rested. "Please keep your head down, sir. Don't leave me in charge of this cluster fuck. I would be tempted to tell that company commander to go fuck a duck."

"No, you won't. You will do your job and take care of our Marines, but I'll keep my head down," Stevenson said. "Asian socialists aren't good enough to kill me. It's going to have to be some green alien bastard that kills me."

"Yes, sir," Mathison said as the lieutenant tapped on Jennings' shoulder and pointed up. The lance corporal understood and cupped his hands together to boost the lieutenant out of the hole. He launched the lieutenant out of the hole and went back to digging as Mathison went back to looking at the spy eyes scrutinizing the distant jungle.

A shot rang out. On Mathison's heads-up display, the icon for Lieutenant Stevenson flashed and went red, indicating death.

"You are now acting platoon commander," Freya reported.

* * * * *

Get “Gods of War” now at: https://www.amazon.com/dp/B0B5WJB2MY.

Find out more about William S. Frisbee, Jr. at: https://chriskennedypublishing.com.

*****

Made in the USA
Las Vegas, NV
07 August 2023